Tears and Tequila

Tears and Tequila

LINDA SCHREYER AND JO-ANN LAUTMAN

PROSPECTA PRESS

Prospecta Press
P.O. Box 3131
Westport, CT 06880
www.prospectapress.com

Book design by Barbara Aronica-Buck
Cover art and design by Tracy McGonigle

Paperback ISBN: 978-1-935212-29-4
Ebook ISBN: 978-1-935212-28-7

In memory of my mother
Greta Schreyer
bright light
— LS

I dedicate this story to all those who have allowed me
to be "THE TRUSTED PASSENGER"
on their long journey toward hope and healing.
— Jo-Ann Lautman

HOW WE
<u>WANT</u>
GRIEF TO
WORK

HOW GRIEF
<u>ACTUALLY</u>
WORKS

Part One

Part One

Chapter One

All she could see was the emptiness.

No flowers bloomed beside the gray stones. No weeping willows reached down to caress the ground. The trees were bare. The sky was gray. The air held a mix of cold and snow.

From the back of a taxi, Joey Lerner's eyes took in the endless lines of gravestones snaking out over the brown winter grass of Pinelawn Cemetery on Long Island.

She toyed with a balsa wood plane while the taxi flew past a sign: GRAVE SITES #750–#1249. She checked the slip of paper in her hand and yelled, "Stop!" The taxi screeched to a halt. "Over there," she said, pointing to another street. The driver put the taxi in reverse and drove, stopping at another sign: GRAVE SITES #1250–#1749.

"Be right back," Joey said, untangling her long legs. "Then JFK, please."

The driver flicked the meter to "waiting." Joey stormed across the graveyard in a green winter jacket, purple scarf, jeans, and red cowboy boots. The wind whipped her long, dark hair across her face as she walked over a gravestone poking up from the grass. "Oops," she said. There was another one next to it and another in front of her.

"Sorry," Joey said to one of the stones as she tripped over it, barely righted herself and began to hopscotch over some of the graves, walking on others set in the grass like stepping stones, until she was standing on a new, plain gray stone in the family plot, bearing her grandmother's name: *Josephine Lerner 1929–2011 Beloved Mother and Grandmother.* The words sent a flush of warmth through Joey's body. She stepped aside.

"Death is not sexy, Nonna," Joey said. "Take it from me. Death is a four-letter word. Right, Dad? Grandpa?" She looked around at her father's and grandfather's markers before sitting in a heap in the family plot. "So," she said, "you're all in here. And I'm out here. And we all agree, don't we? Death sucks." She stopped, her throat suddenly tight with emotion.

"Dad," Joey said to her father's stone. "You always said I should find a job worthy of my talents. And you," she said to her grandfather's stone, "told me I need to become who I am." Turning back to her grandmother's marker, she said, "And you always said life begins at the end of your comfort zone, Nonna. So that's what I'm doing. Taking a flying leap into the unknown. Sure, I'll probably land on my ass. But when I do, I hope you'll be there to catch me."

Her voice caught. Every cell in her body remembered how many times she'd been there. But today she needed to pretend, to act as if she didn't feel the crushing sorrow that engulfed her.

Her fingers traced the letters of her grandmother's name one last time. "I miss you. More than I can ever say."

Joey stood and pulled the homemade balsa wood glider out of her purse. *Josephine Lerner* was written across the wings in red nail polish. "This one's for you, Nonna," Joey said in a wobbly voice as she tossed the glider into the air.

She watched as the glider soared higher and higher above the graveyard until it seemed to merge with a plane winging its way across the sky and the sound of the engine filled Joey's ears. She didn't notice the tears falling on her cheeks until the cold air hit them.

Hours later, Joey was tucked into seat 32-C, the last row in Coach on AA flight #32 to LAX, her hands white-knuckled as she sat amidst a topsy-turvy scene of turbulence.

"We've begun our descent into L.A.," the captain said over the intercom, "and this is just a Santa Ana condition, folks. No cause for alarm."

Joey sat erect, her mouth in a tight line, looking out the window at the landscape below. Her first sight of Los Angeles was a brown layer of smog above a flat valley of strip malls surrounded by mountains. Houses made of ticky-tacky. No real towns, just one big sprawl. It was a landscape as foreign to her as the moon.

As turbulence hit again she squeezed her eyes shut until the plane landed safely. Joey slung her heavy carry-on over her shoulder and rushed to the women's room, elbowing past deplaning passengers.

"Sorry," she said. "Late for an interview."

She ducked into a stall and pulled a change of clothes out of her carry-on. Wedged into the stall she managed to take off her winter clothes without dropping something into the toilet. She put on a sleeveless white shirt, a short denim skirt, and platforms that made her long legs seem even longer. She walked out of the stall and checked the washroom mirror, patting down the top of her long curly hair, a mane that looked different every day. Today it had a bad case of the frizzies as if it too were nervous about what she was doing. She looked into her slightly desperate eyes through her new pink-tinted sunglasses.

Smile, she instructed her reflection, even if she couldn't help but notice the dark circles under her eyes. And she saw no point in thinking about waking at 3:00 AM and wondering why she was moving to a place where she knew exactly one person.

You need this job, she reminded herself, reaching into her purse for her cell phone. She read a text with a name and address, panicked when she saw the time, and raced through the airport, her carry-on slipping off her shoulder. She yanked a small canvas duffle and an oversized suitcase off the carousel and ran outside.

The warm Santa Ana wind blew her hair into her eyes. The temperature was in the high eighties. "Taxi," Joey yelled, hailing the first cab she saw.

"Goddammit, that's mine," said a small, plump blonde who cursed at Joey in an Australian accent as she pushed a fully loaded luggage cart.

"Sorry," said Joey, stepping out of the way before the cart ran over her foot.

As the woman streaked past, Joey noticed she wore long, turquoise feather earrings and a black sweater with a belt cinched a bit too tight, red leggings, and Ugg boots. She commanded the driver to load her bags into "the boot," slammed the door, and the taxi pulled away.

Joey took the next one.

"Where to?" the driver asked, lugging Joey's suitcase to his trunk.

Joey read off the text on her cell. "Oasis. And hurry, please. I'm late for an interview."

"And where is Oasis?"

"Something Oaks," she said, handing him her phone. "Thousand Oaks? Million Oaks? Quaker Oats?"

"Sherman Oaks, lady," the driver said, handing it back as he pulled out of LAX. "Your first time in L.A.?"

"How'd you guess?" Joey settled into the seat as the driver took off for the 405 freeway north. She checked her phone. She was 10 minutes late. She thought of calling, but decided to ignore the churning in her stomach and just show up.

On the way she passed the time looking out the window. Spindly palm trees were blowing in the wind; a pink neon sign read LIVE NUDES. There was a different gas station on every corner, low buildings and snow-capped mountains in the distance. Red or purple or white flowers bloomed in every front yard or in pots on porches. No subway signs. Four lanes of traffic that crawled on the 405. Drivers with heads bent, texting while they drove or talking on cells. By the time the taxi got off the freeway and followed a sign to Ventura Boulevard, Joey felt like a stranger in a strange land.

"Are we almost there?" she asked the driver, checking her phone again. She was now 45 minutes late.

"Think so," he said.

"Hope so," she said. "I'm late."

"Made it here in record time," he said.

When they got caught at a traffic light, Joey glared at it, willing it to change, even though she didn't know which way they were going. Impossibly, as she looked at the other side of the street, she saw a corner lot with towering pine trees and a sign: *Oasis: An Adventure in Learning.*

"Thank you," she said to the job gods who had, for once, smiled down upon her.

"You're welcome," said the driver as he drove across Ventura Boulevard and pulled into a pothole-riddled dirt parking lot in front of an old bungalow court on a large property. A dozen brightly painted rundown cottages ringed the parking lot, with hand-lettered signs: *Hummingbird, Nasturtium, Birds of Paradise, Pink Ladies,* and more. Joey noticed that each bungalow also bore a painted mural: deep-sea corals swayed with the tide; lusty women danced in forest glades; jungle warriors leapt hand in hand with lions and tigers.

A group of teenagers played guitar beneath the pines. Women of various ages painted at easels. Men and women were drumming in a circle or fencing in pairs. A list of the day's classes was scrawled on a chalkboard in neon-colored chalk; tie-dyed flags blew in the Santa Ana wind; spider plants hung from macramé holders.

Joey felt as if she'd landed at the Woodstock-1969 stop on a Disneyland ride.

She emerged from the taxi and drew herself up to her full height, imagining a string pulling her head skyward. She was picturing herself acing the interview when a tall man drove in on a Triumph Bonneville T100 motorcycle and parked next to the taxi. He smiled at Joey and pulled off his helmet, revealing a thick head of black hair with a streak of gray. She noticed he wore a motorcycle jacket, black jeans, and flip-flops.

Joey felt a tug of attraction. She shook it off as she slung her small duffle bag over her shoulder while the taxi driver wrestled her giant suitcase out of the trunk. She paid him, and he drove off. By the time she stepped onto the pothole-riddled parking lot the tall man was walking down a path through the trees. She took another step, only to be trampled by the tiny feet of a small gray lizard that used her shoe as a bridge to flowering red bushes beyond.

"Aaarrggghh."

Joey's ankle turned in her platforms. Her carry-on slipped off her shoulder. She went down, sunglasses flying off her nose, last shred of dignity gone.

"Are you okay?" someone called across the parking lot.

The inquisitive face of an older woman peered at her from behind an easel. Mortified, Joey called back. "I'm fine. A— . . . a lizard ran over my foot . . . " She picked up her belongings and set off again, pulling her enormous suitcase behind her.

"We've got a million of 'em," the woman said as Joey approached. "We even named a cottage in their honor. See?" She pointed with her paintbrush to a sign on one of the bungalows. Joey looked over: *Leaping Lizards.*

"Um. Cute," she lied, as she arrived, dusty and out of breath, at the painter's easel. "Can you tell me where the office is?"

"Over there." The woman paintbrush-pointed to a small stucco building with a sagging clay tile roof.

"Thanks." Joey was about to rush off, but the woman's soft European accent reminded her of Nonna's and the warmth in her voice was the most comforting sound Joey had heard in months. The woman's pink shirt was dappled with drops of lavender paint. A small leaf had fallen into her upswept light brown hair. She looked as if she was in her eighties, but her skin was porcelain and, when she smiled, her face lit up. Then Joey caught a glimpse of the artist's watercolor.

"Wow. I love the colors you're using," Joey said.

"It's coming along. I'm Berta, by the way."

"Joey."

"Are you here for the job?"

"Drama teacher? Yes."

"It's filled."

"What? When did that happen?" Joey asked, shoulders sagging, all the air let out of her balloon of hope.

"About an hour ago, and it's too bad, if you ask me. The woman they hired is a phony."

"How do you know?" Joey asked.

"Because she also told me my painting was nice, but she didn't mean it."

"Then I might as well leave," Joey said, reaching for her suitcase.

"What are you dragging around in that huge suitcase? A dead body?"

Joey laughed ruefully. "More like my old life."

"Why not leave your life with me and go to that interview?"

"Because the job's taken."

"So? They have all kinds of classes and groups here. Go for an interview. If they don't have a job for you, you can suggest one they *should* have."

Joey hesitated.

"What do you have to lose? Go on," Berta urged. "It's right over there." An image of her bank balance flashed before Joey's eyes. "Leave that monster of a suitcase with me while you go see Daniel."

"Daniel Wyndham?" Joey asked, checking the text on her cell. "The director?"

"The director and owner of Oasis."

"Can you tell me anything about him?"

"Sure." Berta painted a flamboyant line of turquoise watercolor across her paper. "He's a triple threat. Smart. Sexy. Single. And he's got a great ass."

Joey laughed. "Too bad I'm not in the market."

"Why not?"

"I've picked so many jerks," Joey said, holding up her forefinger, "I decided my picker's broken."

"Nonsense. You're too young to be an old maid," Berta said, returning to her painting. "See you later."

Joey left her suitcase next to Berta's red cloth bag, which was decorated with a green appliquéd parrot. She headed to the office with her small canvas duffle slung over her shoulder, passing blue-and-white glass wind chimes that jingled in the Santa Ana wind. "Go get 'em," Berta called across the parking lot with a wave of her paintbrush, splattering paint drops into the air. Something about the woman's enthusiasm gave Joey the courage to straighten her shoulders and rehearse what she would say: *I've done so many different jobs, I can do anything.*

Don't tell him about all the jobs, she corrected as she climbed three rickety steps to a wooden porch. *Or all the moves. And for God's sake, don't tell him Nonna said you have gypsy blood.*

Joey took a deep breath and knocked on the paint-peeling front door.

Chapter Two

The office door was yanked open by an ample African-American woman with a pencil stuck in her messy updo and a wrench in her hand.

"The damn toilet's flooding in *Pink Ladies*," she said, on her way out. "Name's Marjorie. Office manager. Just sign the roster if you're registering for a class and we'll get back to you." She began to leave.

"Oh. Um," Joey said. "I'm here for a job interview. But I'm late, so . . . "

"No worries. What's your name?"

"Joey."

Marjorie smiled. "I like that. Daniel!" she yelled down the hall. "Interview's here. Name's Joey."

"Just a sec," a man with an Australian accent yelled.

"Go have a seat," Marjorie said. "And welcome to Oasis—the land of never knowing what the hell to expect next." She wrapped Joey in a bone-crushing hug and ran out the door.

Joey stood in the doorway, flummoxed. Should she stay? Go in? Run? She hesitated before closing the door behind her, and stepped into a tiny foyer in the low-ceilinged bungalow.

The water-stained wood floor creaked under her feet as she squeezed through a gap between two empty desks. One held a large green laptop, the other a listing stack of purple-and-white Oasis catalogues. She walked into a tiny waiting room where a red-and-blue Tiffany lamp provided the sole light in the dim space. It was perched on a fake-wood bookshelf littered with well-thumbed paperbacks, rumpled magazines, beat-up toys, knitting needles in a basket of wool, a plastic pail of sea shells, and other assorted objects. Two red beanbag chairs, a cookie-crumbed shag rug, and a sagging blue futon couch with no legs completed the haphazard décor.

As soon as she sank into the couch on the floor Joey realized her mistake. When she tried to rise she was too low to get up. Trapped on the lumpy low couch, she began to sweat when she heard footsteps coming towards her.

Joey skootched her behind forward until her legs were splayed out in front of her. Knock-kneed and in the most awkward position possible, she tried to stand. She couldn't. She'd just realized she'd have to crawl on her hands and knees to get up when she heard the voice with the Australian accent call her name. "Joey?"

"Yes," she said, rising unsteadily. Her carry-on slipped off her lap and onto the floor. While she teetered on her wedges a tall, black-haired man reached out a hand to steady her.

"Where I come from, a Joey is a baby kangaroo," he said, retrieving her carry-on. "Crikey. That's a heavy load."

It was the man on the motorcycle. The top of her head barely grazed his chin when she regained her footing. He looked about fortyish and fit, with a just-got-out-of bed face, tanned skin, and laugh wrinkles around green eyes with flecks of gold. His thick black hair, with its wide gray streak, curled over the neck of his blue sweater.

While Daniel's hand held onto hers for a moment too long, Joey breathed in the scent of his lemongrass cologne. Then the familiar pain of rejection roiled in her gut. *Damn you, Jack,* Joey thought, moving her hand away. "I'm named after my grandmother," she said, flustered. "Josephine. Joey Lerner."

"Daniel Wyndham," he said. "Come on back."

Joey followed him down the hall to a messy postage-stamp-sized office. A portrait hung on the wall: a slender, gray-haired woman wearing a sari over white pants stood beneath an enormous tree bedecked with ribbons, apparently in the process of marrying the young couple before her. Daniel strode to a seat behind his desk. It was piled high with papers. A silver AirBook was perched precariously atop the pile. Oddly, there were bars on the windows, Joey noticed as she sat.

"I came about the Drama Instructor job," she said.

"I'm afraid that's already filled."

"I heard," Joey said.

"From who? Oh, Berta, of course," Daniel said.

"Yes, well," Joey said, tamping down her desperation, "maybe there's something else I could do here." She handed him a résumé, careful not to let her hand touch his.

"You minored in psychology at Skidmore?" he read.

"Yes."

"Where's that?"

"Upstate New York," Joey said.

"Is that where you're from?"

"No. Actually, I've moved around a lot."

"And I see you've led different groups—Active Seniors, Acting Out Teens. Oh—and you've worked in hospice and recently interned with a psychiatrist in New York, co-leading groups."

"And I taught Drama para Los Ninos to tiny tots in Mexico and walked dogs in Boston and worked in a bookstore in Manhattan and . . . "

Daniel handed her paper back. "That's one wacky résumé."

"I guess so," Joey said. "I've always preferred to move around. Try something new. Keep it fresh, you know?"

You sound like an idiot, she told herself. But every second she held his interest was another second he might think of a job for her. So she talked on as Daniel cocked his head and listened. He listened as if every detail mattered. Joey couldn't remember the last time an attractive man had paid such close attention to her. She was aware of sweat on the back of her neck when Marjorie ran in.

"The water's hitting the high-water mark, Boss. Pipe's about to burst."

"Dammit," Daniel said, rising. "This bloody place is falling apart." He ran out after Marjorie. Joey hesitated a moment before picking up her carry-on and running after both of them, still pitching herself for a job, any job.

Five minutes later, Joey, Marjorie, and Daniel were crammed into the tiny pink-tiled bathroom of *Pink Ladies* where Joey sat on the closed lid of the leaky toilet, handing a wrench to Daniel as he attempted to fix the pipe. "So I—yes, I've moved around a lot in the last 12 years. My dad was an English professor, and he moved us from job to job when I was a kid. My grandmother used to say I inherited Dad's gypsy blood. . . . " *Oh God,* she thought. *Shut up, Joey. Shut up.*

At that moment the pipe burst. Water shot out, soaking Joey, Daniel, and Marjorie.

"Shit," Daniel cursed. "Call the plumber." He rushed out to shut off the water main.

Marjorie pulled out her cell. "Call Perry," she told Siri. "We're sending his kids through college," she told Joey. "Hello," she said a minute later, walking outside for better reception. Joey sat alone on the closed toilet seat in the bathroom. Her shirt was wet. She wondered how she looked. She wondered what she should do next. She'd just flown 3,000 miles, and there was no job. Plus, Daniel was right—the place was falling apart.

So Joey did what she always did at times like that. She opened her duffle bag and took out the only thing in it, a well-worn leather tool-belt outfitted with a leather-handled hammer, wrenches, pliers, work gloves, utility knife, tin snips, a level, soldering iron, solder, and an impressive assortment of pipes and nails and screws and a hacksaw—and got to work.

By the time Daniel returned Joey was sawing through the portion of burst pipe.

"What the hell are you doing?" Daniel asked.

Joey kept on sawing. "Like I said. My dad was an English professor. But Grandpa could do anything with his hands. He taught me about plumbing and left me his tool-belt."

Daniel stared at it. "Those tools are for a lot more than plumbing."

"Yup," Joey said, plugging in a soldering iron. She painted a thin layer of soldering paste onto a new piece of pipe, uncoiled solder from a spool, and began to solder the new pipe to the old. As always, working with tools calmed her. "My grandfather taught me how to use them all."

Flabbergasted, Daniel said, "You seem to have forgotten something in your résumé: Handyman."

"Handywoman," Joey countered, tightening a compression nut on the pipe.

"Handyperson?" Daniel asked.

"Whatever," said Joey. She packed up her tools as Daniel went out to turn the water back on. The plumbing job was done, the toilet flushed. Joey put her tool-belt back into her carry-on. "I'm sorry there's no job at Oasis," she said when he came back with Marjorie. "I would've liked to work here. The place is . . . unique."

"Hang on. What else can you do?" Daniel asked.

"What do you mean?"

"Can you fix wooden stairs with dry rot? Patch a leaky roof? Put up dry wall?"

Joey scoffed. "My grandfather taught me to build cabinets out of hardwood with mitered joints. We installed hundreds of feet of crown molding when we renovated their apartment."

"Jesus f-ing Christ," Marjorie said.

"I've put in a hot water heater and a new boiler and . . . "

"You're hired," Daniel said.

"As what?"

"Look around," he said. "We're in shambles. You're our new handyperson."

"Thank God," Marjorie said, pulling out her phone to cancel the plumber.

"But I'm not a licensed professional. I'm just an amateur fix-it person."

"I can help," Daniel said. "We'll work together." Joey felt a flutter in her stomach at the thought. "When can you start?"

"What's the salary?" Joey asked.

Daniel quoted a figure as they walked out of the cottage. "I know it's not a lot but I'm hoping it will be more soon. We're making a lot of changes," he said, pointing to *Hummingbird Cottage*. "Like the experimental program that starts there tomorrow night. But the porch steps are rotten and I haven't had a chance to fix them. Will you take the job? Can you start now?"

Joey thought for a moment. "Yes. And no. I'll take it. But I can't start now." She pointed to her suitcase next to Berta, who was still painting at her easel. "I just got off a plane from New York. I've got to get to my friend's place and settle in. Can I start tomorrow?"

"If we're still standing," Daniel said with frustration. "Where does your friend live?" he asked as they walked towards her suitcase.

"She's the manager at Ferndale Apartments."

"That's not far," Daniel said. "Need a ride?"

They were at Berta's easel. Joey looked from Daniel to his motorcycle to her giant suitcase. "Um. How will you . . . ?"

"Yes, Daniel, she needs a ride," Berta said. "And while Daniel figures out how to transport your 'life' let me show you where I teach." She squinted at them. "You two get into a water fight?"

Joey followed Berta to a small cottage. *Berta's Bungalow* read the sign above a painted mural of Berta at an easel. She opened the door and they walked inside.

Paint-splattered tables and easels were scattered throughout the room; painted and unpainted canvases, large and small, leaned against the walls; metal shelves held jars and coffee cans filled with brushes, palette knives, and Chinese bamboo ink pens; large brown ice cream containers contained rolls of drawing paper; tubes of oil paints and watercolors, pastels and palettes were in aluminum pie-plates and shoeboxes; ceramic pitchers and Japanese cloths for still lifes lay on a table alongside an old mandolin and a three-foot ceramic spotted leopard.

"Wow," Joey said.

"Isn't it a sweet mess?" Berta said proudly.

Joey noticed that one window was covered with film. "To bring out the play of light and shadow," Berta said, following her eyes, "depending on where you stand." A tall, slender woman in purple jeans poured different-colored paints onto a wet canvas from small plastic cups. The colors ran together, creating intriguing designs.

"Nice, Judy," Berta said.

In the center of the room three women were making charcoal drawings of each other, a vase of sunflowers in the middle of their small circle. Joey recognized "Bohemian Rhapsody" coming from an iPod.

"Queen?" she asked, surprised.

"Oh yes. I loved Freddy Mercury," Berta said. "Yet another fine artist lost to AIDS. Thank God that's behind us. At least, I hope it is. So, how do you like my home away from home?"

"Smashing," Joey said.

"Indeed," Berta agreed, her eyes sparkling. "You'll have to try painting sometime. Take one of my classes."

"Painting's not one of my talents. Unless it's a wall."

"You're a house painter?" Berta asked. "How exotic."

"Painter. Plumber. Amateur carpenter. I'm Oasis's new handyperson."

"Fabulous," Berta said. "And you'll be doing more here, too."

"How do you know?"

"I have a feeling about you," Berta replied with a smile. "And I always trust my feelings."

"Thank you," Joey said, feeling Berta's warmth wash over her.

Chapter Three

Joey was riding on the back of the Triumph, her arms around Daniel's waist, her suitcase attached to the bike by a complicated bungee cord contraption. She tried to sit back far enough so her breasts weren't pressing against his back.

"Come closer," Daniel called back to her. "Before you fall off."

She held on to him, the front of her wet shirt against his back, and leaned with his muscular body as he banked around curves and wove through the traffic until they pulled into Ferndale Apartments.

She dismounted, noting several pastel-colored three story apartment buildings, some with balconies, some without. She handed the helmet to Daniel.

"Thanks," she said.

"No worries," he said.

As he freed her suitcase she spotted a shimmering pool surrounded by lounge chairs. They were almost all occupied with people her age talking on cells, reading on iPads, listening to music on earbuds, typing on tablets.

"Serious vacation vibe," Daniel said.

"Don't these people have jobs?" Joey asked as two women in string bikinis with washboard midriffs walked past, slowing to catch Daniel's eye.

"Sure they do," he said with an ironic smile. "And they're doing it.

It's mating season." At the pool a group of tanned women on lounge chairs giggled hilariously as they looked at something on a screen. "Probably checking out some poor bloke on OkCupid," Daniel said.

Joey laughed, feeling like an idiot. She'd been on the site just last week.

"Who'd you say you know here?" Daniel asked.

"My best friend since sixth grade. Kat. She's the manager." Another woman in a Puma tennis skirt smiled at Daniel, looking him up and down. Joey suddenly felt overdressed and out of shape. "I'd better find Kat," she said, reaching for her suitcase. "And you'd better skedaddle before you're mobbed."

"Are ya all right?" Daniel asked. "Want me to wait till you find her?"

"I'm good," Joey insisted. "Thanks for the ride."

"You're all dry," he said, gesturing to her shirt.

Joey wondered what she'd looked like before. "So are you," she said.

"See ya tomorrow." Daniel smiled. He got on his motorcycle and wove into the traffic. Joey watched him for a moment, feeling a tug she didn't want to feel. Then she lugged her bags to the manager's office, a large sunny room with white orchids on an oversized glass desk and several tan leather club chairs. A coffee pot and donuts sat on a counter. Signs on large metal easels advertised *Ferndale Apartment Complex: Your month-to-month home away from home on a 10-acre resort-style property with two pools, a man-made lake, a tennis court and clubhouse. VACANCIES AVAILABLE.*

A blonde walked in wearing a bikini top, a striped towel, and bejeweled flip-flops. "Hi," she said, heading to the coffee.

"Hi," Joey said, feeling travel-weary. "Any idea where I can find the manager?"

"What?" the woman asked, removing her earbuds.

"Do you know where Kat might be?"

"Oh, she's usually around. Or in her apartment." The woman walked Joey out and pointed to a unit nearby.

Joey rang Kat's bell. No answer. She rang again. No answer. She knocked before she opened the door to the apartment and found Kat *in flagrante* on the floor with a pale, naked bespectacled man.

"Really?" Joey said. "Like every weekend in college?"

She closed the door and waited. Laughter floated towards her from the pool. The sickly-sweet smell of jasmine filled her nose. After a moment, Kat opened the door to her apartment wearing an orange tee and purple shorts, her long red hair streaming down her back. She wrapped Joey in a welcome hug without a shred of embarrassment.

"Why didn't you call me?"

"Long story," Joey said. "It's been an action-packed day."

Kat held her at arm's length. "You don't look too bad for a jilted girlfriend."

"Don't start."

"I'm serious. Come on in. I want you to meet Neil. Then I want to hear everything." She pulled Joey into the apartment where the boyfriend, Neil, was coming out of the bathroom. He had the indoor pallor of a hard-working nerd, dark hair, and black-rimmed glasses. A white V-neck T-shirt and corduroys hung on his rail-thin frame. Kat introduced Joey. "My best friend since we met in the girl's room in fourth grade."

"Where Kat was smoking," Joey said.

"And Joey was wearing an Indian fringe costume with a feather in her hair."

"I was in *Indian Princesses* with my dad," Joey said.

"In New York City, for God's sake," Kat told Neil.

Neil shook Joey's hand. "Good to meet you."

Kat put her arm around Neil's waist. "Neil's the editor of *The People's Weekly*, a paper I'm dying to write for."

"I feel like I already know you," Neil said, peering at Joey before Kat rushed him out the door with a hasty kiss.

"Why does he think he knows me?" Joey asked.

"Because I've told him all about you, silly," Kat said, "I was so excited you were coming." She pushed Joey down to the couch. "Now talk," she said. She began picking up the clothes strewn all over the floor and putting them in a pile. Joey told her about the flight and the job interview. Kat listened with half an ear, as usual. "And this," Kat said, queen of the *non sequitur.* "This is where you're going to sleep." She indicated the couch Joey sat on. "It's not the most comfortable but . . . " Kat tossed a red bra onto the pile.

"But it's free," Joey said. "Thanks."

"Of course, sweetie," Kat said. She gathered up the pile of clothes and threw it into a closet. "So. Tell me more. Did you get the job?"

"No. I just told you," Joey said. "But I got another one."

She was repeating what happened at Oasis when she sneezed. She looked down at Kat's long haired calico cat, Mufflepaws, who was snaking around her ankles. "Kat has a cat," Joey laughed before she sneezed again. "Dammit."

"What?" Kat asked. "Oh, shit. I forgot you're allergic to cats."

Joey sneezed again. "I can't stay here. Now what?" she asked, as exhaustion smacked her in the face.

Kat thought for a minute. "There might be an opening at Ferndale . . . "

Joey began to panic. "How am I going to pay rent when I owe for the flight out and I'm still making payments on those goddamn student loans and—"

Kat grabbed a bunch of keys and began to wheel out Joey's suitcase. "Come with me."

Joey followed, protesting. They squeezed into the tiny elevator with the giant suitcase and got off on the third floor. Joey was still protesting when Kat unlocked the door of a spotless, modern two-bedroom furnished with highly polished black lacquer furniture. "This could work. No?"

Joey balked. "Are you crazy? I can't afford this."

Kat took off her shoes, eying the peach wall to wall carpet. "Better take yours off."

Joey shed her sandals. "Like I said, I can't afford something like this."

"Relax," Kat said. "This belongs to Bud Zellner. He's been here 18 months and just went to visit his daughter in Arizona for a month."

"And . . . ?"

"If you can keep it immaculate he'll never know I let you stay in it."

"But," Joey said, "you know I'm a slob. And I may be staying longer than a month." She felt overcome with jet lag, and utterly lost.

"Sweetheart. Nonna's apartment is rented. Right?"

Joey nodded, miserable.

"All her furniture and art are in storage, right?"

"Right," Joey said. "Along with 3,000 of my dad's books. Another damned expense."

"And you said you couldn't face another Arctic winter after you ran into Jack and the blonde at Gracious Home on Broadway and you started seeing them on the crosstown bus and in the planetarium. And when you walked down to Riverside Park on 76th Street. Right?"

Joey nodded, more and more miserable.

"But it was never them. Right? So you flew all the way out here because you said New York was starting to feel like . . . "

"A chilly steel prison," Joey admitted crankily. "And I was a stalker of phantoms. I know. I know. But why do I have to stay in this . . . black lacquer mansion?"

"Because you can't sleep in Kitty City. And I'm the only one you know out here. So where else are you going to stay?"

The question hung in the air, making Joey's stomach ache with fear and loneliness. After a long moment she wheeled in her suitcase and shut the front door.

Arms and legs touching, Joey and Kat sat on the black leather couch, the TV blaring. They talked as they ordered Chinese takeout (which Joey thought bore no resemblance to New York Chinese). They talked as they ate Mu Shu pork and lobster fried rice with chopsticks until Joey couldn't stop yawning and Kat went to work wresting the sheets off Bud Zellner's bed and putting out clean towels while Joey rummaged through her suitcase for PJs and a toothbrush.

"See you in the morning," Kat said, wrapping Joey in a hug before holding her at arm's length. "You look exhausted. Go to sleep."

But Joey couldn't sleep. Everything about the place gave her the creeps. The master bedroom was spacious and airy enough, with a balcony and skylights that let in streaks of moonlight, but the California King bed with its black lacquer headboard seemed as vast as the Pacific Ocean. Across from her was a black lacquer wall unit with a 53-inch HDTV. Everything was so shiny and clean Joey could see herself in it. And what she saw kept her tossing and turning.

Her long hair was tangled. Her face was tear-stained and pale. Her eyes hurt, her feet hurt, her mind wouldn't shut down. She finally fell asleep, only to be jolted awake at 4:00 AM by the alarm on the Bose. Disoriented, she knocked it to the floor, sweeping her glass of water along with it. By the time she'd cleaned up the spill she was wide awake again.

Joey laid her head back on the pillow. A tear rolled down her cheek when she thought about sleeping in the maple sleigh bed in her grandmother's seven-room apartment on the Upper West Side. And tears puddled in her ears when she remembered making love with Jack in that bed on their first anniversary.

She got up and walked out on the balcony. The air was still warm. The wind was rustling through the palms. As she looked down on the sleeping village of Ferndale she wondered what she'd done. Nobody was around. Not a soul. All she could see was the emptiness.

Chapter Four

The next morning, in a leafy green canyon across town, Tamara Salvo opened her eyes. The clock read 7:11, but she doubted this would be her lucky day. Her mouth was dry, her eyes burned. She wanted to sink back into a dreamless sleep—not that she spent much time there these days.

She stretched her legs beneath the eight-pound weight of Boots, her silky black-and-white tuxedo cat, carefully sliding out of bed so he stayed asleep on the chocolate brown blanket.

Leave it to Bruce to pick browns and greens for the bedroom after I decorated the rest of the house with color, she thought. *He'd said they were soothing. They sure as shit weren't soothing enough.*

Tamara walked into the bathroom and looked at her reflection. *Note to self: Redo bedroom in reds and purples. Note to self: With what money? Note to self: Call Bruce's boss. Find out what's delaying payments from the accounts. Note to self: File suit against life insurance company that won't pay because he killed himself. Note to self: Stop making notes to self.*

She was exhausted, and she'd been awake for only five minutes. As she walked back to the bedroom her steps felt slow and heavy. She looked at the bed. She thought about how many nights she and Bruce had slept in separate tight balls, each clinging to their own side of the king-sized bed, an ocean of space between them. She remembered how many nights she'd woken at 2:00 AM and adjusted to make sure no part of her was touching any part of him, or looked over and seen him sleeping as far away as possible.

For the last couple of years, even in sleep they'd often been defended against each other. One day they'd be fine. The next day they'd get into an argument. Neither would apologize, and soon they weren't talking to each other again. Then, after a day or a week, they'd start sleeping closer again, make love, hold hands in the movies, and the fight would be over.

Tamara had thought they were in a better place a few months before Bruce died. She'd thought their marriage was working. *Guess the joke's on me,* she thought as she headed down the stairs, happy to hear no morning sounds from her daughter Maya's room. She wasn't ready for a skirmish yet. *Coffee.*

Down the stairs she went, padding along the light wooden floors, feeling the chill. When she turned up the thermostat she glanced at the embroidered red and orange pillows on the white leather couch and the purple orchids blooming on the turquoise glass coffee table. *How can I live with so much color and feel so much darkness?*

She walked into the kitchen and went straight to the sliding glass door, opening it to look out on the back yard. She'd done that every morning since they'd moved there nine years ago.

Their Spanish two-story sat on a corner lot on a tiny street off a curvy canyon road. Jacaranda trees formed a leafy canopy over the street. When they bloomed, their fallen purple blossoms decorated the lawn like the morning after a party.

This was their "starter house," the one they'd moved to when Maya was four, with the backyard Tamara had landscaped with pink and purple lantana and white iceberg roses. Where they'd hosted a decade's-worth of parties and barbecues with other families. Where the parents had toasted their luck with rounds of piña coladas while their kids played on the yellow swing Bruce had hung between two eucalyptus trees.

Now, the grass was littered with fallen eucalyptus leaves and ragged strips of rough gray bark. The yellow swing hadn't been used in months. The vegetable gardens were a tangle of weeds. The roof leaked. The gutters needed cleaning. Tamara needed coffee.

As her orange mug caught the first drips she heard Boots thump down the wooden stairs, all eight pounds of him hitting the floor with a thud, thud, thud. He slunk into the kitchen.

"You think you're a panther," she told him as he walked to the back door. His ears pointed forward as she opened the door and Boots flat-bellied onto the Spanish tiles of the covered patio.

"He speaks English," she always told Bruce, who would roll his eyes before he disappeared back into his crossword puzzle.

Automatically, despite everything she knew, she looked over at Bruce's empty chair at the kitchen table. She felt the silence that infused the house.

Tamara thought about silence. She thought about the way she and Bruce would stop talking after a fight, sometimes for days at a time, until the words they didn't say were louder than those they did. She thought about how, even when he was alive, silence swept their house like a dry wind across the desert. She thought about how silence became their weapon of choice and how it had turned out to be a lethal weapon. Because it was during one of those three-day silences that Bruce had killed himself.

Tamara wanted to believe their bitter fights were not why he'd done it. Sometimes she did, in the daytime. Then came the hours after 2:00 AM when she lay awake, wondering why he'd wanted out of her life and how he could have left Maya; why he'd stopped taking his meds and where and when he'd bought the gun; how she could not have known he was in so much pain; and did he kill himself to pay her back? Which always led to the question she hated most: *What is wrong with me?*

Her 13-year-old daughter's sleepy voice floated down the stairs. "Mom?"

"In the kitchen . . . "

Tamara got busy. She opened the fridge and pulled out frozen waffles. She was putting them in the toaster oven when Maya stumbled in, her mouth open in a yawn, cell phone in hand.

Maya's hair used to be blonde and had hung down her back. Now it was spiky black with pink tips and smelled of stale cigarette smoke. Mismatched striped socks were on her feet and she wore a neon-green nightgown Tamara didn't remember buying for or with her.

There was a lot Tamara didn't remember these days, like where she'd put her prescription sunglasses or Maya's homework. Last week she'd left the house without her purse. The toaster oven rang. She took out the waffles. "Maple syrup, honey?"

Maya settled onto a kitchen stool, busily texting. Tamara poured syrup on her waffle and handed her the plate. "There you go," she said brightly.

"It's a little early, Mom," Maya yawned.

"For blueberry waffles? They're your favorite."

"For your Shirley Partridge imitation." She texted furiously.

Ouch.

Tamara took her mug to the coffeemaker for a refill. She knew Maya and her friends watched *The Partridge Family* on YouTube. They loved making fun of the show. Tamara thought about Shirley Jones's recent revelations about her sex life. She decided not to say anything. She looked out the glass door at the rain. Maya chewed and texted in sullen silence.

Tamara wanted to say, "Next time you talk to me like that, young lady, you're grounded." But she was silenced by her guilt. Because Maya used to wear red, green, and purple outfits. Now she dressed in black, as if she were going to a funeral every day of the week. *And maybe she is,*

Tamara decided, *because Maya didn't just lose her favorite parent. She lost the one who's left. I'm not all here anymore.*

As she sipped her coffee Tamara recalled when Maya was six and would run into Tamara's office after school to tell her that Katie hadn't picked her for kickball and ask, if Adam and Eve were the first people, who were the first animals?

My sunny, chatty daughter. Where did she go? Down the drain with the rest of us, Tamara decided.

"Buenos dias," Rosalba called out, closing the door to her room.

"Buenos dias," Maya and Tamara called back.

"You sleep good?" Rosalba asked, walking to the sink.

"Okay. You?"

"I always sleep good, Meesy."

She said that every morning.

Rosalba had worked for them since Maya was two. She had graying hair and a large mole on the end of her nose that Tamara didn't even notice anymore. She was short and round, with an easy laugh. As soon as Rosalba walked into a room the house became a home. She was the unconditionally loving, un-psychological mother Tamara had never had.

When Rosalba's husband died and her daughter moved to Stockton, Tamara told her she'd always have a home with them. She'd cried, of course. Rosalba always cried. These days she was the one person who did, because the house had become a no-tears zone where Maya and Tamara ricocheted off each other in angry, dry-eyed circles of pain.

Rosalba turned on the teakettle and started unloading the dishwasher. Maya brought her plate to the sink, opened the fridge and, drank orange juice out of the carton. Tamara resisted the urge to order her to get a glass.

"Are you going to that thing tonight?" Maya asked Tamara.

"Grief Group? Uh-huh."

"What's the point?"

There isn't one, Tamara thought.

"Um. Being with other people who've lost a husband or wife . . . "

"Daddy didn't get lost," Maya said. "It's not like we can find him. He killed himself, remember?"

Ouch.

"I need a ride after school. I've got guitar."

"I thought it was tomorrow."

"Art just texted. He changed it. I hate him. He keeps making us play stupid folk songs."

"Great. That means driving you to Oasis, picking you up, gulping down dinner, *and* going back there again."

"Forget it." Maya said, walking out. "I'll hitch."

"I'll take you," Tamara called after her.

"Your lunch," Rosalba hurried after Maya with a brown bag.

"Thanks," Tamara heard Maya say from the living room. "Love you."

"Love you, honey," Rosalba said.

As Maya galloped back up the stairs, Tamara braced for the slam of the door and ear-splittingly loud Metallica. She was not disappointed.

"Pobrecita," Rosalba clucked with concern as she came back into the kitchen. "Too much feelings."

Tamara agreed, dumping the rest of her coffee in the sink. "Too much feelings" pretty much described it all.

She walked back through the living room, where she felt the suffocating silence again. The house line rang. She braced herself for another call from another collection agency. Or her mother.

It rang again.

It was early for her mother.

It rang again.

Tamara couldn't stand the silence anymore.

She answered.

"This is Tamara."

In his apartment on Sawtelle Avenue Dave spoke into his cell.

"This is Dave Collier. I called Oasis to find out who else is coming tonight. They gave me your number. I wondered if I can get a ride . . . ?"

The woman at the other end of the phone said nothing.

"You know. Tonight. Are you going?" Dave asked.

"I'll be there. I've got to run," the woman named Tamara said, sounding annoyed.

"Okay. But can I get a . . . "

She hung up before he could finish.

". . . ride?" Dave said out loud before he hung up. *What a bitch,* he thought. He checked the time: 8:03 AM. Past time to get ready for work.

Dave used his arms to pick up his legs, swung over to the edge of the couch and grabbed his poles; walked to the kitchen, turned on the coffeemaker and the TV, upped the volume so it drowned out the nasty hiss of his thoughts, poured coffee into a cup; walked into the living room and bumped into the coffee table.

Every morning, same routine. It should be a boring life, Dave thought. But it wasn't. Not when, with every tortured step, he was doing penance.

Caro, wherever you are, forgive me.

Dave's morning coffee sloshed over the edge of his Lakers cup as he walked down the hallway in his faded blue velour bathrobe. From behind thick lenses, in frames held together with a paper clip and Scotch tape, he surveyed the photos on the walls.

His dead wife, Caro, laughed, head thrown back; she windsurfed in Hawaii; she leapt across a stage in a flowing blue skirt; she waved at her sisters from the Martha's Vineyard ferry, her brown hair blowing in the wind.

Caro in action, fearless and alive.

Dave swallowed the sour misery that rose in his throat. Blue light from the TV filled the dark room. The shades were drawn. It made every day look the same. Which it was.

Check, check, check.

Chapter Five

In Bud Zellner's apartment Joey was slumped over a cereal bowl, struggling to swallow another bite of Raw Alive Granola.

She'd woken up feeling like someone had hit her over the head. After she showered in the black tub, taking care to pluck her hair out of the drain, she'd dried her wet footprints on the peach-colored carpet with a hairdryer.

She'd hung up clothes on the four yellow wooden hangers that had survived all of her moves and scrounged for something to wear to work. She'd even made an attempt at making the apartment homey, pulling six of her father's favorite books out of the suitcase, lining them up on the black lacquer bookshelf next to a purple orchid she'd thought was real until she'd touched its dry silk flowers.

Fake, she realized. Joey had walked onto the balcony and looked down. *Fake,* she thought. Everything about Ferndale Apartments looked artificial, from the sparkling turquoise water in the kidney-shaped pool to the fake-tanned, fake-stacked blondes. It was enough to make her feel like hiding under the covers.

Instead, she'd raided the cabinets, but all the food was gluten-free, nut-free, live-dried, and high in fiber with no trans fats or cholesterol. She'd poured a bowl of Raw Alive Granola and taken a bite. It tasted like sawdust.

Kat walked in as Joey was slumped over the cereal bowl. "Brought you some Smart Water for your first day," she said, plopping the bottle on the counter. Joey's tired eyes met hers. "C'mon, sweetie," Kat said. "It's going to be okay."

"How do you know?"

"How many times have you moved? How many new jobs? You've always made it work." Joey was silent. "Talk to me," Kat said.

"I know how many places I've lived," Joey said tightly. "But until now someone was always in New York."

"This is about Nonna," Kat said.

Joey fought tears. "She was like a magnet."

"She was your true north," Kat agreed. They stood in silence for a moment. "Family is overrated, if you ask me."

They didn't need to talk about Kat's parents, who'd divorced when she was three. They didn't need to talk about Joey's mother, who'd left when Joey was five, leaving four yellow wooden hangers and a hole in her daughter's heart. Ever since they were 10 they'd bonded over their shared abandonments. There was not much more to say. Joey took a bite.

"Like Bud's cereal?" Kat asked.

"Seriously? How do I replace this crap with real food?"

"Whole Foods," Kat said. "Later. Anyway, you look good."

"Ha," Joey said. She was wearing a turquoise T-shirt, jean shorts, the tool-belt on her hips and work boots with the laces untied.

"But you've got to go," Kat said.

"*We've* got to go."

Kat spread her hands wide. "Can't go with you. Got a deposition on that stupid lawsuit."

Joey searched her mind as she carried her bowl to the sink. She vaguely recalled Kat telling her last night about a frivolous lawsuit that had been brought against her by a former employee. "How am I going to get there? How do you get a cab around here?"

"You don't need a cab."

"There are buses?"

Kat shook her head vehemently. "Never, never take the bus. Never. Come with me."

She reached for Joey's hand. They walked past the postage stamp-sized Fitness Center where several young guys in T-shirts and shorts pumped iron, and three women in yoga pants wiggle-walked on tread-mills. A heavy older man, in a Disney T-shirt, Bermuda shorts, and black socks with sneakers, pedaled an Exercycle.

"Typical Ferndale morning," Kat said, hurrying past.

"I thought everyone here was under 30."

"That's just the pool party set. We service all ages here."

"That sounds dirty," Joey said.

"As if," Kat replied, walking faster.

"Where are we going?"

"Here," Kat said as they arrived at the garage. She pulled out her phone. "Smile," she said, snapping a photo of Joey in front of a 1990 red Chrysler Le Baron convertible.

"Why are you taking my picture?"

"I'm taking a picture of the Red Baron," Kat said. "Bud's pride and joy. All you have to do is drive it carefully, no fender benders, keep it washed, and he'll never know you used it. The photo is to remind us how it looked when you got it."

"What's with 'he'll never know?' He'll know when I break his Bose and clog his drains and dent his car. And besides, how the hell do you get around here?"

"Relax," Kat said. "You need wheels. You're broke. This will work. But the car's too old for a navigation system. You can use the GPS on your phone or this." She handed Joey a spiral-bound book of maps.

Joey eyed it suspiciously. "What is it?"

"It's called a Thomas Guide. Used to be the bible of L.A. It's Neil's. He's seriously old school." She opened it to a page she'd dog-eared and highlighted. "I marked your route to Oasis. Between that and your GPS you can't get lost." Kat handed Joey the keys. "You know how to drive stick, right?"

Fifteen minutes later, with a terrible noise of grinding gears, Joey pulled out of the garage and merged into traffic. Ten minutes after that she was driving around in circles on streets with names *(Sepulveda?)* she couldn't pronounce.

As she gripped the wheel she glanced over at the Thomas Guide, splayed open on the passenger seat. All she saw were big red lines that looked like veins or arteries bisecting green squares with tiny unreadable squiggles of street names.

Who could figure out how to use the damn thing? And where did all those arteries and veins go? Where was the heart of the sprawling organism they called L.A.?

So many questions. So few answers.

Joey pulled over, checked the text with the address of Oasis on her phone and set off again. Bud's radio was set to an oldies station, and the Motels sang about loneliness. Joey wasn't going there.

I'm going to my first day on a job I never planned to take at a place I know nothing about, she thought.

Soon she was flying past the Reseda Boulevard exit on a highway called the 101 in a town named, of all things, Tarzana.

Only in L.A. would they name a place after a man who palled around with apes. Or call a highway the 405 or the 101, as if the road were an animate object.

By the time she pulled into the front courtyard of Oasis she'd made several more wrong turns, in spite of the GPS, and realized she might have underestimated her need for a place with a layout she understood.

She was 30 minutes late.

Across the packed parking lot she saw Daniel talking with two older women. One was tall, with long gray braids piled high atop her head. She wore a flowing red caftan and looked a little like Oprah Winfrey. The other was short, with frizzy, dyed red hair and wore a purple velour pantsuit.

Joey ran towards the office in a long-legged dash, hoping to avoid being discovered by Daniel.

"Joey," he called out. "Over here."

Shit, she thought as she walked over to him. Daniel wore a green sweater that brought out the color of his eyes. *Shit.*

"I'm sorry, she said. "I got lost on the freeway."

"Your first day. Of course," Daniel said with a smile. "I'd like to introduce you to the FMs."

Joey smiled politely. "FM? As in radio?"

"As in Founding Mothers of Oasis," said the African American woman in the caftan.

"This is Arbela Kayne," Daniel said, "and this is Bunny Forestall. They founded Oasis with my grandmother. Ladies, Joey is our new handyperson."

Bunny, of the velour pantsuit, eyed Joey's tool belt with concern. "Be careful, honey," she said. "You might hurt yourself."

"Don't be silly, Bunny," said Arbela. "She knows how to use those tools. Welcome," she said imperiously.

"You can do your paperwork with Marjorie," Daniel said. "She's waiting for you in the office."

But Marjorie was walking towards them. "Morning, ladies. Hello, Sweet Pea," she said to Joey. "Daniel? Can I talk to you for a minute?"

"Sure."

"The leader of tonight's group just quit."

"What group is that?" Daniel asked.

"Grief Group One. Should we cancel?"

"Absolutely not," Arbela Kayne said. "It's part of the outreach you promised Oasis would do when you took over. Not to mention the jobs you need to create to keep your EB-5 status."

"I'll find someone else to lead it," Daniel said. "No worries."

"Come on, darl," Marjorie said to Joey. "Let's get you signed, sealed, and settled."

Joey followed the office manager as she made her way through the colorful chaos of students coming and going. Soon Joey was sitting across from Marjorie at her desk, filling out paperwork.

"What's Grief Group One?" she asked.

"A pilot program for young people. A Grief Group that meets outside of a church or hospital."

"How old are the people?"

"Your age," Marjorie said, shuffling through stacks of papers. "All of them just lost a husband, wife, or partner."

"Oh God," Joey said. "That's tough."

"For sure," Marjorie agreed, frowning at the mess.

"Does Oasis offer a lot of groups like that?"

"Nope." She pulled out the paper she was looking for. "Aha. Here's the enrollment for tonight." She tossed it into a wire basket. "Daniel found out that most Grief Groups meet at a hospital or a church, and very few are for young people who lose their spouses or partners. Okey dokey," Marjorie said, rising. "Let's get *Hummingbird* up and running for tonight. I haven't been in there for years."

They walked down the path, turned right and climbed another set of rickety steps to another sagging wooden porch. Marjorie opened the front door and began to laugh. "*This* is the waiting room? Now there's a euphemism if I ever heard one."

Joey looked around the postage-stamp sized waiting room. It was unfurnished, dark, dingy, and dank.

"Follow me," Marjorie said, barreling down the hall to another room, where she threw open a door. "The den," she announced. "Where Grief Group will meet."

It was about 14-by-20 feet square, with a scraped wooden floor, dirty beige walls, and a nonworking fireplace.

"Wow. Depressing."

"Totally," Marjorie agreed.

"There's a lot of work to do before tonight," Joey said.

"I know. But all we can do today is furnish this dump. C'mon." Marjorie grabbed Joey's hand and walked out the back door of the den. "It's pillage and plunder time."

"Vikings pillage. Pirates plunder," Joey murmured, struggling to keep up with Marjorie as she strode across the grounds.

"What?"

"It's something my dad always said."

"The English professor?" Marjorie raced up the steps to *Birds of Paradise*.

"You remembered?"

"Of course. That was the most fun job interview ever. Leaky toilet. Burst pipe. You and your tool belt. Awesome."

"How long have you worked here?" Joey asked as they carried out a rickety coffee table.

"Practically since Genesis," Marjorie said as they lugged it up the steps to *Hummingbird*.

She'd been the office manager since the original one quit 15 years ago, she said. "This place was started 31 years ago by Daniel's grandmother Zora. A real peach. She was a midwife in Australia until her husband died.

Then she came to the States and carried on with an artist in Big Sur until she moved down here and midwifed this place into being, along with the FMs." Marjorie ducked her head into another bungalow and walked right back out, finger to her lips. "Memoir Writing's in there."

"What's with the FMs?" Joey asked as they located a wicker rocking chair in another bungalow.

"Oasis was started with a gift from Zora. Then she got matching sums from Chip Forestall as an outlet for his wife's cockamamie ideas, and from their best friends, Alexander and Arbela Kayne, the entrepreneur couple who are terrific do-gooders. They all became the Board of Directors, together with six of their pals."

"What do they do?" Joey asked as they carried in two standing lamps.

"Get apoplexy when other people park in their parking spaces. Meet in the board room every few months. Wear stale lilac perfume that gets into the paneling. Play canasta and do as little business as possible while drinking as much Sauvignon Blanc as they can swill," Marjorie huffed as they dragged three chairs out of *Leaping Lizards*. "But Oasis was mismanaged and neglected as Zora and the FMs got older. So after she died Daniel came from Australia."

"When was that?"

"Six months ago," Marjorie said. "He promised his grandmother he'd take care of Oasis, so he sank his own money into the place. About half a mil so far." Joey whistled. "Daniel's here on some fancy visa. He gets a green card after two years if he sinks a certain amount of dough into a failing place and creates a certain number of jobs there. One of those jobs is yours."

"Wow. I'm glad of that."

"Me, too. But we're bleeding money. Plus, he has to answer to the FMs, who pretend all's well while we're really just one step ahead of the bogeyman. It's supposed to be a great big secret. Except that everyone around here knows. Like everyone knows *everything* around here," she warned as they moved in a red plaid couch. "So watch your back."

"Watch yours!" Joey called as Marjorie swung the couch around and smacked her back against a bookshelf.

"Ouch!"

They scraped the wooden floor. Though it was scraped before they got there. And the walls were begging for a fresh coat of paint. They arranged the half-dozen mismatched chairs in a circle completed by two worn red plaid couches. The rocking chair sat at the far end of the room.

"It looks . . . " Joey searched for the right words.

"Early Salvation Army?" Marjorie said.

"Exactly."

"Good enough," Marjorie said.

When they walked out Joey almost tripped on one of the steps. "I'd better replace those rotten boards before tonight," she said. "Is there a workshop with tools, by any chance?"

"If you can call it that." Marjorie pointed to a metal Quonset hut lettered with LSMFT in fading red paint.

"What does LSMFT mean?" Joey asked.

"Lucky Strike Means Fine Tobacco. It was here when Zora bought the place." They walked towards it. "Can I give you a suggestion, darl?"

"Okay."

"I recommend you look for another job."

"Instead of working here?" Joey asked, confused.

"On top of working here. We can't always make payroll."

As Marjorie walked away Joey's heart sank. She'd thought she'd found a place to land. *Not so fast,* she told herself as she walked into the ramshackle hut.

Chapter Six

While Joey oiled the moldy woodwork in *Leaping Lizards*, the parking lot began to overflow. She was replacing a broken window pane in *Birds of Paradise* when a group walked into Tarot Cards. As she fixed the railing on the steps leading up to *Pink Ladies*, she listened to a teacher named Ashana playing Crystal Singing Bowls. She was patching the leaky roof of *Nasturtium* when she looked down on a dozen silent women in Mindful Meditation and hastily stopped hammering. Yoga students came and went; potters potted; weavers wove; drummers drummed.

"This place is like hippie summer camp," Joey told Berta when the artist shared her home-made lunch in *Berta's Bungalow*. "Pot roast sandwiches, kugel, and pumpkin bread? When do you find time to cook like this?" Joey asked. She took a bite and looked around at Berta's colorful paintings.

"Painting is my life's work," Berta said. "If I don't do it I feel like there's something wrong with me. But you can't eat a painting. So cooking? Cooking is my hobby."

Joey silently finished her pot roast sandwich.

"Jet lagged?" Berta asked.

"I guess so," Joey said, falling silent again.

"Are you usually this quiet?"

Joey laughed. "Never." She stood. "Thanks for lunch. I'd better get back to work. And I need to find a second job."

"In case we close."

"Yeah."

"So you're worrying."

"I have to make money."

"Worrying has its place, but only if it motivates you to do something about it. You also need some fun. Tomorrow night I'm taking you to Margaritaville at the Sagebrush Cantina."

"What's that?"

"A big barn with a live band. Line dancing. Thursday night specials on Margaritas and tequila shots. Let's invite that friend you're staying with. And Daniel, too."

"Why Daniel?" Joey asked.

"He likes you."

"He does?"

Berta nodded. "And you?

"I . . . he . . . he's my boss."

"Yes. Of course. Not proper at all," Berta twinkled. "I learned a long time ago that doing the right thing sometimes leaves you lonely. So—are you?"

"What?" Joey asked, flustered.

"Lonely."

"I've only been here a day."

"And you have a lot of friends here, do you?"

"Nope. Kat is my entire social life."

"Got room for another pal?" Berta asked.

Joey was confused for a moment. "You mean you? Of course!"

"Thank you," Berta said.

"Thank YOU," Joey said. "But about tomorrow night, I'm off the market, remember?"

"Why? I've had four husbands, and I'm still *on* the market." Joey shifted uneasily as Berta mixed watercolors on her palette. "He must have hurt you badly," she said.

"He who? Oh. Jack. My ex?"

"What did he do?"

"It's a long story, Joey said.

"I'm in no hurry," Berta said.

Joey was 27 when she relocated to New York City on the first day of winter, after her father died of a sudden heart attack at the age of 58. She was blowing like the wind from one job to the next when she moved in with her grandparents. Their rambling seven-room apartment in a prewar building on the Upper West Side became her home for the next five years.

It was there that her grandfather taught her how to fix what was broken and preserve what had been neglected. Until he died. It was there that Nonna taught Joey about aging with grace, as Nonna herself declined over the next years. Until she died.

It was only after her grandmother was gone that Joey discovered her family had been her true constants. She missed them the way she would have missed air.

When loneliness ate at her soul she put family photos on the floor-to-ceiling bookshelves in the living room and went for long walks through Central Park, where she watched fat squirrels jump from branch to branch. By the time she got home she was lonelier than ever. Even the squirrels had more family than she.

She got a job at a bookstore on Broadway at 89th Street. She was unpacking a delivery when a man with black eyes and prematurely silver hair came in asking for a book called *The Enneagram Personality System*. His name was Jack.

Joey found him geekily handsome in a loose-tie-and-rumpled-jacket way. Over the next three months they became a couple. Over the next two years they morphed into Joey's first long-term relationship.

"You defy the Second Law of Thermodynamics," he'd whispered as she lay beside him.

"What's that?" she asked, breathing in his scent of ginger and cardamom.

"It means everything changes over time," Jack replied, his hand stroking her stomach. "Heat becomes cold. Order becomes chaos."

"And why do I defy that?" she asked, trailing her hand down his back.

"Because you're as hot as the day I met you," Jack replied, rising on his elbows to look in her eyes before they began to make love.

"Life is never boring around you," he'd declare at many a Sunday brunch as he wolfed down banana pancakes at "their" table in Sarabeth's Kitchen on Amsterdam Avenue.

"Apparently I was too stupid to notice that Jack was getting bored with me. But how could he leave me for a seriously boring blonde named Mandy with highlights and lowlights in her stick-straight hair? And a closet-full of Ferragamo stilettos in every color that she wears to her seriously boring job on Wall Street? How could he do that? How could I not see that coming?" Joey agonized.

Berta painted a purple flower on the paper.

"So many questions, so few answers," Joey said, trying not to sound morose. "Or maybe there are answers. But I never wanted to think about them." Her stomach hurt from telling the story.

"I'm sorry about your family," Berta said, shading the purple flower. "But that fellow—Jack? He wasn't enough for you."

"How do you know?"

"A little plaque in the arteries, a little wisdom."

Joey's face fell.

"Oh. Did I upset you?" Berta asked with concern.

"No. Not at all. I just . . . I haven't talked to anyone like you since my grandmother died. I'd forgotten what it was like."

"And I haven't had a sparkling young friend like you to talk to in some time," Berta said with a smile. "You may be off the market, dear, but Daniel is not. I saw the way he looked at you, even in those work boots. Even with those untied shoelaces of yours. I'm inviting him to join us. Can we trade phone numbers?" she asked before Joey could say another word.

Daniel was filling potholes in the parking lot when Joey walked back to *Hummingbird*.

"How's it going?" he asked.

"Too many termites, too little time," she answered. "I've got to go and replace those rotten steps."

"Can I ask you to do something first? Come with me," Daniel said.

Joey walked behind him to an area beneath the tall pines. A large terrarium holding two huge tortoises stood on the ground.

"Meet Lexus and Armani."

"What?"

"That's their names," Daniel said.

When Joey bent to take a closer look the tortoises pulled their gray necks into their translucent brown shells. "They look about a million years old. Where did they come from?"

"Arbela's grandkids got them as little guys. They grew too big for their home and now they belong to us. That's where you come in."

"What am I supposed to do?"

"Build a habitat for them."

"You're kidding."

"I'm serious."

"But there are so many more important things to do."

"Arbela Kayne is our biggest donor. And she asked that you build it,"
he said firmly. "So draw up some plans and show them to me, will you?
I'll be filling potholes for a while." He walked away.

Lexus and Armani looked steadily at Joey. "Seriously?" she asked
them. They stared at her with hooded eyes. She sat on a log, pulled out a
small notebook from her tool belt and began to sketch plans for a large
wooden box with a hinged, screened top. She was walking over to show
it to Daniel when a group of yoga students walked by, mats in hand. One
of them, a small, plump blonde, stopped in her tracks.

"Oh my God!" she shrieked in an Australian accent.

Daniel looked astonished. And not at all pleased. "What on earth are
you doing here, Heidi?" he asked.

"I've been in L.A. for months," the woman said. "I only just got up
the nerve to visit Oasis." As Joey approached she saw that the woman had
spiky blonde hair and a cleft in her chin, and wore yoga clothes that were
too tight. An alarm rang in Joey's mind. *Where have I seen her before?*

"What do you want?" Daniel asked the woman, his mouth set in a
hard line.

"Peace. I want us to be friends. We have so much history."

"Yes, we do," Daniel agreed. "And so much of it is shit."

Joey hung back. Whatever was going on was none of her business.
From their heated exchange, she learned that Heidi was Daniel's ex-wife,
they'd had a bitter divorce, he hadn't seen her since, and good riddance.

"I hope you don't mind if I come here for yoga," Heidi said brightly.
"Sara is an amazing teacher."

"I can't stop you. It's a free country," Daniel said with an edge.

"Thanks," Heidi said smoothly. "And congrats on taking over Oasis.
Grandma Zora would be so proud." She put her hand on his arm.

"Don't," he said, pulling his arm away. He saw Joey hanging back and
motioned her over.

"Can I show you this?" she asked.

"Go ahead," Daniel said, turning away from Heidi. She looked at Joey with interest.

"I'm Heidi Berne. Wyndham. Daniel's ex-wife," she said to Joey with a smile. Joey saw that her teeth were uneven.

"Hello," Joey said.

"Joey's our new handyperson," Daniel said.

Heidi smiled a crooked smile. "Isn't that darling!"

She walked away as Daniel looked over the plans.

Heidi sat in her rented Chevy Spark, the cheapest car she could have gotten, and watched Daniel talking to Joey. *You're not going to blow it now,* she thought as she drove away. *Not over Daniel and his next victim.* She willed herself to forget that, long ago, when she was 17, she thought she and Daniel would always be together. *Not now, Heidi, she scolded herself.*

She had waited 10 years and flown 7,500 miles to get to this moment.

An hour later Heidi pulled into the underground garage of a gleaming office building on Wilshire Boulevard. She strode through the lobby, holding a large paper bag. She pulled down the jacket of a hot-pink mohair Fendi suit she'd snapped up online for 75 percent off. It was uncomfortably tight and made her feel like a sausage. But she was satisfied by the click-clack of the metal-tipped heels on her stilettos. They sounded like a machine gun as she walked to the elevator.

Her hands shook as she pressed the elevator button. She got on and hit the button for the 14th floor. Checking the mirror, she saw that a small black river of mascara was running down her cheek. She hastily fixed her makeup as the elevator dinged. She walked through the double glass doors facing her, with a large gold crown insignia and the words: Regency Properties.

"I'm Miss Berne," she smiled at the Asian receptionist. "I'm here to see Jonathan Caroon."

"He's in conference. Do you have an appointment?"

"Of course," Heidi said, heading down the hall. "This way?"

Before the receptionist could stop her, Heidi came to a glass door leading into a conference room where four men sat around a polished redwood table with a base in the shape of a dollar sign. She pushed open the door.

"Hello, gentlemen," she said. "I'm Heidi Berne Wyndham, and I have an exceptional opportunity for you."

Over their protests she explained that she had just come from Australia because there was a large and valuable piece of property in the Valley that hadn't been up for sale in decades. "And I alone can deliver it."

The men exchanged glances. Heidi explained that her ex-husband had recently inherited the property, "with strict codicils in his grandmother's will. But I know exactly the type of buyer he'll accept."

"So you're on good terms with your ex, are you?" one of the men asked.

"The best," Heidi said. "Daniel will want to work with me." Before they could stop her she took a seat at the table. She pulled a stack of pamphlets out of her paper bag. "I took the liberty of having these printed up." She passed them out. "Will everyone please open to the first page?"

The men's expressions told Heidi they thought she was a kook. She didn't care. She opened her pamphlet to a photograph labeled: "The New Oasis." It showed a black glass 30-story office building. "I like to call it the Tower," she said. "And when the right buyer is secured it will be built on the site of the current Oasis."

"Is that the place on Ventura Boulevard? The one that's been there forever?"

"Yes, indeedie," Heidi said.

"Big property. What goes on there?" asked Jonathan Caroon.

"Nothing of value, trust me," Heidi sniffed. She proceeded to explain her plan.

Chapter Seven

That evening, in the parking lot of Oasis, Tamara, the first member of Grief Group One, sat in her black BMW. She eyed the list of evening classes written in chalk on a blackboard: Astronomy for Lovers, Vegetarian Masterpieces, Dance like Isadora Duncan, Pottery and Poetry. Grief Group One.

Who flunks Grief Group? Tamara asked herself. "I did," she said aloud as she prepared to meet the second Grief Group she'd joined since her husband died.

From the moment she'd entered the first group, Bereavement for Widows and Widowers, in the fluorescent-lit classroom at Beth Amir Synagogue, Tamara had had one foot out the door.

Had she imagined it? Or had the 50-ish leader, Renata, with false eyelashes, a plaid red kilt that gapped open at the waist, and a syrupy "nice" act, actually started the first group with the words: "We're here to make peace with our losses. To find the silver lining in the glum gloom of our deceased's demise."

Had Tamara been the only one who wanted to run screaming out of that room? Apparently so. Aside from all that awful alliteration, Tamara knew there was no silver lining to be found in Bruce's death, that all he'd left behind was a mountain of bills, no note, and a bundle of unanswered questions. Turned out she'd been the only heretic among the bereaved.

"Now, let's go around the room and say one nice thing about our loved ones who passed," the leader had chirped.

One by one, the mish-mash of men and women, aged 30 to 65, had recited anecdotes about puppies brought home as a Valentine's Day surprise and camping trips where favorite songs were sung around a campfire. *His* sweater found after death and worn to keep a widow warm; *her* vitamins in the fridge that still couldn't be thrown out even though they, too, had expired long ago.

The leader had listened with sympathy and dispensed tissues. Tamara had listened with half an ear. All she'd thought about was how bad Bruce's morning breath had smelled.

When it was her turn she passed, saying it was just too emotional, which it was, but not the emotions everyone else felt as they sniffled; all Tamara felt was the volcanic rage that had consumed her since Bruce died.

She'd lasted until Session Five, knitting a long fringed scarf of Peruvian brown yarn for Maya while the leader decided she was the "silent minority."

"But don't worry, dear," she'd assured Tamara and the rest of the Group. "Everyone gets through the Doldrums of Demise eventually. And so will dear Tamara."

Tamara never made it through the Doldrums of Demise. But by the time she left she'd gotten through Maya's scarf and the back of a plum-colored sweater for Rosalba. And she'd learned nothing about how she was supposed to get through bereavement or how to get her daughter through it either.

So why am I here? Tamara asked herself as she pulled down the vanity mirror to put on lipstick. She knew the answer. She was going to her second Grief Group to appease her mother, Sheila the shrink, who'd sent her to the first one too. *But as soon as I can,* Tamara told herself, flipping the mirror back, *I'm getting the hell out of here.*

A blonde in a red VW bug pulled in and parked next to her. She looked like she was texting. Resentful and reluctant, Tamara put on sunglasses, slammed out of her BMW and headed down the path to *Hummingbird.*

Joey had just finished replacing the rotten boards on the steps when a brunette woman walked up them. She was wearing sunglasses despite its being already dark.

"Is Grief Group meeting here?" she asked.

"Yes," Joey said.

The woman entered *Hummingbird.* Joey quickly collected her tools and walked down the path. On her way to the Quonset hut she passed several more people heading to Grief Group.

A small blonde with messy hair, wearing a baggy orange sweater that stretched to her knees, leggings, and motorcycle boots walked by. *She looks like an overgrown teenager,* Joey thought. A wiry, curly-haired doctor in green scrubs and tortoiseshell glasses stalked towards the cottage, talking loudly on his cell. Joey passed a tall woman with a pale halo of frizzy blonde hair who wore an oversized flannel shirt and carried a bundle under her arm, and a disheveled-looking man who walked with braces on his legs, his hands in metal poles.

They're all my age, she realized as she got into her car. *Good God.* She started the engine and turned on the radio. She couldn't get out of there fast enough. She rolled down the windows to let cool night air into the stuffy car.

"Joey," Daniel called. She looked over. He was striding toward her, looking frazzled. "I'm glad you're still here. I've called everyone I can think of. I can't find anyone to lead Grief Group tonight. So I thought of you."

He talked to her through the open passenger window.

Joey eyed him, stunned. "Me? Why?"

"You said you minored in psych, co-led groups with a psychiatrist, and worked in hospice. You're a natural."

"I'm not a grief counselor," Joey said with indignation.

"Hey. You've done everything. Can't you do this? For one night? Please?" He ran his hand through his thick hair.

"No," Joey said.

"Why not?"

"Because . . . " she fumbled for reasons. "I've lost my whole family. And I hate deathbed promises and funerals and the casseroles people bring. I've eaten enough tuna noodle casserole to audition for the next *Flipper*."

Daniel blinked. "Flipper's not a tuna. He's a dolphin," he said reasonably.

"Whatever," Joey said. "I hate death. And I don't believe in a Grief Group."

"Why not?"

"Because everyone grieves differently," Joey said with passion. "Grief can't be shared. Everyone carries it alone. It's a foreign country with no roadmap." She looked over at the book on the passenger side. "No Thomas Guide. No GPS. No rules."

"That's why you'd make a great leader," Daniel said. "You follow your gut."

"Puh-leaze," Joey said, fastening her seatbelt. She wanted the conversation to be over. Now.

"I can't find anyone else at this hour."

"So call it off."

"Do you think that's fair? After what these people have been through? It was tough enough for them just to get here."

"So lead it yourself."

"I have no idea how . . . "

"That makes two of us."

"I don't think so," Daniel said.

"I'm not doing it," Joey said. "Sorry. No."

Daniel looked at her steadily.

"No way," Joey repeated.

Daniel looked at her. Joey looked back. His eyes were dark with intensity.

"Please," Daniel said softly. "I need your help." In his quiet tone she heard undertones of sorrow. *Who has he lost?* she wondered, startled. "Please," he repeated.

Twenty minutes later Joey was sitting on one of the plaid couches in the den of *Hummingbird,* feeling wildly uncomfortable.

"Hello, my name is Joey, and I'll be your leader for tonight," she said as she faced five silent young widows and widowers. "Um. We're here to listen and share. Let's go around the room and everyone say their name."

"DelMaggieTamaraDaveAlli," they said.

Joey struggled to match names to faces. "Okay. And, uh, say the name of the person who passed."

"Shawn didn't *pass*. He died," said Del, the wiry doctor. His voice was intense. His eyes were pegged on Joey.

Alli, the small messy blonde, had an inappropriate fit of giggles.

"Died," Joey said. "Will you please say the name of your person who died?"

Maggie, the tall woman with military posture, looked across the room with a blank stare. "His name was Jeff."

Tamara looked down at her knitting, sunglasses covering her eyes. Her needles click-clacked in the quiet room. She said nothing.

"Caro," said Dave, the man with braces on his legs and a vacant expression behind thick glasses.

"His name is Rod," Alli said with a sigh.

"How old are you?" Tamara Sunglasses asked Joey sharply. "What are your qualifications for leading a group like this?"

Joey started to sweat. "I'm . . . uh . . . 32 . . . and I . . . uh . . . I know how you feel because I, um, lost people I love."

"How can you possibly know how I feel?" Tamara said. "Did you find your husband in a motel room with his head blown off?"

"No. Oh, God. Of course not." Joey wanted to crawl out the door. "No. You're right, I can't begin to understand your pain and grief but my heart goes out to you. So let's talk about you and why you're here tonight."

A slender man walked in, carrying a diaper bag over his shoulder and something in his arms. He had sandy brown hair and bags under his eyes, and he looked like he hadn't shaved in days. He didn't seem to notice the others in the room.

"Hello. Please take a seat," Joey said.

The man blinked at her words. He looked around the room as if choosing a seat was a bigger decision than he could possibly make. Finally, he walked to one of the plaid couches and sank down across from Joey, cradling the bundle in his arms like a carton of eggs.

His eyes were red-rimmed, his cheeks sunken. When he adjusted the bundle, Joey realized he was carrying a newborn baby. Then she saw that he and the baby were wearing hospital wristbands.

Time slowed as thoughts rushed into her. *Why is he coming straight from a hospital to a Grief Group?* Joey tried to swallow but the possible answers to that question stuck in her throat.

Before she could speak, Del, the doctor, strode across the room to stand over the father and baby. "This baby is—what? Two days old? What's it doing in a public place, man?"

The father's eyes focused on the distance. Joey realized she was holding her breath. She forced herself to speak. "Why don't you sit down, Del?" she said to the doctor in scrubs.

The father said nothing. Del shrugged and went back to his seat. Joey was struggling to find the right words when the baby began to cry. The father clenched a container of powdered formula in his hand and an empty bottle.

"I see you have powdered formula," she said. "You need some water for that. Anyone else need water? I'll get some and be right back."

She walked to the door and reached for the knob. It came off in her hand. Joey looked at it for a moment, making sense of the fact that they were all locked in together. And her tool belt was in the office. She turned to face the group. Everyone but the man with the baby was staring at her.

"Oh, boy," Joey said, the first words that came to her. "Here we go."

Chapter Eight

Doorknob in hand, Joey said, "I'll get it open."

"In what century?" Tamara asked. She threw down her knitting, walked to the door and pulled on it. It held fast.

The baby cried louder. Tamara took a bottle of Purell out of her knitting bag, cleaned her hands, took a bottle of water out of the bag and walked to the father. She mixed it with the formula and shook the bottle as the father watched, frozen. "May I?" Tamara asked him. No answer. She reached for the baby and began to feed it.

Del tried to open a window. It was painted shut. "Find local locksmith," Del said to Siri on his iPhone.

"We don't need one," Joey said. "I'm the new handyperson here. I'll get the door open. It will just take some time."

"Handyperson by day?" Alli asked.

"Grief Group Leader by night?" Del scoffed, closing his phone. "Some credentials."

Joey's nails dug into her palm.

"Tell us," Del said. "Why should we trust you as our leader?"

"I . . . um . . . co-led therapy groups with a psychiatrist in New York."

"Awesome," said Del.

"And . . . like I said, I've lost a lot of people I love . . . "

"Like your husband?" asked Maggie, the tall woman.

"Were you married?" Alli asked.

"Me? No. God, no. No," Joey said. Her leg started to jiggle.

"Kids?" Tamara asked.

"No. Nope. No." Joey forced her leg to stop jiggling. She watched Tamara feed the baby. The Group watched Joey. "I mean, almost. I . . . uh . . . lost a baby. A year ago. I didn't lose it. . . . It's not like I left it on the bus. . . I had a miscarriage. At eight weeks. I didn't think it would mean much. I wasn't ready to be a mom. And *he* definitely wasn't ready to be a dad. The doofus. Oh God," she clapped her hand over her mouth. "How insensitive of me, when you all lost your husbands or wives. I'm sorry. I know I should shut up but it's just, it was better for the kid. I mean, who'd want me for a mom?" *Stop talking*, she told herself. Everyone was staring at her. She looked down at her feet in work boots. "I still don't tie my shoelaces . . . I move around from place to place . . . and job to job. Anyway, I just . . . never realized. I didn't know it would mean I wouldn't have this." She reached out and touched the baby's tiny bootie.

The baby slept, its steady breathing audible. Nobody said a word. The father began to talk in a hoarse voice. "I'm Sam. This is Andrew. I brought him here tonight because I didn't know what else to do. I'm not thinking straight. My wife, Melanie had a stroke right after she delivered Andrew. She died two days ago."

The room reverberated with shock and horror.

"Oh, my God," Alli said.

"It was her second. She'd had the first stroke during her first trimester. Her ob-gyn said it might have been related to her gestational diabetes but they couldn't treat her because of the pregnancy. Then she seemed okay," he said, his voice filled with disbelief. "Mel was a nurse, She'd never been sick before. Until she went into labor and next thing I knew . . . " He stopped, stared straight ahead, unseeing. "I stayed at the hospital until they made me leave. I'm afraid to go home. I can't go into the nursery she decorated. We were waiting on the crib because we wanted the baby to sleep with us. In our bed. Until it was bigger. We were going to be a family . . . " His tears fell on the small white hat on the tiny baby's head.

Waves of pain flowed towards Joey. She checked her seat. *Am I sitting evenly on both sides of my butt? No, of course not.* She was leaning in Sam and Andrew's direction.

She straightened so both her butt cheeks were evenly weighted on the seat. Until she leaned towards none of them. And away from none. Centered in her own space. The most valuable lesson she'd learned from Jack about how to run a Group.

Alli reached for Sam's hand. Her fingers traced the hospital band on his wrist.

"I'm so sorry," she said.

"I am, too," said others.

A blanket of silence hung over the room. Joey made herself think about being bamboo. Being hollow and at ease, open to whatever happened next. "Would anyone else like to talk?"

Tall Maggie stood. "I was hanging Jeff's dress socks on the line when a Pontiac drove up with two uniformed soldiers. They told me Jeff was killed in a training accident. And they gave me this." She reached for the bundle next to her on the couch and started to unfurl an American flag. When a corner of it touched the floor, Del dove to hold it up. "Sign up to serve your country," Maggie said. "Die before you can, and your wife ends up with a prize—a folded flag—red, white and fucking blue? What a crock." She sat, looking numb, gathering the flag around her.

The heavy silence returned to the room, broken by a giggle from Alli.

"Why are you always laughing?" Tamara asked.

"I do that when I'm nervous," Alli confessed.

"When I laugh I feel guilty," Maggie said.

"I don't know what there is to laugh about," Tamara said.

The door opened. An Asian woman glided in. She wore a black peplum suit and carried a Louis Vuitton purse.

"Is this Grief Group One?" The woman started to close the door behind her.

"Stop!" everyone yelled.

Joey ran to keep the door open. "The knob worked from the other side," she explained. As Joey took off one of her work boots to use as a doorstop the Asian woman plopped down on the rug in the center of the circle, still managing to look put-together.

"My damned mother in law is out to get me," she said.

Everyone looked stunned.

"Huh?"

"My husband was a Jewish lawyer. He died a month ago. Left three sperm donations to me. Now his Jewish mother wants to give them to the daughters of her mah jongg group. What the hell do I do? Who's the leader here?"

Everyone looked at Joey as she sat, one boot on, boot off. She wished she were a million miles away.

When Grief Group ended Joey walked to the office to pick up her tool belt. Daniel was at his desk, paying bills.

"How ya goin'?" he asked.

"Not good. So much sadness in that room."

"Aaah," Daniel said. "I'm sorry."

Joey's palms were damp as she spoke. "I probably did more harm than good in there tonight."

"I don't agree. Ya done good."

"How do you know?"

"Because nobody left."

"Of course nobody left. They were locked in with me." Joey plunked the doorknob onto his desk. Daniel began to laugh. "It came off the door. I'll fix it tomorrow," she said, reaching for her tool belt.

"No, you won't."

Joey looked at him, worried. "Am I fired?"

"Are you kidding? You just did two jobs on your first day. Go home, take tomorrow off and when you come back we'll see what broke while you were gone."

"But there's so much to do . . . "

"And time to fix it."

Joey nodded. She felt drained from the stories she'd just heard. Daniel seemed to sense that as he walked her to her car.

"What do you need?" he asked.

Joey wanted to say she needed him to put his arms around her, to tell her everything would be okay. *Stop it,* she told herself.

"Know how to get back to Ferndale?" Daniel asked.

"I don't have a clue," Joey admitted.

"How'd you get here this morning?"

"GPS," Joey said. "But I'm too tired to figure out how to use it to get home."

"Give me your cell," Daniel said.

Leaning on her car he fiddled with it until he'd accessed voice navigation that would give her turn-by-turn directions.

"Thanks," Joey said.

Daniel opened the car door for her. "G'night," he said, shutting the door.

As Joey drove away she looked through her rear view mirror. Daniel was heading back to the office with his easy walk. She caught herself wondering if, in this season of dying, the man might become part of her new life.

Chapter Six

The next morning Joey woke up at 6:00 AM. *Jet lag,* she thought as she felt the blanket of loneliness that covered her.

She found herself thinking about mornings with Jack on the Upper West Side and the love they'd made in their early morning bed. She remembered their quiet walks on rain-washed morning streets.

Enough, she decided. She threw off the covers, grabbed her goggles from her still-unpacked suitcase, wriggled into her bathing suit and headed down to the pool in flip-flops. The white gate to the pool creaked as she opened it. A mockingbird responded with a burst of song. Ahead of her, mist rose from the water. She looked up. *Never have I seen a wider sky,* she thought. *Or maybe it was the same in New York and I never looked.* As two hummingbirds buzzed a wall of magenta bougainvillea the beauty of Los Angeles began to reveal itself to her for the first time.

She put her towel on a lounge chair, pulled off her robe and put on goggles, walked to the edge of the pool, and dove in. She swam the length of the pool underwater, gasping when she reached the other side before she turned to swim back. Head in the water, Joey turned her neck, breathed, head back in water, turned, breathed. Her arms pulled her forward. Her legs fluttered. The sound of her own breathing was all she could hear. She swam as she always had—in New England lakes and the

Atlantic Ocean and in every pool she'd dived into since she was eight years old.

When she was done she toweled off and listened to the silence. Ferndale had slept on as she swam for what seemed like forever. Something about that made her smile. The *New York Times* awaited her in front of the door in its blue plastic wrapper. A post-it note from Kat read: *Here's a New York fix. Gotta go back to that damn deposition. See you tonight at MARGARITAVILLE! XO.*

Later, Joey sat on her balcony, an open copy of the paper on the little white table. She had the day off from Oasis and needed to find another job. She was about to start looking online when the phone rang.

"I can't believe you took off and left me again, Kat," Joey said. "You know I can't find my way around! And that damn Thomas Guide is a joke."

"Don't tell me you're using the Thomas Guide," said an older woman's voice. "It's an antique jumble of boxes and lines. More like an abstract art piece than a finding aid, dear."

It was Berta. Joey said good morning, happy to hear from her.

"Don't you have CBS? Or whatever it's called?" Berta asked.

"GPS?" Joey started to laugh. "Yes, I've got it."

"Then use it to take you to that second job you need," Berta said. "I just got back from buying primroses at a place that's hiring. It's called Pygmalion's Covenant Plant Nursery but everyone calls it Miss Piggy's."

"Who owns it? A fat pink lady?"

"Not exactly," Berta said.

An hour later Joey was standing in a greenhouse watching Demetrios Pygmalion Phillippousis, a bear of a Greek man with thick dark hair and caterpillar eyebrows, as he talked to the leaves of a lady's slipper orchid.

"Tell me why you're dying. *Parakalo* (Please). More water? Less water?

More sun? More shade? What ails you, my little darling?" he cooed, his large fingers delicately stroking its yellowing leaves. "Sir? I . . . I think it needs water," said one of the other potential employees.

"Ssh!" Demetrios commanded. "I am listening." He studied the orchid with intense concentration. "Opa! Iron. She needs iron!" He paced down a greenhouse path and disappeared before returning, a small dark bottle in hand. "Iron," he glowered at the young man who'd spoken up. "She wants. She asks." He pantomimed wilting. "You want to work here? You listen. *Kahtelavo?* (Understand?) Two-hour trial starts now," Demetrios ordered. "Go!"

Joey and the other applicants began to transplant tiny tomato seedlings according to Demetrios's instructions. He peered over Joey's shoulder.

"No, no, no. Firm up soil around roots or roots rot. Like this," Demetrios told her, his large hands moving rapidly. "Now, you."

She did as told. He moved on.

Later, everyone was wheeling wheelbarrows of soil to a vegetable garden planted between the spokes of a giant wooden wheel. Joey was rushing, trying to make a good impression. Her wheelbarrow turned over, spilling the dirt and pitching her into it. Demetrios looked over, bushy eyebrows raised. Joey, filthy, got up, began to shovel the dirt back into the wheelbarrow, and started all over again.

At the end of the two-hour trial, Demetrios stood over Joey's wilted transplants.

"You have black thumb," he pronounced.

"That's not what my grandmother used to say," Joey shot back. "I helped her put in a garden in every place we lived. I'm the one you should hire."

Demetrios showed her how to fix the wilting transplants. When she did it right he nodded approvingly.

"You know how to learn," he said and surprised Joey by hiring her on the spot.

By the time she got back to the apartment, Joey was exhausted and filthy. She showered and changed into a black dress and ballerina flats. Then she knocked on Kat's door. No answer.

"Ready for Margaritaville?" she said as she walked in and found Kat *in flagrante* with Neil. Again.

"Really?" Kat asked, unfazed.

"Really?" Joey retorted before turning on her heel and walking back up to Bud Zellner's apartment.

She was reading emails from friends in New York when Kat came in 20 minutes later. She wore a scarlet miniskirt, a fringed white-and-red shirt, and a turquoise suede cowboy hat.

"Didn't know we were going to a costume party," Joey said.

"Hey. It's line dancing, babe," Kat said, sitting next to Joey. "And you're seriously underdressed."

"Look who's talking about being seriously underdressed."

Kat laughed. "What else do you have to wear? You look like a nun."

"I look fine," Joey said, yawning.

Kat started rummaging through Joey's suitcase. "Are you ever going to hang this shit up?"

"Nope. Never," Joey said.

Kat held up a yellow crocheted dress. "Now, that looks like Margaritaville."

"Margaritaville," Joey said, yawning again. "The last place I feel like going."

"Didn't you say that guy Daniel was coming?" Kat asked.

"Yup," Joey said. She stood, suddenly motivated to change into the yellow dress and her red cowboy boots.

Loud country music blared at the Sagebrush Cantina, a big barn-like club with high ceilings, wagon-wheel chandeliers, a live band, a couple of hundred drinkers and line-dancers.

"One tequila, two tequila, three tequila, four," barflies shouted as Berta, Joey, and Kat sat at the U-shaped bar and downed another shot.

"Again," Berta said. The bartender poured yet another shot. Berta downed it and stood up. "Time to dance."

Joey shook her head.

"Come on," Berta said. She was dressed in a denim shirt, black pants, and black Latin dance shoes. Joey shook her head again. Berta moved onto the dance floor. A man in a Stetson hat took her arm.

"Come on," Kat said to Joey, standing unsteadily.

"I can't," Joey protested. "My head's spinning."

Berta pulled Kat onto the floor into a line-dance. Joey laughed as she watched Berta, a natural, and Kat, a klutz, dance. When they said go left, Kat went right. At the end of every dance segment, Kat was facing the opposite direction from everyone else.

Joey was still laughing on her barstool when Kat swung by and pulled her out onto the dance floor. At first Joey followed the steps, then she fell back and danced, arms and legs flailing, behind a burly man in a green-and-black checked shirt who didn't know she was dancing behind him. Kat and Berta stopped dancing to watch.

"What's she doing?" Berta asked, winded.

"She's always done that," Kat said. "She's a mad dancer. Look." Joey was now dancing behind a middle-aged couple. Kat pulled out her cell phone and took a video. "I'm going to put that on YouTube," she said. "Bet it goes viral."

"She's great," Berta said.

"She's bad-ass," Kat agreed.

"A true original."

"That's what she says about you," Kat said.

"That's why she's perfect to lead Grief Group. Believe me, I've been in plenty of them."

"What were they like?" Kat asked.

"Some were awful; some were okay," Berta said. "I never had a leader like your best friend."

"Why? She has no training. What could Joey do that's so spectacular?"

"It's not what she does," Berta said. "It's who she is. She's sensitive. She has solid instincts. A great sense of humor and a heart of gold. That's what grievers need the most." Kat nodded thoughtfully as they watched Joey dance. "What do you do?" Berta asked.

"Manage an apartment complex. And write."

"Who do you write for?"

"Myself. I have notebooks full of my own bullshit."

"About you?"

"No. Other people. I write human interest pieces about people I know or see."

"I'd love to read them. Where are you published?"

"Nowhere," Kat admitted. "But my boyfriend is the editor of *The People's Weekly*. I keep showing him pieces. He keeps saying they're flat. I'm looking for the right person to write about. Hey, maybe I can write one about you."

"Why don't you write one about your friend?" Berta said.

"Joey?" Kat said, surprised. "How did you know I've been writing about her?"

"Well, why wouldn't you? Like I said, she's an original."

"I was reading something to Neil tonight but I can't find a hook for it."

"How about this? What happens when a woman with losses of her own ends up leading a Grief Group of people her own age?"

"Where's the suspense?" Kat asked.

"Everywhere," Berta responded. "Will she stay or will she go? And what about the young grievers? Will they fight to the surface or drown in the river of grief? That's plenty of suspense for you."

Kat thought it over as they watched Joey mount a fake horse and begin to attempt to "rope." "But what's the hook? That's what my boyfriend always asks."

"They're doing it backwards. Going from death to life," Berta said. "There's your hook."

Kat's eyes widened. "That's good."

"So tell the boyfriend."

"I will," Kat downed another shot. "I just hope I remember that in the morning."

"Why wait?" Berta asked. "Take that to the boyfriend now. Call him."

"Actually, he's at my place," Kat said.

"So go tell him now. I'll make sure Joey gets home safely," Berta said, her eye on the door. "I've enlisted the help of Tall, Dark, and Handsome over there," she said, waving Daniel over. "Go home," she told Kat, "and introduce yourself to Daniel on the way out."

"So that's Daniel," Kat said approvingly, eyeing him. "Will do."

As Berta watched, Kat and Daniel said hello before she left. He walked over and Berta welcomed him with a shot of tequila.

"That was Joey's friend, Kat," Berta said.

"Carrot top and freckles," Daniel said. "Ferndale. Are you fixing her up with me?"

"Not on a bet." She looked over at Joey. "I have an assignment for you."

The cheers of the crowd rang in Joey's ears as she made a successful throw. She was teetering on the fake horse when someone took her hand and whispered in her ear.

"Time to go."

It was Daniel. "What are you doing here?" she asked, trying to focus on his face.

"Taking you home," he said, helping her off the horse.

"But . . . Berta and Kat . . . " Joey looked around for her friends. They were gone. He took her by the hand and led her out of the bar and to his motorcycle.

"Hold on tight," he said when they got on. And she did. When they got to Ferndale, Daniel asked if she could find her way to where she was staying.

"Nope," Joey shook her head vehemently. "I need help."

She took his hand, led him into the elevator and down the hall to #303. She fumbled for the keys and watched him unlock the door. She was dimly aware of him walking her in, taking off her cowboy boots and tucking her into bed. Utterly wasted, she pulled him down to her and kissed him deeply once, then again.

"So, Daniel," she said, trying to sweep her arms wide. "How do you like my lion's den?"

"I like it," he said. But Joey didn't hear. She was out like a light.

Joey called Kat as soon as her eyes opened. "I threw myself at him," she said. "Get over here. Please."

Kat appeared, supplies in hand. "Coconut water, wheat grass shots, spirulina. Mix, drink, hangover gone."

"Ohhh," Joey moaned, her head in her hands. "Why did I do that? The last thing I need in my life is another man."

She got lost again on the way to Oasis and arrived 20 minutes late. As she ran across the packed parking lot to the Quonset hut she half looked for/half tried to avoid Daniel.

"Hey there," a voice rang out. "You're not going to like my news." Marjorie was steaming toward Joey, plunger in hand.

"What's up?" Joey asked, her eyes red behind sunglasses.

"The sink in the office is backed up," Marjorie said. Berta's red Corvette pulled into the lot.

"Oh, man," Joey said. "I'll get the tools in a sec."

Berta walked over to them. "Why so serious?"

"The sink in the office is backed up."

"Again?" Berta said. Marjorie nodded. "Good luck," Berta told Joey. "Those pipes are older than me, dear. Gotta go. I've got a couple of nude models and a group of students in there."

"A couple?" Joey asked.

"Mmhmm. A guy and a girl. Gotta keep mixing it up," she said, heading to *Berta's Bungalow.* "Which reminds me, tell me later how it went with you and Daniel."

When Marjorie shot her a look Joey headed to the Quonset hut. Soon she was struggling to unblock the pipes using a rusty snake she'd found in a back corner. By noon they were unclogged but Joey was cooked.

"You don't look so great," Marjorie said, eyeing her green face.

"Jet lag," Joey said.

"Jet lag, my ass," Marjorie said. She opened a drawer, took out two aspirin and put them in a cup of coffee. "Best hangover cure in the West."

"Is Daniel here?" Joey asked, drinking it down.

"In meetings at the bank," Marjorie said.

"Problems?"

"Payroll problems, property taxes overdue, mortgage problems. You name it."

"Sorry to hear that," Joey said, wondering about her job security.

Later that afternoon Joey was fixing a screen door when she saw Daniel pull in on his motorcycle. He was wearing a tight-fitting Italian suit and black motorcycle boots.

"*Shit,*" she thought, looking down at her unlaced work boots as he approached.

"Hey," he said.

"Hey."

Daniel it a cigarette and offered one to her.

"No thanks."

"How's it going?" he asked, taking a drag.

"Slow," she admitted. "Thanks for taking me home last night. I was pretty wasted."

"My pleasure," Daniel said, his eyes on her.

Joey felt her face reddening. "How's your day going?"

"Pretty crappy."

"Money troubles?" she asked.

"Keeping this place afloat is costing a mint." He gestured toward tree roots that were buckling the cement. "A goddamn mint."

"Anything I can do?" Joey asked.

"You're doing it," he said with a tired smile. "And hey. You rope a mean bull."

Daniel stepped on his cigarette. She watched as he walked to the office. His shoulders looked like they were in knots. Joey found herself wishing she could rub them.

Heidi, Daniel's ex-wife, was seated in the front row of Green Real Estate 101, listening to the owner of the school. She was taking classes to get her California real estate license. And she was there to troll for a willing partner.

"'Red-tagged' does *not* mean it is not livable or inhabitable," the instructor said. "There is a wide array of problems that can get a property or a structure red-tagged. One as minor as a fence built a foot too high."

Heidi raised her hand. "Mr. Green?"

TEARS AND TEQUILA · 75

"Yes?"

"What if a property has lots of issues?"

"Like what?" asked the instructor. Gus Green was about five feet six, with thinning rusty-brown hair and a paunch. Heidi noticed he wore khakis, loafers, and a tie, as if he was trying to look preppy, but he'd forgotten to wear a belt, which made his pants sag.

"Like umpteen pot holes in a driveway. Big tree trunks that make bumps in the pavement. No fire hydrants, just hoses hooked up to faucets." She smiled. "What's the responsible thing to do with such a rundown property?"

"Residential or commercial?"

"Commercial," she said.

"That sounds like a perfect candidate for a red tag, Ms.—"

"Berne," Heidi smiled. "Heidi Berne." She wriggled in her seat and hiked her miniskirt higher up her thighs. She saw the instructor take in her stilettos, black fishnets, and red bra beneath a lacy black camisole. "I want to make sure to do everything by the book."

"It's not that simple to get a property condemned. Why don't you see me after class?" he said. "The red tag will provide information about the date of the inspection, the inspector's identification, and a brief comment on the problem. The red tag is also recorded on your title, if the red tag got posted on the property and somehow got taken down." Heidi took copious notes in red ink on her lined yellow pad.

Chapter Ten

A week later Joey, dressed in an oversized purple "Miss Piggy" T-shirt, baggy jeans, and sneakers, was sowing carrot seeds in peat pots with a sharp pencil, the way Demetrios had taught her. She moistened the lead end, stuck it into the seeds to pick up one or two, painstakingly moved them to the little pots.

At first Joey had been astonished by the depth of her boss's love for living organisms. By now, she was used to the fact that Demetrios, who liked to feed everyone, whether they were hungry or not, was devoted to every plant in his nursery.

"Athelfos" (Brother), he called the sunflowers.

"Athelfee" (Sister), he sang to the red geraniums.

"Seezigos" (Wife), Joey once heard him quietly intone to that rarest of orchids, the Red Moon, kept under lock and key in what he called his *sanctum sanctorum w*here nobody but Demetrios could admire (or steal) its fabled red-striped flowers.

Joey observed that most customers came for Demetrios's exquisite flowers or bushes or his greenhouses full of exotic orchids. Others came for his Greek wisdom, which he never tired of dispensing. And everyone tried to come at 4:00 PM on Wednesdays, when Demetrios's wife, Agatha (Aggie), and his three sons served platters of homemade spanikopita or baklava.

Like everyone else who worked there, Joey did what he told her, no questions asked, because Demetrios ruled his two-acre nursery like a Mycenaean kingdom: with endless kindness (towards plants) and a firm hand (towards humans.)

Now, Demetrios moved on to a lively argument with the Latino gardener who'd worked there since Day One. Joey waited for the right time to ask her boss for a favor. She approached as he was complimenting Perfecto on wiping out white flies on a yellow hibiscus plant.

"Demetrios?"

"Oh! Josefina!" he answered, bellowing at his own joke, which she'd heard about a hundred times by now.

"I, um, was wondering, could I leave an hour early today? I'll make it up on Friday."

He regarded her imperiously. "Why you leave?"

"I need to help my friend. She's the manager of an apartment complex and there's a leaking hot water heater."

"Come late, leave early. What story? Why you always late?"

"No story," she apologized, embarrassed. "I keep getting lost."

"What you do when get lost?"

"I try to get found?" she replied, hoping that would end the conversation.

"No." Demetrios shook his head vigorously. *"Ochi.* No."

"What do you mean?"

"You need be like bird. How birds learn to fly?" He moved his arms up and down.

"They flap their wings?"

"Ochi (no)." Demetrios mimed pushing.

"The mother and father push them out of the nest?"

"Ne (yes). And then?"

"And then they fly?"

"Then they *fall*," Demetrios corrected. "*Then* they can fly. See?"

"No."

"Come." He walked her to his tiny, cluttered office. It was wallpapered with index cards from floor to ceiling, lettered in thick black magic marker in Demetrios' hand. The cards held poems by ancient Greek poets and verses from the Bible, quotes by "The Boss," Nikos Kazantzakis, alongside photos, posters, postcards, and prints. Demetrios breathed heavily with concentration as he searched for an index card. He found it on the back wall. "Rumi. Read!" he commanded.

She peered at hieroglyphics on the index card. "I can't read this," she said. "What language is it?"

"Ancient Persian," Demetrios replied with an impatient gesture. "It says . . . " He began to translate.

Joey heard something about love and birds that learn to soar after they fall. It was hard to understand his Greek-accented translation of ancient Persian.

"You see?" he asked when he was finished. "The great poet, he understand your problem. You need fall. Then you fly. *Kahtelavo* (Understand?)"

"No. You think I should fall . . . in love?" Joey was completely confused.

"How you say in English. Do what love?"

Joey thought a second. "You mean do what you love?"

Demetrios nodded. "English wrong. Not do what you love. Love what you *do*," he said, gesturing to his plants. "Fall head over feet in love. With life. Oh! Josefina. Don't be afraid. Get lost. Until you *love* lost. Maybe then you get found," he pronounced.

"Hmmm. Okay," she said, trying to sound casual but feeling the emotion in her throat. "Thanks."

Demetrios nodded twice. "Back to work," he commanded.

Joey returned to planting carrot seeds. She found herself wondering if he was talking about finding her way around L.A. or about being afraid to fall in love again or to make any commitment at all. She suspected that Demetrios knew more about her than he had any right to know.

"Customer," Demetrios told Joey, walking back into the greenhouse. "Take flower order."

Collecting a sales pad, Joey went out to meet the customer.

It was Sam, the newly widowed father from Grief Group. "I'm here to order flowers for my wife's memorial. It's tomorrow," he said.

Joey took a step backwards, shocked. "Do you live nearby?"

Sam looked dazed. "I live in Pasadena but my mother-in-law lives down the street. She's got the baby. She told me Miss Piggy's does the best funeral arrangements in town. But I don't know how many arrangements I need or what color or anything. Can you help me?"

"Of course." Joey wasn't sure if he even recognized her. "Come into the greenhouse and let's take a look together."

Joey picked out flowers, checked prices, and made arrangements for the flowers to be delivered to the sanctuary.

"Thank you," Sam said as he started to leave, one slightly unsteady foot in front of the other. Then he looked back at Joey, as if he'd just remembered how he knew her. "See you in a couple of nights."

"Oh, sorry. I won't be there," Joey said.

Sam was already gone.

Kat was writing by the pool when Joey arrived at Ferndale. After a quick swim she told Kat about running into Sam. "I can't believe his wife's memorial is tomorrow," she said, toweling off. "And he thinks he'll see me at the next Grief Group."

Kat put down her writing. "The poor guy's counting on you."

"Daniel's going to get someone else to lead it."

"You should keep doing that group."

"Easy for you to say."

"Why can't you? You've done every other job under the sun."

Joey thought about that as she combed her long, wet hair. "I don't know why, but I can't talk to those people. I don't know what to say or do for them. I have nothing to offer them."

"Of course you do. You're on the same path as they are."

"So?"

"So all you have to do is stay two steps ahead of them. You don't have to be all the way healed to help them."

Joey shrugged. "I don't want to do it."

"Fine," Kat said. "So leave. You love to leave. You should leave right now. They won't even miss you." Kat went back to her writing.

"Why should I stay?" Joey asked. "In the end you lose everyone."

Kat kept on writing.

"What are you writing?" Joey asked after a minute.

"Another essay nobody will publish," Kat said acidly. She closed the notebook.

"Still need help with that hot water heater?" Joey asked.

"Umm hmm," Kat said, walking away. After a moment Joey followed silently. Between Demetrios and Kat she'd heard enough for one day.

Two days later the rain sounded like golf balls on the metal roof of the Quonset hut. Joey wore goggles as she finished sanding a table and six chairs. Lexus and Armani were walking around the workshop on wrinkled legs. Occasionally Joey would look up and see two pairs of orange-ringed eyes looking back at her as the turtles stretched their long necks.

Joey had organized the Quonset hut the way her grandfather had taught her: she'd hung pliers, hammers, wrenches and saws on the pegboard walls, their shapes traced to mark where they belonged; her grandfather's old Estwing leather-handled hammer had a place of honor. A row of colored plastic bins lined the floor, filled with odds and ends. Paint cans were labeled by color; brushes and rollers were hung neatly. Now, Joey took out a labeling gun and began to label jars of screws and nails on the workbenches.

Through the dirty window she saw the drum circle pounding away on bongos around the fire pit, where, despite the rain, a fire sizzled. She was washing up to go home when Marjorie appeared, looking troubled.

"You're not going to believe this."

"What?"

"The daughter of the woman Daniel found for Grief Group just called. Her mother tripped over a cement barrier in Walgreen's parking lot and shattered her elbow. She's going into surgery right now."

"So?" Joey asked, not liking the sound of that. "Daniel must have someone else to back her up."

"I can't reach him. He's not answering his cell and Grief Group's arriving. I need your help," Marjorie said.

Joey looked over at the path to *Hummingbird* with misgivings. The woman named Tamara was already walking down it.

Chapter Eleven

Sunglasses in place, Tamara shook the last drops of rain off her trench coat and walked into the den of *Hummingbird*. *What a dump,* she thought. The room smelled dank. Everything she saw she wanted to paint, reupholster, or refinish. She saw the father sitting on the red plaid couch, holding the baby and reading *The Hero with a Thousand Faces*. "Hello," he said as Tamara walked to the rocker in the corner. His face still looked drained.

"Hi," she replied in a hoarse whisper. She couldn't think of his name.

"Sounds like you've got a cold."

"Laryngitis," she lied. "My doctor said it's not catching—probably from all the stress." She pulled out a ball of hunter green wool and began to knit. "You look like you haven't slept since the last meeting."

"Does anyone sleep when they have a newborn?"

"Of course not, but my husband and I took turns." She stopped herself. "I'm sorry, I forgot you're the mom *and* the dad."

"I can't believe it myself. I never imagined doing this without her. I'm a professor." He trailed off, overcome.

Tamara changed the subject, ashamed of her crassness. "What do you teach?"

"Classics. Claremont College."

She knit a row, impressed. "That's one of the top schools in the country."

"Uh-huh," Sam said, looking down at the sleeping baby. "I'm sorry, I forgot your name."

"Tamara."

"Sam."

He returned to his reading. She worked the needles, sneaking glances at him. *What was his wife's name? Christ, he just lost her two weeks ago. How is he going to manage this?*

She noticed the simple gold band on Sam's left hand. Automatically, her hand went to her ring, hanging on a chain hidden underneath her sweater, as if she and Bruce were going steady. She thought about the love in Sam's voice when he talked about his wife. She thought about the last time she'd seen Bruce.

She needed air.

"Excuse me."

Tamara charged out of the room, walked through the small waiting room and emerged onto the porch

A cloud of cigarette smoke drifted up to the yellow light over an old picnic bench. Tamara recognized a few people from the last meeting. The messy little blonde sat next to the Asian woman with the Jewish mother-in-law problem, who was decked out in a Burberry raincoat, not one black hair out of place. The disheveled man stood next to the bench, resting on his poles as he smoked. When he saw her he called out.

"Good thing you're wearing shades. Wouldn't want the light to hurt those eyes."

"Thanks," Tamara rasped. *Instant allergy*, she thought. She pointed to the NO SMOKING sign on the porch. Dave took another puff, ignoring her.

"What happened to your voice?" asked the blonde.

"Laryngitis," Tamara repeated. She saw no reason to add that it was a good excuse to get out of telling Bruce's story tonight. "Sorry, can't remember your names."

"Daisy," said the Asian woman.

"Alli," said the small blonde.

"Dave," said the man with the poles.

"Tamara," she added.

"Tell her," the blonde named Alli said to Dave.

"Why didn't the chicken skeleton cross the road?" Dave asked Tamara.

"I give up."

"Because he didn't have enough guts."

Alli tittered. Daisy laughed. Tamara barely smiled.

A curtain of water cascaded off the sagging wooden roof. In the midst of the downpour she heard the crunch of gravel. Then the tall woman from the last group ran across the parking lot, up the steps, and slipped.

"Don't worry," she said, righting herself, "I still haven't grown into my legs. I trip over them all the time," she said, closing her umbrella.

"I never *did* grow into my legs," Dave said sardonically, indicating his poles. "Lower limb deficiencies." Everyone looked blank. "Birth defects, people," he added.

Tamara moved to the far side of the porch as the tall woman said her name—Maggie—and the rest stood around talking awkwardly. She had no intention of getting to know any of them. She'd be bailing soon enough. She checked her phone for messages from Maya.

"Have you ever noticed how fast you shut down a conversation just by showing up?" she heard Dave say.

Everyone stopped talking.

"I thought it was me," Daisy said.

"People don't want to be around death. They think it's catching," Dave said.

"Does anyone call you anymore?" Daisy asked.

"No," Maggie said.

Alli said, "They stopped after a couple of months."

Tamara listened despite herself. She and Bruce had played "Be Nice to Each Other in Front of Company," so none of their friends knew how miserable they were. They were all shocked by his suicide. They'd all stopped calling.

"Anyone invite you to a Superbowl party?" Dave asked.

Silence. Tamara was listening.

"Nobody knows what to do with us," Maggie said.

Daisy said, "I guess that's why we're here."

"There's nowhere else I can talk about my husband," Alli said. "People just don't get it."

"Like, when I dropped my clothes at the cleaners last week the guy asked, 'How's your wife?'" Dave said. "I said, 'She died.' He said, 'Just tell her she can pick them up on Friday.'"

"I keep getting Rod's *Sports Illustrated* in the mail," Alli complained. "Even though I told them to cancel the subscription because he's not reading them right now."

"I told *Playboy* to send his subscription to his new address. Forest Lawn," Tamara said from the other end of the porch.

Dave laughed.

"It's like we're living in another country," Daisy said.

"Another planet is more like it," Maggie said.

"Planet Grief?" asked Alli.

"Better than Uranus," Dave replied. "Up yours," he yelled. "That's what I have to say to people who blow us off. And how about that stupid groundhog seeing his shadow yesterday?"

"Six more weeks of winter," Alli said glumly.

"Screw the shadow," Dave said. "Who gave that little weasel the right to tell me I'm supposed to grieve for six more weeks?"

Awkwardness descended. Tamara looked down at her phone: "6:55."

Dave stubbed out his cigarette. "Wonder where our leader is."

They filed into the waiting room. *Our own little band of losers,* Tamara thought as the screen door banged behind her.

Joey had come through the back door of the den where she'd found the father and the baby sitting on the couch.

"Hello," she said. He nodded at her and went back to his reading. She wondered how his wife's memorial had gone. She lit a few candles and the rest of the group filed in. Everyone had come back except the doctor.

"Well, it's me again," Joey said when they were seated in the same seats as before. "But this is the last time. I'm, like, a sub."

"Great," Tamara said, pulling out her knitting.

"When are we getting a real person?" Dave asked.

Joey smiled tightly. "Next time, for sure. A few of you talked last time. Does someone else want to talk about their spouse? Who he or she was and how he or she died?"

"Is," Alli said. "Not was."

"Sorry," Joey said. She wanted to disappear.

"I'll go," said the man who walked with metal poles. "The name's Dave."

Joey looked at him, waiting. It looked like Dave was waiting, too, to find the right words. "What is your wife's name?" she asked, careful to use present tense.

"Caroline," Dave began. "Caro. She taught kindergarten. She was also a dancer." Dave's eyes watered. He stared at the flickering candles on the table. Everyone stared back at him. "I lost her in November." He paused. "Three months ago. Caro was just . . . at the wrong place at the wrong time. She was walking across the street when a truck came barreling off the highway. A drunk driver. Hit and run." His face crumpled. "Sorry. Didn't mean to . . . "

Alli, Maggie and Daisy regarded Dave with sympathy. Sam looked down at the sleeping baby. Tamara knit, needles clicking.

Dave reached for the pitcher of water. "My mouth's dry."

"Thank you for telling us," Joey said.

Alli raised her hand. "I'll go next. I'm Alli. My husband is Rod. We met at Stanford." She paused. "He drowned. At least, that's what they say happened." She bit her lip as she looked around the room. "Any of you guys ever been to the Sea of Cortez? That's where my husband's sister and brother-in-law live. We went for July Fourth and the guys went fishing in Sal's boat—*Number Nine*, like the Beatles' song. They even went when a big storm was coming in."

Alli's bangs covered her eyes. "I was standing on the dock, waiting for them to come in. These huge waves were soaking me up to my knees but I was staring at the horizon as boat after boat came back. I was sure I'd see *Number Nine* if I looked hard enough." Her voice grew softer. "Everyone told me the boat must have sunk and the guys drowned. But Rod swam like a merman. What if he and Sal took off for somewhere? You know, they were sick of being married and headed to Hawaii? It could happen—right?"

Nobody said a word.

"He's out there somewhere. One of these days he'll come walking through the front door," she said. The room was silent. "I have Rod's passport. His Harley's parked in the garage. The one thing I don't have is his body. So how am I supposed to believe he's dead?"

Alli was looking at Joey. Someone's cell phone rang.

Joey sat frozen, caught in a memory.

She was ordering a mocha latte at a Starbucks near Boston Common when her cell phone rang. Her father had dropped dead of a heart attack on West 57th Street in New York. He'd just taught a Creative Writing class at the School of Visual Arts.

Ever since, Joey often imagined him crashing to the pavement, a tall tree falling, forever stilled. Every time she did, she felt her world shift on its axis.

What would I have done if Dad had disappeared? she asked herself now. *Would I have thought he wasn't dead? Would I have waited for him to come home? Yes,* Joey realized. *That's exactly what I would have done. I'm no different from Alli,* she thought with a sinking heart, *so how can I possibly help her?*

Dave was watching Joey. *The good news is she doesn't know what she's doing. So she's not likely to find out why I was ordered into grief counseling. The bad news is she doesn't know what she's doing. So she's not likely to help any of us.*

"You have no idea how to help us, do you?" Tamara asked Joey.

Joey blew out a long breath. "I'm not sure," she admitted.

The room was silent, except for Tamara's knitting needles.

"You hear those stories. About people whose husbands die. I never thought I'd be one of them," Alli said.

Silence.

"I thought, after I married Jeff, everything was going to be perfect . . . ," Maggie said.

Silence.

"That's what life does to you," Dave said. "Fucks you over when you least expect it."

Silence.

The rain had stopped. Smoke from the bonfire came through the cracks in the windows.

"Does anyone else want to talk about their spouse?" Joey asked tentatively.

"No," Tamara said hoarsely and with hostility. "Not tonight. Not ever."

"Okay," Joey said.

Silence.

The pounding of the drums reverberated in Joey's ears. An idea came to her. *No,* she thought. *It's disrespectful. Wrong.* She looked at the silent group. She had nothing to say. She didn't know how to lead them. She had nothing to lose.

Joey stood. "I've got a totally weird idea." She walked out of the room and went to the fire pit. She began to circle around the fire in a slow dance. In a few minutes she saw the group filing towards her.

"What are you doing?" Tamara called over.

"I don't know how to help you. In there. But there's a difference between a funeral and a wake," Joey answered. "So I'm going to celebrate the lives of my loved ones." She continued to dance, twirling to the beat of the drums. "Come join me."

Some of the group said no, it's too soon, it's too weird. Then, surprise, surprise, Del the doctor arrived.

"You're late," Dave said.

"I'm here," Del said. He ran to the fire pit and began to dance. As Joey kept dancing, the drums kept pounding. In time the Grief Group joined the dance until they were all dancing around the fire, together and alone. Sam covered the baby with a blanket and moved slowly.

The drumming got louder and faster. The group began to dance around the blaze. Joey danced behind some of them without their knowing, arms and legs flailing. Others gathered to watch. Some started to dance too. Marjorie appeared; Berta joined in, grabbing Marjorie by one hand, holding Joey's hand in the other.

When Daniel appeared, Berta beckoned him over. Then they were all dancing, holding hands, not holding hands, as the fire sparked and the drums roared and Grief Group One took over Oasis as they mourned their losses without words.

Heidi was watching with a group of yoga students.

"Let's join them," said a Samoan woman.

"Seriously," agreed a tiny redhead.

"Looks like fun, but gotta go," Heidi said to the others.

She got in her car and spoke into her iPhone. "Look up 'Fire code for commercial premises'" she told Siri. Then she pulled out her lined yellow pad and began to write in red ink.

A few days later at Ferndale, Kat was reading her new piece to Neil as they lay in bed.

"She's been my best friend since fourth grade and I love her. But she can be pretty maddening," Kat read nervously. "She says she has gypsy blood. That's supposed to explain why she never settles in one place for long. Or one job. It's supposed to explain why she prefers tequila to tears, laughter to dwelling on sorrow. So what happens when a gypsy meets a Grief Group of people her own age? And the hard truth of their losses smacks her in the face?"

As Kat was reading, Joey was working at Oasis, pulling old furniture out of bungalows, including an old crib. She began to break it down for trash, looked at it for a while, thought better of it, and walked to the office to get an address before she loaded the crib into the back seat of the Le Baron.

At Ferndale, Kat read aloud to Neil: "She says she can't think of one reason why she should be a grief counselor. She thinks she should just keep doing what she knows how to do—fixing things that are broken.

She doesn't realize her gifts might include fixing people who are broken, too."

In Pasadena, Joey stood in front of Sam's house, crib in hand. He opened the door.

"Hey there," Sam said, surprised.

"I thought you could use this," Joey said. For a moment, Sam looked from her to the repaired crib. Then he carried it into his house, passing the baby sleeping in his car seat. Joey cast a long look at the child. At Ferndale, Kat read to Neil: "There are moments when you have to choose your one true thing. And getting through grief might just be Joey's. She's had a lot of practice."

In Pasadena, Joey and Sam were in the blue nursery his wife had painted and stenciled with soft white clouds. It was luminous with life and love. As Sam put the sleeping baby into the crib Joey looked down at him.

"I'm sorry for your loss," Sam said.

"What do you mean? Oh. My miscarriage?" Sam nodded. Joey was stunned. "How can you say that? After all you've lost?"

"It's not a contest," Sam said softly. "Everyone loses. We start losing from the day we're born." He walked Joey to the door. "See you next week?"

At Ferndale, Kat read to Neil: "So what does a woman like that do? If I'm right, you'll find her at Grief Group One at Oasis on Wednesdays, seven to nine. If I'm right, my best friend will keep doing it her own way and her Grief Group won't be like anyone else's. If I'm right, my best friend, the professional gypsy, will stay put. Finally."

In Pasadena, Joey answered Sam at last.

"See you next week."

Kat came to the end of the piece she'd written. Neil pulled her into his arms.

"That one I'll publish," he said.

"Oh, my God," Kat said. "Really?"

"Really."

She started to kiss him.

"What's the title?"

Kat pulled away long enough to look him in the eye.

"'Tears and Tequila,'" she said before he kissed her again and they began to make love.

In Pasadena, Joey drove away from Sam's house. She got on the 134 Freeway West to Ferndale.

This time she didn't get lost.

Part Two

Chapter Twelve

Ten days later, Tamara sat on the white leather couch in her living room, answering Sam's question and playing with the fringes on her hand-knit black and white afghan.

"What was the worst thing about the day Bruce died? The way Maya kept saying, 'Where did he go? Where did he go? One minute he was playing Guitar Hero on the Wii with me, next minute you told me he was dead.' By nighttime she was screaming it. 'Where did he go?'

"My mother's doctor had to sedate her before she could sleep. Me? I was icy calm. I couldn't stop shaking, but I couldn't cry either. How are you supposed to feel when you find your husband in a motel room, dead from a gunshot to the head?"

"I can't imagine," Sam said. "What a nightmare."

Tamara looked over at him, a little startled. Sam was sitting on her couch, leaning against the red pillows, filling the silent house with warmth. She'd been so caught up in telling the story that for a moment she couldn't remember how he got there.

Tamara had seen Sam and the baby at Oasis when she went to pick up Maya from her guitar lesson. Sam looked sad. Maya looked her usual shade of miserable until Andrew smiled at her. Soon Maya was begging Tamara to let them come over so she could babysit, which was ridiculous because Maya didn't babysit and it was a school night. And Tamara had vowed not to get to know anyone in Group, since she wasn't going back.

But it had been months since Tamara had last seen Maya smile, and she knew Rosalba had made home-made taquitos and she felt terrible for Sam. So he and the baby had come for dinner, and now Andrew was asleep in Maya's room, and Tamara and Sam were sharing a pitcher of Rosalba's sangria.

"You mean, you had to organize the funeral after seeing that? How could you do it?" Sam asked.

"I just did what had to be done," Tamara shrugged, ticking her actions off on her fingers. "Called my mother, my sister, Bruce's boss, and his mother, Rhonda, who told me I had to tell everyone Bruce died of a sudden heart attack. 'I'm telling the truth,' I said. She said he was going to hell because of me. Bruce was Italian Catholic from the San Fernando Valley. I'm a Jew who grew up in West Los Angeles. Rhonda never got over him marrying me." She poured refills of their drinks. "Heard enough?"

"I have, if you want to stop. Otherwise, I'm here."

"You don't want to hear this story," Tamara said, taking a sip and waiting for Sam to say he had to go.

"You have to tell someone," he said. "You can't keep all this bottled up inside. Tell me."

Tamara hesitated. Sam was still in shock over his wife's sudden death. He looked as if he couldn't take a breath without it hurting to be alive. "I shouldn't be doing this," she said. "Not after what you've been through."

"We've all been through hell," Sam said. "Haven't we?"

"You're right," Tamara said. "You're very understanding."

This is sick, she thought, looking at him over her glass as she took a sip of her drink. *I'm flirting. Is death-and-funeral-speak some kind of foreplay for grievers? Why the hell didn't Joey tell us about this in Group?*

"So—the drama queen. Your mother-in-law?" Sam looked at her inquisitively.

Is he just being polite or does he really want to know? Tamara's head felt woozy from the sangria.

"Rhonda? She kept shrieking at me. 'Everyone knew how miserable Bruce was with you. He stayed because of Maya. He was going to leave you because you're such a bitch.'"

"Good Lord."

"She kept screaming until I started screaming back. I said something about how it had felt to find him, and why didn't Rhonda go down to the morgue and check out how the left side of his face was missing?" Sam's face reflected the horror of her tale. Tamara told herself to shut up, but now that she was talking she couldn't stop. "My mother-in-law was yelling louder and louder until she hung up on me. That's when I saw my mother standing at the top of the stairs with Maya."

"Oh, God."

"I never wanted Maya to hear any of that. For one thing, she was Daddy's girl. My mother, a shrink, raced over here right after he was found. She made sure to tell Maya, 'Your father had an illness. A mental illness. That's what made him kill himself. It was not your fault.'"

"Was he ill?" Sam asked.

Tamara took a deep breath. "Bruce had been depressed, off and on, for years. Sometimes he took medication for it. Sometimes he didn't." She paused. "A couple of months ago I noticed he'd stopped taking his pills. Again. But I didn't say anything because I thought it wouldn't make any difference. He'd say he'd take them, like always. Only he wouldn't. Because he didn't like the way they made him feel." A headache began to throb above Tamara's right eyebrow. "Anyway," she said. "After I realized Maya had heard what I said to Rhonda I went to the top of the stairs and wrapped my arms around my daughter. I said I was sorry, but she didn't hear me because she was sedated. My mother ended up putting Maya to bed while my father helped make the arrangements for the funeral."

"What a horrible, horrible day."

Tamara, nodded, feeling numb.

"So, the funeral?" Sam asked.

"It was a blur. Some friends came. Others stayed away. It didn't matter. I wasn't there."

"You didn't go?"

"I went. There was nobody home." She pointed to her head. "I don't remember a word of it. At least I got out of going to the graveside service by saying I had a blinding migraine. I still haven't visited his grave."

Sam looked at her steadily.

"On the ride home Maya had one question: 'Who's going to take me to the Father-Daughter Dinner Dance?' That was when I started to get mad. I was so mad at Bruce for doing that to her. I still am. And at myself. For not realizing how much pain he was in. . . . "

On she went, gulping sangria and blabbering to the kind, sympathetic, nice-looking man who was a virtual stranger and still in shock from his own loss. She knew she was behaving badly. She knew she should ask about his wife's funeral, but she couldn't stop talking.

An hour later they were both yawning when Sam walked to the door, carrying the sleeping baby in his arms.

"I can't believe I told you all that," Tamara said, feeling both grateful and embarrassed.

"I'm glad you did." Sam gave her a weary smile. "See you at Group."

"I'm not coming back."

"Why not?"

"Who wants to hear this story?"

"Who wants to hear any of our stories? We're all in the same boat—remember? Come back and tell it to the Group."

Tamara paused. "I'll think about it," she said finally.

After Sam had driven off she closed the door and leaned against it. *I'm shnockered,* she realized, as Boots the cat padded in and looked at her curiously. "Plastered," she said to him while she carried the glasses into the kitchen, turning on the radio as she washed up. When a dance tune came on, in an inexplicable moment Tamara found herself shaking her hips as she dried the dishes.

Out of nowhere, she remembered making love with Bruce. She imagined making love with Sam. She pictured talking with him afterwards as they lay side by side in bed, his hand on her breast.

Heat rose inside of her until she had to hold onto the sink, because there it was again. The crushing silence. The fucking silence.

Whispering to her about all she hadn't said.

Chapter Thirteen

The sign on the closed wooden door read *Los Angeles Department of Building and Safety.* Heidi stood in the hallway, the third person in a long line of men waiting to go in. She was the only woman there. She checked her cell phone: 7:15.

"They open at 7:30—right?" Heidi asked the Hispanic man behind her, a lanky 40-something in well-worn jeans.

"Si," he said.

"Gracias," Heidi said with a smile, turning away when she saw the man was looking at her strangely. She pulled her long red sweater down over her ass and shifted impatiently from one gray Ugg-booted foot to the other.

She looked at the notes on her lined yellow pad and the printed papers clutched in her hand: *Is the property up to code? Building codes include rules regarding parking and traffic impact. Fire codes are rules to minimize the risk of a fire and to ensure safe evacuation in the event of an emergency. There are requirements for specific building uses (for example, setting a fire). . . .*

The words swam before her eyes. There were so many ways that Oasis was not up to code. So many important ways. Heidi felt as if she'd fallen into a pot of gold. But all that writing about fire made her want to light up a cig. She turned to the man behind her.

"Can you save my place in line?"

"Si," he nodded.

Heidi walked outside the building. She put the papers in her vintage studded leather purse. Her hands shook as she lit up.

Why am I nervous? she asked herself. *Because I'm about to bury Daniel and his pet project. Stay focused,* she scolded herself. *He deserves this. He* more *than deserves this. You're doing this for your family. You deserve the money you'll make.*

But Heidi remained rooted to the spot. Because despite her lust for revenge she had loved Daniel once. *Once upon a time,* she reminded herself as she took a long drag. *And now you're broke and he's got bank, so move your ass and get back in there.*

Heidi ground her cigarette under her boot and resumed her place in the line just as the wooden door opened and the line filed in. The first two men went over to the clerk. Heidi felt a tap on her shoulder.

"Senora?" said the man behind her.

Heidi turned.

"Yes," she said.

"Perfecto," said the man, "is my cousin. He know you."

"Huh? Do I know *you?*" Heidi asked.

"My name Oscar. My cousin—Perfecto—works at Oasis on Sundays. Sometimes I help him. I hear you talking there. You have—*cómo se dice?*" He spoke Spanish with his neighbor while Heidi pulled up her collar and tried to disappear. The last thing she needed was someone from Oasis hearing what she was up to. "You have accent. From another country."

"Yeah," Heidi said gracelessly. "I'm Australian."

"Next?" said the clerk.

Heidi, relieved to get away from Oscar, walked up and slid her written papers over to the clerk.

"I'm filing violations," Heidi said, indicating her pages.

"You can file online, " the clerk said.

"I know, but I wanted to find out how soon you can act on this. It's about a dangerous property."

The clerk silently perused the list of violations and began to enter them into his computer.

"Sir?" Heidi said.

"Yes?"

"What happens if the building is in breach on a bunch of codes?"

The man continued to type. "They have to bring it up to code."

"And if they don't?"

"Anything from a small to a hefty fine to a—"

"A red tag?"

"Exactly."

"Good," Heidi said. "I mean for the community."

The clerk handed her a printed receipt. "These have been filed. An inspection will be set up soon."

"When is soon?" she demanded in a loud voice.

The man looked at her impassively. "As soon as we get to it. We have a backlog of buildings to investigate, ma'am."

"Then I need to speak to your supervisor. These violations need immediate attention."

That night, when Joey pulled into Oasis she carefully avoided the deepest potholes. After she parked she checked her cell phone. She was actually early. As she walked towards *Hummingbird* she saw a light burning in *Berta's Bungalow*.

Berta was at her easel in a paint-covered smock. Her red bag with the green appliquéd parrot sat on a nearby chair. She was painting a blue, yellow, red, and purple watercolor of a blonde woman riding a black panther.

Joey watched for a moment, afraid to break the mood.

"Good evening, dear," Berta said without looking up. "What do you think of it?"

"It's striking," Joey said.

"Think so?" Berta said, taking a step back to assess it.

"I've never seen anything like it."

Berta laughed. "Look around. It's my own personal mythology." She gestured to stacks of watercolors and oils scattered all over the bungalow. "Kind of an obsession." Berta went back to her work. Joey walked over to the other paintings. In some, the blonde woman danced with the black panther in a dance of love and death. In others she slept beside it in what looked like the Garden of Eden. The works were brilliantly colored, mysterious and dream-like.

"What's it all about? Sometimes the panther looks protective, sometimes it looks downright wicked," Joey said.

"Exactly," Berta said.

"So what do the panther and the woman symbolize?"

"Good and evil. Light and dark."

"I don't understand."

"Making peace with our dark side. Our panther. Know what I mean, jelly bean?" Berta asked.

"I have no idea," Joey said. Then she thought for a minute. "Do you mean what Nonna used to say when I had a nightmare?"

"What was that?"

"'Take the monster for a walk around the block. By the time you get home you won't be scared anymore.'"

"Exactly," Berta laughed. "Take the monster out for a walk. Tell that to Grief Group, dear. They should relate."

"Okay," Joey said without much conviction.

"Are you ready for tonight?" Berta asked.

"No . . . "

"But you're doing it."

"I'm doing it," Joey said, standing a little taller. "But I don't know what to expect. What's normal for a Grief Group?"

"Anything and everything."

Joey felt a stab of panic. "How am I going to do this?"

"The Group will let you know," Berta said, her voice firm but gentle. "Just remember—grief is necessary. But I've found that many things I lost came around in another form. Eventually. Like you."

"Me?"

"You. My daughters moved halfway around the world, which made me quite sad. And now here you are, and your hands look like my youngest daughter's." She took Joey's hands in hers.

Berta's hands reminded her of Nonna's. Joey felt a lump in her throat. "Thank you," she managed, glancing at the clock on the wall. "I'd better go."

"Wait," Berta said. She walked to a table across the room and picked up a large blue plate of chocolate chip cookies. "I baked some cookies for your group. Something sweet along with the bitterness. "

Twenty minutes later the plate of cookies was still being passed around in *Hummingbird*. Joey had told the Group she was going to be their leader, after all.

"For good?" Daisy asked.

"For better or for worse," Joey said before realizing she'd just recited part of the wedding vow which ended with "till death do us part." *Oh, God,* she thought.

"Yay," Alli said, seemingly oblivious.

"I'm glad," Maggie seconded.

Sam, who was giving Andrew a bottle, welcomed her.

Dave cracked a joke.

Del wasn't there.

Tamara sat silently in her usual rocking chair, wearing dark glasses and knitting a deep blue hat. Joey was wondering how to get Tamara to tell her story when Del breezed in, wearing his white coat, with no apology for being late again.

"Hey. Group starts at 7:00," Dave said.

"Hey. I just came from rounds, man," Del bit back. "Saving people's lives trumps being on time for a meeting about the dead. Get it?"

Words flew out of Joey's mouth before she thought about them. "I need to ask you to go outside, Del, take off your white coat and come back in."

"What?"

"Please, just do it."

He threw his hands in the air. "Why the hell should I?"

"Because you're playing the part of a doctor. And you're not a doctor here. You're a grieving spouse like everyone else."

Anger flashed across his face. "That's the stupidest thing I ever heard."

The rest of the Group watched with interest.

"Just do it," Joey said with more confidence than she felt.

Del exhaled in frustration before he left. Everyone else looked at each other.

"He's not coming back," Dave speculated.

"He's probably on the 101 by now," Maggie said.

Joey waited. She'd seen Jack do that with an actress who wouldn't get real in Group.

Del burst back in, coat in hand and resettled on the couch. "You satisfied now?"

"Yes. Thank you."

"What a dumb thing . . . " He rummaged through the cookies.

"Okay, Del," Joey said. "As long as you're talking, why don't you tell the Group why you're here. Who died?"

Del looked fierce. Beat. Beat.

Joey started picking at a hangnail.

Del gripped the plate of cookies. "My partner. His name was Shawn."

"Shawn," Joey repeated. "How did he die?"

He reached for a cookie. "Acquired Immune Deficiency Syndrome."

"Excuse me?" said Daisy.

"AIDS."

Tamara paused before putting a cookie in her mouth. She shared a look of concern with Alli. Which Del saw.

"Jesus, people. It's a cookie. Not semen, for God's sake. This is two-thousand-fucking-eleven. You're not getting AIDS from a cookie I touched."

Tamara forced herself to take a big bite. "I know that."

"I didn't think anyone died of AIDS anymore," Dave said.

"You and everybody else," Del said. "By now it's supposed to be a chronic disease, not a fatal one."

"Can you tell us what happened to Shawn?" Joey asked Del.

Silence.

"We'd like to hear about him," Joey said.

She and Del stared each other down. He blew out a long breath. "What do you want to know? That he was healthy as a horse until he got sick? A marathoner. Tennis player. Six-foot-two, 180 pounds of muscle." He looked around the room with undisguised hostility. "Or would you rather hear he was a flamer who deserved to die of the plague?"

Daisy put her manicured hand on his. "Nobody thinks like that anymore. At least nobody in this room. Same-sex marriage is legal, for heaven's sake. I'd like to hear about Shawn."

"Please tell us about him," Joey said.

Del explained how they'd met in New York at Mount Sinai where Shawn was interning as an anesthesiologist. When Shawn started losing weight and began to have trouble walking, he went to the neurology department. They thought he might have early-onset Parkinson's. Nobody thought of AIDS until the blood test came back. By then, Shawn had a rare, drug-resistant pneumonia and lymphoma that had spread to his bones.

"I got him into every drug trial there was. Nothing I did mattered. He developed hemolytic anemia. He was white as a ghost. At the end he weighed 80 pounds. He couldn't breathe." Del's voice rose. "I'm a trained doctor. It's my goddamn job to save lives, and I couldn't even save my own partner. I'm a fucking failure," he said with rage.

"I was in the same room and couldn't do a thing for Mel," Sam added. "I failed her."

"So did I," Dave said, looking surprised that he'd spoken.

"You're not failures," Joey said. "We're not in control of other people's deaths." That much she'd learned.

"Some say the time of our death is written on our foreheads the moment we're born," Daisy reflected.

"Like an expiration date," Dave said.

"So we're all in the same boat," Joey said.

"Only Rod's boat sank and I don't have his body," Alli added with a hitch in her voice.

They were quiet for an uncomfortably long time. Joey sat, still as a statue.

"I'll never hear him whistle again," Maggie said softly.

"I'll never touch her again," Dave said.

"I'll never smell his hair," Alli said.

"I'll never make love with him again," Daisy said.

"Andrew will never know his Mommy," Sam said, looking down at the baby with sorrow. Everyone turned to look at the sleeping baby, whose loss suddenly seemed so much greater than theirs.

Joey willed herself not to think about the baby she'd miscarried. She breathed in the musty smell of the room. She watched the clock on the wall tick another minute. Then two.

"I never got to say goodbye to Jeff," Maggie said softly.

I never got to say goodbye to my dad, Joey thought.

"God, I hate this rain," Maggie said. "All that water. . . . It feels like it's in my bones."

"What about *their* bones?" Daisy asked in a high-pitched voice. "Do you think this rain seeped into the coffin? Stu was a runner so we buried him in a polyester jogging suit. Is it moldy?"

"Is Jeff cold?" Maggie cried.

"And what about worms?" Daisy asked, her voice higher.

"What if it rains so hard all the graves at Forest Lawn go sliding down the hill?" Alli worried. "Maybe I should be glad I couldn't bury Rod."

"Maybe I should've buried Jeff in the wall," Maggie wailed.

Joey listened and watched as they talked over each other. *This is getting out of control,* she worried. Then she slid from the edge of the chair to the center of it, waiting for her instincts to tell her what to do next.

Alli began, "I heard about someone who bought a new mattress after her husband died and it had bedbugs."

"I hate Saturdays," Maggie said. "Those mattress ads in the L.A. *Times*. I never want to replace the one I slept on with Jeff."

Tamara interrupted. "I want to talk about how Bruce died." The room quieted. Tamara took off her sunglasses as if she were laying down her gun. "Happy?" she asked Joey.

"For you, yes." Joey sat up straighter, steeling herself for Tamara's story.

Fifteen minutes later Dave was gripping the sides of his chair until his knuckles were white as he listened to the end of Tamara's story.

"The police said I started screaming when I saw him in that motel room," Tamara continued. "I don't remember. I can't recall what the room looked like, just a lot of blood everywhere and a coppery smell, like a penny. The police said that was the blood, mixed with the sulfury smell of gunpowder. It was disgusting. I can still smell it."

Dave's chair was on casters, and he'd been using them to push himself out of the circle. He'd been putting distance between himself and Tamara since she began her story. *Bottom line,* he thought, *she blames herself. No matter how mad she says she is at Bruce.* With everyone looking at Tamara, nobody noticed him inching his chair towards the door.

"How disgusting is that?" Tamara asked. "That the most vivid thing I remember from that hideous day is the horrible, awful smell of his blood."

As Tamara paused, Dave noticed Sam leaning forward slightly. *Like there's an invisible line between them and he's holding her up.*

"That's it," Tamara concluded. "The story of my husband's ultimate 'Fuck you' to me and my daughter. I hate him for doing that to us. I hate how he used his mind, that brain of his that he blew out. I mean, he planned it." Tamara stopped, spent.

"Thank you," Joey said.

Dave saw her look around the room and discover how far back he'd wheeled himself. Her eyes widened. "Where are you going, Dave?" she asked. "You're almost out the door. What don't you want to hear? Or say?"

Dave saw Joey looking at him.

He remembered Caro's scream shattering the night as the truck hit. Once again, as in his dreams, the edges of his world grew dark.

"Dave?" he heard Joey say.

He opened his mouth to speak.

And then. And then.

An angry voice piped up. "I'm sick and tired of talking about what's-their-names," Del said.

Saved by the Del, Dave thought.

Chapter Fourteen

Joey saw it when their eyes met. The truth flickered across Dave's face for an instant and she knew he had a secret. Her palms began to sweat as she realized he was about to reveal it.

"I'm sick and tired of talking about what's-their-names," Del repeated. "They get every second of airtime in here. Well, they're dead, dead, dead."

"Wow. You're cold, man," said Dave.

"Seriously," Sam agreed.

Joey couldn't believe Del had just taken them on a U-turn. She held Dave's eyes for one more second. *What is he hiding?* Then Dave looked away and she reluctantly turned to Del. "What *do* you want to talk about?" she asked.

"Us," he chided. "I want to know more about us. Didn't they teach you anything in grief school? Didn't they tell you to focus on the living, too? Why can't we move on already?"

One minute he's shattered about Shawn. Now he wants to move on? What's with this guy? Joey wondered.

"I'm not ready to move on," Maggie said.

"Neither am I," Alli agreed.

"What's wrong with you?" Sam asked angrily.

"What's wrong with all of *you*?" Del snapped. "We need to get our lives back. Look to the future, man."

"Of course we're going to talk more about your spouses," Joey said. "What do you want to know about the Group, Del?"

Del paused.

"That I couldn't get on a plane to visit my family for Thanksgiving because I was so freaked about coming back to that empty house?" Maggie said.

"That I put Rod's favorite frozen French fries in my cart last week and paid for them before I realized?" Allie added.

"That I can't go to the grocery store to buy milk without thinking I should call Mel to ask what else we need?" Sam said.

"I don't care about any of that shit," Del said.

Joey felt her hands turning to fists as she tried to lasso Del. "So what do you want to know?"

"You all know what I do," Del said. "What about the rest of you?"

"Jesus, how superficial can you get?" said Dave.

"All right, let's do it and then we'll move on," Joey said to Del, who seemed amped up.

"I'm a decorator," Tamara said. "Or I was. Maybe I should become a 'death decorator' and specialize in funeral parlor décor."

Sam told them he was a classics professor. Daisy was a realtor in Beverly Hills. Maggie was a paralegal who hoped to go to law school some day. Dave was an amateur photographer who pushed paperwork at the VA. Alli was studying psychology at UCLA Extension and owned a horse in Malibu. They were back to Del.

"What's your specialty, Doc?" Dave persisted. "Besides being a royal pain in the ass?"

"I'm an ER doctor," Del said.

"Like I'd want to see you if I had a heart attack," said Dave.

Joey sat back and listened as the evening continued on the same feisty, divisive note.

The air was chilly by the time she'd finished cleaning up the den. She was heading to her car, absorbed in thoughts of the meeting when she saw Daniel striding to his bike, wearing a motorcycle jacket, jeans, and boots. He stopped when he saw her.

His eyes traveled down her body. Distracted, she stepped into a pothole. He caught her before she went down.

"Steady there." He put his hand on her arm.

"You keep doing that," she said.

"My pleasure. How was Grief Group?" he asked, not letting go of her arm.

"They were fighting like siblings," Joey admitted, wondering if her hair was wild. *His hand on my arm.* "It was kind of out of control."

"Is that good or bad?" Daniel asked. "Being out of control?"

"Neither, probably."

He let go of her arm. "I reckon they're all angry and just getting comfortable with each other."

"You're right," she said.

"Good on ya," Daniel said, translating when he saw her eyebrows furrow. "It means 'well done.' Are you feeling more confident?"

"Not exactly."

"Want to talk about it over a drink?" Daniel asked. "Sounds like you need someone to talk to about this Group. No?"

"Yes. But *should* I talk about them? Or is this supposed to be confidential? God, I really don't know what I'm doing."

"You're doing it like you do everything. By the seat of your pants," he said. "Right?"

"Right," Joey said.

"So? A drink?"

She hesitated.

"It's just a drink," he repeated. "After all, I've already put you to bed.

Remember?" He leaned toward her. She smelled his citrus cologne. She felt the warmth rising from him.

"All right, yes," Joey said.

It's just a drink, she rationalized as they walked to a neighborhood bar around the corner, where a crowd lounged in comfortable seats around the fireplace, some eating sandwiches, most just talking. Joey was glad it was a casual conversation bar with a decent juke box turned low, dim light, and a couple of TVs behind the bar for solo drinkers. *It's not a real date,* she repeated to herself as her legs brushed against his when they settled into a booth near the fireplace and Daniel ordered drinks for the two of them.

"Two rum and cokes."

"You mean Cuba Libres?" the barmaid asked.

"Sure," Daniel laughed. "If that's what you call them here." After she left, he said, "Rum is more than a drink Down Under. It's practically a religion. The drink of choice for the first settlers and convicts."

"Where in Australia are you from?" Joey asked, feeling tongue-tied as he studied her across the table.

"Byron Bay. The Gold Coast." Seeing her puzzled look he added, "Near Brisbane. In Queensland."

"Oh."

"Never heard of any of it, have you?"

"No," Joey admitted.

"Brisbane's only the capital of Queensland and the third biggest city in Australia, but that's all right."

"Sorry," Joey said. "I'm a geography retard."

"Oy," Daniel said. "Let me draw it for you." He took out a green pen and drew a map of Australia on a napkin. "Over here," he said, making an X on the east coast, "is Byron Bay. And this is Wategos Beach. The sweetest surfing spot on the whole flippin' continent."

"You surf?" Joey asked.

"All my life."

"So . . . you surf in L.A., too?"

"You bet."

Joey was at a loss. "So you—what? Surf on weekends?"

Daniel smiled. "I'm out there every morning."

"What?"

"Six AM. I've got to do it."

Joey was mystified. "Why?"

"Think of it like crack," he said with a laugh. "It's my addiction. I'll take you long-boarding one day. You'll see."

"What's long-boarding?"

"Long-boarding is soul-surfing. Anybody can do it."

"Don't be so sure," Joey said as she looked into his eyes. Once again he was looking deeply at her. *He's flirting with me,* she realized with a rush as the waiter brought their drinks.

She felt the power of Daniel's eyes gazing into hers when she talked about tonight's Group and told him she'd suspected one of the members was keeping a secret. He listened to her intently, as if he didn't want to miss a word. It made her heart race. "But I missed my chance to talk about it with him when another person took over. So frustrating."

"What are you planning to do about that?"

"I don't know. I'll have to see," she admitted.

"Taking time to think about things sounds right. So, tell me. How does it feel to be in there after losing your family?"

Joey was startled by the question. She took another sip of her rum and coke. Her body began to feel warm and her legs loose. "I'm not sure, but I see myself in them," she admitted.

Daniel nodded. "'Course you do. You're a survivor."

"I'm a fighter," Joey said automatically, her tongue loose from the rum. "No, I'm lying. I'm still not over my family dying."

"Takes a while, I know," he said, draining his drink. "My parents died when I was 23. Car accident."

"Wait. You lost your family, too?"

"Almost. I have a sister."

"Is that why you offered Grief Group? Because of what you went through?"

Daniel hailed the barmaid and ordered another round. "I could have used a group like that when my parents died," he said. "I had nobody to talk to. Nobody understood. Then I had a surfing buddy whose wife died of a heart attack at 32 and nobody wanted to hear about it. That was so much worse than what I went through. So, yeah, that's why I put Grief Group in the catalogue."

"I had no idea," Joey said.

"And I had no idea that offering Grief Group would mean you'd come to lead it."

Joey's breath caught. The last time she'd been on a date, or whatever this was, with a man she was attracted to had been with Jack.

"So. Is this the first nonprofit you've run?" she asked, making conversation.

"Yes."

"What did you do before?"

"Depends on the decade. In my 20s I worked at a surf shop, played piano in a cocktail lounge in the evenings, and taught at a distance school in the Outback. I moved around a lot until I hit my 30s and grew up. Got into the venture capital business. Following in my dad's footsteps. In a way." A flash of anger crossed his face.

"So . . . your father was . . . "

"An investor. And a crook," Daniel said. "He lost a pile of money for a lot of people. Including my ex-wife's father."

"Heidi?"

"One and the same," Daniel said.

"The woman you were talking to at Oasis."

"Yes. Bad blood."

"Oh?" Joey wanted to know more.

"The woman's rigid as a stick and obsessed with rules. I like to follow my gut." He picked up the menu. "We were a pretty disastrous combination."

"How long were you married?"

"Seven years," Daniel said. "Seven miserable years."

"Sounds like you two are polar opposites. What drew you together?" Joey couldn't help asking.

"How long you got?" Daniel said, putting down the menu and lighting up. "We grew up practically next door to each other. Heidi used to be a spitfire. Sky diver; river rafter, dirt biker. She was a regular scrapper. Had a great laugh." He blew out a long puff of smoke. "Then she became a shrew."

"Why?"

"Family dramas. Life changed her."

"How long have you been divorced?" Joey asked although she knew she should shut up.

"Three years. Shall we order something to eat? I'm famished."

As he studied the menu she studied Daniel. She took in his generous lips and dark eyes. Her eyes roamed over his crooked nose and square jaw. *Thank God he's a smidge short of gorgeous,* she thought. Gorgeous made her nervous. As the waiter took their order Joey's eyes stopped on Daniel's strong fingers and the band on his left hand.

"Why do you still wear your wedding ring?" she asked after the waiter left.

"This isn't a wedding band," he said quickly. "It's a saltwater-freshwater ring."

"A what?"

"It's made from an Aboriginal design. See?" He took the ring off and put it in her hand. It was still warm. "I've always been keen on places where the river meets the sea," he said. "Like Cairns, Northern Australia, where the mangroves grow."

"What are mangroves?" Joey asked.

"Trees." Daniel's fingers rubbed the small vertical lines etched all around the band she held in her hand. Joey was unnerved by the touch of his fingers. "Mangroves live where rivers meet the sea. Masses of life grow in their tangled roots. See these little pink diamonds?"

"Yes."

Daniel traced the pink dots along the ring. "Those are symbols of the eggs laid by fish and birds that are protected in the mangroves and nurtured by the waters."

"So . . . why do you wear it again?" She handed the ring back to him, feeling the warmth of his hand leave hers.

"First off, it's a beaut," he said as he slipped it on. "Second, I like the story it tells, and I have a deep respect for the Aboriginal culture. Third, my sister designed it."

"Your sister's a jewelry designer?" Joey asked.

"*Adopted* sister. Yes," Daniel said. "Long story. Know much about the Aboriginals?"

Joey noticed how fast he changed the subject. *He must be estranged from his sister,* she thought.

They drank their second round of Cuba Libres while Daniel talked about the Aboriginal culture in Australia. Then they talked about places they'd lived, jobs they had worked at, the way she kept getting lost in L.A. and how exhausted she felt after Group. It was superficial conversation, she knew. They didn't talk about who'd loved whom and had been hurt by them. Or whether either of them still thought love was possible.

By the time they left Joey realized she was crazy about the way Daniel talked and the way he looked at her when she talked. *Nobody's paid so much attention to me,* she realized as they walked back to Oasis, *since Dad and Nonna.*

In the parking lot the glitter of streetlights lit up the branches of the giant pines.

"You sure you can find your way home?" Daniel asked.

Joey hesitated. "I think so."

He stepped on his cigarette and opened her car door. "I'll lead you there. Follow me."

Joey drove behind Daniel, watching him weave between lanes with confidence and sway with the curves. She pulled into Ferndale and waved at him as he drove away.

Watch out, she thought as she walked to the apartment. *Don't rip that Band-Aid off your heart too soon.* Then she wondered when Daniel would ask her out on a real date.

Chapter Fifteen

"Hot date last night?" Dave's co-worker, Gary asked him as he walked into the lobby of 11000 Wilshire Boulevard, aka the Federal Building. Gary worked in the next cubicle, and they shared the same sick sense of humor.

It was Thursday, the morning after the latest Grief Group and Gary knew full well where Dave had been. Most people he toiled beside knew what had happened to Caro that night. They were aware he'd been ordered into grief counseling after his work tanked.

While Dave waited for the elevator with Gary and a host of others, Janice from Personnel walked in, sporting jeggings and thigh-high black boots.

"Happy Day," she chirped brightly.

"Mayday, mayday, mayday," Dave said in a doomsday voice. Gary snickered. Janice shot him a dirty look as the elevator dinged and they all piled in.

Dave had worked at the VA for the last seven years. He was not the most popular employee among his government brothers and sisters, a mostly unambitious group of nine-to-fivers content to push papers and, hopefully, help vets along the way. With a few exceptions.

"Hold it," yelled one of the exceptions as the elevator doors began to close.

A pudgy hand reached in. The doors reopened. In marched Lannie, Dave's 47-year old Brooklynite boss, who looked 50 and dressed 30. She anointed her brown hair with an explosion of hairspray, mousse, and any gel that would make it stand up in spikes. She favored turquoise eye shadow, press-on silver nails, and skin-tight jeans. Dave thought she had the backside of a baby elephant but nobody asked his opinion.

Lannie was not Dave's cup of tea. For one thing, she'd mastered the art of doing the least amount of work possible while jockeying for the most power. To that end, she would arrive an hour before everyone else, supposedly to "catch up on the workload." Dave knew she spent that time poking around other people's offices, gathering tidbits to trade up.

Lannie barhopped every Wednesday night, as all the employees on the 12th floor were aware, because she bored them all in the lunchroom every Thursday with her latest adventures. Now, as she yakked to Yolanda in HR about last night at a club called Scream, Dave shrank against the sides of the car, hoping to avoid her searchlight eyes.

"I swear, I danced until I was a sweaty pile of flesh."

Dave stared at the floor numbers as they rose, trying hard not to picture that. He got off the elevator and headed for his cubicle, hoping to avoid Lannie's attention. But the sound of his metal poles on the linoleum floor gave him away.

"Dave. Office. Now," she yelled at his receding back.

When he entered she was perched on a chair, talking on the phone. Her belt was cinched so tight that a thick roll of fat hung over it. Her floor featured stacks of papers and piles of manila file folders. Her beige visitor's chair was occupied by unopened mail. *So much for "catching up on the workload,"* Dave thought as Lannie hung up.

"I got a call from Cindy in HR. Someone's here who requested you. Personally."

"To do what?"

"Coordinate benefits for a widow. The file's right here."

Her chubby silver-nailed hand plowed through files and managed to extract the right one.

"Lieutenant Jeffrey Bodi," she read. "Friend of yours?"

"Nope."

"His widow just asked for you." She handed him the file. He opened it and read the name.

Maggie.

Mascara-blackened tears had streamed down her cheeks as Maggie cried through most of last night's meeting. Dave noticed she was wearing the same oversized blue and green checked flannel shirt. So did Joey, who asked if it had been her husband's.

"Yes. I always wear Jeff's shirt. I even sleep in it."

That was all it took. Maggie looked down, fighting tears. By the time she'd looked up again her face was taut with pain.

And what had Dave thought? *Great photograph. Mr. Sensitive.*

When Joey asked if Maggie wanted to talk more about Jeff she told the Group how they'd met.

"I'd just dropped out of high school and was waitressing in an all-night diner in Bozeman, Montana, about a 45-minute drive from my parents' place. The girls used to ask if I was scared driving home alone at three in the morning. When I said no, they thought I was brave. I wasn't. I always knew that if I broke down Jeff would drive out and find me. He'd fix whatever was wrong with that car—and me, too."

"He took care of you?" Joey asked gently.

Maggie nodded, sniffling. "Jeff was the biggest, strongest man I ever met."

She sounds like a teenager, Dave thought, *but she is the baby of the Group.* She probably wasn't much older than 28.

"He got me to go back to high school and then to community college. He thought I could do anything. I can't. But Jeff was brave enough for both of us. Now what do I do when he's not here and there's so much to be brave about?"

"Like what? Tell us. Maybe we can help," Joey said.

Maggie paused. "Like I don't know where my next rent payment's going to come from. I'm scared I'm going to be put out on the street. And have to live in my car."

"Don't you get benefits from the VA?" Del asked.

Maggie's face contorted. "Yeah. Maybe. I don't know." She mumbled something about red tape, forms to fill out, waiting on hold for 30 minutes, talking to some asshole.

Del cocked his head in Dave's direction. "Don't you work for them?"

Dave looked out the window at the lights in the building across the street. "Yup," he answered. "That's not my department, but I'll see if someone there can help." In truth, Dave wasn't eager to have Maggie talk to a coworker who might spill the truth about what happened the night Caro died. So he wasn't planning to talk to anyone. Then he caught Joey looking at him, and he wondered what she was thinking.

Maggie sobbed through the rest of the meeting until used tissues lay in sad little piles all around her. It pained Dave to see her hurting so badly, but not enough to get him to help her.

Five minutes before the end of the meeting, while Joey read, "There is a time to live and a time to die . . . " a cry came from deep within Maggie.

"I'm pregnant," she announced to the Group.

"Dave?" Lannie's voice cut through his fog.

"Sorry."

"I asked if you know this woman."

Lannie stared at him as Dave closed the file.

"I'll take care of it."

Questions bubbled to the surface in the round pond of Lannie's face.

"Is there anything you want to tell me? Because if you're having a personal relationship with her, you might want someone else to take the case."

He read her loud and clear. Lannie was fishing for a juicy story, something she could spread through the lunchroom. The-poor-cripple's-got-a-new-gal story.

"No," Dave said and walked out of her office.

In his cubicle he stared at the cursor blinking on his computer. This was supposed to be a regular, boring day, like all the others.

Maggie was there.

He had calls to make. He started to dial but it wasn't working. It was his hands. They were shaking.

Maggie was there.

Dave hung up, grabbed the file and went over to Gary's cubicle.

"Can you take this case? I'll trade for one of yours."

"Okay."

Dave handed him the file. "I've got a doctor's appointment," he lied. "Cover for me with Lannie, will you?"

He took the coward's way out, down the back elevator to the garage, to make sure he didn't run into Maggie. He sped to Point Dume, the beach in Malibu where he often went at daybreak, after a sleepless night, to shoot photos of the ocean. It reminded him there was something bigger than his own misery. Today, the ocean only reminded him of the vastness of the nothing he called his life.

Sitting in his car, Dave took out his new Leica-M camera. Click. Click. Click.

A few evenings later he was parked near Maggie's shabby bungalow in the East Valley. The garage door was broken, the lawn unmown, dried stalks of last summer's sunflowers poked through the dirt.

He'd been sitting there for 20 minutes, trying to screw his courage to the sticking place. God knows, he didn't want Maggie coming to see him at the VA. It would have been easier to stay out of this entirely. If only Maggie weren't a woman he liked and one he might be able to help.

Out of nowhere, his father's voice rang in his head. "Only chickenshits lie to get out from under."

Dave walked up to her front door. Maggie opened it, wearing Jeff's checked shirt. "Sorry to surprise you like this," he said.

She looked at him, hard. "How did you find me?"

Dave showed her his iPhone. "The list of the Group's contact info. I just thought . . . I wondered if you needed help filling out forms for the VA."

"Those fucking forms." She looked past him to the empty street. "When I asked for you, they said you weren't there. Then somebody said you'd been there but you'd just left." Dave's courage wilted under her steady look. He had no idea what to say next. Luckily, Maggie spoke first. "Come in. I hate all these damn forms. Especially that box I have to check."

"Which box?"

"The one that says 'Widow.'"

Dave understood. Maggie opened the door, and he walked into her cramped living room, sat beside her on her corduroy couch and noted the folded flag nearby—the flag that had escorted the body of Lieutenant Jeffrey Bodi to his grave.

There it sat, on its own seat, as if it were alive. Dave wondered if he was the only one who heard what it was saying. Was he the only one who heard the words of reproach from Maggie's brave, upstanding, very dead husband, Jeff?

Liar. Liar. Liar.

Chapter Sixteen

The following Saturday afternoon gumball-sized hail bounced off Joey's head as she ran across the parking lot to Gelson's Market. She was picking up frozen pizza for a lonely Saturday night dinner-and-Netflix. Kat was going to Big Bear with Neil. Joey was trying to keep from obsessing over Daniel.

Twice that week she'd gone to talk with him at Oasis only to discover Heidi, his ex-wife, monopolizing him, her hand on his arm. Joey knew Daniel detested Heidi, who seemed to regard him as her property.

Marjorie came up alongside Joey as she watched them.

"That's one's a mess," Marjorie said.

"How do you know?"

"Daniel. He says she's a mega-bitch. And trouble is her only friend."

Later, Joey was fixing a broken fence when she suddenly realized where she'd seen Heidi before: she was the woman who'd beaten Joey to a cab the day she'd landed in L.A. Heidi, she remembered now, was arriving with a mountain of luggage. Yet she'd told Daniel she'd been in L.A. for months. Why would the woman lie about that? Should she tell Daniel?

She told Berta instead. "I don't know what she's up to," Joey added. "Probably nothing. But . . ."

"I'd say, trust your instincts," Berta said.

"My instincts say stay away from her," Joey said. Berta nodded.

When in doubt, do nothing, Joey reminded herself as she ran across the parking lot to Gelson's in the hail. She was happy to see some actual weather in Los Angeles even if the innocent blue sky looked like it had nothing to do with the ice balls it was throwing down.

She raced to the store, barreling past the announcement: "Pet Adoption Today." She spotted a newspaper box filled with stacks of the latest *People's Weekly*, stuck one in her cart, and walked into the upscale supermarket.

She'd discovered Gelson's a few weeks earlier, ducking in to pick up Fuji apples and Brie. After that, she'd gone back to look and to buy a few things when she could afford it.

She went for the flowers that greeted her as she entered. Refrigerated glass cases with clusters of red tulips and radishes; thin green stalks of pink lilies tied with crisscross pink ribbons like ballerinas in toe shoes; gardenias that floated in miniature lily ponds.

She went for the fruit: immaculate tiers of ripe Bartlett pears and rows of perfect plumcots and pomegranates. She went for the produce man in his green apron, who greeted her cordially while trimming celery as if it were the rarest of roses. She went for the Eastern European women behind the bakery case, small red hats on their short dark hair, who presided over displays of Linzer cookies and Princess cakes like empresses of a small kingdom. They reminded her of women at the Éclair, Nonna's favorite Eastern European bakery on West 72nd Street in New York.

She went to Gelson's because everything had a place, every place had a thing, and she was responsible for none of it. It was a strange obsession, Joey knew, and pricey, too, but it was cheaper than Valium.

Today Kat had given her money to buy coffee creamer for Sunday, when Joey would be manning the manager's office while Kat was away.

She'd also requested a couple of cinnamon persimmons, which Joey had neither seen nor tasted. She asked the produce man. He selected two ripe orange ones at $5.99 a pound. As she put them into the cart Joey noticed a front-page article in the *People's Weekly*: "Tears and Tequila," by Kat Jenkins.

Standing in the produce aisle, Joey began to read. At first she was excited for Kat. Then she was incredulous. Then she was furious. *How could Kat write this without telling me?*

She whizzed the cart to the checkout counter, snatched a chocolate bar, and opened it even before she'd paid. She couldn't wait to get back to Ferndale and clock Kat with a cinnamon persimmon.

The hail had stopped when Joey emerged from the market. Chaos reigned in the area outside the front entrance, which was filled with a jumble of crates and wire enclosures that held yapping puppies and assorted canines. Joey steamed past it into the parking lot. She was unlocking her trunk when she heard someone call her name.

"Joey!" Alli from Grief Group was waving from the dog area. "Joey! Over here!"

Joey fought the urge to drive away. She walked back to Alli instead. Alli was crouched on the ground, a small shivering Cocker Spaniel puppy in her arms, tears streaming down her face.

"Rod's dead," Alli sobbed. "He's dead. And this little dog is the one who told me."

"What do you mean?" Joey asked, dumbfounded.

"I just came from seeing a medium," Alli said, holding onto the dog for dear life. "I asked if Rod was still alive and she channeled him so fast I was stunned. Rod said he had drowned. And if I didn't believe him I should believe the dog that had eyes just like his. He said I'd know which dog he meant when I heard three short barks. I didn't know what to think, so I came here for groceries and passed this little dog. And he barked at me. Three short barks. He has Rod's eyes. Exactly," she said. "It's Rod talking to me from the other side. He's saying he's dead, but he's come home to me . . . in another form." She smothered the tiny pup's face with kisses. "I don't know whether to laugh or cry."

Joey didn't know either. But she kept that to herself, murmuring support and encouragement. *If Alli believes Rod has come back as a dog, who am I to doubt her?*

Within minutes Alli was filling out an adoption application, and Joey was saying goodbye. Until Alli clutched her arm.

"Now that I know he's dead, I need to have a memorial for Rod. Will you help? No, wait!" Alli exclaimed. "Will you deliver the eulogy?"

"Me?" Joey asked. "No," she said. *Dear God, no.*

The first funeral was her father's. She'd declined to give a eulogy, so Grandpa Eugene had delivered it. The next funeral was Grandpa Eugene's, where Nonna and his friends spoke. By the time it was Nonna's funeral, the clergy at Frank Campbell knew Joey didn't do eulogies.

She found it impossible to give a loving tribute to the family she'd loved and lost. She could barely face the fact that they were gone and knew she'd break down. So it was left to Nonna's lifelong friends to memorialize the woman Joey had loved more than anyone in the world.

Although Joey had been raised to be brave about things a little girl shouldn't have to be brave about, she'd remained frozen in her seat in the oak-pewed sanctuary, wordless and miserable as others spoke about her beloveds.

"Please?" Alli said, breaking into Joey's thoughts. "I really need your help. I don't know who else to ask." The dogs barked shrilly. Joey smelled their wet fur. "I mean, I could ask his parents or his best friend. But everyone is so broken up about this . . . and they're mad that I didn't do it before. . . . " Alli was biting her lower lip. Joey saw the dark circles under her eyes. "Please?" Alli repeated.

Joey's stomach clenched. *How bad could it be to talk about someone you never knew?*

"I need your help," Alli pleaded. "Please?"

"Okay," Joey said, against her better judgment. "But you'll have to tell me all about Rod."

Alli wrapped Joey in a tight hug. Joey wondered what she'd just done.

On the way to Ferndale Joey passed Kaye's Donuts, where Heidi's real estate instructor, Gus Green, was reading from the *People's Weekly* while Heidi dunked a maple-glazed donut in her coffee. She'd slept at his place last night. It was a tiny one-bedroom in North Hollywood, but it was better than the hole she was living in.

"Isn't this the place we're targeting for a red tag?" he asked, reading aloud: "*So what does a woman like that do? If I'm right, you'll find her at Grief Group One at Oasis on Wednesdays, seven to nine. If I'm right, my best friend will keep doing it her own way and her Grief Group at Oasis won't be like anyone else's.*"

"Give that to me," Heidi said, tearing the newspaper out of his hands. She began to read. The more she read, the wider her smile grew. "*She can fix things that are broken?* I bet I know who that is." Heidi started to laugh. "All roads lead to Rome," she told Gus Green, slamming the newspaper on the table.

"Are you going to Rome?" he asked.

"Let me put it this way. There's more than one way to skin a kangie."

"A cat, you mean?" Gus was confused.

"Oh, for God's sake," Heidi said. "There might just be more than one way for us to get Oasis," she said. "From here on, they've got a number on their heads."

"So the plan is . . . ?" Gus Green asked.

"Phase 1. Get the place red-tagged, bring the price down. Phase 2. Find the right buyer. Phase 3. Laugh all the way to the bank."

For emphasis, and because she was in a good mood, Heidi played footsie with him under the table. Gus Green was a tool. But she needed him.

Kat was checking bookings on her iPad when Joey walked in. "Hi," Kat said without looking up. "Did you get the cinnamon persimmons?"

"Yes," Joey said, setting the bag on the desk and unfolding the *People's Weekly*. "And I got this: *My best friend thinks she should just keep doing what she knows how to do—fixing things that are broken. She doesn't realize her gifts might include fixing people, too. Maybe even including herself. . . .*"

"Where did you get that?" Kat asked, jumping up.

"Gelson's. There's a huge stack of them."

"Omigod," Kat said, reaching for the newspaper. "Neil didn't tell me it was out yet!" She grabbed her car keys. "I've got to get a bunch before they're all gone. Be right back. Watch the office." She started to run out.

"Are you kidding me?" Joey said. "What were you smoking?"

"What do you mean?" Kat stopped, her hand on the door.

"How could you write about me and not even tell me you were doing it? And how could you write *that*—?" she waved an impatient hand at the newspaper. "That bullshit?"

"It's not bullshit. I thought you'd be happy it's published."

"Do I look happy?" Joey asked, livid.

"Happy for me, I mean. It's my first published piece. God, you can be such a selfish bitch," Kat said.

"Oh shit, you're right," Joey said. "Of course I'm happy for you. How does it feel to be published?"

"Good. Bad. I don't know. I feel . . . exposed," Kat said.

Joey nodded. "I know what you mean."

"You're right," Kat said after a moment. "Sorry."

"You made it seem like I've decided to be a grief counselor for the rest of my life."

"But you're doing Grief Group," she said. "You committed to it."

"I did," Joey said. She felt as if she was being squeezed in a vise. "But I don't need the whole world to know. I might change my mind."

Kat shook her head. "You should've worked with a good dog trainer."

"What?"

"You never learned 'Stay.' You only learned 'Go.'" Kat pushed the door open. "Back in a jiff."

Joey sat at the desk. Unsettled by the conversation, she checked her email as the phone rang.

"Ferndale Apartments," she said.

"Kat?" said the voice on the other end.

"Sorry, she's not here right now. Can I take a message?"

"Tell her Bud Zellner called."

"Yes?" Joey said, her heart beating fast.

"Tell her I'm coming back. Soon."

"Um. How soon?" Joey asked.

"I'll be home next Friday. Tell her to make sure to have my apartment cleaned. Spic and span. Number 303," he said.

Joey hung up, frozen in place.

"Time to move," she said when Kat walked in with a stack of newspapers and a grocery bag. Kat put a dozen copies of the paper on the desk and took out a box of Krispy Kreme donuts while Joey filled her in on Bud Zellner's call. "Now where do I go?"

"I've got an idea," Kat said, arranging the donuts on a tray.

"A cheap idea?" Joey asked, feeling desperate. "I'm not exactly flush."

"Cheap. A place you can stay for a while and actually feather your nest." Kat opened a drawer and pulled out a large set of keys. "Come on."

"I don't feather nests," Joey said as they got into the elevator.

"Of course not," Kat said, punching the button for the second floor.

"Nesting is overrated," Joey insisted.

"Then this should be perfect for you," Kat said, turning the key in the lock of apartment #291. They walked into an immaculate studio apartment. "It's one of our model units. A 'Color-Coordinated Designer-Chic Unit,' to be exact," Kat said as she walked around the 500 square-foot room. "See? The walls are 'ecru' and the carpet is 'sand.' The couch is 'fawn,' those two armchairs are 'camel,' and the coffee table is 'blonde'. And here's the bed." She opened a mirrored closet and pulled a Murphy bed out of the wall.

Joey began to laugh.

Kat sank into the couch. "So how does it look?"

"Like baby shit," Joey said, sitting next to her.

Kat laughed. "That's what I call it. 'The Baby Shit Suite.'"

Joey put her feet up on the coffee table. "I like it. How long have I got here?"

"Until the manager catches you," Kat said.

"And the rent?"

"For you? Minimal."

When Joey walked back into Bud Zellner's apartment she looked around at the gleaming space. It was messy enough, but she'd been living out of a suitcase for the past six weeks.

She jumped in the shower. In spite of herself, Kat's words resonated. Annoying as she was, Kat was the one person who always spoke the truth, even (especially) when Joey didn't want to hear it. As the water ran down her body she remembered taking showers in Nonna's apartment. Half a continent away, the pale yellow walls of her grandmother's apartment held her in their stately arms.

Home, Joey thought, shampooing vigorously. As she reached for conditioner a voice whispered softly in her ear: *But you never made it yours.*

When she got out of the shower, she realized the rest of the weekend stretched before her with nothing to do. She was firing up her laptop to check on Netflix when her eyes fell on the *People's Weekly.*

"Oh, shit," she said. Oasis was all over that article. She decided to tell Daniel about it, in person, before he heard it from someone else. *Or maybe it's just an excuse to see him,* she thought as she started up the car and checked out her hair.

Saturday afternoon classes were winding down as Joey pulled into Oasis. A Faery Hunt had just ended, and adults dressed as colorful faeries waved goodbye to little girls wearing wings and carrying wands; painters were cleaning brushes and folding their easels; a couple of dark-haired women collected pads of paper from writers in Memoir Writing under the Pines; the fencing class was on its final duel of the day.

Berta made one last sweeping brushstroke of yellow as Joey walked up to her and showed her the article.

"That's terrific," Berta said after she read it.

"What's so terrific about it?"

"It's great publicity for Oasis."

"Oh," Joey said. "I didn't think of that."

Berta said, "It's just what we need."

"What do we need?" Daniel asked, joining them.

"This article Joey's friend wrote about Grief Group. You know—Kat? The woman you met at Margaritaville?" Berta asked.

"Long red hair, turquoise Stetson?"

"That's Kat," Joey said. The mournful wail of an instrument floated across the lawn. "What's that?"

"A didgeridoo," Daniel said.

"A what?"

"A wind instrument played by the Aborigines of Australia," he explained, beaming. "I brought one with me to remind me of home, and now we've even got a didge class up and running."

As if in reply, several more instruments played in lusty unison, woefully off-key.

"How's that?" yelled the teacher to Daniel.

"Ace, mate," Daniel yelled back. "Ace all the way."

"Why don't you two go to the office so Daniel can read the article in peace?" Berta gave Joey a thumbs-up as she and Daniel headed that way. Soon Joey was sitting in the chair opposite his desk while he read Kat's article.

"A great portrait of you and your work. It just might help us. Thanks."

"Don't thank me. I had no idea she was writing it."

"Still, you were the inspiration."

Joey looked around as he rummaged through papers on his desk.

"What's with the bars on the windows?" she asked.

"Ugh. Those. Old-fashioned burglar prevention. One of these days we'll have to get those off." Daniel grabbed his satchel, and they walked out together. He locked up the office. "What are you doing this afternoon?" he asked.

A burst of hope began to flood Joey. "I have some errands."

"You reckon you can get out of them and go to the beach?" Daniel asked.

"I haven't been to the beach since I got here," she admitted.

"All right, then. Let's get your car back to Ferndale. I'll take us on the bike."

Soon she was riding behind Daniel on his Triumph motorcycle, her arms wrapped around his waist, her breasts against his back, her heart in her throat as he wove along a narrow, winding canyon road cut into a rocky blue mountain.

Trust, she told herself, the wind whipping her long hair from beneath the helmet as they emerged into the light from a tunnel cut through the rock.

Trust, she repeated as the road curved sharply to the left and she eyed the distant blue creek at the bottom of the ravine.

Trust this man, she echoed as she breathed in the heady scent of his cologne. She wrapped her arms tighter around him, willing herself not to envision flying off the road and falling 300 feet into the canyon.

Daniel turned left at a sign—Paradise Cove—and drove down a mile-long driveway to a parking lot. They paid 10 bucks and walked to a small, pristine beach in a cove with a restaurant and a badly damaged pier.

"The last rains did that," Daniel explained.

"What do you call rain in Australia?" Joey asked as his hand brushed against hers.

"Rain," Daniel replied.

It sounded like "rine" to Joey. Which for some reason made her giggle. Or it might have been the salt sea air on her face. Or the crystal blue water in the pretty cove with bluffs that rose above it, topped by tall trees. Somehow the stress of the morning fell away. She forgot about the article, she forgot about the eulogy she'd promised to do and the move she had to make. She forgot about everything but the moment.

For the rest of the afternoon they walked along the beach.

"Could you surf here?" Joey asked.

"Not much of a wave," Daniel said. "I'll take you to Topanga Point one of these days when it's gentle and teach you to surf."

"I'm a klutz," Joey said.

"What's a klutz?"

"Someone who trips over their own feet. Like when I came for the interview."

"You're only a klutz when you're nervous," Daniel said, pronouncing it "klotz." "I saw you dance. You're brilliant."

They took off their shoes, and freezing water soaked the bottoms of their pants as they watched the waves breaking close to the shore with a gentle splash. They talked about other beaches and other places, while steering away from the mention of other people they'd loved.

They wandered away from the crowds and jumped from rock to rock and stared at barnacles opening and closing in tide pools. They saw pelicans swoop down, catch fish, and swoop back up, the beating of their large wings echoing off the bluffs. Seagulls squawked. Joey smelled the seaweed and salt in the air.

They sat on a blanket in the sand and talked until the sun began to set, the air cooled, and the fog rolled in. Joey buttoned her jacket.

"My first L.A. beach sunset," Joey admitted.

She tried not to feel a stab when she thought about orange and pink sunsets on Fire Island with Jack. She tried not to think about leaning back in his arms, with their familiar warmth.

"Homesick?" Daniel asked.

"Kind of," she said.

He reads me. Joey was amazed.

The heat of Daniel's hand found hers as they made their way to the cheesy restaurant ("Paradise!") with red leather booths and photos from *Gidget* and *Beach Blanket Bingo*, which the owner informed them were filmed at Paradise Cove. They shared a bucket of greasy fried calamari in a booth in front of floor-to-ceiling windows overlooking the ocean.

They ordered baked potatoes and had seconds from the salad bar as they watched a Lakers game on the TV over the bar. They drank Bloody Marys and split a huge slice of red velvet cake before it began to rain and Daniel put his jacket over both of them, but they still got soaked as he drove through the downpour to Ferndale.

It had stopped raining by the time they pulled into the parking lot.

Joey had decided she was going to ask him up for a nightcap and wherever that led.

"Thanks for a great afternoon," she said, dismounting. He got off, too. She handed him her helmet. "Do you want to . . . ?"

He pulled her close, lifted her chin, and looked into her eyes. "I want to . . ."

He kissed her, his lips cool and moist. She tasted the night air on them as her body melted into his. Daniel's urgency and her own took her by surprise. She hadn't known how much longing she had until it was met with his.

"Nightcap?" Joey asked, still in Daniel's arms.

He reached down and touched her face. "Next time. Surfing at 5:30 AM tomorrow. Rain check?" He smiled.

"Rain check," she said.

As Daniel drove away Joey felt the disappointment in her chest. She inhaled deeply, her lungs filling with the cool air she'd just tasted on his lips.

Chapter Seventeen

A wild wind blew Joey's hair around as she stood on the dock outside the lounge of the Del Marina Yacht Club. Hundreds of white-masted sailboats bobbed in the water. Yacht club pennants flapped in the breeze as she practiced reading her eulogy for Rod, Alli's husband.

Joey looked out at the waves and tried to talk herself off the ledge. *This isn't that big a deal. You're not going to break down. No one will judge you.* The sliding glass door opened. A uniformed employee of the yacht club looked over at her.

"Alli's ready for you."

You'll be fine, Joey told herself as she walked into the packed lounge where Rod's favorite song was blaring through the speakers: *This is a Ma-a-a-an's World,* James Brown sang, *Man made the boat for the water like Noah made the ark . . .*

In the back of the room she passed a dozen men wearing navy blue blazers and white captain's hats. She smelled Scotch in the air as she walked past the polished oak bar where the members of Grief Group perched uncomfortably on wooden stools. She passed the friends and families of Alli and Rod seated on club chairs around small tables. The glazed blue eyes of a mounted swordfish stared back at her as she made it to the front of the room.

A poster of Rod aboard *Number Nine* stood on an easel. Next to that sat Alli, in a micro-mini red dress, red fishnets, and motorcycle boots. Her Cocker Spaniel puppy sat in her lap, Rod's motorcycle goggles around his neck. Alli shot Joey a grateful look as the song ended. Joey looked out at the crowd and took a shaky breath.

"I'm Joey Lerner, a friend of Alli's. I never met Rod but I feel like I know him. I know he loved his life, his friends, and his family. Most of all he loved Alli. And he was just too young to die . . . . " She went on, doing her awkward best, talking about Rod and Alli meeting at Stanford, how he went into his father's business and built homes in Malibu, how he loved to sail and fish and ride his Harley. She talked about their wedding, the snorkeling trips they took together, their love for each other. She used what Alli had told her and embellished it as best she could.

When she ran out of things to say she reached for an embroidered pillow on her seat that Berta had handed her before the memorial. "This is for you, Alli. It's from Berta at Oasis. It says: 'Oh, God, be good to me. My boat is so small and thy sea is so great.'"

Alli teared up, reached for the pillow, and wrapped Joey in a tight hug. Joey sat while Alli stood, holding the Cocker Spaniel puppy in her arms.

"Most of you know I wasn't going to have a memorial for Rod," Alli said softly. "I mean, how do you have a memorial without a body? Then this little dog told me Rod was dead." She kissed the puppy. "Look at his eyes. Aren't they just like Rod's?"

Joey looked out at the crowd. Alli's friends and family looked confused. The skippers looked soused. Grief Group looked miserable.

"He's come back to me in another form," Alli said. "So would everyone please raise your glasses?" Everyone held up tumblers of Scotch. "To Rod," Alli said, holding the Cocker Spaniel high, her voice ragged. "We're so happy to be with you again."

The room was silent for a mystified moment. Then a hearty voice rang out: "To Rod!" It was one of his sailing buddies, dressed in a skipper jacket. The half-dozen men in skipper jackets and captain's hats marched up to the dog, saluted him, and marched back. Then everyone was drinking and sharing stories about Rod, and Alli was surrounded by people, including her mother and sisters. She introduced Joey to everyone as the bartender started to serve bar fare—fish 'n' chips, buffalo wings, and sliders. Joey managed to slip away and walked straight to Grief Group, where everyone but Maggie was swilling Scotch.

"Weird memorial," Del said.

"It's strange to do this without a body," Tamara agreed.

"It's sad. I can't imagine Rod leaving Alli like that," Maggie said.

"I know," Joey said, reaching for a badly needed Scotch. She checked her watch and wondered how quickly she could leave.

"Speaking of leaving," Daisy said abruptly. "I am."

"You are . . . what?" Joey asked.

"Leaving. L.A."

"When?" Del asked.

"In a week."

"Where are you going?" Maggie asked.

"Up north. To Walnut Grove. To live closer to my family."

"But I'm just getting to know you," Maggie said, looking stricken. Her hand went to her belly. "I'm not ready to lose anybody else."

How exactly do I deal with this? Joey wondered. "Will you be at the next meeting?"

"Yes," Daisy said.

"Why are you leaving?" Dave asked.

"Is Group not doing it for you?" Del asked.

Daisy shook her head. "Group is great. I just need to be near my family right now."

"So we'll say goodbye at the next meeting," Joey said.

"Maybe we should do it like this." Maggie gestured to the food. "Like after a funeral. When you stuff your face."

"Except nobody died," Joey pointed out.

"So let's go to Chinatown and have a feast," Dave said.

"Did you ever wonder why there's so much eating after a funeral?" Joey asked, looking around. People were piling their plates like they hadn't eaten for a month.

"Maybe if everybody keeps their mouth full they don't have to say what they're feeling," Maggie said.

"Because there aren't words for those feelings," Sam said.

"So let's not do that," Tamara said. "Because Daisy's leaving isn't a sad goodbye."

"It's a bittersweet goodbye," Maggie said. "So let's have a dessert party. With bittersweet chocolate."

"Or a sweet goodbye," Joey said. "Since the others were bitter."

"I'll bring a special dessert," Daisy said.

Alli arrived breathlessly, clutching the Cocker Spaniel tightly. "I feel like this is a performance, and I can't do it anymore."

"What do you mean?" Maggie asked.

"I'm trying to play the perfectly sane widow. Because Rod's family thinks I'm nuts. But you guys understand me. Right?" Alli looked bleary-eyed.

Joey thought about a cartoon she'd just seen: "How grief is supposed to go" (a straight line); "how grief really goes" (squiggles and mess.)

"We understand you," she told Alli.

"Fuck 'em," Dave said. "Let's blow this joint and find the best margaritas in L.A."

Everyone agreed. As they walked out together Del checked Yelp on his cell. "Margarita Cantina," he said, striding to his Porsche. "See you there."

"I'll go with you," Alli said, racing to keep up with him.

"You coming?" Tamara asked Joey.

"Can't. Sorry. I'm busy."

She drove out the gate, feeling like her heart was skipping every other heartbeat. She had somewhere to go and someone to be with.

Daniel.

Chapter Eighteen

An hour later Joey pulled into Oasis wearing a red sweatshirt and jeans. Daniel was up on a ladder, painting the outside of *Birds of Paradise*.

"I thought you were going to wait for me," she said.

"I decided to get a jumpstart. There's plenty more to do. How did it go?" Daniel asked.

Joey shrugged. "It was okay. I was lame."

"Well, you did it. That's more than most people would've done." He ran a roller of beige paint with a hint of gray down the wall. "Can you believe they call this color 'Going to the Chapel'?"

Joey laughed.

"Come on up," Daniel said, pointing to a ladder on the ground. "That one's got your name on it. And after we paint we get to fix the gutters that are hanging off the roof."

"Exciting. Be right back." She walked to the Quonset hut feeling like a teenager. Her palms were sweaty, her face felt flushed. *Stop it,* she told yourself as she rounded up tools. *He's just being friendly. Professionally friendly.*

But by the time the two of them were painting side by side on ladders it was clear that he was being more than professionally friendly. Within five minutes of her starting to paint he'd asked her out to dinner.

TEARS AND TEQUILA · 145

"Or are you busy tonight?" he asked.

For a moment Joey thought of playing hard to get. Then she stopped herself. "I'd love to go to dinner with you."

"Perfect," Daniel said, smiling. "I've been planning this for a while."

Joey wanted to reach over and kiss him, but she stayed on her own ladder. They were almost done when they heard a man's voice below them.

"I'm looking for a Daniel Wyndham."

Joey and Daniel looked down at a burly man with an official-looking clipboard.

"That's me, mate," Daniel said. "What can I do for you?"

"I'm Ed Groenig," the man said. "From the Los Angeles Department of Building and Safety. We got a complaint about—" He looked down at his paper. "Osis."

"Oasis," Joey and Daniel corrected. Daniel climbed down his ladder. Joey followed suit.

"Yeah," said Ed Groenig. "So we need to schedule an inspection."

"Who made the complaint?"

"Sorry. Confidential."

"Well, what's the complaint about?"

The man read from his clipboard. "No fire hydrants on campus, just old hoses with leaks. No fire extinguishers on the premises. Large tree roots causing pavement to buckle on paths to cottages. Pot holes in parking lot. Danger to inhabitants . . . "

"Nobody lives here," Daniel said impatiently. "This is a community center."

"For kids?" The inspector asked, looking around. "Because, from the look of things, you're going to be in for a whole lot more violations."

"For adults," Daniel corrected. "And occasionally kids."

"You're going to have to correct these items," the inspector said. "This place is clearly not up to code."

"Fine," Daniel said. "Will you give me a copy of the report?"

The inspector handed him a yellow copy, asked Daniel to sign and date it, and scheduled an inspection in two weeks.

Joey's heart sank as the man walked away. She forced herself not to think about all the work that needed doing: the archaic heating system that sounded like a jackhammer; the water leak in the office; windows that were painted shut; curtains that covered broken window panes; the bars on the windows in Daniel's office, which were a fire hazard; the sewer line that needed replacement. The list was long. As charming as Oasis was on the outside, its infrastructure, Joey knew well, was as rotten as the state of Denmark.

It could be a losing battle, she thought. *And God knows the cost.* But she wasn't about to say that to Daniel. Because strong, capable Daniel was looking down at the list of violations, crushed. Joey came up alongside him.

"Who do you think filed that complaint?" she asked.

"It could be anyone. And they're not wrong. We need fire extinguishers and we have to fix those bumps in the pavement. I just wish whoever it was had talked to me first."

"Me, too."

"Once you get in the city's crosshairs, it's tough to get out."

He frowned.

"We can fix this," Joey said.

"I know we can," Daniel agreed. "But it's just the tip of the iceberg, eh?"

Joey had to nod.

"I made a deathbed promise to my grandmother that I'd keep Oasis going," he said. "I'm beginning to wonder if I can."

Joey put a hand on his arm. "Time to get to work."

"You're right," Daniel said, coming up for air. "There's life in the old girl yet." He started to close the paint cans. "Let's go."

"Where?"

"Home Depot," Daniel said. "Romantic for a date, what say?"

A date, Joey thought as they drove off together.

Half an hour later they were in Home Depot, where Joey felt she'd died and gone to heaven. It was the biggest hardware store she'd ever seen, and she insisted on going up and down every aisle, regaling Daniel with stories of hardware stores she'd gone to with her Grandpa when she was a kid.

Soon they were wheeling a flatbed piled high with sheets of drywall and drywall mud, sections of gutters, fire extinguishers, bags of cement, cans of paint, putty knives, panes of glass, spackling compound, and two acetylene torches.

When they checked out, the cashier asked if they were fixing up their house.

"Right-o," Daniel said with a straight face. "Now, here's the address for delivery. . . . "

It was dark by the time they ducked into the Quonset hut. Daniel looked around, impressed by Joey's improvements. Screwdrivers, hammers, hatchets, pliers, wire cutter, glue, crescent wrenches, staple guns, saws, files, and chisels were hung on hooks. Extension cords were coiled perfectly. A drill press, vise, and power saws were clean and ready. Rows of white plastic plant pots (from Miss Piggy's), separated by size, were filled with wood screws, machine screws, and nuts and bolts.

"Wow," Daniel said. "Good one."

"Thanks," Joey said happily. "Time for dinner," she told Lexus and Armani. She opened their box and fed them lettuce.

"Looking fine," he said, coming up beside Joey.

"Aren't they?" she said.

"I mean you." Daniel tucked a strand of her hair behind her ear. "Let's go."

"But I'm not dressed," Joey said, reaching to wipe a smear of paint from his cheek. "I thought we'd go to Ferndale first."

"You look perfect the way you are," Daniel said, reaching for her hand as they walked out.

The penny dropped. Daniel was into her, Joey realized. She felt like skipping all the way to his motorcycle.

An hour later they were sharing a pitcher of margaritas at the famous Mexican restaurant El Cholo.

"*Los Ninos y los locos dicen las verdades,*" Joey said.

"And that means . . . ?" Daniel asked.

"Kids and crazy people speak the truth."

Daniel laughed. "Where did you learn to speak Spanish?"

"I lived in Mexico for three months."

"When you taught *drama para los Ninos.*"

"How do you know?" Joey asked, pouring refills.

"I remember seeing it on your résumé when you came for the interview. I remember all the groups you did before this one."

Her face felt hot. "You do?"

"Yup."

"Wow," Joey said as the waiter brought them guacamole and chips. She felt seen. She felt heard.

They began to talk about Oasis and how to renovate it with as little money as possible while getting the building inspectors off their back.

"How about some new ideas for bringing in students," Joey said. "To increase our revenue stream."

Daniel looked at her. "*Our* revenue stream?" he said. "I like it."

After two pitchers of margaritas, it was easy to go from mariachis to planning a Mardi Gras at Oasis.

"We could do a parade of dogs in costumes," Joey said. "And a float pulled around by a motorcycle."

"I know where we can get our hands on a Triumph," Daniel said.

"It'll be a fabulous way to bring in new students."

"It could get us great publicity," Daniel agreed. His hand reached for hers. "So. We're in this?" His eyes stared into hers.

"Together," Joey said.

"We're in this together," Daniel repeated.

"Together," Joey echoed. The words sent a flush of warmth through her body.

It was almost 11:00 when they got to Ferndale, where they walked around the man-made lake and Daniel called to the nesting swans. When the swans swam over, Joey laughed at the sight of him surrounded by adoring females, as usual. They ended up with Joey in a bathing suit in the Jacuzzi under the stars and Daniel in black briefs, icy Foster's beer cans in hand. Joey admired Daniel's lean, muscular body. She was glad she'd been swimming laps when she saw the hunger in his eyes as he looked her up and down.

"Please?" she begged, more than a little bombed. "Will you *please* teach me to speak Australian?"

"You're banged," he said, amused.

"Nooooo."

"All right. You say a word with a consonant at the end. I'll say it like an Aussie."

"River," she said.

"*Rivah,*" he corrected.

"Together."

"Togethah."

"Paid."

"Pide."

"Stop sounding so damn superior," Joey said.

"Can't help it," Daniel replied.

"I'll never get it."

"Just keep your tongue flat on the roof of your mouth."

"Want to show me how?"

He did. And after he kissed her she was breathless.

"No worries about pronunciation," Daniel said. "Australia was settled by convicts, so Aussie sounds kind of rough. It's messy. Not too proper." He reached out and ruffled her curls. "Like you, Joey."

They kissed again, a long, lingering kiss that lit up the sky. *No, actually, those are stars,* Joey realized when she leaned her head back against his chest and looked upward.

"What do you Americans say when you see the stars? Make a wish?"

"Right," Joey said.

"Roite," Daniel corrected. "Got a wish to make?"

Joey climbed out of the Jacuzzi and reached for his hand. "I think my wish is about to come true."

They walked up to her new place, where Daniel dried her with a towel. He slipped her suit off and caressed her body from head to toe before slipping off his briefs and letting her caress him. Soon Joey was caught up in the feel of his touch and the way Daniel surrendered to hers, and they were making love on the living room rug. She let go of everything as their bodies mingled, and her heart raced, and they came together.

"Chemistry," Daniel said later as they lay in the Murphy bed, her back nestled against his chest. "We've got chemistry." He pulled her tighter, and she closed her hands over his. "You can't fake it. You can't fight it. And we've got it."

TEARS AND TEQUILA · 151

As Daniel fell asleep, his arms around her, Joey's fingers felt the ring on one of the hands that had just driven her wild. Once again she found herself wondering why he wore it. Then she settled deeper in his arms and fell asleep.

Across town, Heidi was lying in bed next to Gus Green.

"Married?" she asked him.

"Nope. You ever been married?"

"Yes. To my father's enemy," Heidi said.

"Really?" Gus propped himself up on his elbow.

"Really. His father ruined mine."

"So why did you marry the guy?" he asked.

"A little love. A lot of revenge," Heidi said.

"Did you get it?"

"Not yet," Heidi said. "But I will."

Chapter Nineteen

Over the next two weeks Joey and Daniel labored to fix the violations. She was grateful there was no Grief Group scheduled until after the inspection, because she and Daniel arrived at 7:00 AM and worked until midnight under rented work lights set up in the parking lot. On the days she worked at Miss Piggy's, she joined him in the evening.

Fire hydrants were installed. Gutters were hoisted. Daniel rented a large cement mixer from Home Depot, and for three days he and Joey spread the cement themselves. Wearing goggles, overalls, and work boots, they worked with Perfecto and his cousin Oscar, while Marjorie took over the running of the office. Students, who had to park on the street, rubbernecked at the goings on as they walked to and from classes.

When Heidi passed by, she saw Daniel's hand brushing Joey's. She recognized the look in his eyes when he watched her climb a ladder. *Daniel is sleeping with his handybitch*, Heidi realized, *while Oasis is getting fixed for a pittance.* Things were not going according to plan. When she caught Perfecto's cousin, Oscar, looking over at her Heidi hurried to her car. She couldn't afford Oscar mentioning that he'd met her at the Department of Building and Safety.

By the end of the first week the parking lot was paved; the biggest bumps from tree roots were patched over. By the end of the second week the falling rain gutters had been nailed up; roofs had been reshingled; railings and rotten porches had been repaired.

At the end of their long days Joey and Daniel soothed their sore muscles in the Jacuzzi at Ferndale. At night, they lay in bed, too sore to move. Until Daniel reached over to touch Joey and she came alive.

The night before the inspection they worked until 2:00 AM. "Are we done?" Joey asked as they looked around the property with flashlights. The paint on most of the bungalows was no longer peeling. The potholes were filled. Mostly.

"As done as we're going to be," Daniel said. "Anyway, I'm out of funds. For now. "

"Here's to passing inspection tomorrow," Joey said, raising her flashlight.

"Here's to us," Daniel said. "A team."

Joey's breath caught in her throat. He pulled her to him. They kissed under the lights in the parking lot before driving home separately to get a good night's sleep.

Her phone rang at 5:48 AM. She reached for it blindly.

"The ceiling in the waiting room of the office fell down," Daniel said. "It triggered the burglar alarm. I just got the call."

"I'll be right there."

By the time she arrived everything in the waiting room was covered in plaster dust, including Daniel. Joey worked with him and Perfecto to carry out the furniture, then patch, paint, and plaster before the inspector showed up. They moved the furniture back in at 5:00 PM. Ed Groening arrived at 5:20. Luckily, Oasis was his last appointment of the day.

"Fresh paint, eh?" he said, sniffing as he walked in.

"Fresh everything," Daniel said, walking him outside before the inspector could see signs of the ceiling having fallen. "Let me show you."

Joey watched as Daniel walked the inspector around, showing him

154 · LINDA SCHREYER AND JO-ANN LAUTMAN

the fixed violations. The inspector checked off some boxes on his paper and circled others.

"We'll get back to you," he said as he walked to his car and drove away.

Daniel joined Joey. "What does that mean, you think?" she asked.

"It means we take the night off," Daniel said, brushing plaster dust from her hair. "Nothing more we can do, and God knows we've earned it."

The following night, every muscle sore, Joey entered *Hummingbird*, where she found an edgy Grief Group staring at a white coffin-shaped box perched on a bed of fake grass on the scarred wooden coffee table. The room was still as everyone pondered the possible contents of the box.

"What's that?" Joey asked, taking her seat.

"A little joke for you to remember me by," Daisy said. "Open it. We were waiting for you."

Joey felt the room hold its breath as she opened the coffin box. A small piece of folded paper lay on top of purple tissue paper; it looked like a fortune inside a fortune cookie.

"Read it," Daisy said.

Joey read aloud: *Ancient Chinese Proverb say inside coffin find sweets.*

Daisy moved the purple tissue paper aside and pulled out a cake with white frosting garnished with foil-wrapped coins depicting a panda and a splashy comma of Chinese characters written in red jujubes.

"What the hell?" said Tamara.

"It's Chinese sticky-rice cake," Daisy explained. "For special occasions."

"What about the coffin box?" Sam asked.

"Isn't that what you meant by 'gallows humor'?" Daisy asked Dave.

"Nope. I think it's what you meant about Chinese parents not raising their kids with a sense of humor," Dave said.

"I dig the box, Daisy," Del said with a laugh.

"God, it scared me," Maggie said.

"Let me cut the cake," Daisy said. "I've got to go soon. I need to finish packing."

"So sudden? Oh, wow," Alli said, taking the piece Daisy handed to her. "Can I say something I learned from being with you in Grief Group before you go?"

"Why not?" Joey said.

"It's your lipstick. I love the way you do your lips," Alli said.

Maggie and Tamara laughed. Daisy nodded politely. She passed a piece of cake to Maggie, who said, "You're the best-dressed widow I ever met."

"A touch of class," Del said. "That's what you brought to this Group. I'll miss you."

"Love the Jewish lawyer sperm thing," Dave said. "What are you doing with it?"

"Taking it with me, of course. I can't wait to see what Airport Security makes of those three little vials."

Everyone laughed. Then it was Daisy's turn. "One of the things I got is that it's okay to be miserable. In here I never had to pretend that I'm not. I'll miss that. I'll miss you."

"We'll miss you, too," Joey said, noting that Daisy was picking at her manicure. "Anything else you want to talk about?"

"The ICU," Daisy said, blowing out a long breath. "How can anyone get well when the lights are on night and day?"

"They're on so that patients can be monitored," Del said.

"How do you stand that smell?" Daisy asked.

"The Lysol?"

"The vomit," Daisy said with passion. "The Lysoled vomit. Stu was in there for 10 days. All those machines. Beeping endlessly." Her face filled with misery. "I can't forget any of that." Then she stood, her business-like mask in place again. "I've got to go." She started to pack up the coffin box. "Unless somebody wants to keep this."

"No, thanks," Joey said.

"Are you going to be okay?" Maggie asked Daisy.

"I don't know."

"Why don't you look for a Grief Group where you're going?" Joey asked.

"Better yet," Dave said, "we can Skype. We'll put an iPad on your chair. It will be like you're still here."

"Perfect," Alli said, clapping her hands.

Daisy stowed the coffin box in her Louis Vuitton bag. "The town where my parents live has lousy Internet."

The room went silent.

"You don't want to be with us," Alli said.

"It's not you. I don't want to be with this." She indicated the coffin box with a wave of her hand. "It's too sad. I'd rather not talk about this so much. I want to forget, not remember. So long," she said. And she was gone.

She left as abruptly as she arrived, Joey thought, remembering Daisy plopping down on the rug at the first meeting.

A silence settled over the room.

"I feel terrible," Alli said.

"What didn't we do for her?" Maggie asked.

"I'm pissed." Tamara said. "I'm hurting too, but I don't want to run away from it."

"She's just different," Del said. "Cut her some slack."

"Let's give her time," Sam said. "Maybe she'll email one of us."

"I know what she means," Alli said. "There are so many things I don't want to think about. Like how Rod's body must have looked . . . . "

The room fell silent. Joey saw something out of the corner of her eye.

A woman was looking in the window. When Joey looked again the woman was gone.

"I touched her," Sam said quietly.

"You what?" asked Tamara.

"I touched Mel. In her coffin," Sam said. "She looked like a wax statue. Her hands felt like . . . rubber."

"I didn't eat anything for five days after Jeff's funeral," Maggie said slowly.

"I couldn't stop eating," Tamara admitted.

"My hair started to fall out," Alli said.

"I didn't comb mine for a week," Dave added.

"You still haven't combed it," Del said.

"I never thought I'd be choosing a *casket,* did you?" Dave asked.

Sam agreed. "God, that was awful."

"Did you get the coffin at Costco?" Dave asked.

"Did you ride in the ambulance?" Maggie asked. "I've always wondered about that."

"Her toe had a tag," Dave said in a tight voice.

"She was ice cold," Sam added.

"With all of my training, how could I be surprised?" Del said.

"About what?" asked Alli.

"That Shawn's ashes would have bone fragments," Del said. "How could that surprise me?"

"Last night I dreamed Jeff was alive," Maggie said. "I woke up feeling great. Then I realized he was dead."

"I've had those dreams," Sam said.

"When is that going to stop?"

"What about closure?" Tamara asked. "When do we get that?"

"Closure is for bank accounts," Joey said. "So they say . . . "

The door opened. A woman walked in. "Excuse me," she said.

It was Heidi.

Chapter Twenty

Joey jumped to her feet. "This is a private group."

"Oh, sorry" Heidi said, looking around with hungry eyes. "I thought yoga was meeting in here tonight."

"This is Grief Group," Dave said. "Come on in. Everyone's dying to join."

Alli giggled.

"You need to leave," Joey said.

"Of course. I'm so sorry." Heidi walked out the door.

Joey sat, wondering what that was about. *Yoga always meets in* Rising Lotus Cottage. *What was Heidi doing here?*

The Group began to talk about Rod's memorial. Dave said he'd show Alli how to make a Memorial Facebook page for Rod. He said he'd help if she wanted to post pictures of him on Instagram.

"So many ways to keep his memory alive," Del said.

"Are you feeling any better after the memorial?" Maggie asked Alli.

"Not really."

"They say time heals," Sam said. "But I'm not so sure."

"I don't feel time's helping me at all," Maggie said.

"Me, neither," Tamara agreed.

"I feel as raw as the day I heard Rod drowned."

"The walking wounded," Del said.

"I don't feel like other people our age. I feel like I'm scarred or something," Maggie said.

"Maybe our scars are the most authentic parts of us," Sam said.

Word, Joey thought, thinking of her own losses.

By the time she headed to the deserted parking lot the fog was rolling in. Daniel and Marjorie had gone to a Chamber of Commerce meeting. The other classes had ended earlier.

Joey was almost at her recently purchased 1996 gray Honda when the streetlights illuminated a figure standing next to a dark blue Chevy Spark. The person wore a fake fur-trimmed green anorak with the hood over his or her head.

"Hello?" Joey called out.

"Oh, thank goodness," said a female voice with an Australian accent. She pulled down her hood. Heidi's cell phone was in her hand, and she was looking at her car with dismay. "I've got a flat tire. I think someone slashed it."

"What?" Joey asked.

"Look." Heidi pointed to her rear tire.

Joey peered through the darkness. "I can't see anything."

"Here," Heidi said, flicking on her lighter. "Is that better?"

"No," Joey said. "Do you have the flashlight App on your phone?"

"It's dead," Heidi said. "I couldn't even call the rental company."

"Hang on," Joey said.

She had no reason to try to help Heidi. No reason at all. But her handyperson instincts kicked in as she opened the door of the Honda, stowed her things and came back to Heidi's car, flashlight in hand.

"Hold this," Joey said. "Shine it there, and let me take a look." Joey knelt on the ground and saw a two inch gash on the outside wall. "You're right. Somebody slashed it."

"Why would anyone do that?" Heidi asked, upset.

"Daniel said there's been some vandalism at Oasis recently," Joey said. "They graffiti'd one of the murals on the bungalows."

"Poor Daniel," Heidi said, handing the flashlight back to Joey. "He's got his hands full."

At the mention of Daniel Joey became aware that it was his ex-wife who was handing her a flashlight and that she had lied to Daniel about when she arrived in L.A. Questions chased each other in Joey's mind. *Why did Heidi lie? Why did she barge into Grief Group? What was it like being married to Daniel?* She was curious about Heidi but the fog made Joey shiver in her pea coat. So she looked at the flat and asked if Heidi had a spare.

"I don't know." Heidi looked completely helpless.

"Pop the trunk," Joey said. She hunted around for the spare. "Got it." She started looking for a jack. But there was no jack in Heidi's car. And, inexplicably there was none in the Honda "I don't believe this," Joey said, frustrated.

"So we can't change the tire?" Heidi asked. "Should I call Uber car service and get them to give me a ride home?"

Joey didn't answer. She was thinking about changing a tire without a jack. Despite whose tire it was, the challenge appealed to her.

"Let me see what I can find in the workshop." She started for the Quonset hut.

"Wait for me," Heidi said, looking around nervously as she fell into step. "I don't want to be out here alone."

As Heidi peered with distaste at Lexus and Armani, Joey rummaged through tools until she found a Coleman lantern, work gloves, a lug wrench, and two shovels. She handed one to Heidi, and they walked back to the parking lot.

"You sure work late hours for a handyperson," Heidi said.

"I also lead Grief Group. As you know."

"Yeah. Sorry about walking in. I read about that in the paper. I didn't realize the leader was you."

"Why did you come in?"

"I was just curious. I've never seen a Group like that before," Heidi said. "I'm really sorry."

"Right," Joey said, not sure whether or not to believe her. "So here's the drill," she said, dropping the tools onto the ground. "We're going to have to make a substitute for a jack." She lit the Coleman lantern. Its brilliant light illuminated the parking lot, making Heidi's face look a bit like a ginger cat's. "We can fix the flat if we dig a hole under the tire so it doesn't touch the ground. Then we take off the flat and put on the new tire. Get it?"

Heidi's eyebrows furrowed. "Um—what do we do first?"

"Get in your car," Joey said. "Drive it onto that dirt over there. I'll show you where to stop."

Heidi followed the instructions. "Now what?" she asked from the driver's seat.

"Get out," Joey said.

Heidi stepped out, tripped over the tools and righted herself. "Oopsie," she said. "Now . . . ?"

"Now," Joey said, handing her a shovel, "we dig a ditch under the tire."

"How do you know what you're doing?" Heidi asked as she dug.

"My grandfather made me change a tire without a jack in the driveway of our house in Maine when I was 10."

"Amazing. But I meant how do you know what you're doing in Grief Group."

"I don't," Joey admitted.

"Are you following those seven stages of grief?" Heidi asked.

"Not exactly," Joey said. "When my grandfather died I thought I was flunking grief because I stayed in 'anger' for four years. So I'm not going to do that to anyone else. Shovel." Heidi handed her the shovel. "No. Dig over there," Joey said, pointing to the dirt.

"So you're a licensed contractor *and* a grief counselor. So many talents," Heidi said as she dug.

"I'm not a licensed anything," Joey said. "I just know how to fix things that are broken."

"Including people," Heidi said. "That's what the article said."

"I'm just doing the best I can."

"Aren't we all?" Heidi agreed. "Like, I don't know how to hammer a nail. But I can screw," she laughed.

Joey thought about Daniel with Heidi. It gave her the creeps. "What about you?" she said, digging the ditch wider. "What do you do for a living?"

"A little of this, a little of that," Heidi said. "I'm working freelance at the moment. Are we done yet?"

"I think so." Joey said. She was distracted by the sight of the tire suspended in the air above the ditch. "Hand me that tool, will you?" She pointed to the lug wrench.

"Working late, aren't you?" a voice said. Joey looked up to find Berta standing beside her.

"What are you doing here?" Joey asked.

"I was hanging the art show and lost track of time. What are you two up to?" She looked from Joey to Heidi.

"Hi, I'm Heidi," she said, sticking out her hand. "I've seen you around but we've never met."

"Hello," Berta said, her voice cool.

"Someone slashed her tire so I'm changing it," Joey said.

"Aren't you something, dear heart? Look at you, a regular grease monkey."

Joey looked at her orange sweater. There were grease stains on both cuffs.

"Oh, no! I'll pay for the dry cleaning," Heidi said.

"But why on earth are you re-inventing the wheel here?" she said, gesturing to their ditch.

"Because there's no jack in either of our cars," Joey said.

"Pish tush," Berta said. "Come with me." She walked them over to her car, which was parked on the street. She opened the trunk and pointed to a jack. "Voilà."

"God," Joey said.

Within minutes Joey finished changing the tire; Heidi thanked her profusely and drove off.

"That's Daniel's ex-wife—right? Well, she did it herself," Berta said, her eyes on Heidi's disappearing tail lights.

"Did what?" Joey asked.

"She slashed her own tire. I saw her do it earlier this evening," Berta said. "Very strange."

"But why would she do that?" Joey asked, stunned.

"That's what I want to know," Berta said, her face grim.

Heidi pulled into the paint-peeling carport of her single-story bungalow in Van Nuys. She got out of the car, reached into a corner of the carport, and put the jack she'd taken out of the Chevy back into the trunk.

"I knew she wouldn't be able to resist a challenge," Heidi said aloud.

Then she walked in, and Scout, her black-and-white mutt, whirled in circles, greeting her with kisses. She put kibble in his bowl and took him out. She had plenty to think about as she walked down Magnolia Boulevard to In and Out Burger.

She'd learned what she needed to know tonight. *Not a licensed anything,* she thought as she ordered a Double Double with Cheese. *How lucky can a girl get?*

Chapter Twenty-one

Two weeks later mockingbirds sang as Tamara opened the trunk of her BMW and lifted out Maya's baby swing and circus mobile. The birds loudly imitated one birdsong after another. Tamara was unsure what to carry first up the stairs to the small gray-shingled Craftsman bungalow where Sam lived.

They were in the third month of Group and they were starting to bond. At the last meeting Joey had said she could feel a shift: "You've gotten through Easter and Passover. You're beginning to stand on your own two feet. Of course, there will be good days and bad days."

Tamara had a feeling this was going to be one of the good days. She closed the trunk on five bags of Maya's unisex baby clothes, four hand-knit angora blankets, and a box of stuffed animals. She picked up the baby swing and mobile and made for the stairs, trying to ignore the butterflies in her stomach.

Calm down, she scolded as she climbed the steps to the porch, passing the FOR SALE sign. *This isn't a date. This is a good deed* (a mitzvah, as her mother called it.) Still, Tamara's hand tugged her denim shirt down and over her butt.

Even if this wasn't a date, even if Sam and she weren't romantic, whether or not she'd had fantasies about him, spring was here, and she was feeling a little frisky. And she wanted to look her best.

She rang the bell, willing herself not to think about the date: April 15. She tried not to obsess over how big a tax bill she might owe or worry about why Bruce's boss hadn't returned any of her calls.

The door opened. Alli stood in the doorway, barefoot and balancing Andrew on her slim left hip. Her Guess jeans were so tight she couldn't squeeze a five-dollar bill into a pocket. Tanned cleavage peeked out from beneath the see-through white tee that drifted off one shoulder, *Flashdance*-style.

Since the memorial Alli had started dressing like a sexpot and sleeping around. She had a hot body and she knew how to use it. "Rod wouldn't want me to be a nun. My therapist says I'm sexualizing my grief," she said one night in Group. "And that's fine."

"Hi," Alli grinned at Tamara. "When's Maggie coming?"

"I . . . I'm sorry . . . ? What?"

"I guess all of us women Groupies want to mommy this darling little boy," Alli laughed, opening the door wide. "Come on in."

Tamara froze, feeling fat in her baggy jeans and shapeless denim shirt.

"Need a hand?" Alli asked.

"I've got it." Tamara deposited the baby gear on the light wood floor.

"Tsk, tsk," Alli clucked. "We should have talked. I already brought my nephew's baby swing."

Tamara felt ridiculous. "Where's Sam?" she asked briskly.

"Putting together the swing and a highchair I brought. I was just stashing some of my nephew's baby clothes and stuffed animals in the dresser." Alli eyed her with concern as Tamara's face fell. "Oh, no. You brought those, too?"

"Yeah."

"We *really* should've talked, girlfriend," Alli said, bouncing Andrew on her hip.

"Oh, well, I'll go get the Pack 'n' Play. Unless you—?"

"Nope. Didn't bring one. Need help carrying it up?"

Tamara eyed Alli's toned upper arms. She could easily have lifted the Pack 'n' Play with one hand while balancing Andrew with the other.

"I can do it," Tamara insisted. But Alli came anyway, chatting Tamara up all the way down to her car. "So when Sam said Andrew only had clothes and stuff for the first three months I had to do something for this little mousie—right?" Alli buried her face in Andrew's neck and he squealed happily.

Like he does when I do that, thought Tamara miserably as she headed back up the stairs, *only now I'm not Andrew's special friend. I'm Martha the Mover, lugging a playpen behind Alli's tight behind. When did she get there? This morning? Or—please God no—last night? Did the little slut bed Sam, too?*

They crossed the threshold into the living room.

"I'll tell him you're here," Alli said, heading down the hallway to a bedroom. She looked far too familiar with the layout for Tamara's taste.

She could hear Sam whistling and decided to bail before he saw her. She cast a practiced eye around the cozy room before she left—Mission furniture, built-in bookshelves, Art Nouveau prints—a room decorated with a woman's touch. As she headed to the door she saw a red jacket (Melanie's?) on a coat-rack and (Melanie's?) floppy straw hat. Tamara's hand was on the antique brass doorknob when she heard Sam's voice.

"Hey." Sam was barefoot, wearing a gray cotton T-shirt and faded jeans. He looked younger than she'd ever seen him.

"Hi," Tamara said. "I brought some stuff for Andrew." She indicated the pile on the floor. Alli walked in, still carrying the baby. "Sorry. Gotta run."

"Tamara, wait . . . ," Sam called out. But Tamara tramped down the steps to her car and couldn't hear his next words over the blood that pounded in her ears, making a loud *whoosh whoosh* that drowned out everything else. She peeled out without noticing that Sam was standing on the street looking after her.

Tamara was almost on the 134 Freeway when she realized the rest of the baby gear was still in her trunk. *God, I'm pathetic,* she thought as she ran a light that had just turned red. When she saw the flashing lights of a cop car she was relieved to have a real problem to take her mind off the pain.

Across town Joey sighed as she breathed in the fragrance of the purple hyacinth. "My favorite flower," she told the young couple who were shopping at Miss Piggy's.

"Do you have any white hyacinths?" asked the wife.

"Absolutely. Let me show you."

She led them past row after immaculate row of vibrant spring flowers—tulips, crocuses, daffodils, irises and narcissus—to Demetrios's latest display: dozens of hyacinth plants arranged in a multi-colored heart on a nursery bench.

"Look," said the young woman, grabbing her husband's arm. "How sweet is that?"

Joey agreed, happy beyond reason to see the blooming pink, white, and purple hyacinths. It was one of many sights, sounds, and smells that fed her senses on the warm Saturday morning at Miss Piggy's. The woman took out a few white plants.

"But now the heart looks broken," her husband noted.

"No worries," Joey said, parroting Daniel. She reached for replacement plants. In a moment the hyacinth display was mended, the couple was loaded with plants, and Joey was leaning against the nursery bench lost in a reverie of love, lust, and last night.

She'd ridden with Daniel at dusk as he wound down a long dirt road and stopped outside a rugged wooden building.

"This is the place," he said.

"Where are we?"

"Back o' beyond," he replied, pointing to a sign written in hand-painted orange letters on a rusty metal coal wagon.

"The Place," she read aloud. *"Steamed Clams. Wine. Steak."*

Wafts of wood smoke perfumed the cool air. Late afternoon light filtered through the sycamores. The deep quiet was broken by loud meows echoing through the canyon.

Joey felt as if she'd traveled to another world.

"Peacocks," Daniel explained. "They were tame, now they're wild." He put his warm hand on her back. "A bit like you."

Hand in hand, they walked up creaky wooden steps into a dark, crowded room with a crush of people on tractor-seat stools lining a 20-foot-long hand-hewn oak bar that doubled as a giant dining table.

"Joey," Daniel announced to the regulars as they walked to the bar. The guys, wearing jeans and Stetson hats, eyed her with interest; the women, wearing Western shirts and bouffant hair, gave her dirty looks.

Why are they looking at me like that? Joey wondered. She felt ridiculous in her short blue dress and ankle boots. Daniel pulled up a tractor-seat stool for her and called to the bartender.

"Rick. Couple of Foster's Oil Cans for me and the lady. Tom," he yelled into the kitchen, "can you toss some salmon on the barbie, mate?"

"Get your arse in here," the cook yelled back.

"Be right back," Daniel told Joey with a grin.

As she waited, the bartender poured her a glass of Foster's beer. She heard a raucous conversation from the kitchen before Daniel came back, walking past the backslapping guys and eyelash-fluttering women.

"Tom's the cook. A real gem," Daniel announced, sliding onto a stool. "Rough around the eddies but good with the tucker. So what do you think o' the place?"

"I think you think you're back in Brisbane," she said, laughing. "I've never heard you talk like that before."

"Right-o," Daniel said. "I slip back into that whenever I'm here." The bartender poured him a foamy glass of ale. Daniel took a sip. "Like it here?"

"It's interesting," she said before lowering her voice. "But why are the women glowering at me?"

"Because everyone in here is a regular except for you."

"Including you?" she asked, taking a sip.

"Especially me," Daniel answered. "I was here every weekend. Before you . . . "

"Are you the mystery woman? The reason he's been gone?" asked a man in a Stetson.

"Where've you been hiding him?" asked his neighbor, a buxom redhead in a skin-tight cowgirl shirt.

"Did he tell you about the night he taught Tom to cook Jolly Jumbuck in a tucker bag?" one of the women asked.

Joey asked Daniel to translate. He did, with the help of several of the regulars. An hour later, their salmon was demolished and she'd gotten an earful about him.

An older woman called to Daniel from the other end of the bar. "When are you going to play the piano, Danny boy?"

Joey had never heard Daniel play the piano. She'd never heard him ask for anything in a tucker bag. *How well do I really know him?* she wondered.

"Y'all right?" Daniel asked, seeing the look on her face.

"I think so." She watched him as he took a long swig. "I'm just wondering what this place means to you."

"Home away from home," Daniel said. "A family of sorts. Until you came along."

He drained his glass and kissed her before ordering another round of drinks and taking his over to the piano, where he began to play soft jazz. His eyes were closed and his face lit by amber light. His hands glided over the keys. Joey had never seen him so happy or so much at home.

"This one's for Joey," he said before he started to play a jazzy version of *New York, New York.*

Joey smiled back at him. Then she realized: Daniel had just welcomed her into his world.

Leaning against the nursery bench at Miss Piggy's, Joey's memories were interrupted by Demetrios calling her name.

"Oh, Josefina!"

Joey was astonished when her boss walked towards her, holding the hand of a small, older woman. "Berta!" she exclaimed with surprise. "What are you doing here? Aren't I coming for tea in a few hours?"

"Yes, dear. I had to see what was blooming on this April morning and I figured I'd say hello to you, too."

Demetrios wagged a large finger at Joey. "I knew you Greek," he scolded.

"What?"

"Why you no tell me Madame Berta is your *Yia-Yia* (Grandmama)?" he glowered. "She my best customer."

Joey looked past him at Berta, who was grinning impishly.

"My . . . *Yia-Yia?*"

"*Ne* (yes.) When she ask for you I see resemblance right away. Madame Berta is Greek lady." He swept her under his arm. "If she Greek, is mean you Greek." He gathered Joey under his other arm and displayed them to every customer in the nursery.

"I never said I was your grandmother," Berta informed Joey, trying not to laugh.

"You're *Greek?*" Joey asked quietly, wondering why she fell for Demetrios's ploy.

But Berta nodded. A red-and-orange scarf was wrapped around her neck, making her look even more like a colorful bird than usual. "My husband was Greek. Giorgio. My last husband."

"First, last, same thing," boomed Demetrios, overhearing. "Her husband is born in my city. Heraklion. *Kritti* (Crete.) Like the Boss."

"Excuse me, Dimi," Berta said. Joey had never heard anyone call him *that* before. "Who's the Boss again?"

"*Ehlahto* (come)," he commanded, setting them both free to follow as he strode to his office.

Joey and Berta entered to find Demetrios looking at a photograph of the epitaph on the simple gravestone of Nikos Kazantzakis: "I hope for nothing. I fear nothing. I am free."

"Mr. Kazantzakis," said Berta.

"Of course," Demetrios said.

"Didn't he believe that everything in the world has a hidden meaning? Something about men and animals, flowers and stars being symbols?" Berta asked.

"Yes. First time you see them, you not understand," Demetrios said.

"You think they're actually men and animals and flowers and stars. Until years later . . . " Berta said.

"Years later," Demetrios repeated, "you see. These are life!"

"These are pieces of heaven!" added Berta.

"Opa!" Demetrios yelled exuberantly. "*Kahtahlaveno* (she understands)!"

Joey silently watched Demetrios and Berta—two Greek peas in a pod. She had nothing to add to their conversation.

"Excuse me?" a customer called out. "Is it too early to plant petunias?"

Joey left Demetrios and Berta to assist the April hordes with planting fever. As soon as she could, Joey returned to the office where she found the two standing in respectful silence before a photograph of a young boy.

Joey wondered if it was Demetrios's son, a boy who'd died when he was five, or so she'd heard. As she watched for a moment, loath to interrupt, she yawned. A huge yawn.

"Late night, dear?" asked Berta, peering at her with interest as they left the office together and walked to Berta's car. "When you come over for tea you can tell me all about last night. With Daniel."

"How did you know I was with him?" Joey asked.

Berta regarded her with amusement as she closed the car door. *"Kahtahlaveno (*I understand), *"* she sang out, raising her hands skyward, Demetrios-style. "I'm Greek, remember?"

As Berta drove off, Demetrios came up alongside Joey.

"Sophia," he intoned, waving to Berta.

"Berta," Joey corrected politely.

"Sophia," Demetrios insisted. "Your Yia-Yia Berta, she is Sophia. Is mean 'wisdom.'"

At Oasis, Heidi looked around before using the key she'd made to let herself into the office bungalow. She'd found out that Daniel and Marjorie were at an off-site meeting. She made sure nobody was close enough to notice her unlocking the door. She walked through the tiny waiting room, sniffing at the cookie-crumbed shag rug and lumpy low couch before walking down the hall to Daniel's office and unlocking his door with a key hanging on a hook in the hallway.

"Great security," she laughed as she replaced it.

His AirBook was perched atop a listing stack of papers. She logged on and quickly figured out Daniel's password (*Zora20*). After a steely glance at his grandmother's portrait Heidi opened a file labeled TO FIX and took a screenshot of every potential violation at Oasis. Then she opened FINANCIAL RECORDS and took more screen shots. She was reading updates about Daniel's EB-5 Visa status when her cell phone rang. The display read: Gus Green.

"Meet me at the Formosa Café," he slurred. "And wear that red Suzy Wong dress, will you? I've got news. And hurry. Desserts are half-off today."

Heidi slipped away from Oasis, now certain about the steady decline of the finances of both Oasis and Daniel. She drove home, walked Scout, and barely squeezed into her Suzy Wong red dress with the thigh-high slit up the side.

As soon as she walked into the Formosa Café she smelled the liquor-laced air and immediately knew why Gus wanted her to wear that dress; it matched the dragon décor of the old place. She was looking at black-and-white photos on the red brocade walls—Marilyn Monroe, Lana Turner—when Gus called to her from a red leather booth.

"Yoo hoo! Heidi! Over here."

Heidi smelled the stale air as she walked over to him. He gave her a sizzling look of admiration while she slid into the booth, hoping her Suzy Wong wouldn't rip.

"Hot stuff," Gus said.

"Thanks," Heidi said, noting the lineup of empty cocktail glasses with limp umbrellas. "So what's the news?"

"Welllll," he said, taking a sip of his Mai Tai, "I think I have a buyer for us."

"You do? Who?"

"A group of investors that might be interested in acquiring Oasis."

Heidi's heart beat faster. "Can you . . . can you tell me their names?"

"They're called the Foundation," Gus said, signaling the 100-year-old waiter.

"The Foundation? Sounds like a nonprofit group."

"Doesn't it?" Gus grinned. "A great cover. But until they're in the bag, keep on filing those violations. Gotta fight this war on every front. We're in a turf war," he said. "Know what I mean, pretty little Sheila?" He squeezed her knee under the table. Heidi let his hand travel up her thigh.

"I'm working all the angles, Gus," she said as his hand traveled higher. "And all by the book. Including outing one of their unlicensed professionals."

"Attagirl."

The Foundation, she repeated to herself as he forgot about her thigh and ordered another round of Mai Tais and two hot-fudge sundaes. She turned the word over and over in her mind. *The Foundation.* Whoever they were, they sounded like the perfect group to bamboozle Daniel into selling Oasis.

Chapter Twenty-two

Tamara was calmer by the time she pulled her car into the garage and parked next to Bruce's pride and joy, the dark green classic Jaguar XJ-S he'd bought last September. Rosalba had taken Maya to a band rehearsal, so nobody was around to see Tamara open the door to Bruce's car and slide into the passenger seat.

For a moment she breathed in the scent of the still-new leather and Bruce's woodsy cologne. She imagined herself sitting beside him as he drove them to a party, back when she was a wife instead of a deliverer of baby bribes.

She lit a cigarette, inhaled deeply, retrieved the key from under the seat and turned on the radio. Miles Davis's trumpet played cool jazz on Bruce's favorite station. Tamara sat until she heard the phone ringing in the empty house. She ran to get it.

"Hi, Tamara," said Marty.

"Finally," she said to Bruce's boss.

"Sorry it's taken so long," he apologized in a sorrowful tone she ignored.

"It's April fucking 15th, and I have no idea what to do about taxes, let alone what's happening with payments from our investment accounts. . . . "

Marty talked as she listened, standing beside the tiger oak table she and Bruce had gotten in Half Moon Bay, where they went antiquing on their fifth anniversary weekend. Then she sat, splayed in the Bargello-upholstered chair they'd found at a garage sale in Camarillo, while Marty explained how Bruce had lost one client after another until there were almost none left. How he'd run through their savings and sold all the stocks in the portfolio and taken out a second mortgage on the house that she knew nothing about.

Tamara wanted to scream. She had always let Bruce manage their money, no questions asked, just as her father had done.

"That's why it took so long to get back to you. I kept searching for some good news. I was hoping to find funds for you, hidden somewhere."

"And . . . ?" Tamara held her breath.

"Nothing."

"Nothing?"

"Nothing."

Shock waves blurred her vision. Boots snaked around her ankles, meowing. For once, not even he could make her crack a smile.

"What do I have left, Marty?"

"The house."

"That's it?"

"I'm afraid it's your one asset."

Tamara's temples began to pound. "But how much would I get if I . . . if I sold it, if Bruce took out a second mortgage?"

Marty paused. "Not a lot."

As he droned on she could feel her heart battering her chest.

Homeless. Maya and I and Rosalba will be homeless . . .

"I'm sorry for giving you this news on April 15th. I guess it does boil down to death and taxes," Marty concluded. "They're the only certainties in life."

"Very comforting," she spit as she hung up.

I've lost everything, Tamara realized. Icy cold snaked up her spine. Stupefied, she thought back to all the mornings when Bruce had left the house saying he was going to the office, dressed in the good clothes she'd bought for him to wear in client meetings. *Did he go to the office? Have any meetings?* Fewer and fewer, according to Marty.

But Bruce was always busy.

All at once she realized what he'd been busy doing: deceiving her; making it look like he was still working when he wasn't; hiding the web of ruin he was spinning and wearing those clothes to make it look good.

To whom?

To her.

Horror and outrage fought for space in her brain.

Boots crawled under the turquoise coffee table as Tamara stomped up the stairs and into their brown and green bedroom. She flung open Bruce's closet doors, ripped his good clothes off the rails, and started throwing them on the floor.

Hangers flew as she seized dress shirts, slacks, and jackets and hurled them. She slammed open his drawers and lobbed socks, underwear, and ties onto a multi-colored pile that bloomed on the carpet. She heaved sweaters and suits and silk pocket-squares to match his ties. She ravaged his casual clothes, pitching his green windbreaker and sweatshirts. She started in on his collection of baseball caps. She was so busy reaching, grabbing and hurling she didn't notice the sweat until it rolled down her forehead. Panting, she swept her bangs off her brow and her eye went to the window. In a flash she'd opened it and looked out on the backyard that would soon no longer be hers.

Down into the yard the clothes flew.

Striped ties flapped and dress socks sank to the lawn. Long sleeves of shirts floated, arms out, dancing in the breeze. Sports jackets cascaded, landing beside a cluster of daffodils with a satisfying thump near the brick barbecue, which gave her an idea. As she slammed down the stairs and out to the backyard Boots slithered under the couch to get away.

The lid to the grill opened with a squeal. It was in need of maintenance, like everything else around there, including herself. She rolled newspapers into logs and mounded them over with charcoal. She grabbed lighter fluid and squeezed the can several times as she basted the newspapers like a Thanksgiving turkey. She snatched a box of long-handled matches, lit several and tossed them onto the grill.

With a *crack* a three-foot crescendo of orange flames shot toward the sky, licking the lower leaves of the eucalyptus trees. Tamara stepped back, wondering if she should call the Fire Department, but the flames died down. She squeezed the can of lighter fluid again, blind to the danger, getting the fire as hot as she could without setting the entire canyon ablaze.

She stood close, mesmerized by her beautiful creation, watching its carroty flames stretch, spread, curl, and subside. She contemplated tearing her clothes off and dancing around the fire, naked and howling. Sweat poured down her face and she wiped it away with a swipe of her charcoal-blackened hand. When the fire banked and the coals glowed red, a pink Brooks Brothers shirt landed in the blaze and smoldered, leaching a tornado of black smoke before it burst into flames. She threw on another shirt. Then another. She watched them seethe in the flames, twisting and writhing as they burned. Again and again, she squeezed the can of lighter fluid, urging on the inferno.

Sweaters. Slacks. Vests. Ties and T-shirts. Smoldered. Wriggled. Hissed. Burned. Turned to ash.

Black smoke clouded the backyard. The air before her was blurry from the heat. Her hands were sooty. Her hair was flecked with ash. She was emptying the last of the lighter fluid onto the fire when she heard a scream from behind her.

Maya hurtled out the kitchen door. "You killed him, now you're burning him? I HATE YOU."

"Meesy?" Rosalba cried, confused.

Tears coursed down Maya's face. She ran to the pile of remaining clothes and threw herself on it, clawing at Bruce's sweaters and his green windbreaker. Red-faced and furious, she swiped a baseball cap out of her mother's hand before she could immolate it.

"You're nuts. I HATE YOU," Maya cried, in case Tamara had missed it the first time.

As Maya ran back into the house, arms laden, Tamara tossed a suit jacket they'd bought at Carroll & Co. onto the blaze. She felt nothing.

"Wait, Meesy, wait," Rosalba said with enormous concern. She hustled to the pile of unburned clothes and started rummaging through pockets. "Wait. There could be money . . . "

"There is no money," Tamara said as she threw another sock on the fire for emphasis. "Not a penny. Bruce spent it all." Rosalba looked up, uncomprehending. "He left us nothing. Not even this. "

Tamara threw her arms open wide, embracing the air in their backyard as if she could cradle it and her beloved home in her limbs. She started to turn in a circle, looking, looking, turning as she looked until she stopped.

"It's all gone," she gulped. "Everything, even the house."

The word stifled in her throat. Tamara dropped the clothes she was holding and raced into the kitchen where she barely made it to the sink before she began to throw up.

Chapter Twenty-three

Following Berta up the winding dirt path to the Labyrinth was like trailing after a goat, Joey decided. By the time she'd caught up, Berta was pointing into the woods.

"Look over there," she whispered. "See?"

Joey looked. Two deer were taking long-legged steps down the canyon.

"Beautiful," Joey said softly.

"Just a little further," Berta said, beginning to climb again.

They were headed for a clearing where sacred circles of rocks lay beneath a stand of old-growth eucalyptus trees. The Labyrinth, Berta called it. It had been created by her and a group of women in the Canyon.

"It's the perfect place to continue our conversation."

Their conversation had begun on the brick patio beneath a canopy of mission oak trees behind Berta's home and studio on a tiny canyon road. Seated at an overturned wine cask that served as a table, Berta poured them tea brewed from twigs, and they munched on a plateful of her favorite cookies—Pepperidge Farm Mint Milanos.

Flowing water burbled from a stone fountain beneath a chattering pair of lovebirds in a Chinese cage. In Berta's house, a tree grew straight through her living room. In her studio, her vivid paintings hung floor-to-ceiling on deep-red walls.

A stone statue of St. Francis of Assisi stood next to a golden Buddha beside a collection of clay menorahs. Framed drawings of nudes leaned against floor-to-ceiling bookshelves lined with art books in English, French, German, and Greek. There were books on philosophy, history, poetry. The windowsills were crammed with photographs of Berta, young and old, with her children and grandchildren, her four husbands, and numerous friends. Prisms rainbowed the light through the seven-foot studio windows.

"Amazing," Joey told her.

"It's home," Berta replied.

"How long have you lived here?"

"An eternity to a gypsy like you," Berta laughed, taking Joey's arm and walking her to the patio. "About 40 years."

Joey asked about the St. Francis, Buddha, and menorahs.

"I'm a Bu-Jew," Berta explained.

"A . . . what?"

"One who follows both Jewish and Buddhist belief systems. I throw in a little St. Francis for good measure. Anything for inspiration," she added, leaning forward to whisper. "You know what I do before I paint?" Joey shook her head. "I dance," Berta proclaimed in a tone of great excitement. "It's a meditation."

How cool is this woman? Joey marveled before she asked about Berta's daughters. One lived in Bali; the other in Chile.

"Is that hard for you?" Joey asked.

"Yes and no," Berta said. "I wish they were closer but the older I get the smaller the distances become. I always tell them, 'You're in my heart and I'm in yours. So we don't have to be together to be together.' You know?"

"Actually, I don't." The familiar twinges she felt told her she was no more settled than ever about losing her family. "How did you deal with the death of your husbands?" she asked Berta.

"Like everyone else," she said. "I cried. I wailed. I raged. I hid. I picked myself up and went on living. So, what's with the Aussie from Queensland?" Berta leaned forward eagerly.

"I think I'm in love," Joey blurted.

"Good! He is a sexy one, that young fella."

"Yes, he is," Joey agreed as she dunked a cookie in her tea. She remembered waking up beside Daniel that morning.

"How are you feeling about your romance?"

"Thrilled. And a little scared."

"Don't be afraid, darling. Some things just have to be lived."

When Berta's hand reached for hers, Joey felt the raised veins beneath Berta's silk-soft skin. She wished she could seal the moment in a bottle and keep it forever: the earthy smell of the twig tea, the chattering of the love birds, the warmth of Berta's hand in hers.

A flicker of fear fired in Joey's chest. Loving Berta was crazy. She had to be in her 80s, at least. *I can't lose anyone else,* Joey thought.

"Our lives are a collection of days," Berta said, as if she read Joey's thoughts. "This is a good one, so let's enjoy it. No need to worry about tomorrow." Berta stood up suddenly, sniffing the air.

"Fire," she said with alarm. "We have to be terribly careful around here."

She stared at the sky for a few more minutes before deciding there was no danger.

"Come, dear," Berta said. "There's something we need to talk about. Let's go to the Labyrinth."

Down the road in the same canyon Rosalba had helped Tamara upstairs and into the shower. From her bedroom window, Tamara saw

Rosalba wipe away her tears as she closed the grill and let the fire die, while gathering the rest of Bruce's clothes. Her compassion touched Tamara and she knew she could learn a thing or two from Rosalba's quiet resolve.

Me? I feel nothing, Tamara thought. *I don't dare look around at anything. It's all no longer mine.* In a moment the color and life of her home had become her wound.

Twenty minutes later the afternoon sun streamed in through the kitchen window as Tamara sat at the table looking at the water spots on the glass. She was wearing sweats and drinking the tea Rosalba had made for her.

Tamara knew that somewhere inside her there lived a woman who cared that her daughter was in tears and that she'd just immolated her husband's wardrobe. That woman had feelings Tamara could no longer find—compassion, sorrow, kindness. She cried the tears Tamara could no longer shed. So she shut that woman out again. *Because if I start crying I'll never stop.*

She was sitting at the kitchen table and staring, unseeing, when Rosalba came in, biting her lip.

"Meesy. Please. You need to come with me."

Tamara followed her reluctantly, past the rooms she'd decorated with love, with Bruce. Up the stairs she went and down the hallway, carpeted with silk rugs they'd brought back from Burma, to Maya's bedroom door with its hexagonal hand-drawn STOP sign with YOU in the middle and a diagonal slash through the word.

"She's in the shower," Rosalba said, opening the door.

Maya's room was the usual rat's nest of clothes, clean and dirty, three deep on the floor, along with school papers, old lunches, art projects, photos, CDs, crumpled magazines, postcards from kids she'd gone to camp with last summer. Lights were burning; her laptop was on the bed beside wet towels that stained the expensive pink and green duvet Tamara had picked out; packs of Kool cigarettes were in plain sight.

Tamara went in there as little as possible.

Rosalba picked her way across the piles littering the floor. She headed straight for the bed where she lifted up the duvet that hung down over the sides like icing melting off a cake.

"Lookee," Rosalba said ominously, motioning for Tamara. Rosalba inclined her head, showing her where to look under the bed.

Tamara saw a small mountain of clothes with tags still on them and more piles of ripped-off tags with no clothes attached.

"What's all this?"

"I don't know. I just found it. I think . . . maybe she took them from the store, Meesy."

Could a day get any more hideous? Tamara stared at the evidence. *Maya. Shoplifting. Another secret I didn't know.*

"You need-a talk to her."

"I can't," Tamara blurted, running back into her bedroom, where Bruce's side of the closet gaped open, empty. She walked into the bathroom and closed the door. She stared at herself in the mirror. *Death. Taxes. Secrets. The certainties in* my *life. Like father, like daughter.*

She needed to talk to someone.

Who can I call? Sam? Alli will answer. My mother? Who won't fall apart when they hear my latest sob story?

Then she knew.

In the same canyon Joey clambered over the last hill and found Berta waiting in a large field of blooming purple wildflowers. Her back was to Joey. Behind her small frame lay a glade of trees.

As she walked towards her, Joey passed the Labyrinth—circle upon circle of small river stones set into the field of flowers. Stones were laid in curving paths that led to the center. When she looked back at Berta the late afternoon sun that streamed through the trees was turning her silhouette to gold.

Joey got the chills. This was a magical place, and she wasn't sure what she was supposed to say or do. When she arrived at Berta's side she took Joey's hand, and they began to walk towards the Labyrinth.

"What do you do up here?" Joey asked.

"Not much, now that most of us have gotten old, but we used to meet here often."

"Women who live in the canyon?"

"Other artists, mostly. Some of them are kind of woo-woo," Berta laughed. "We'd dance by the light of the moon in feathered costumes or bring up a jug of wine and laugh our heads off. Once, when we came to scatter the ashes of one of the women in our group, a young couple came over the ridge to get married here. We were their witnesses."

"Cool."

They were at the entrance to the Labyrinth. "Now, we walk. Are you ready?"

"I don't know," Joey answered. She had no idea what to be ready for.

"These circles of stones represent our journey in life, dear. Some say that when we walk the Labyrinth we are travelling to the center of our own soul. They like to take a long time doing it. Others think that's a load of crap. They walk it in five minutes."

Joey laughed.

"I leave it to you to decide whether to walk fast or slow. You can ask yourself a question, one you would like the answer to when you are done. Just follow me. And remember. The way in is the way out. And vice versa."

What does that mean? Joey wondered, but Berta had already begun to walk slowly between the lines of stones, following the winding path towards the center.

186 LINDA SCHREYER AND JO-ANN LAUTMAN

As Joey walked behind her, looking down at the flowers, her mind traveled. To New York. Nonna. Her dad. Her grandfather. Jack. The faces of the Group appeared in the purple flowers. Daniel. Berta. She asked herself a question, but her mind stilled until she got to the center and had no more thoughts. No thoughts at all.

When she turned around to go she began to follow another path out. Then she remembered: *The way in is the way out.* She retraced her steps, got back on the path she'd taken and made it out. Berta was waiting for her on an old picnic bench in the glade of trees.

"How was it?"

"Fantastic. I feel like I just woke up."

"Yes," Berta said. "You are glowing, my dear."

"So are you."

"Now," Berta said. "We have something to talk about. Something quite serious. There's a storm coming. You will need to take cover."

Joey looked at the sky.

"Not here." Berta paused. "There is someone who wants to hurt Oasis. And Daniel."

"What do you think this person is going to do?"

"I don't know what they're up to but you, who are daring and revolutionary; you, who have big ideas and are rather careless about rules; you, who have always been a comma, not a period . . . "

Joey smiled at the description.

"You will be caught in the eye of the storm."

Joey startled.

"Not now," Berta said. "It will happen one day. Maybe a month or a year from now. Maybe 10."

"So what am I supposed to do? Start following the rules?"

Berta laughed a throaty chuckle. "Never! But when it happens, I want you to remember what you learned when we walked the Labyrinth."

"Which was . . . ?"

"The way in is the way out. And vice versa."

"Okay," Joey said, with no idea what Berta was talking about. This felt very *Lord of the Rings* but, as with everything Berta, she had to admit it was pretty cool.

"Now, enough proclamations for one day. Tell me, dear, what does this work you're doing mean to you? This is a good place to talk of such things."

"I love it. I don't know why, but I do."

"What is it you love?"

Joey thought for a moment. "I love being part of these people coming back to life. Does that sound conceited?"

Berta shook her head vigorously, as if that was the perfect answer. "You're very good at that. And you're coming back to life at the same time. Yes?"

"Yes," Joey said, surprised at the truth of it.

"There's a song that wants to be sung through us, and it will haunt us forever until we sing it. Have you ever heard that?" Berta asked.

Joey shook her head.

"You've found your song, darling. The work you were born to do. One day, perhaps you will learn that loss is a gift. Never one we want but still, a gift. It's made me appreciate every special person I know, especially someone as special as you.

Joey inhaled deeply.

"So tell me, if you had a dream, what would it be?"

"To do Grief Groups," Joey replied to her surprise. "To do them again. And again. And again."

"Perfect," Berta said.

They talked until the sun began to set over the distant ocean and a woman came up over the hill. As she walked towards the Labyrinth, dressed in sweats, her gait looked familiar to Joey.

It was Tamara. Joey was astonished when Berta greeted Tamara like an old friend.

"We know each other from Oasis and living in the same canyon," Berta explained. "Did you smell fire before?" she asked Tamara.

"I had a barbecue," Tamara said.

There was more to it than that, Joey could see. So could Berta, apparently. "I'll see you back at the house," she said.

After Berta headed off, Joey listened to the events of Tamara's day.

"How awful," Joey said.

"Yes," Tamara said. "Awful." She looked out at the darkening sky. "I thought it was my fault. That he killed himself. Now at least I understand why he did it."

Joey stayed quiet.

"I wonder if I ever really knew him," Tamara said.

"Do we ever really know anyone?" Joey asked.

"Right," Tamara agreed. "I guess the only good thing about today is that it made me realize I've got to get help. For myself. And for Maya."

Later, as Joey bushwhacked down the trail in the growing darkness, she had a flash that took her breath away. Jack was walking shoulder to shoulder with the blonde in Central Park, carrying a little boy in his arms.

The image lasted a mere second. The baby they had created, the one Joey had lost, was something she hated to think about. It was just too painful.

Now, the flash made Joey remember her question in the Labyrinth.

Why is this Grief Group so important to me?

She found the answer.

Family. Grief Group is my family.

Part Three

Part Three

Chapter Twenty-four

On May Day, colorful flower baskets lined the paths at Oasis where ribbons hung from branches of the giant pines. A maypole dance was in progress on the lawn as Grief Group met.

"I hate the friggin' calendar year," Tamara said.

"What do you mean?"

"May Day. Mother's Day. What do we have to celebrate?"

"Nothing," Sam agreed. "Andrew will never know his mother."

"This baby will never know its father," Maggie said, her hand on her belly.

"I doubt Maya's planning to bring me breakfast in bed this year," Tamara said.

"When I took a walk in the park someone had dumped old trunks on the track," Alli said. "I wished I could hide in one of them until Mother's Day was over." She bit her lip. "By this Mother's Day we were planning to be pregnant."

An idea began to form in Joey's mind. Before she had thought it through, she opened her mouth to speak. "It sounds like Mother's Day's going to be hard for some of you. So I was wondering," she said before she lost her nerve, "how would it feel to be together? We could have a Mother's Day swim party at Ferndale, where I live."

The Group stared at her. Joey knew she was crossing boundaries. She went on anyway. "They have a couple of pools and a clubhouse we could use for a barbecue. Unless that sounds like a bad idea."

"It's a great idea," Sam said. "I had no plans."

"Especially the swim party," Alli said. "Won't it be hot to be together without all these clothes on?"

Joey hadn't thought about that.

The following Sunday, Joey opened her eyes on Mother's Day morning. Daniel was sitting on the edge of the bed, checking the surf report on his cell.

"Sssh," he said, reaching to stroke her hair. "It's early."

"Hang 10 . . . " she murmured sleepily.

"See you tonight," he said. Her eyes closed with the touch of his hand. When she opened them again the apartment was empty.

"Daniel?" she whispered.

Sunday morning cartoons screamed through her open apartment windows. The scent of jasmine wafted in on the May breeze.

"Daniel?" she called.

Her hand reached over to feel the dent in the pillow next to hers where his head had lain.

He's gone, whispered a little voice in her head.

Don't be ridiculous, argued another voice. *Remember how his lips felt on yours.*

But is he yours? the little voice whispered.

Joey threw off the covers. Why was she having such negative thoughts? Then she remembered it was Mother's Day. Her least favorite day of the year. Her heart felt heavy as she walked to the bathroom and saw that Daniel's wetsuit and bag were gone.

He'll be back, she told herself as she turned on the shower.

He's not your mom, she told herself as she stepped into it.

Everyone leaves you, the voice insisted as water ran down her tired body.

She made herself stop listening to her thoughts and focused on her body as the hot water cascaded over her tight shoulders. She had a black-and-blue mark on her thigh and Band-Aids on both thumbs from the work she and Daniel had done, fixing the latest round of violations.

"I feel like the guy who rolls the rock up the hill every day and while he sleeps it rolls back down." Daniel had said last night as they lay side by side in bed. "That's how it is with these damn violations."

"Who do you think is filing them?" Joey asked.

"Could be a neighbor with a grudge. Or any one of hundreds of students who've been in and out of here and noticed how rundown we are. If I knew who it was," Daniel said, "I'd knock the bloke to kingdom come."

Now, under the shower, Joey heard the phone ring. She ignored it. It rang again. She turned off the shower, grabbed a towel and ran naked through the living room.

"Happy Mother's Day," Alli said.

"Same to you," Joey replied, juggling the phone as she toweled off.

"About the party. Can I bring a date?"

"Sure," Joey said. "It's for Grief Group, family, and friends, remember?"

"Can my date bring gin and tonics?"

"Sorry," Joey said. "That's a no."

"Okay. See you soon," Alli said.

Joey hung up and checked the time. The party would start in an hour. She finished drying off, pulled on a black bathing suit, and reached for a red sarong hanging on one of the yellow wooden hangers her mother had left behind. Remembering her mother made her feel worse.

Joey shook off her thoughts and grabbed towels to reserve lounge chairs.

An hour later Tamara was knitting by the Ferndale pool, watching a buff widower named Rick play in the water with his nine-year old twins, Trevor and Moira. Maya, who went to school with the twins, had invited them to the Mother's Day swim party.

"It's for family and friends—right? So they're my friends, and their mom died a couple of years ago," Maya had told Tamara. "I thought they should come to your stupid Mother's Day party. And bring their dad, too."

"Go!" yelled the dad, Rick, as he tossed his red-haired, freckle-faced daughter to the other end of the pool, her arms and legs flailing.

"Cannonball!" yelled her brother, jumping in with a massive splash.

The twins surfaced, their heads shiny as otters' as they raced back to Rick. From behind sunglasses Tamara watched him shot-put the winning twin across the pool. He stood in the shallow end, his upper body glistening in the sun.

"What a lovely man," murmured Berta, Joey's "family" for the day. She began sketching Rick and his twins.

"Muy guapo (handsome)," Rosalba said, fanning her face.

Maya lounged on a lounge chair, earbuds in her ears, eyes closed, her feet tapping to a heavy-metal tune.

Tamara returned to her knitting. She'd decided to be Madame-De-fucking-farge today, passionately purling in her turquoise and white cover-up and wide-brimmed white hat while the rest of the Groupies flirted and frolicked in the pool.

From the way they're acting you'd never know what day this is, Tamara thought.

Del lazed on a blow-up raft; Sam sat on the steps at the shallow end, balancing four-month-old Andrew on his knees. Next to him, to Tamara's chagrin, sat Alli in a teeny pink bikini. Joey played a fierce game of ping-pong with Maggie, whose small baby bump topped her mile-long legs.

Tamara was feeling self-conscious about being with everyone outside of Group, in bathing suits no less. She lit up a Newport and glanced at Maya, who was wearing one green sock and one red and white striped one.

"Socks aren't supposed to match," Maya had told Tamara earlier that morning, after wishing her a terse "Happy Mother's Day" and giving her a little hug. Little, like the amount of progress they were making, despite the therapists they were both seeing.

"Hey!" a voice called out.

Tamara saw Dave walking in slowly. His khaki parachute pants looked like they'd been balled up in the back of his closet for months. She watched as he pulled up a chair poolside and began to crack yet another bad joke.

Loser, she thought, needles clicking.

An hour earlier Dave had been juggling two flowering hyacinth plants at Forest Lawn as he made his way to Caro's grave.

"Happy Mother's Day," he said, with not a hint of sentiment.

He placed the plants, one pink, one blue, in front of her stone. One card read, "From Kevin." The other, "From Melissa."

A wave of misery swept over Dave with so much force he had to hold tightly to his poles. Then he swallowed the wave and slowly walked back down the hill.

At Ferndale Tamara continued to knit.

"Tamara! Come on in!" Alli and Maggie yelled from the pool.

"Later," Tamara called back. She planned to stay where she was, knitting and chain-smoking.

Around her, several lounges were occupied by women in thong bikinis. In the pool, Sam and Alli looked like a couple as they played with Andrew. Tamara's face burned as she watched Alli gently splash water on the baby's feet. Tamara looked down, thinking about how fat she was and how trim Alli was. *Any red-blooded man would prefer her over me.*

"Come on in. Water's great." She looked up to see Sam standing in front of her, dripping wet in green board shorts. Andrew was in his arms.

"No. That's okay."

"Come on." He put out his hand.

"No thanks," she said, ignoring his hand as she reached for another Newport.

"Please," Sam said, taking the cigarette out of Tamara's hand. "No more cancer sticks. Okay? I'd like you to be around for a long time."

Tamara was completely taken aback. "I'm not in the mood to have fun," she admitted,

"Neither am I," said Sam. "But I'm doing it anyway. We all spend too much time alone and sad. Come on."

"Sorry," she replied, mortified to reveal her body to Sam.

"Please?"

"I've got to finish this afghan before . . . "

"I'll hold that, Meesy," Rosalba said, swooping the knitting out of Tamara's hands before she could protest.

"Want to take Andrew?" Sam asked Maya, pulling one of the earbuds out of her ear. Tamara was surprised to see Maya smile as she reached for the baby with joy.

Why can't we say no to Sam? Tamara wondered as she reluctantly slipped off the muumuu and chucked the hat while Sam wiggled one of Maya's toes.

"You're next in the water," he said.

"Don't hold your breath," Maya smiled back.

"Looking good," Sam murmured to Tamara as they walked to the pool.

"Thanks," she stammered. *Didn't he see my Jewish thighs?*

"Hey!" Alli and Maggie said when Tamara stuck her toe in the water. "We missed you."

Tamara submerged her hot face in the pool. She swam a few strokes and remembered how good it felt to stretch her body in the water. Before she knew it she'd forgotten how fat she felt, that Maya was in trouble, and that she was too. After a while, between the warmth of the sunlight and the splash and feel of the water, she was jumping around with the rest of Grief Group.

Dave sat at the edge, taking pictures and cracking jokes: "What did one goldfish say to the other? I've already made arrangements to be flushed down the toilet."

Click.

He watched the bevy of beautiful widows through the viewfinder.

Widows, he thought. *Black widow spiders. Old Greek women in black.*

Click.

That's what I think of when I think of a widow.

Click.

Not these beautiful babes.

He shot. As Alli played ring-around-the-rosy with Moira. As Tamara swam with Sam. As Maggie got out of the pool and walked towards him in a yellow terry playsuit, drying her hair with her hands. All six feet of her pale skin glistening in the sun.

Click.

"I hear there's a lake," she said. "With swans and turtles. Want to take a walk?"

"Sure," Dave said, slowly getting to his feet. "As long as you don't mind going at a snail's pace."

Off they went, as he wondered why she wanted to walk with him. And how fast she would run if she knew the truth.

Berta watched Joey cook lunch beneath the awning outside the clubhouse, a cedar-shingled two story building with a party room up a flight of stairs. It had an oversized stone fireplace, corduroy couches, dark wood bookshelves, and a pool table.

"Where's your friend Kat?" Berta asked. "I was looking forward to seeing her."

"She was invited to New Hampshire for the weekend, to meet her boyfriend's parents."

"Sounds serious," Berta said.

"I guess it is."

Joey focused on the hamburgers and hot dogs.

"Your Group is having a great time," Berta said.

"I hope it's not weird for them to see each other outside of Oasis," Joey said.

"I'm sure it's weird. And sexy, too, after being so covered up. But it's lovely to see them acting like young people."

Laughter floated over from the pool. "I've never seen them having fun before," Joey said.

"It's good for them," Berta said. "Mother's Day must be a heartbreak." Joey bit the inside of her lip as she turned the burgers. "Looks like a hard day for you, too."

"How do you know?"

"As I said the first day we met: you've got loss written all over you. So many of us do, dear," Berta continued. "Are you missing your mother today?"

Joey looked up. "I've always missed my mother."

The call of the loons on Pushaw Lake in Northern Maine woke five-year-old Joey in the middle of the night. They sounded like they were laughing. She heard the sound of her bedroom door opening, then quiet footsteps as someone walked across the room to her bed. She felt the soft brush of her mother's long black hair across her face. Joey wrapped her arms around her mother's neck.

"I love you," her mother said.

"I love you too" Joey said sleepily.

The next sound she heard was tires crunching on gravel. *Someone's driving down the driveway,* Joey thought before she fell back to sleep.

When she came down for breakfast her father looked tired as he drank stale coffee from the blue cup with the chip. "She's gone," he told Joey flatly.

It would be a long time before Joey realized that her 25-year-old mother, a graduate student who'd married her 40-year old English professor, Joey's father, was never coming back.

"Nonna came instead," Joey told Berta. "She moved to Maine from Europe a few months later. Then Grandpa Eugene came. They raised me together with my dad."

"Did you ever see your mother again?"

"Never," Joey said.

"Did you ever try to find her?"

Joey shrugged. "No. It's not like she ever tried to find *me.*" She realized her hands were shaking as she turned a burger.

Berta came up alongside and put a kind hand on her arm. "You don't have to hide how you're feeling, dear."

"I just . . . It was a long time ago . . . but . . . "

"But sometimes it feels like yesterday."

"Yes." Joey wiped her eyes. "It's not like I have good memories of my mother. Actually, I barely remember her."

"Maybe that's why it hurts so much."

"I never thought of that."

The women were silent for a few minutes. Joey focused on cooking lunch. Berta looked out at the pool. "I've often wondered," she said, "which is worse. Having good memories of your mother, like that little redhead who's sketching there—" Joey looked at Rick's daughter Moira, her head bent over a sketch pad. "Or no memories at all."

"How do you know she has good memories?" Joey asked as she transferred burgers to a platter.

"She came over when I was drawing by the pool. She watched for a while, then she told me her mother had been an artist before she got sick. I asked if she'd like to borrow some paper and a marker, and her face lit up. She said she wanted to make a drawing of her mommy. In heaven. You can imagine how fast I gave her my pad."

"Thank you for that."

"That little girl tries to hide how sad she is. Her twin brother looks angry. And that poor teenage daughter of Tamara's. They're all hurting. How I wish you had a grief group for them." Joey said nothing. She put more hot dogs on the grill. "Joey?" Berta asked.

"Could I do a kids' group?" Joey asked. "Or am I too broken?"

"We are broken in order to heal," Berta said, her voice gentle and firm. "That's what we're here for."

When the food was laid out in the upstairs room Joey headed down to call everyone to lunch. She was almost out the front door when Del strode out of the men's room, an open pill bottle in hand. He was about to down a multicolored handful when he spotted her.

Del's angry look told Joey she was not supposed to have seen that.

Chapter Twenty-five

"Lunch!" Joey's voice rang out. She looked for Del but he'd disappeared. Over at the pool, she saw Sam take Tamara's hand to help her out of the water. She saw the water drip down the bodies of Grief Group as they grabbed their towels and wrapped them around themselves. Their feet made sopping, dark footprints all the way to the clubhouse.

She thought about Daniel's lean, muscular body balancing on his board in his black wetsuit. She thought about seeing him later. A flicker of desire fired inside her.

"Great party, Joey," Alli said, breaking into Joey's thoughts. A handsome African American man stood next to her. "This is my date. Jacques, Joey," Alli said.

"Welcome, Jacques," Joey said as they walked into the clubhouse.

"Thanks, Joey," Sam said, coming in next. "I can't imagine what this day would be like if I wasn't here." He walked upstairs behind Tamara, who looked sunburned and uncharacteristically happy.

"I appreciate your letting us join the party," Rick, the new griever said, his voice rough with emotion. "It's great for my kids."

"Why don't you come to the next Grief Group meeting?"

Rick nodded gratefully. Joey noticed the dark shadows under his eyes. He offered Berta his arm as she climbed the stairs to the party room.

When she paused to catch her breath he held on tightly. "Young man, you are a gentleman and a hunk," she said.

Rosalba came in carrying Andrew; Maya, along with Moira and Trevor, Rick's twins, streamed in, dripping in wet towels; Dave and Maggie wandered in from the lake, jabbering about turtles and ducks.

Joey waited for Del before heading upstairs. When he didn't appear she joined the others. In a few minutes Del walked in, and Joey realized he'd been deliberately late. He knew she wouldn't talk about what she'd seen in front of the others.

Tamara was finishing a burger when she saw Dave go over to Maya and tap her on the shoulder. "Who are you listening to?" he asked.

Maya pulled out her earbuds. "Lizzy Borden. Alice Cooper."

Tamara waited for Maya to put her earbuds back in and tune Dave out.

"Metal, huh?" Dave said. "So you must like Kiss."

"Love *love* them."

"Black Sabbath? Joan Jett and the Blackhearts?" Dave asked.

"'I Love Rock 'n Roll' is my all-time fave. I want to *be* Joan Jett," Maya said. Then she smiled. An actual smile.

What's going on? Tamara wondered.

"Actually, you kinda look like her," Dave said.

Tamara saw Maya's face redden with pleasure.

"The other kids think I'm weird to listen to heavy metal," Maya said matter-of-factly. "So old-school."

"They thought I was weird, too. Taking pictures all the time." Maya looked at Dave like she wanted to say something. "I know," Dave admitted. "I'm still weird."

When Maya laughed, Tamara realized she couldn't recall the last time she'd heard that sound.

"She looks happy," Sam said, moving closer to Tamara.

"She does," Tamara agreed, feeling the warmth of his naked leg next to hers.

"Are you eavesdropping?"

"You bet," Tamara said. "Maya doesn't talk to me about this." *How long has it been since I've sat next to an attractive nearly naked man? What would it be like to make love with him?*

"Go for it," Sam said.

Startled, Tamara looked at him for a moment, wondering if he'd read her thoughts. Then she saw him looking over at Maya. Tamara went back to eavesdropping as Maya told Dave about the indie music she loved.

"Abe Vigoda. Ancestors. Captain Ahab."

She listened to Dave telling Maya about the hot clubs his boss frequented.

"I can't wait till I'm old enough to go to those clubs," Maya said.

"How old are you?" Dave asked.

"I'll be 14 in August."

Dave laughed. "Couple more years and you can drive yourself there." He shot a look at Tamara, which told her he knew she was eavesdropping. "You'll be driving your mom nuts soon, don't you worry."

"I already am," Maya replied with a wicked grin.

"Hey," Dave said, "ever been to The Smell?"

"What's that?" Maya asked.

"A club for kids your age," Dave said. "No booze. No drugs. Great place to hear indie bands."

"Wow. Cool," Maya said. "Maybe I can go with you some time."

"Maybe we'll see what your mom thinks about that," Dave said.

"I don't know my own daughter anymore," Tamara said to Sam. "If Bruce were alive he'd know everything she just told Dave."

"It's tough," Sam said.

"What is?"

"Being mother and father to these kids." He looked at Andrew, asleep in his stroller. "I have no idea how I'm going to pull this off."

"Me neither," Tamara admitted. Somehow, sharing that with Sam made her feel a bit better.

Joey was eating lunch with Berta when she saw Alli's date, Jacques, handing her a beer.

"I'm sorry," Joey said, quickly at his side. "We can't drink alcohol at a Grief Group event."

"But we're not at Oasis," Alli said.

"And I got that at the bar downstairs," Jacques said with a smile.

"How about if anyone wants a drink they go downstairs to buy it?" Alli suggested.

"I can't stop you," Joey said after a long minute and against her better judgment.

An hour later most of the Group was soused and all of them were laughing at sick death jokes. Even Rick and Jacques, Berta and Joey were howling with laughter.

"So he, like, fell into a vat of chocolate and drowned!" Alli said.

"No!" Maggie said.

"I swear to God," Alli declared. "That's how Mr. Hershey's Chocolate died. Cross my heart and hope to die."

"I've got one," Del offered, his eyes bright. "These three guys go to heaven and God takes them to the edge of a cliff. 'You've been so good you get to be anything you want now. You just have to jump off the cliff and say what you want to be.' The first guy runs to the edge and jumps into the air: 'I want to be an eagle!' Poof. He's an eagle and off he soars into the sunset. The second guy jumps off: 'I want to be an owl!' Poof.

He's an owl. The third guy runs towards the edge of the cliff, trips on a rock, shouts 'Oh, shit!' and jumps off. Poof . . . "

There was a moment of silence. Then Maggie started to laugh, a loud, high-pitched howl. That set the rest of them off, even Joey. She'd never heard Maggie laugh before. Soon Maggie was laughing so hard she was getting up and running out of the room.

"Where's the bathroom? I'm going to pee my pants!" Maggie disappeared down the stairs.

"Me, too," Alli yelled, running off, followed closely by Tamara.

When they came back they decided to play charades. Then they decided to play dirty charades. Alli gave a command performance acting out "orgasm."

"So. Orgasms," she said, nestling close to Jacques. "Who's having them? Besides me? I mean, with other people . . . . "

"I'm not ready to go to bed with anyone else," Maggie said.

"Why not? Going to bed with someone is easier than holding hands. Too intimate."

Dave began to tell another inappropriate death joke. Joey listened to the raucous laughter. She knew the party was off the rails. She didn't know what to do about it.

"You're not in control," Berta told her softly.

"I know," Joey said. "But shouldn't I be?

"Let it go. Laughter is the best medicine."

Joey looked over to see tears rolling down Rick's face.

"My wife, Jess, would have loved this," he said softly.

Alli looked over at him and grew quiet. "Rod, too. My husband."

Sadness settled over the Grief Group like a layer of ash over flowers. Alli teared up, then Maggie. The others looked down or away, except Del, who looked fierce.

They were silent for a few minutes.

206 · LINDA SCHREYER AND JO-ANN LAUTMAN

"Oh, shit," Alli said finally.

Maggie started to giggle, then Tamara, then Sam, until the clubhouse was filled with roaring laughter.

Del stood up. "You guys are nuts."

He walked out, which made the Group laugh harder.

Oh, shit, Joey thought. She ran after him. "Del," she called as he strode towards the parking lot.

"Time to go," he said, walking faster.

Joey sped up until she was walking next to him. "I need to talk to you."

"Later," Del said, hitting the remote to unlock his car. The Porsche responded with two beeps.

"I saw what you were taking," she said. "And I've wanted to talk to you about it before."

"Gotta go," Del said.

"Look. There are times you seem a million miles away. Or you're revved up to the max. I know I have a confidentiality agreement with all of you . . ."

"You do?" Del looked amused.

"It's not written down. And I would never say anything about this unless you were in harm's way."

"It's none of your fucking business, Ms. Unlicensed Grief Group Therapist," Del snarled.

Joey was shocked by his tone. "I'm concerned about you—"

"Then let me go," Del said, getting into his car. "I've got rounds."

He drove away, leaving Joey on the parking lot, feeling like an idiot.

Chapter Twenty-six

A few weeks later Joey and Daniel were sitting in the Jacuzzi on the deck of his guesthouse on Skyline Drive. It was sunset. They were looking across the twinkling red and white lights of the Valley to the mountains beyond.

"What color would you call them?" Daniel asked, pointing to the peaks in the distance.

"Indigo," Joey said, twining her feet around his. "Indigo blue with furrows of deep purple aubergine."

"Whoa," Daniel said. "When did you get so artistic?"

"Berta's teaching me how to see, that's all."

"Those are smart names for colors, woman," Daniel said, his foot stroking hers.

"I'm not smart, trust me," Joey said. "I still can't find my way around. Navigation system or not."

"Look," Daniel said, pointing. "That's the top of Fernwood and Old Canyon Road. Over there's Lost Hills." He pointed in a different direction. "Eagle Rock, where we hiked last week."

Joey blew out a long breath of frustration.

Daniel reached for the bottle of Yellow Tail Shiraz and refilled their glasses. Then he turned her around until her naked back was to him. "Sit still. I'm going to draw a map of L.A. on your back."

"I hate maps," she protested.

"Sssh."

Joey felt Daniel's hands moving around her back.

"This is Topanga," he said, stroking her left shoulder blade, "and there's the beach where we went long-boarding. And your right shoulder's Silver Lake, where we had breakfast yesterday." He moved his hands up to the base of her neck. "That's the San Fernando Valley. And Oasis." He moved his hands all the way down her spine. "And that's the airport. Way down there. Got it?"

"Thanks," she laughed as his hands kept on traveling, moving back up her spine.

"If I were to fly due north," he said, cresting her shoulders, "I'd fly over the horizon and see beautiful mountains." His hands descended to her breasts. "And once I found twin peaks I'd fly around them for as long as I liked."

"Thanks," Joey laughed as his index fingers circled lightly around her nipples. She stopped laughing when Daniel started kissing the back of her neck.

"From here on you're never lost," he said softly, "even when you can't find your way."

"Why not?" She was having trouble concentrating.

"Because—" He kissed her shoulder. "I've got your back."

It would have felt cheesy if someone else had said it. But between Daniel's Aussie accent and his caress, it was lovely. Joey turned to kiss him back, feeling desired and desiring him.

"I love you," Daniel said in her ear.

Joey froze. The last man who'd said that to her was Jack.

She thought about how Daniel had taken her long-boarding at Topanga Point that morning and patiently taught her to set her board on a trimline and gently glide over a wave. She thought about how he hadn't made fun of her when she fell off the board and came up with a mouthful of sea water.

Now, as her body melded to his she smelled the ocean on his skin, and she knew if she licked him he'd taste salty.

She'd gotten used to sleeping in his big brown bed. She'd grown accustomed to the smell of his guest-house, the scent of pine trees and apples. Daniel was beginning to feel like home to her.

"I love you, too," she said.

They made love by the amber glow from the candles. Later, Joey fell asleep in his arms.

She was dreaming about riding a horse on a dirt road when she heard a phone ringing. It rang again. Joey looked over at the time. 3:13. It rang again. "Daniel," she said, touching his arm. "Phone."

Daniel awakened and picked up the phone. "Hello," he said, his voice rough with sleep. "Yes? Who's this?"

Joey tensed. A 3:00 AM call was never good.

"Oh, God," Daniel said sharply. "When?" He sat up, fully awake.

Joey looked over. He was sitting on the edge of the bed. His shoulders were up around his ears.

"What kind of an accident?" Daniel asked.

As he listened Joey pulled the covers around herself, suddenly cold.

"Tell her I'm coming. Tell her I'll be there as soon as I can. Tell her I'm taking the first plane out. Make sure you tell her that, mate."

Who is "her"? Joey wondered. When Daniel hung up she asked him.

"My sister. Lara," Daniel said in a tight voice she'd never heard before.

"What happened to her?" Joey asked.

"She was in an accident," Daniel said. "She's in the ICU."

"Shit," Joey said.

"Shit doesn't cover it by half," Daniel bit back. "I have to get back there. Now. And the timing couldn't be worse. With Oasis targeted by some nutcase."

Thrusting off the covers he leapt out of bed, slipped into a pair of jeans and savagely pulled a sweater over his head. He walked to the front door, threw it open, and went out into the night. After a minute, Joey pulled on one of Daniel's shirts and followed, a little afraid.

An owl hooted in the canyon. Daniel stared out at the darkness, his chest heaving. Joey came up behind him and slipped her arms around him until he calmed down. He was breathing hard.

"I've lost everyone else in my family. I can't lose Lara."

Something about the way he said "Lara" split the air into shards.

"You won't," she said.

"I can't," he repeated. "I can't lose Lara."

"Tell me about her," Joey said, despite her nagging fear. "Tell me about your sister."

"She's Aboriginal."

"What?"

"I told you I have an adopted sister. My mother had a strong sense of social justice, so my parents adopted an Aboriginal child. A stolen child."

"Wow." Joey didn't know what to say.

When Daniel turned to face her his expression was carved in stone. "Lara was beaten and abused. She'd been horribly mistreated. My parents took her in when I was 15 and she was 12. We grew up together. When they died I promised to take care of Lara. I taught her how to surf. I told her she could be a champion. . . . " He turned away from Joey and looked out over the canyon. "Last month I told her she should enter the Big Wave Surf contest. This morning she got tangled up on the reef and broke her back. All because of me." He waved his hand in the air with agitation.

"Oh, God," Joey said, knowing the words were meaningless. She let the revelations sink in as her hands closed over his and she felt the ring.

Every nerve ending in her body was on high alert. A terrible feeling rushed up inside of her. "Is that why you wear this saltwater-freshwater ring? To remind you of Lara?"

Daniel flinched. "No."

Joey flinched at his reaction. "But she designed it?

"I told you she did," he said impatiently.

Joey heard doors shutting around his heart while Daniel looked at her as if she were a stranger. "Why are we talking about this?" he said. "I've got to get on a plane."

Joey stayed out on the deck as Daniel went back into the house. She heard him call the airline. She wanted to ask if he wanted her to go with him. She wanted to ask what his adopted sister meant to him. *He just told you he loved you. Let him go and he'll come back to you,* she told herself.

So she helped Daniel pack and held him through the rest of the night and into the early morning. She drove him to the airport and walked him to the security gate where he put down his bag and held her in his arms.

"Hoo Roo," he whispered in her ear. "That's Aussie for 'so long.'" He put her hand on his heart. "You're in my heart until I'm back."

Passengers formed a wave around them as Joey held onto Daniel, breathing in the citrus scent of his thick hair, his skin, feeling his strong hands warm on her back. Then he let go of her, picked up his bag, and walked through the gate.

Joey missed him the minute she walked away.

On the drive home she decided she believed he loved her. She believed he'd be back soon.

Then she walked into her apartment and looked at her tired face in the mirror as an unwanted thought flew into her head with the speed of a gathering storm.

He's gone. Just like dear old Mom.

Chapter Twenty-seven

At first they talked or emailed every day. Daniel Skyped from the house where he'd grown up, walking around to show her the giant banyan trees his grandmother had loved and the view of Byron Bay from their patio. He Skyped from the ICU where all Joey could see was a blurry figure in a bed with monitors beeping and the sound of a ventilator.

Lara, he said, was still in critical condition. She'd had two surgeries with three rods and four titanium screws put into her back. She was in terrible pain. The doctors didn't know when she might be stable.

Daniel needed Joey's support, and she gave it freely, over the phone and online. She tamped down her misgivings and soldiered on at Oasis, fixing whatever she could and running Grief Group. Between that and working at Miss Piggy's, her life was full. In her free time she swam laps at Ferndale and hung out with Kat, Neil, and Berta.

Despite going to bed alone and waking in the middle of the night to check emails from Daniel, she told herself she was lucky. Unlike the members of Grief Group, the person Joey loved wasn't gone forever. She thought she was keeping her emotions in check. Then Rick came to the next Grief Group and his words broke Joey wide open.

"My wife's name is Jess. She had ALS," he said, his voice taut with emotion.

"Amyotrophic lateral sclerosis," Del said. "Also known as Lou Gehrig's disease."

"*Tuesdays With Morrie*," Sam said, shocked.

Joey was stunned.

Rick spoke slowly. "We met in drama club in high school. Jess played Nellie in *South Pacific*. I was Emile. We got married when we were 19. We finished Cal State together. We had the twins when we were 25. Jess was only 28 when she got sick." He paused. "It started with tingling in her right arm, then her speech slurred. When the doctors did tests they said she'd had a stroke. They said she'd get better with time. The doctors were wrong."

Joey saw Rick's jaw clench as he looked over at Del.

"It got harder and harder for her to talk. Then it got hard to breathe. On Jess's 30th birthday she couldn't even blow out her candles. The kids had to do it for her."

Joey felt the tears behind her eyes. "Finally, they diagnosed ALS. But there was no cure. A year later she started wearing a mask with tubes pumping air to help her breathe."

Oh God, Joey thought.

"Within the next six months Jess couldn't talk or hold her head up. By the twins' seventh birthday she couldn't swallow." Rick stopped and stared at the carpet. "Jess died a month before her 32nd birthday." Tears rolled down his cheeks. "She knew all along exactly what was happening to her. Anyone who says life is fair is a friggin' imbecile."

The members of Grief Group bowed their heads in sorrow.

Rick was quiet for a long time. When he looked out at them he seemed to be become suddenly aware he was talking to a roomful of strangers. "Jess was an artist," he said. "She knew all the words to *Brigadoon*. We ran triathlons together. Now, all I ever say is that she died of ALS."

Alli put her hand on his knee. "I understand."

"I know what you mean," Sam said.

"We know what you're going through," Dave said.

"We're glad you're here," Joey said.

A heavy silence settled over them. The sorrow in the room was palpable. For a moment it felt like their first meeting to Joey, when all they could think about were their own losses.

Daniel, she thought before she could censor it.

Then it was June.

"Daisy sent an email. She's getting married. She'll be a June bride," Maggie said.

"Wow," Alli said. "That was fast."

"We had a June wedding," Sam said.

"Father's Day is coming," Del said unexpectedly.

"Graduations," Tamara said glumly.

The goddamn calendar year. Every month, a new enemy, Joey thought.

"I need to talk about something," Maggie said. "I have to move out of my place."

"Me, too," Sam said.

"I've put the house on the market," Tamara said.

"I don't know what to do with Mel's clothes and books and . . . " Sam tapered off, looking overwhelmed. "I can't take everything. But I don't know if I can give it away."

"I love having Jeff's clothes around," Maggie said. "And his tools. But where am I going to put them when I move to a smaller place?"

"You could give them to Goodwill," Dave said.

"Take it to the thrift shop for cancer research," Alli said.

"Better yet, the one for AIDS," Del proposed. "Out of the Closet."

"You could do nothing if you're not ready," Joey said.

"I still can't go into Jess's closet," Rick said. "And it's been almost two years."

"You could rent a storage locker," Alli said.

"I don't have the money," Maggie said.

"When in doubt, throw it out," Dave said.

"Or burn it," Tamara deadpanned. Everyone knew what she'd done on April 15.

Maggie bit her lip. "I'm not ready to joke about this."

The Group fell silent.

"You may treasure their things forever and never part with any of it . . . but it's not Caro," Joey pointed out. "Or Jeff. Or Shawn or Jess or Mel or Bruce or Rod. They're *things*."

"*Their* things," Maggie sniffled.

"But does a part of the world ever leave the world? How does wetness leave water?" Joey said. It was something her father used to say.

"What's that supposed to mean?" Del asked with an edge.

"I think," Rick said, "it means their stories aren't in their stuff."

"Because their stories are in *us*?" Alli asked.

"As in the mingling of our atoms over eons of time," Sam noted.

"So let's do a Group garage sale," Alli said. "Between us all, we've got to have enough stuff. Like, I could sell Rod's Harley. And those yards of books he collected. And that damn fishing equipment that killed him." Her voice caught.

"And Bruce's telescope and his butterfly collection," added Tamara.

"Butterflies?" Sam asked. "Seriously?"

"Seriously."

For the rest of the session they talked about what to do with cameras and jet skis and iPads loaded with thousands of photos of happier times. About boxes of stuff in their bedrooms, living rooms, and garages. Things they couldn't bring themselves to look through.

"Her journals," Sam said.

"His high school yearbooks," Alli said.

"His ratty hiking boots," Maggie said. "Jeff loved those."

"Maybe, while we sleep, their stuff sits around breathing in the air and choking the life out of us," Tamara said.

"Don't get poetic on us," Del said. "It's just . . . "

"Stuff," Alli said. "Seriously, why don't we do a garage sale? All of us."

"We could call it 'clothes and stuff to die for,'" Dave said.

"We could do it on Father's Day," Maggie suggested. "So we could be together."

"In my garage," Tamara said.

There was a long silence. Joey wasn't sure what to say.

"I can't decide what's worse," Rick said for all of them. "Living with it or letting it go."

Joey had no answer to that.

The next morning as she walked to the Quonset hut, Joey passed Heidi sitting on a bench. She was deep in concentration as she wrote in red ink on a lined yellow pad. Next to her sat a white canvas bag with a logo, a small gold crown.

"She's up to something," Marjorie said to Joey, catching up with her. "Always writing in that yellow pad.

"Maybe it's her journal," Joey said as they walked into the Quonset hut. She fed a live worm to Lexus and Armani.

"That's the problem with your mother," Marjorie said to the tortoises. "She's too trusting. Me, I like a good conspiracy theory."

"Like what?" Joey asked, pulling out a table with two broken legs.

"I don't know yet," Marjorie said. "But she's up to no good. Trust me."

At the next Grief Group, when Joey walked up the steps to *Hummingbird* she found the Group on the porch, huddled around a large white box with a plastic window. Alli was smoothing the plastic, tears in her eyes.

"What is it?" Joey asked Maggie.

"Her wedding dress," Maggie said quietly. "She found it when she was looking through a closet."

Joey looked at the bright yellow tissue paper that filled out the bodice of the white dress. She could picture Alli in it, standing next to Rod, two beautiful young people starting out together on the happiest day of their lives.

"Do you want to bring it into the den?" Joey asked. "You can tell us about the wedding."

"I'm going to sell it," Alli replied. "Time to move on," she said as she picked up the box and they all filed in.

Soon they were talking about the garage sale on Father's Day. Dave said he'd drunk two bottles of Pinot Noir as he packed up Caro's dance outfits. Rick said he downed close to a fifth of single-malt Scotch after he found a drawer-full of Jess's bright cotton bandannas and yoga clothes. Del said he had three hefty snifters of cognac while he sorted through Shawn's colorful ties and found loafers still in their boxes. Joey knew he'd had more than that. But Del wasn't willing to talk with her about it.

Everyone talked about jamming Tamara's garage with bags and boxes and stacks of books, a treadmill and two beach cruisers, Rod's Harley, Bruce's golf clubs, Jeff's chainsaw, and Jess's easel. They talked about selling unused wedding gifts—a dozen shrimp cocktail glasses from Tiffany's, a set of Fiesta ware, carved wooden masks from Bali, mid-century vases, and a designer beech wine-rack from Australia that was supposed to be as mesmerizing as the waves on Bondi Beach.

Daniel, Joey thought, falling down the wormhole.

They talked about how it felt to make trip after trip up the winding road to Tamara's blooming purple jacaranda-lined street, carting carloads of their spouses' things. They talked while Joey's mind stayed stuck on thoughts of Daniel.

The night before the sale she joined them in Tamara's garage, where they went through pitchers of Rosalba's sangria and set up the sale. Alli had a meltdown and decided not to sell the wedding dress; Del got furious at the idea of pricing Shawn's suits and drove off; Rick suggested they price each other's things so it didn't feel so bad. Tamara distracted everyone with the swirling colors of the paper-thin insects in Bruce's butterfly collection. Dave ended up sitting in a corner looking at every butterfly.

They folded Nike sweats and skinny jeans and Lululemon yoga clothes; hung up black leather jackets, including a suede one of Bruce's that Dave eyed for himself. They filled racks with little black dresses and pencil skirts and tops in every color of the rainbow; chiffon scarves and paisley scarves; hobo purses, Louis Vuitton knockoffs and Kate Spade wallets. They lined up corduroy jackets and black suits. They arranged Asics sneakers and Frye boots next to ballerina flats and Jimmy Choo stilettos alongside Bruno Magli loafers.

"It looks like the ghosts of our spouses are ready to party," Dave said. "This isn't so bad."

"This is brutal," Alli said.

Joey left at midnight, listening to them call their good nights to each other into the cool canyon air, their voices mingling with the howls of coyotes. As she drove away she felt she'd done a good job of helping them let go of some of the material weight of grief. Then she thought of her grandmother's oversized felt hats and her fur-trimmed red wool coat, still in storage in New York. The weight of her own unresolved grief resettled onto her shoulders.

The next morning June gloom was fogging the canyon when Dave pulled up at 8:30. A dozen cars were already parked on Tamara's street. Curious eyes followed him as he walked to the front door and Rosalba threw it open. "Meesy Tamara went to the hospital."

"Is she all right?" Dave asked.

"Si," she said.

Maya appeared. "Mom got a call from Sam. Baby Andrew's sick. She went to meet them at the ER."

Dave saw they were both scared. "I'm sure he'll be okay. Babies do that, y'know. Snot factories and all . . . "

Maya broke into a crooked smile. "Snot factories. I like that. You're funny."

Alli, Maggie, Rick, and his kids arrived, and Maya helped Rosalba serve coffee to the grownups and cocoa to the twins. Del was working, Dave learned. He told the others Tamara was with Sam and Andrew.

It was almost nine when Dave went into the garage to look around. When he turned, Maya was behind him.

"This is weird. My mom burned most of my dad's stuff."

"So I heard."

"Which ones were your wife's?" Maya asked.

Dave indicated some clothes nearby.

"What happened to her?" Maya asked.

"She was hit by a drunk driver."

Maya looked at him, hard.

"What?" Dave said.

"You look like me when I'm lying to my mom."

Dave was struck silent.

"Sorry," Maya said. "That was stupid."

He wanted to tell her it wasn't stupid at all, that she was the first person to see right through him. Then he saw the pain on Maya's face.

"Do you think my dad is in heaven?" she asked. "He killed himself, you know."

"What do you think?"

"I hope so. He used to take me to Burbank airport on Sundays. We'd watch the planes take off—" She stopped, her voice choked. "My mom doesn't know I watch home movies of us sometimes so I can remember his laugh. And his voice. He was a great dad."

"He sounds like one," Dave agreed.

"Andale," Rosalba said, appearing behind Maya. "Your friend's waiting."

At nine o'clock they opened the garage door. In swarmed the garage sale locusts, strangers who, in a flash, picked through the Group's precious "stuff," tossing it to the floor.

"Tell me about the person who wore this jacket," said an older Hollywood Wife with Botoxed lips and false eyelashes, as she waved a 50-dollar bill in front of Dave's nose.

Dave wondered what he should say to someone paying 50 bucks for Shawn's black Armani bomber jacket, the one Del said cost $900. That Shawn died of AIDS at the age of 30? That his partner had a chip on his shoulder the size of China?

"He was a doctor," Dave said finally. "An anesthesiologist."

"Oh, good," said the woman, plunking down her money. "The jacket comes with a pedigree."

Dave kept his head down and made change until Maggie gripped his arm in panic.

"I can't do this." She gestured frantically at the acquisitive horde. "I can't stand seeing that guy's hands all over Jeff's red chamois shirt."

The man held up Jeff's shirt, a couple of his wrenches, a denim jacket, and a power sander. "How much for everything?"

Maggie's eyes were filling.

"I'll do it," Dave said. "You take care of yourself."

She fled into the house, weeping, as Dave walked to the man, gave him a price and took his money. Then he took money from the next person. He found refuge in his role as cashier. It was better than feeling what he felt whenever he looked around—the chasm between him and the rest of the Group. The guilt and shame he felt compared to their sorrow.

"Where's Joey?" Alli asked as she came to the cashier table. "She should have been here by now."

Joey had stopped at Oasis on the way to the sale. She was on the floor under Daniel's desk in his office, fixing the sticky lock on his drawer, when she heard footsteps.

"Marjorie?" Joey said from under the desk.

"Jesus, you scared me," said a woman's voice. "Who's there?"

Joey banged her head as she came out from under the desk. "Ow," she grumbled. Then she saw Heidi. "What are you doing here?

"Shit!" Heidi said, startled. Her white canvas bag was in one hand and a key in the other. When she dropped the bag the door slammed behind her. It slammed so hard the door knob fell off.

"Not again!" Joey yelled as the knob clattered to the floor.

Chapter Twenty-eight

"Excuse me," Tamara said as she pushed through the crowd at the ER. She scanned it for Sam and baby Andrew but couldn't see them.

"Askavian," a triage nurse called out from behind her. "Mila Askavian?"

"Yes," replied a short man who helped a plump woman to stand up.

"Have you admitted a man and a little boy?" Tamara asked the nurse. "About four months old with a high fever?"

"We see a lot of those," the nurse frowned, opening a door and ushering the couple into the treatment area.

Before it closed behind them Tamara slipped in, too.

"Sam?" she yelled at the line of blue-curtained cubicles. A white suited orderly appeared at her elbow. "Ma'am?"

"Sam, it's me. Tamara," she yelled again, ignoring the orderly. "Are you in here?"

"You need to wait out there," the man insisted, taking her arm and leading her to the waiting room.

"In here," a male voice called out. Down the hall a curtain parted to reveal a worried Sam in a wrinkled pajama top and jeans, holding a limp Andrew in his arms.

Tamara wriggled out of the orderly's clutches and ran to him. "Thank

God. I got here as soon as I could. How is he?"

Sam let out a long breath. "I don't know. He's so hot. . . . "

She reached out to touch Andrew's forehead. The baby was burning up.

"He was throwing up all night long. And then he had diarrhea. I don't know what's wrong with him."

Tamara noted that the bottle of formula in Sam's hand was almost full. "Is he drinking?"

Sam shook his head, worry radiating off him in waves. "Not any more. And he's barely peeing. God, I wish Melanie was here."

"We've got to get someone in here. Now. Nurse!" Tamara yelled, barging into the corridor. She knew about sick kids with high fevers and dehydration, which fueled her to poke her head into other cubicles, pissing off two nurses and a doctor before she collared a handsome Hispanic intern who hadn't met her yet. "Please," she said, reading the name on his tag. "Please, Robert. We need help."

She grabbed him by the arm and dragged him to Sam's cubicle, explaining what was going on.

"How long has he been vomiting?" asked the intern, scribbling on a chart.

"Since last night . . . " Sam answered vaguely.

Robert scribbled again.

"Will you just take his temperature?" Tamara interrupted, reaching for his clipboard. The intern took it.

"104.5."

"What was it the last time?" a worried Tamara asked Sam.

"103," he answered, his face ashen.

Sam's in shock, she realized. *This must remind him of the last time he was in a hospital.*

"When's a doctor going to be in here?" she demanded.

"As soon as possible," said Robert, backing away.

"Not good enough," Tamara snapped, blocking his exit. "Look at this baby. He's limp. He's not drinking or peeing." Her voice rose. "He could go into convulsions any minute."

"A doctor will be with you soon," sputtered the intern. "Sunday mornings are a zoo around here."

"*I don't give a shit.* We need help! *Now!*"

"What's going on?" asked a familiar voice from the other side of the curtains. A familiar, arrogant voice. "Sam Morrell?"

"In here," Sam called back.

The curtains parted and Del walked in, stethoscope around his neck, white coat-tails flapping. "I saw your name on a chart. What's wrong with Andrew?" He peered at the drooping baby in Sam's arms while Tamara shocked herself, Sam, and Doctor God Himself by bursting into tears of relief.

At the garage sale Alli whispered in Dave's ear. "There's a Special Delivery from Doctor God Himself."

"And what's in there?!" Dave asked.

"C'mere," she said, reaching for his hand.

Dave gave his cash box to Rosalba and followed Alli to the back of the garage. A black Ford pickup had just pulled away, driven by a beefy young man who said he was Del's neighbor. He said Del had asked him to bring some things over: a 10-speed Peugeot bike, two large Chinese vases, a decorative urn, a black lacquered coffee table, framed posters and a number of boxes.

Alli opened a flap on one of the boxes. "Sex toys," she said to Dave. "An entire box of sex toys. Look!"

Dave gaped. "Jesus," he said, taking an awkward step back, bumping into Rick.

"What's going on?"

"Check this out," Alli crowed, doing a quick show-and-tell.

They opened more boxes filled with Del's collection of gay porn, XXX rated books, and kinky magazines. When a nosy older woman peered in and let out a small scream, they closed ranks around the boxes.

"What do we do with these?" Maggie asked.

"Sell 'em," Dave said. "Put them out and sell 'em. We'll get good money."

"Close 'em up. Now," Rick urged as Trevor ran in their direction.

Rick headed off his son; Alli, Maggie and Dave grabbed black plastic garbage bags. They scrambled to disappear the XXX stuff and price the rest of Del's G-rated delivery while a new wave of prospective buyers stormed the garage.

"Where are they all coming from?" Dave asked.

"I put ads on craigslist and garagesale.com. I tweeted the address and papered the city with Xeroxed posters," boasted Alli. "You get a lot done when you don't sleep more than three hours a night."

"I get it," Dave said.

Back at his cash box, he rang up sales and fielded questions from customers who kept asking about the "Clothes and Stuff to Die For" signs.

"You're actually *selling* your dead spouses' things? That's cold," pronounced an ice-blonde in a pink Ralph Lauren polo as she bought some of Jess's clothes.

"He won't need these in the place he's in," said a man with thinning brown hair who loaded up a shopping bag with Shawn's clothes.

"It was God's will," clucked a rail-thin matron, swooping up a watch that had belonged to Bruce.

"I'm sorry for your loss," croaked a red-headed harridan who drove a hard bargain with Alli.

Some buyers made the Top10 List of Things Not to Say to the

Bereaved. Others were more sensitive. By noon the sale had made $1600.

Berta drove up. "Happy Father's Day," she exclaimed. "This is a big step for all of you. It's about a lot more than overcoats and umbrellas." She swept her hands wide. "How is it going?"

"Okay, if you don't think too hard," Rick said.

As Rick's daughter leaned against her father, Dave saw the sadness in her. So, apparently, did Berta.

"Come," Berta said to the little girl, holding out her hand. "Are your Mommy's art supplies here?"

Moira nodded.

"Maybe I need some." Berta headed into the garage hand in hand with Moira. As she passed Dave, she said, "Joey must be very proud. Where is she?"

"See anyone out there?" Heidi asked Joey, desperation making her voice shrill.

Joey craned her neck to look out the window. Between the wires that crisscrossed the glass in diamond shapes and the bars outside it was hard to see anything at all. "Not a soul."

"My turn," Heidi said, pushing Joey aside to take her place at the window. "Why is this place built like a fricking fortress? There's nothing of value in here."

Joey resumed her seat on the floor, back against the wall, legs outstretched. She looked up at the portrait of Daniel's grandmother and silently sent out a message of help.

Heidi took a seat on the floor opposite Joey, which wasn't very far, clutching her white canvas bag to her chest. Joey noticed her face was red and her foot twitched.

"Why can't you fix that doorknob?" Heidi asked.

"I told you. I don't have the tools."

"I thought you're some sort of a handygenius."

Joey shrugged.

"Can't you cut through those window bars?"

"With what?"

"A nail file?" Heidi asked.

"You've seen too many prison movies," Joey said.

When the doorknob had clattered to the floor, leaving a useless shaft in the door, Joey's first thought was, *What is Heidi doing here and where did she get a key?* Then she realized they were locked in on a Sunday. In a small office with nobody around until Monday morning.

First, Heidi panicked about her dog. Then she panicked about having no exit. Next she hogged the window. "I can't help it," she said. "I'm claustrophobic."

Helpless, dishonest, and *claustrophobic,* Joey thought.

Now, they'd been stuck for over an hour, having rejected all the ways they could get out: fix doorknob (impossible, it had snapped off the shaft); pound on door and scream for help (useless); climb through window (forget it.)

Joey made a mental list of what they had: half a bottle of water between them (hers), three sticks of gum, and a jar of Vegemite (in Daniel's desk). She made a list of what they *didn't* have: a toilet, a phone (they'd left their purses in their cars), a laptop or a book or magazine to read.

"What about the laptop that's always in here?" Heidi asked as if she read Joey's thoughts.

"Already looked." She wondered how Heidi knew about that. "Marjorie must have taken it home for the weekend," Joey said. "Where did you get the key to this office?"

"It was hanging on a hook in the hallway. What's it to you?" Heidi asked, her voice rising.

Joey, realizing that was true, said nothing. She looked over at Daniel's grandmother's portrait instead. "Okay, Zora," she said. "Work your magic. I heard she was some sort of Saint Midwife," she told Heidi.

"Crikey," Heidi laughed mirthlessly. "She was a mercenary bitch who slept around."

"Really," Joey said, not believing a word.

"And her son stole from my father. And they all lived like that didn't happen, except my father left us and my family got screwed." Heidi's leg jiggled restlessly.

Joey checked her watch. "I've got to get out of here. My Grief Group is having a garage sale," she said.

"'Clothes and Stuff to Die For.' I saw the signs around here," Heidi said. "Selling their dead spouses' things? Is that in good taste?"

"It was their idea."

"And that swim party? Was that their idea, too?"

Joey was startled. "How do you know about that?"

"Everyone knows what goes on here," Heidi scoffed. "How did that go?"

"Fine. They had fun," Joey said firmly. "They deserve it."

"Why? Life isn't fair. It doesn't give a shit."

Silence.

"Why do you care?" Joey asked.

"About what?"

"Grief Group."

"Everyone's curious what you do in there," Heidi said. "You're so . . . *innovative.*"

Something about the way she said the word made Joey's flesh crawl. "You make *innovative* sound like a communicable disease."

"Maybe it is. It's not like you trained for this." Heidi picked at a loose thread of her sweater. "And your insensitivity! The way you insist they talk about things that shouldn't be talked about. I couldn't believe what I heard the night I walked into your Group. *How did she look in her coffin?* Nobody should have to remember that." She screwed up her face like she'd just tasted cat food. "And people shouldn't see grievers selling their dead wife or husband's clothing."

"Why not?" Joey was mystified. "What's it to you?"

"Grief is private," Heidi insisted, her voice rising. "There are rules, and you break all of them. There are ways to behave, and you act like you can do anything you want."

"So?"

"So the world runs on rules. Like the way to act about grief. It belongs in the home. You don't talk about it the way you do or make jokes about it or throw a garage sale like that. That's why the stages of grief were such a brilliant breakthrough. They're meant to be followed, one stage at a time. In order. Exactly in order . . . "

As she continued her litany of grievances, Joey began to see what Daniel meant. Heidi was troubled *and* trouble. She was tightly wound and officious as hell. Joey stopped listening and watched Heidi's lips move instead. Her face was red with excitement, as if she were on the roller coaster ride of her life, speeding down the rails, running over Joey's body.

"What happened to you?" Joey interrupted Heidi mid-spew.

"What *happened* to me?"

"What made you like this?"

"Like what?"

"So tough."

Heidi waved her hand in the air. "People like you and Daniel make people like me the way we are."

"What did we do?"

"Don't get me started on him. And you? You have no respect for appropriate behavior. You think you can make things up as you go along.

People like you need people like me to keep them in line. To protect others from your disruptive influence."

"What the hell are you talking about?" Joey asked.

Heidi's voice raised even higher. "I knew you were a phony the minute I saw you, but you're so much worse than I could have imagined. You're a dangerous amateur who's done those poor people harm with your made-up, New Age claptrap," she yelled.

Before Joey knew it she was yelling back. "What's *your* problem? Why did you lie to Daniel about when you got here? Why do you snoop around, writing in that yellow pad? What are you always writing, anyway?"

Heidi's hand went to her white canvas bag, where Joey saw the yellow pad sticking out. She reached for it. Heidi pulled it back. The pad ripped. Pages flew out, filled with tiny cribbed writing in red ink. They scattered across the floor like flowers of evil.

As Joey reached for them Heidi grabbed for her arm. Joey saw crisscrosses of scars on Heidi's wrists. She held onto them and looked into Heidi's eyes. "What did you do to yourself?"

Heidi's face paled as she regarded Joey with astonishment and several things happened at once. Heidi gasped for breath. She struggled to speak. Then she stopped breathing.

Chapter Twenty-nine

Boy, put a guy in a white coat and look what happens, thought Tamara as she watched Del in the ER. Doctor Del in action was a different person from the condescending jerk in Group.

"When did this start?" he asked Sam, paying close attention to his answers.

"Let's give a listen," he said, putting the stethoscope in his ears and unwrapping the baby's shirt to listen to the breaths that came in rasps from his tiny chest.

Tamara stood in the background, marveling at Del's bedside manner. If she didn't know what an asshole he was outside this hospital, she'd think he was a great guy. After he examined Andrew, Del quickly diagnosed a virus raging through the baby's small body. Within minutes, he had given the intern a list: blood tests for backup, an isolette crib and IV supplies, STAT.

"We're going to fast-track this," he told Sam. "We'll treat Andrew in the ER instead of admitting him. Save you all that red tape."

"Thanks," Sam said in a hollow voice.

Within a few minutes a nurse and an intern hurried in with the isolette and Del began prepping Andrew for an IV of anti-virals and fluids for dehydration.

Tamara watched as Del took Andrew from Sam's arms and lowered him gently into the crib. The baby's eyes fluttered beneath bluish-veined eyelids. His chest rose and fell rapidly.

Tamara saw that Sam was impaled by what was happening. *Here he is, on his first Father's Day, for God's sake, watching his beloved boy labor to breathe.* She inched over to his side. She stood beside him as Del worked on the baby, who cried when they stuck the IV into his tiny hand. She saw each weak, thin little mew strike Sam like a blow from a 50-pound mallet. Tamara moved in closer.

Moments later the IV was in, and two bags of clear fluid hung from a pole, dripping into Andrew's veins. Plastic sides draped over the crib. Steam emanated from within, creating an instant steam tent. "That ought to help," Del said, stripping off his gloves. "But he'll need to be in here a few hours before we see any improvement. Settle in," he told Sam. "This could take a while."

Del left on rounds. Andrew slept in his steamy world as the IV dripped anti-virals and healing fluids into his body. Sam moved a hard chair alongside the crib, reaching his hand beneath the plastic sides to touch his son's chest.

"How are you doing?" Tamara asked.

He didn't answer.

She touched his shoulder gently. Sam regarded her blankly. *He's forgotten I'm here.* "Why don't you go outside for a minute and get a breath of fresh air?"

"I'm not going anywhere."

From the look on his face she could tell he was in shock.

"How about a cup of coffee from the cafeteria? I think we could both use one," Tamara asked gently.

Sam looked at her again and blinked.

"How about it?" she repeated. "I'll stay here with Andrew."

"Okay," he said, as if emerging from a dream. He walked slowly out of the cubicle in his wrinkled pajama top and jeans. He looked years older than the Sam she'd come to know.

Tamara took his seat on the still-warm chair and reached through the opening in the plastic to place her hand on Andrew's chest. Through the white T-shirt she felt his heart fluttering like butterfly wings.

As she stroked his downy head, Tamara remembered.

Maya. Barely two and barely breathing after a long day of high fever and a frightening night of croup. Tamara and Bruce alternated sitting up with her in their bathroom, where all the mirrors and windows fogged from the hot shower, and steam dripped from the ceiling onto their heads. All night long, holding her in their arms, they braced for the sharp bark of her cough. They waited for her fever to break until early morning light seeped through the windows and the thermometer hadn't budged and Maya started turning blue and they raced to the hospital.

Tamara remembered how, for two days and two nights, she and Bruce slept beside Maya's isolette while she lay in her own steam tent with her own IV, Sleeping Beauty in a nightmare. When the danger was finally past, they went home and crawled into bed together, grateful for the miracle of modern medicine.

Now she sat beside another steam tent in another hospital with another man and another baby on Maya's first Father's Day without Bruce. The bitter irony was not lost on Tamara.

At Oasis, Joey was dealing with a full-blown crisis.

"I. Can't. Breathe," Heidi panted, in the middle of a panic attack in Daniel's office.

Joey quickly realized how terrible things could get if Heidi became a 911 call in a room with no phone. In a flash she searched for a paper bag and found one in the trash can. "Breathe into this," she said, handing it to Heidi.

Heidi pushed it away. "Not from the trash." Joey held it up to her face and soon Heidi was breathing into it and out. But her eyes remained unfocused, and her face was losing color.

It wasn't working. *Now, what?* Joey wondered. Her mind reeled all the way back to a psychology book Jack had given her long ago, with a technique on how to get present by focusing on your senses.

"Listen to me," she said as Heidi's breath came in ragged gasps and her hands loosened their grip on the bag and her eyes began to roll back in her head. "Listen to me," Joey shouted. "Look around you. Tell me what you see. Name the colors. Like this. Brown desk." Joey pointed to Heidi's clothes. "Orange shirt. Come on. You do it."

Heidi didn't.

"Do it *now*. Name the colors you see."

"Beige file cabinet . . . " Heidi panted. Her eyes darted to Daniel's orchid plant, a gift from Joey. "Purple orchid . . . "

"Go on. More."

Heidi glanced at Joey's finger. "Turquoise ring . . . "

Joey remembered Daniel buying it for her after she'd admired his turquoise inlaid belt buckle. She turned her attention back to Heidi, who was looking up at the window.

"Black iron bars . . . " Heidi's breath began to even out.

Fifteen minutes later Joey sat on the floor, leaning against the wall. She closed her eyes. Sweat rolled down her forehead. When she wiped it with her shirtsleeve she realized how trying the past hour and a half had been.

Once again she thought about the Grief Group. She wondered how they were doing at their sale. She wished she were there.

"Thank you," Heidi said quietly.

Joey nodded, eyes closed. She wished she could slip into a dream without Heidi in it. She heard Heidi gather the pages of her yellow pad from the floor.

"I don't know what you thought you saw," Heidi said.

"Forget it," Joey said.

"I put my hand through a glass door when I was 14."

"Uh-huh."

"It was Daniel's fault."

Joey said nothing. Apparently, everything was Daniel's fault.

"After his father ruined mine, my dad left the family and mum had a breakdown. I had to take care of my younger brother. He was deathly allergic to bees, but one afternoon he forgot his bee-sting kit and I saw him get stung. I ran to give it to him. I forgot the glass door was there."

Joey said nothing.

"He had Down Syndrome. His vision was impaired."

Joey opened her eyes. Heidi looked miserable.

"What's his name?" Joey asked after a long silence.

"Theo. He died." Heidi's face was full of sorrow.

Joey swallowed. The small room was warm and close. She had no desire to spook Heidi, who was finally acting like a human being.

"He liked to dance to ABBA," Heidi said. "He hated pineapple and eggplant. We had the same toes."

"I'm sorry."

"So I know about grief. I know all about it."

"I understand."

There was a moment when Joey thought they might have connected. *Maybe that's why Heidi is the way she is. Maybe she never grieved for her brother.*

"So I know all about going through those stages. In order," Heidi bristled. "They worked. And I don't need your sympathy or your pity,"

Heidi said. "I just wanted to clear that up, since you seemed to think I'd tried to kill myself. My telling you doesn't make us pals."

The bitch was back.

"And it's your fault we're locked in here. If you hadn't scared me I wouldn't have slammed the door," Heidi said.

"If you hadn't slammed the door the knob wouldn't have broken off," Joey said reasonably.

"Of course it would have," Heidi said. "This place is falling apart. It's dangerous." Heidi brushed imaginary dirt off her pants.

A bell began to ring inside Joey's head.

"What were you doing in here on a Sunday?" she asked.

"Sara wants to do a yoga retreat. She asked me to put flyers about it in the office."

"Is that so?"

"Of course," Heidi said, indignant. She reached into the canvas bag and pulled out the flyers. "See?"

Joey looked at the flyers, thinking.

"If you had to be locked in with someone you're lucky it's me," Heidi said. "Those iron bars are a fire hazard. There are people in this town who'd think this place should be shut down."

Joey thought about that while Heidi put the yoga flyers back into her canvas bag, the one with the crown on it. She was still thinking about it when a paper fell out of the bag and Joey reached to pick it up.

It was a map of Oasis. With red x's for every place a violation had been filed.

"It's you," Joey said.

Heidi looked up, her eyes black with rage.

Chapter Thirty

At the hospital Sam looked up with gratitude when Tamara walked back into the ER cubicle from the bathroom.

"Hey," he said. She was relieved to see the color had returned to his face. "I don't think I've thanked you for coming when I called."

"I'm just glad I could be here."

"All night long I thought, what do I do?" Sam shook his head in disbelief. "What do I do? Mel was the nurse in the family. I was just supposed to be the dad."

"But you did the right thing. You got him here in time, and look, he's doing better already."

They looked at the sleeping baby in his steam tent. Andrew's chest rose and fell with a slower rhythm, and they could no longer hear his rasps. An intern entered to monitor him. As he reached in to take his temperature, the young man looked at Sam and his wrinkled pajama top with sympathy.

"Some Father's Day. I guess you and your wife had a better plan than spending it in the ER."

Sam looked down and said nothing. Tamara looked down and thought about Maya.

"What do you want to do tomorrow?" she'd asked her daughter the night before, standing in the hallway outside her room after knocking on the closed door with its hideous STOP (YOU) sign.

Maya's therapist insisted she could keep her door closed to Tamara despite her (valid) desire to police her daughter's every action and every inch of her room for new stolen clothes.

Maya cracked open the door. "Yes?" she said coolly, as if she didn't know it was her mother standing in the hallway.

Tamara repeated her question. "Do you want to make plans for Father's Day?"

"I've got plans. And so do you," Maya observed. "Aren't you making blood money from selling Daddy's stuff in the garage?"

"It's not blood money," Tamara said as evenly as she could. "We can't take it all with us when we move to a smaller place."

"Whatever," Maya retorted. "I'm going to breakfast and miniature golf with Janae and her family."

Janae. A spiky-haired, sullen 12-year old who played bass in Maya's band, the Angels of Mercy. A girl Tamara detested, whose mother stage-whispered every time she saw Tamara, "How do you get through the day? I can't imagine what I'd do if Mark did such a thing."

"Is that all?" Maya asked in a dead voice.

"Yes," Tamara said. She peered through the crack in Maya's door at Bruce's green windbreaker hanging on a hook.

"Anything else, Tamara?" Maya asked, using her first name ("Janae calls her mom "Lori" Maya insisted.) It was an obnoxious new habit she knew Tamara detested. Maya started texting on her phone.

"Mom," Tamara corrected. "Yeah, that's all."

"Good night, Tamara," Maya said.

Tamara stood in silence as her daughter's door shut in her face.

Sitting beside Andrew, Tamara wondered what Maya was doing right now. She thought about how, to Maya, she'd become the angry red spot on the couch, while with Sam she was a softer, kinder version of herself: a person she barely knew these days.

"Thanks for coming," Sam said, interrupting her thoughts. "You were the first person I called."

Tamara flushed with pleasure. "I'm just glad you got to me before the sale started."

"Oh, man. We're both supposed to be there," he realized.

"I'll call Rosalba and see what's going on," she said.

"Did you have a lot to sell?"

"Some stuff from Bruce. Maya's highchair and dollhouse and—"

"I didn't know you had her highchair. I would've bought it for Andrew."

"But Alli brought you one. You were putting it together the day I came by." Tamara stopped, her face hot as she remembered burning rubber outside his house, fueled by jealousy.

Sam laughed. "I couldn't get the thing together. She must have lost a few important pieces along the way. That's Alli," he said with a look of tolerance and nothing more for the blonde flibbertigibbet in the Group.

We're bonding, Tamara realized with a little thrill and a lot of guilt as they both looked down on Andrew. *We're bonding while my daughter is out there, celebrating Father's Day with her best friend's family.*

In Daniel's office anger fired in Joey's chest as she looked down at Heidi's map. "You're the one who filed the violations."

"So?"

"Damn it! Why would you do that?"

"Revenge is sweet," Heidi said, reaching for the paper in Joey's hand.

Joey held onto the map. "Revenge? Because Daniel's father lost money for yours?"

"Yes, and—"

"I can't believe you're still hanging onto that," Joey snapped. Their eyes met. There was something unsettling in Heidi's eyes, a flicker of rage that caught Joey's attention.

"That's not all Daniel did to me," Heidi said.

"What else?" Joey asked, shaking her head. "What else are you holding against him and his family? What other excuse do you have for filing all these . . . " She held up the map. "These miserable violations?" Joey walked over to the desk and sat down, as far away from Heidi as she could get. "I can't wait to tell Daniel when I talk to him. You're everything he said you were. A nuisance. A pain in his ass. And now, in mine."

When Heidi swiveled her head to look at her Joey remembered something she'd seen recently.

She'd been lying out by the Ferndale pool when she spotted a large green bug poised on an azalea branch. Its head swiveled slowly as it stared at her with beady eyes.

"Is that a grasshopper?" she'd asked an older man on the next lounge chair.

"A praying mantis," he corrected. "They eat their mates."

Now, as Heidi fixed Joey with a murderous glare she looked like a praying mantis ready to kill. "Not only did Daniel ruin my family," she said. "He jilted me."

"For whom?" Joey asked, knowing she was about to hear another lie.

"For the only woman he's ever loved. His sister. Lara. His *adopted* sister. He's in love with her. "

Joey felt the room tilt and whirl.

"Senora?" A familiar voice called from the other side of the door. "Senora Joey? Are you in there?"

"Perfecto?" Joey ran to the door. "Is that you?"

"Si, Senora," he said.

"We're locked in here. The doorknob broke off."

"We see cars in parking lot and checking cottages," Perfecto said.

Heidi talked through the door. "Get us out of here right now," she demanded.

The garage sale was coming to an end. A few stragglers were still browsing when Dave saw Rick carrying Jess's easel back to his station wagon.

"You're taking stuff *home*?" Dave asked.

"Berta," Rick said, cocking his head in her direction. "She convinced me not to sell it."

"Why?"

"She said, 'I hear your wife was an artist, and now, so is your daughter. Do you know the ritual of an older artist handing her easel down to a younger one?' She said it's a time-honored tradition. So. . . . "

Dave watched Rick pack up the easel and return to the circle of life that awaited him. His two kids. Berta, a grandmother-type. A surge of melancholy swept over Dave. He thought of his own life: wifeless, childless. *A worthless piece of crap of a life.*

Maggie appeared at his side. "How about that Joey?"

"How about her?" Dave agreed, quickly covering his pain. "I'm surprised she didn't show."

"She must have found something better to do today," Maggie said.

"What could possibly have been better than this?" Dave asked, sweeping his arms wide at the mess.

The office door opened with a rusty squeak. Heidi raced past Perfecto to the bathroom in the office bungalow.

"Thank you, thank you," Joey said to him as she ran to the bathroom in *Hummingbird*. While she peed, Joey decided Heidi had lied about

Daniel and his sister to cover her ass about the violations. *The best defense is a good offence,* she thought.

She walked back to the office where Heidi stood on the porch, looking out, cell phone in hand. When Joey came closer Heidi raised her chin, which made the cleft in the middle point right at Joey. The back of her neck started to prickle.

"I thought you'd like to see a family photo," Heidi said. She tapped on a photo in her phone. Before she could stop herself Joey looked.

Daniel stood next to the most beautiful woman she'd ever seen. She had almond-shaped eyes and skin that glowed, voluptuously full lips and a seductive smile. A heart-stopping beauty.

"That's . . . his sister?" Joey asked.

"Yes. That's Lara." Heidi flipped to the next photo.

Daniel's arm was around his sister's waist, and he was looking at Lara the way he looked at Joey. Before she could stop her, Heidi flipped to another photo. Lara was standing with her back to the camera, holding a surfboard, wearing a red thong bikini that left nothing to the imagination.

"Like I said, Lara's the reason our marriage broke up. Lara is the love of his life." Heidi's mouth formed a small, delicious smile, like she'd just sampled the best strawberry ice cream in the world.

Lara is the love of his life. Seven words, and Joey felt her world begin to crumble.

She knew she shouldn't believe Heidi. She knew Heidi lied. But somewhere, in the pit of her stomach, Joey knew it was the truth.

"You poor thing," Heidi said. "Men use you and betray you, It's always the same."

Joey ran to her car and drove away.

Somewhere inside her a word was repeating, over and over again, like the clanging of a bell. The same word that rang out when she'd found out about Jack and the blonde. *Betrayed. Betrayed. Betrayed again, stupid.*

By the time she drove up to Tamara's garage Joey felt completely raw.

"Where were you?" Alli asked.

"We were worried about you," Maggie said.

"Sorry. I was tied up," Joey said, hoping her voice sounded normal. "How did you do?"

"Great," Dave said.

"We made a bundle," Rick said.

"And . . . ?" Joey asked. She looked at their gloomy faces with confusion. "And it was *that* painful?"

"We sold a lot," Alli began.

"Including Shawn," Maggie finished.

"What?" Joey was having trouble comprehending.

Alli, Maggie, and Rick explained they'd figured out that the neighbor who'd brought Del's boxes and the urn that held Shawn's ashes must have taken them from the wrong shelf in the garage.

"But by then I'd already sold Shawn to a hot young guy who said the urn would make a great martini mixer," Alli said.

For a moment Joey forgot about her own troubles. "How do you know it held his ashes?"

"Del showed it to me one night at his house," Alli answered.

At that moment Del pulled up in his Porsche. The Group froze.

"Let me tell him," Joey said. She swallowed her own feelings as she went to greet Del. The Group watched anxiously as she told him what had happened.

"And *who* bought him?" Del asked.

"A hot young guy, apparently," Joey said.

There was a long moment of silence. Then Del started to laugh. Soon the laugh turned into a roar. "A martini mixer? What a great afterlife for Shawn. He would've loved that."

As his loud laughter echoed, Joey wondered if he was high. Then she realized he'd just come from the hospital. Before she could say another word, Del got back into his Porsche and drove away.

"Good job," Rick told Joey. She nodded blankly. "Are you okay?" he asked.

"Sure," Joey lied as Tamara pulled up. She filled them in on Sam and Andrew; Alli thrust a wad of bills into Tamara's hands.

"What's that for?"

"Bruce's junk. His golf clubs fetched a pretty penny."

"Alli was a tough negotiator," Maggie said.

"Thanks," Tamara replied.

"Here," Alli said, handing Tamara some papers. "I found these in the pocket of his suede jacket."

When Joey offered to help clean up the mess in the garage everyone told her to go home. "Whatever you did today, you look more tired than we do," they said.

If only they knew, Joey thought as she drove away.

An hour later, Dave and Maggie were the last people in the garage.

"Now who will tell?" Maggie asked as she crouched on the floor, smoothing a green and black tartan blanket in a box.

"Tell what?" Dave asked.

"Tell about the night Jeff and I camped in Oregon. And we lay on that blanket and named stars for our future kids. Who'll tell that story now?" She looked up at Dave, her eyes bright.

"You will, Maggie. With or without that blanket you'll tell that story to your kid," Dave said.

Maggie wiped her eyes, put the blanket back in a box, closed the lid, and said goodnight.

How do you measure a life? Dave wondered as he looked around at the black plastic bags of their spouses' clothes piled in a corner for the

Salvation Army. Alli said she'd sell Bruce's squash racquet and Shawn's roller blades, the treadmill, dishes, framed paintings, and miscellaneous sports equipment on eBay.

Dave killed the light and for one instant he thought he felt their presence in those items.

"Goodbye," he whispered softly.

As the word winged its way across the garage and into the precious items that had walked the earth with their beloveds, Dave began to feel foolish.

When did I turn into a sentimental slob? he wondered. He closed the garage door and left it all behind.

Tamara pulled her car into the garage. As she looked around, for the first time she accepted that she, Maya and Rosalba would soon be leaving this house. *Home.*

She closed the door to her BMW, soon to be traded in for a Toyota. She walked to one of the piles in the corner and pulled out Maya's highchair to give to Sam. Then she walked into the silent house, where Boots made figure eights around her ankles.

"Hi," she said. "I bet you're hungry."

She fed him and watched as he gobbled up his food. Feeling grimy from the ER, she walked upstairs, went into the bedroom, turned on a bubble bath, and imagined how good it would feel to sink into it.

Boots jumped on the bed as she dumped out the papers Alli had found in Bruce's jacket.

"How about a winning lottery ticket?" Tamara said to Boots.

She tossed her clothes onto the floor and sat on the bed in her bra and panties, scanning the notes written on blue-lined paper in Bruce's left-handed scrawl: *Get cat food. Call eye doc. Mail contract.*

She was taking them to the wicker waste basket when she saw one last unopened piece of paper with Bruce's handwriting. Reflexively, she opened it: *My darling Tamara and Maya. Forgive me. I love you.*

Goose bumps bloomed on Tamara's bare arms and legs. A cry caught in her throat. Bruce had left a note for them in his jacket.

Tamara stared at the paper as water filled the tub. She stared as water overflowed onto the bathroom floor. While the water caused a leak that would cost every dollar she'd just made at the garage sale, Tamara sat on her bed, staring at Bruce's note, her head bowed in sorrow.

High above Topanga Canyon, Joey looked out from the wooden deck behind the guesthouse where Daniel had lived. She'd come straight from Ferndale, where she'd called him, waking him in the middle of the night.

"When are you coming back?" she asked.

"I don't know," he said sleepily.

"How's your sister?" she asked with her own meaning.

"She's supposed to get out of ICU tomorrow. But she'll be in rehab for a long time."

"Good," Joey said woodenly.

"I miss you," Daniel said.

"Do you?" Joey asked.

"Of course I do."

Joey was silent.

"Joey?"

She said nothing.

"Are you there?"

"Yes. I'm here. And you're there with your sister."

"She's the only family I have," Daniel said. "I've got to stay until she's healed. You of all people should understand."

"I think I do," she said. "I think I finally understand."

"Joey?"

"What about your place in Topanga?" she asked.

"They're renting it to someone else."

Chills ran through Joey.

"Goodbye, Daniel," she said. She hung up, feeling hollow.

Now, Joey looked around the wooden deck. Stubs of candles stood in empty wine bottles with Australian labels. As she walked into his bedroom the pain started in her chest and moved up and down her body. She remembered being in Daniel's arms. She remembered his hands caressing her, his voice in her ear.

Several well-thumbed paperback mysteries remained on his nightstand. An ashtray with Daniel's hand-rolled cigarette butts was next to them. Q #435 was scribbled on a notepad: his flight number to Australia.

Joey was surrounded by the detritus of Daniel's life in L.A.

Which includes me.

Her head began to pound, and the pain grew until she had to get out of there.

It was dark by the time she pulled into the winding canyon road. Tears coursed down her cheeks. Hiccups of sobs followed her out of the car and up the path, where, mercifully, a yellow light shone in the window. As Joey raised her hand to ring the cowbells the door was opened.

Berta stood there in a wine-colored velvet robe, her long hair in a braid down her back, her face etched with concern. "What is it?"

"Can I sleep on your couch tonight?" Joey asked, her voice wobbly. "I can't go home."

"What couch? You're family. Come in and tell me everything," Berta soothed, pulling Joey inside.

"He loves her," she wept, standing in the foyer.

"Who?"

"Daniel."

Berta looked confused. "Who does he love?"

"His sister . . . I mean, his adopted sister . . . he's in love with her . . . "

"Oh, I don't think so, dear," Berta said.

"You didn't see her picture," Joey said. "And the way he looked at her. She's the one," Joey sniffed. "She's the one he loves."

"No," Berta said.

"Yes," Joey insisted tearfully. "How awful is that? He's in love with his own sister." She burst into another round of sobs.

"Aaah," Berta said, no longer arguing. "I'm sorry, darling." She wrapped her arms around Joey. "I'm so sorry." Berta smoothed Joey's hair, made her a cup of tea, persuaded her to take a long, hot bath scented with oils from brown bottles with hand-written labels, and lent her a paisley caftan and slippers.

Then Berta sat beside Joey in the cozy kitchen and listened until Joey was talked out.

"I guess that's all there is to say about a man who tells you he loves you and goes back to the woman who's his one true love," Joey said. "His *adopted* sister"

"Is it?" Berta's face brightened unexpectedly. "This may not be the moment to tell you, dear, but there's an old Polish expression for a lover who turns into a louse. My mother used to say it."

"What . . . what is it?" Joey paused. She breathed in the earthy aroma of the twig tea in her hand. An owl hooted in the canyon. It was the perfect moment for one of Berta's pearls of wisdom.

"The cake turned into a pickle," Berta said.

Joey didn't react until she saw Berta struggling not to laugh. When Joey started to giggle Berta joined in and Joey laughed until she cried. Then she and Berta started laughing all over again.

Part Four

Chapter Thirty-one

Summer came, with its longest of days and shortest of nights. Ever so slowly the pain began to ease. Gradually, there were moments, then hours, then days when death wasn't the focus of the Group's lives. Joey watched it happen from her seat in the den. She heard it in the laughter that floated to the sky when they gathered on the porch before and after Group. The spark of life flickered and fired until the faces that huddled together became less lined.

Sam put it best one night: "I realized something the other day. We will never, ever stop loving them. But we will go on."

Three steps forward, two steps back, Joey watched the young widows and widowers inch towards a future carved from stone and watered with tears.

Joey wasn't feeling so optimistic.

She'd stopped taking Daniel's calls. She'd blocked his emails. She'd "unfriended" him on Facebook and deleted him on Skype. She'd told Marjorie that Heidi was the one who'd filed the violations.

"We should ban her from Oasis," Marjorie had said, furious.

"Do whatever you want," Joey said.

"Have you told Daniel?"

"No. Please tell him yourself. From now on, you guys are on your own. No need to keep me in the loop. I'll take care of whatever needs to be fixed. And run Grief Group, of course."

"I don't understand," Marjorie said with a frown. "What happened between you two? I thought—"

"So did I." Joey shrugged. "Shit happens."

"Poor Daniel," Marjorie had said, biting her lip. "He went back to a world of trouble."

"What do you mean?" Joey asked in spite of herself.

"There's some sort of judgment against him in Australia. Not only does he have a sister in the ICU, he's fighting the Australian court system. And it's jeopardizing his EB-5 Visa status."

"Oh," Joey said. "Gotta go."

"Joey?" Marjorie followed her out. Joey turned. "You're not mad at me, are you? We're good, right?"

"Of course we are."

Marjorie pulled her into one of her bone-crushing hugs. "I'm sorry about you and Daniel," she said.

"Me, too," Joey said into Marjorie's hair.

Joey half walked, half ran to the Quonset hut. When she opened the door she allowed herself to feel just how sorry for herself she was. She walked over to Lexus and Armani's habitat and opened their door.

"Who deserts a man in that much trouble? What does that make me?" she asked Lexus, stroking her leathery head. "A terrible person," Joey decided. Armani clacked his jaws as if in agreement.

"You're not a terrible person," Kat said a week later when they hiked in Cheeseboro Canyon, down a mile-long dirt path beneath the graceful boughs of great oak trees. "But why are you believing Heidi? From what you've said, every time she opens her mouth another lie falls out. When did she become a reliable reporter?"

"It's not Heidi. It's me. I felt it in my body when Daniel told me about his sister. Something was off. Those photos just confirmed what I was feeling."

"This isn't about Daniel," Kat said. "It's about your mom leaving. And the guys who cheated on you. And Jack. Sweetie, you've got a hair-trigger reaction to betrayal."

"Or a good nose for when someone is betraying me," Joey countered as they climbed a green hill dotted with purple loosestrife flowers. Joey looked out at the astonishing vista of faraway canyons covered in green velvet, stretching clear to the ocean. It was extraordinarily beautiful, but not enough to melt the ice around her heart.

"Daniel's not with his adopted sister," Kat said. "Not the way you mean."

"How do you know? If Woody Allen can run off with his adopted step-daughter, Daniel can canoodle with his adopted sister."

"Canoodle," Kat said, laughing. "Now there's a word!" She tried to get Joey to laugh, but it was useless.

Joey wished she could agree with Kat. But every time she thought of the photograph of Daniel and Lara, she felt pain in her chest and bile in her throat. She couldn't let it go. The longer Daniel stayed away the more certain Joey became. *He's chosen his adopted sister over me.*

On the first Saturday in July, Joey sat on her balcony, nursing her bruised heart with a lime-laced gin and tonic. With no Daniel, summer stretched before her like a silver slide in the blazing sun. The heat rolled in. Leaves curled and browned. Plants withered in a day. Oasis simmered. The air-conditioning in her car quit. Then it went out at Ferndale. Kat took to sleeping at Neil's place in Hollywood as repairs at Ferndale began to multiply. They were beyond any help Joey could offer.

Soon she couldn't immerse herself in the sparkling blue water of the pool or even stare at it. Because the pools were drained to repair leaks, revealing scarred black cracks in the bottoms. Even the nesting swans deserted the lake, their nestlings zigzagging behind them across the sky. Within a week, green algae bloomed on the water like witches' brew.

Heat, tyrannical and oppressive, stifled the breath in Joey's throat and further crushed her broken wings. It was lying in wait every morning before she opened her eyes. Sometimes the wind fluttered the fronds on the palm trees, but the wind blew hot, and stagnant air came through her screens.

By the end of July she felt as if her brain was boiling. There was nowhere for her to go to escape the heat and nobody interesting to escape it with. Except Berta.

"Where are we going?" Joey asked when Berta pulled into Ferndale in her convertible late on a Friday afternoon.

"A blessed sea view," Berta said. "Besa Del Mar. Kiss of the sea. That's what we need." Joey tossed her overnight bag in the back. "Turn off your cell phone, dear," Berta said. "This is a good old-fashioned vacation." They roared up the coast to a Spanish-style hotel on the beach in Santa Barbara.

They arrived in the dark. Joey smelled it before she saw it: menthol from giant eucalyptus trees, salt in the sea air, the scent of orange blossoms. The minute they walked through the oversized hacienda door into the lobby, Joey fell in love with the deep yellow walls, arched windows, and iron grillwork.

Their luggage was taken to adjacent Spanish-style cottages by a fresh-faced bellman on a bicycle pulling a red wagon. Joey and Berta played cards, ate room-service sandwiches, and went to bed early. Joey woke in the middle of the night to the whistle of a train that rattled the windows and walls.

The next morning at breakfast on Berta's ocean-view balcony, she said the train was one of her favorite things about the place. "Makes you feel alive to wake up with your heart pounding, doesn't it?"

They walked down to a wide gray wooden boardwalk overlooking the ocean. Berta sat at a table under a deep red umbrella and began to draw. Joey stepped onto the flat beach and began to walk. It reminded her of Fire Island beaches.

As she walked she realized her heart no longer ached for Jack. But when she saw surfers in wet suits it ached for Daniel. There was no escaping it, she thought, bending to pick up a heart-shaped rock. Love hurt. When she got back Berta taught her how to waltz in the sand, which ended with Joey dissolving into badly needed laughter.

In the evening they drove to Stearns Wharf, where the tires of Berta's car slapped against the old wooden boards. They ate fresh-caught rock and spider crabs at a picnic table overlooking the harbor. They strolled past the storefront of a gypsy fortuneteller, Madame Rosinka, whose large parrot squawked at them.

"Let's go see her," Joey said.

"No," Berta said, skeptical for once.

Joey managed to convince her and they went in.

Madame Rosinka told Berta she would live three lifetimes in one, minimum.

"I already have," Berta said. "Next?"

Madame dealt Joey a hand of Tarot cards and gazed into her palm. "As low as you go is as high as you go," she said. "So when you go low, dive deep. That is as high as you will go. . . . "

"What was she talking about?" Joey asked Berta when they were back on the pier.

"Tell you in a minute. But I'll be damned if the gypsy wasn't right," Berta said as they stood in line for ice cream. Suddenly, people began to yell and Joey and Berta saw a whale surface between two moored boats. "And that's another sign," Berta said.

"Of what?"

Berta walked Joey to the edge of the dock. "Whales symbolize death and rebirth. It means it's time for you to stop hiding from your grief." Joey was startled. Berta took a bite of pistachio ice cream. "You'll never be fully alive, dear, unless you heal those wounds. As Madame Rosinka said: 'As low as you go is as high as you go.' So go low, dear. Go as low as you need to go."

"I already have," Joey said, frowning.

"Not just about Daniel. Dive deep into the pain of losing your family."

Joey inhaled deeply. "No. I don't want to. I'm afraid."

"You must. Drown in those tears," Berta said. "The ones you're afraid to shed."

"And what if I can't?"

"Then you'll miss it."

"What?"

"The light."

"What light?"

"The light in Daniel's eyes when he looks at you."

"Not him, please."

"The light in your own eyes, then," Berta said. "And mine. It's all around you. It's out there. But you can't see it yet."

Joey looked out over the water. All she saw was the dark of the evening.

While Joey was in Santa Barbara, Tamara dialed every Group member, including Joey. Nobody picked up. Tamara was shaking by the time she reached the last person on her list.

"It's Tamara," she told Dave when he answered. "I've got a problem. Can I come over?"

"Okay."

She ran out of the house without combing her hair and sped to his apartment on Sawtelle. She rushed in, two cell phones in hand.

"What's wrong?"

"My house sold and I was talking to my mother on the phone. I said if I have to pack one more box I'm going to kill myself. Maya must have heard that because the next time I looked she was gone." Tamara was close to tears. She checked one cell, then the other.

"What's with the two phones?"

"This one's mine. The other's Maya's. I found it under her bed. With this on the home screen."

She handed the phone to Dave. A drawing of a man with a gun to his head startled him.

"Maya drew that and put it on Instagram," Tamara said, snatching back the phone. "Then she linked it to Twitter, and here are some of the lovely Tweets she got: 'Let's blow our brains out.' 'Today's a good day to die.' "Die, die, die, Maya.' It says the picture has 48 'likes,' for God's sake, and I don't understand any of this shit or know where she is. Or who she's with . . . "

"Do you think she's run away?" Dave asked.

Tamara took a shaky breath. "I'm sure of it."

"Have you called the police?"

"I filed a report. But they won't do anything until she's been gone 24 hours." Tamara was trembling. "What do I do?"

Dave made her sit down. "Talk to me. Tell me what she's interested in. Maybe we'll figure out where she went."

Tamara told Dave about the punk rock chat rooms she'd discovered that Maya was in. And the meetups she'd apparently gone to. "I knew nothing about any of this until I spent these last two hours scouring her cell. I've been calling and texting everyone."

"Nobody's seen her?"

"Rosalba's visiting her daughter in Bakersfield. My parents are on a cruise in Mexico. I called Maya's friends. Nobody's heard from her. God only knows how old these people in the chatrooms are. Some guy could have her . . . " Tamara's eyes were wild.

"Whoa," Dave said. "Sit down." He poured her a Johnnie Walker. "Drink this and tell me what else she's been interested in. Give me a complete rundown on her."

Tamara downed the Scotch and told him how Maya had played soccer in the park until she was 11; how she loved the Griffith Park Observatory because Bruce had been obsessed with astronomy.

"What else?" Dave asked.

Tamara told him about family trips they'd taken and how Maya used to go to the airport on Sundays with her dad to see the planes take off.

"What's today?" Dave asked, looking at the cell phone display.

"Sunday."

"What airport did they go to?"

"Burbank."

"Let's go," Dave said. "She once talked to me about that."

They found her at the United Terminal, a small heap gathered in a chair by a floor-to-ceiling window. She was tear-stained and grimy but grateful that her mother was still alive and not planning to take her life any time soon.

Tamara folded Maya in her arms, and Dave drove them home. Later that night, after Maya had fallen asleep, Tamara called Dave. "You're a friend," she said shakily. "I'm sorry I was such a shit to you. I haven't had a friend for a very long time."

"That makes two of us," Dave said.

August arrived, a dreamy, pensive interlude with less traffic. It was time when unbroken families went away on vacations and grieving families stayed home. While all the therapists left town, Grief Group met every two weeks.

"Summertime and the livin' is easy," Del sang out one night. "Wrong," he added.

Tamara told them that, when Maya turned 14 on August 16, her first birthday since Bruce died, "she said she wanted to take her cake to the cemetery so Dad could blow out the candles. I made it chocolate. He was allergic."

There was news of other summer birthdays and anniversaries celebrated alone. Then, one morning, Maggie saw her baby on an ultrasound. That evening she asked the Group to be her labor coaches.

"Thanks, but ouch," Tamara said.

"Been there, done that," Del said.

"Can I get T-shirts made up with 'Maggie's Labor Coaches'?" Alli asked.

"Can I be in charge of saying 'push'?" Dave asked.

Sam said he couldn't do it. "Next baby," he promised.

"What about you?" Maggie asked Joey. "Will you come?"

Joey felt anxious at the thought of being present at a birth. She made excuses.

"I'll be there," Rick said steadily. "New life. New hope."

When September roared in with wildfires raging, Maggie moved, with Dave's help; Tamara and Sam moved, to the same red stucco duplex in Westwood: Tamara and her family occupied the second floor; Sam, baby Andrew, and Rosalba's cousin, now Andrew's nanny, lived on the first.

"Do I hear wedding bells?" Dave asked

Sam and Tamara shook their heads. But Joey noticed Sam had started to wear his wedding ring on his right hand.

The kids went back to school. "And there's still no place on those forms for 'widower,'" Rick complained. "Just 'single, married, or divorced.'"

Maya was in a new junior high. "She said she's going to tell her new classmates that Bruce is on assignment in Washington, D.C.," Tamara said. "I didn't know what to say."

Joey wished she could start a kids' Grief Group. But she knew better than to ask for one at Oasis. Because Oasis was in trouble.

Chapter Thirty-two

At Oasis, Joey stared at the FOR SALE sign on the weed-filled lawn.
Then she got into her car in the parking lot. With the windows rolled up
she screamed as loud as she could. Her life, her brand-new life, was going
up in smoke. First Daniel, now Oasis. If it was sold, what would happen
to Grief Group? *What will happen to me?*

She stormed into the office and told Marjorie she wanted to take a
picture of the sign and text it to Daniel with the caption: "See what you've
done?"

"Believe me, it's killing him. But he's done everything he can,"
Marjorie said, her voice cracking. "The balloon payment on the mortgage
turned out to be more than Daniel could afford. Not with all the
additional expenses for his sister and lawyer fees in Australia."

When tears welled in her eyes Marjorie began to reorganize the
organized stacks of paper on her desk.

"Maybe the FMs can help?"

"They're helping plenty. Helping me keep this place running. But it's
more than the biddies can finance." Marjorie walked out to the porch, too
upset to continue the conversation. Joey followed. They stared at the sign.

"Well, it's not sold yet," Joey said. "And it's a lousy real estate market,
so maybe it won't sell." Marjorie nodded, but her eyes looked miserable.

Around the corner at The Counter, Heidi and Gus Green sat side by side eating lunch.

"Yup, my sign is up over there, and I put it on LoopNet."

"What's LoopNet?" Heidi asked, irritated beyond belief.

"Number One Commercial Real Estate Listings," Gus bragged. "And my people want to know the status of the sale of Oasis," he said between bites of his Old School burger. "What's the update?"

Heidi tried not to look at the dribble of relish dripping down his chin. She took a bite of her Stacked B.L.T. and bided her time.

Gus had made his own decision to put up the sign. *Stupid man.* Now he was listing it online? He was a major dunce. And calling them "my people?" He'd become a liability. An ungrateful, self-important little twit. *He's only in on the scheme because of me,* she thought as she chewed slowly, *and he still hasn't introduced me to "his people"—the fucking Foundation.*

"So what's the 411, little Sheila?" he asked.

"Well, as you know," she said, "I stopped filing those violations." She saw no reason to tell him why. "So the place won't be red-tagged. Which means the price won't drop. Luckily, the owner will be tied up in Australia for a good long while. Legal trouble," she said. She briefly explained that the minute Daniel had set foot on Australian soil she'd had her lawyer serve her ex-husband for back alimony.

"A real claim?" Gary asked.

"Not exactly," Heidi said. "But it will take the court system months before they unravel that. Meanwhile, Daniel's EB-5 visa status will expire, and poof! Along with that will go Oasis when we swoop in with the right buyer. Cha-ching! *And* I figured out a way to make myself completely invaluable to Oasis."

"Smart pussycat," Gary purred, reaching for her hand with his clammy paw. "Come to Papa."

Heidi smelled the beef on his breath. She pulled her hand out from under his. "I'm keeping up my end. It's time for us to make a trade," she said. "You introduce me to 'your people' and I'll introduce you to 'my people.' Regency Properties. They're waiting to hear back from me."

Gus frowned. "Why do we need Regency? I can broker a deal with the Foundation myself."

"Not the deal I have in mind," Heidi said sweetly. "We're talking multi-multi-millions. You've never ever done a deal that high, have you?"

"Nope," Gus Green said, grabbing a French fry. "Have you?"

"Of course not. But I've learned exactly what we need to do. First, we need to lie low for a while. So take down that sign, Gus. Let them think nothing's happening with Oasis."

In late September, in a Solstice ceremony replete with rainbow kites, wandering minstrels, and a male harp player whose long hair fluttered in the breeze, Bunny and Arbela bid a flashy farewell to Zora's creation.

Joey watched it all alongside Marjorie and Berta. "Does this mean Oasis has been sold?"

"God, no," Marjorie said. "Nobody's come to see it. And the sign's gone."

Joey realized it was. "What does that mean?"

"No clue. But it's a weak market," Berta said. "And Oasis isn't such an easy sell."

"Why not?" Joey asked, her heart heavy. "It's a huge property. In a prime location."

Oddly, Marjorie began to laugh. "That it is. That it is."

Berta chuckled.

"What's going on?" Joey asked, mystified.

"I just found out from Daniel that Zora added a codicil to her last will."

"It stipulates that whoever buys Oasis must continue to run it in a similar manner," Berta said.

"So a sale isn't exactly a slam dunk," Marjorie said, looking around. "Who's going to buy an anachronism like us?"

"We're a relic," Berta agreed. "A darling and dilapidated relic."

"But . . . what about the money troubles?" Joey asked.

"We've still got those," Marjorie said. "That's why Arbela and Bunny are pulling out. They can't save Oasis, but Daniel's working on it. So I decided to stop worrying. Excuse me," she said, going to help with the raffle tickets to the Moondance.

"You really think Oasis will be all right?" Joey asked Berta. "I've been so worried about Grief Group."

"Just keep on doing Grief Group," Berta said, patting her arm. "Everything will be fine." ·

As Berta went to help her art students hang their work on the fence, Joey remained unsure about what she'd just heard. Then she saw Heidi walking towards her, leading a group of prospective students, like the ones she'd been bringing to Oasis for months. Joey walked in the opposite direction.

Since their time together in the office, Joey and Heidi had given each other a wide berth, two cats stalking the same territory, tails high.

"Daniel should ban her from Oasis," Marjorie sniffed every time she saw Heidi. "She's always spying on everything."

But no more violations had been filed. And Heidi had taken it upon herself to increase enrollment, something Oasis desperately needed.

"I met her at Weight Watchers," said the first several women she brought in.

"At the dog park," said the next group.

"At Marshall's." "At the DMV." "I subscribe to her blog about Oasis." "She posted a yoga meetup online."

Everywhere Heidi went, it seemed, she recruited people to sign up for classes at Oasis.

"Maybe she's done taking revenge?" Joey mused one afternoon as she drilled holes in a board on the lawn while Lexus and Armani sunned themselves.

"Women like that are never done," Marjorie told Lexus and Armani.

When the afternoon skies began to darken early, Joey took to driving the streets to catch the sunset. She discovered she was finding her way around town; she discovered that, even in Los Angeles, the leaves turned.

One afternoon she pulled over on a street lined with flaming red Liquidambar trees. That night she brought in 14 five-pointed red leaves to Group: one for each of them, one for each of their late spouses.

As October came to a close the Group began to talk about Halloween. Gravestones on lawns, skeletons hanging from trees, R.I.P. signs everywhere. Seen through their eyes, Halloween sounded like a waking nightmare.

Joey had never thought about how much death played a part in the holiday. To grievers and their children, she realized, it was about much more than dressing up in costumes and trick-or-treating.

She wanted to help them. But how? She thought about it at night as she lay in bed. Then, one morning as she swam, Joey had an idea. It was wacky, but it was something they could do together on Halloween. It would be a celebration of life in a year of death.

When she mentioned the idea at the next Grief Group meeting it was met with raucous reactions. So Joey went ahead with the plans, even if throwing the party at Oasis on a Saturday night could prove to be dicey.

At an elegant, dark restaurant in Beverly Hills, Heidi and Gus Green were finishing up their meeting with a slender brunette wearing a pinstriped suit. Gloria Morgan, CFO of the Foundation, was pleased with what she'd heard about the purchase of Oasis. She accepted the percentage the Foundation would receive as "straw buyers" for Regency Properties.

"But I have one question," Gloria said. "How do we know the community won't create a flap when we close down Oasis and build on the site? It's been there for what, 40 years? If the community objects to an office building, they could wreak havoc with the zoning board."

"I've taken care of that," Heidi said. She pulled her yellow lined pad out of the white canvas bag. "I've been tracking ethical violations at Oasis over the past nine months. One teacher in particular has been out of control. I'm monitoring the Oasis website for more activity from her. I'm following her every move."

"And the relevance of that?" Gloria Morgan asked.

"When the zoning board hears about these ethical infractions, it should quash any protests about closing down the place. There's plenty of wrongdoing at Oasis."

"Good work, Ms. Berne," Gloria Morgan said.

"Call me Heidi," she said with a smile.

Chapter Thirty-three

"Perfecto?" Joey whispered through the small gap in the locked wooden fence to Oasis on Halloween. No answer from the other side. She peered through the 6:00 semi-darkness. Was that Perfecto unlocking the front door of the board room as he'd promised Marjorie?

Joey struggled for the welcome sound of keys unlocking doors. All she heard was a breeze that rustled the dry leaves and made her button up the pea coat she'd bought at the Army-Navy Surplus in Venice.

Beams of light sliced through the darkness behind her. She turned to face the headlights. Marjorie's battered blue Nissan pulled up alongside Joey's Honda.

When Marjorie opened the car door and stepped out, Joey saw that her friend was decked out in a black wig, a tight red shirt with huge sleeves, ruffled blue bellbottom pants, and white patent leather platforms.

"You look hot," Joey said.

"Thanks. Trying to find something hip in my size is damn near impossible. It's either for a 98-year-old woman or a 14-year-old hooker," Marjorie laughed. "Here," she said, thrusting a bag into Joey's arms. "One mirrored disco ball, one motor, six colored lights, four lava lamps."

"Where did you get all this?"

"www.disco.com. I've got a lot more stuff in the car. How do you like my outfit?"

"I love it. It's *you*."

Marjorie peered at Joey in the dark. "What are you doing in jeans and tennies?"

"My costume's in the car. I'm going to change after we set up the room." She looked through the little gap in the gate. "*If* we ever get in there."

"No Perfecto?"

"Damned if I know. Didn't you give him the keys?"

"I did. But where's his truck?" Marjorie asked. They didn't see it.

"Maybe he's not here."

"Maybe he parked on the street," Marjorie said. "Or maybe he's waiting for me to do the Funky Chicken before he shows." She fluffed out her elbows and squawked loudly, high-stepping around the parking lot. Joey laughed so hard she had to lean against the gate for support. When a hand unlocked it from inside, the gate opened and she almost tumbled in face first.

"Got it, Senora," Perfecto said calmly, one hand under her elbow.

"Thanks a million."

The board room doors were open, lights blazing from within.

"Okay," Marjorie said, talking into her cell. "So," she said in announcer's voice, "we're about to attend the 'First Ever Dirty Death Dance Disco Ball' for every Grief Group member who comes in a disco costume with a killer song to dance to. Think it'll be fun? Stay tuned." She pointed her phone at the board room, shot for a moment and pressed "stop."

"What are you doing?" Joey asked.

"Making a little video. I'm going to put it on YouTube. This is going to be a blast."

Over the next hour Joey, Marjorie, and Perfecto moved the table and chairs out of the center of the room to create a dance floor, hung the mirrored disco ball from the ceiling, hooked up the motor to make it turn, and mounted the red, blue and purple-colored spotlights, positioning them so they hit the mirrored ball at strategic angles.

Marjorie shot video as they set up an iPod disco mix, tossed glitter over the floor, and plugged in Lava Lamps. Beanbags were set up in corners; non-alcoholic punch and cookies went on tables. Marjorie and Joey bumped butts as they danced to the Pointer Sisters while they spread out the last of the disco props. Their final move was to burn sandalwood incense to cover the stale lilac scent embedded in the pine paneling.

"We're wiping out a decade and a half of the FM's Board meetings," she said into her phone with a wink.

Just before 7:00, Perfecto was on his way home and the room was ready. Marjorie turned up the music. Joey hustled to the women's room where she wriggled into her rented scarlet-tasseled disco mini-dress and high-heeled pink patent leather boots. She sprayed pink streaks into her long brown hair before she raced back to the board room, arriving just behind Del.

Marjorie shot footage as Del strode in wearing a slinky maroon shirt with wide lapels, a white vest, and the tightest of black pants. Marjorie greeted him with a jive handshake. To Joey's surprise, he jived her back with a whoop of laughter.

"Whoo hoo," a voice shouted. Joey turned to see Alli roll past her at top speed on orange suede roller skates. She wore a tiny pink, orange, and green-flowered mini, her face and long blonde hair dappled with glitter. Rick slid in after her, wearing a skintight midnight-blue outfit. He caught her around the waist before Alli crashed into the refreshments table.

"This is so groovy, Joey," Alli yelled above the loud music from across the room. "What a fun Halloween party." "We Are Family" came on. Alli pulled Rick out on the dance floor, Del started to boogie by himself, and the party was on.

Maggie, nine months pregnant and due 10 days ago, waddled in wearing a rainbow-hued Mama Cass muumuu with a hundred little pleats that sparkled as she twirled in the colored lights.

Joey crossed to her. "How are you feeling?"

"Like a whale."

"A whalette," Marjorie clucked, joining them and shooting footage.

Maggie scanned the Group. "I thought he'd be here."

She meant Dave.

"Me, too," Joey agreed, trying to cover her concern. "I called several times and told him about tonight. I'm sure he'll come."

Two weeks ago, after Group, a fight between Dave and Del had broken out in the parking lot. They'd heard about it from Rick, the last to drive out that night. Since then Dave hadn't made it to the next Group and hadn't answered any calls, and Del wouldn't talk about it. Joey found that worrisome, but there was nothing she could do about it tonight, so she put her worries aside as someone else arrived.

"Hey there." Tamara stood in the doorway in a tiny and tight white waitress costume, fishnets, and a little white hat.

"You look smokin'," Alli shouted, skating to Tamara.

Maggie, looking like a hot air balloon on flamingo legs, waddled over to join the knot of women.

On the dance floor, Del moved, lost in his own world. His hips swiveled as he swayed and rocked to the music. His lips were parted in a grin. He was a beautiful, amazing dancer.

But Joey grew anxious as she watched him. Because Del was higher than the Hollywood sign, and the party hadn't even started.

Chapter Thirty-four

Three Harvey Wallbangers later, Tamara stood on the sidelines, leaning against the wall for support. Flashing lights glinted off the mirrored ball. Music blared, and the dance floor was crowded with the sweaty, crazed Group. Tamara had no idea how the booze got there, but she'd had plenty of it.

It had something to do with a box Del had smuggled in. When it turned out Alli used to work as a bartender and Maggie's uncle owned a bar in Denver, the Wallbangers began to flow. Then came Tequila Sunrises after Del produced a tank of tequila and some glass beakers he'd filched from the lab for shot glasses. Marjorie captured it all on video.

Tamara had been standing near Joey when somebody spiked her punch with a stiff shot of tequila. Now, Joey's face was flushed, her body loose, and Tamara thought she'd never looked better.

Then again, Tamara thought, *the rest of us look pretty good too. Here we are on a Saturday night, the loneliest night of the week, partying like the last year never happened. Except for Dave and Sam. Where is Sam?* Tamara wondered.

Joey called out, "Will somebody get out there already?" She looked over at Tamara. "Okay, Tamara. Time you showed us what you're doing in that hot little waitress getup. Right, Group?"

"Tam-ra, Tam-ra," Alli started to shout. Everyone else joined in, clapping to the beat of her name. Tamara stepped forward. She was ready to rock to a Donna Summers tune when a male voice yelled from the doorway.

"Yo. My turn, baby!"

John Travolta walked in with long sideburns, tight white suit, black shirt, and shiny black platform shoes. He strode to the Bose, slipped in a CD, and jacked up the volume. A familiar funky syncopated bass, open hi-hat, and lush synth chords boomed. His hips swayed as he strode to the center of the room and posed, his right hand pointing to the ceiling, index finger up, left hand pointing down, right foot beating to the music.

Everyone started to scream as the falsetto voices of the Bee Gees sang "Stayin' Alive" and Tamara watched with wonder as Sam, the straight-arrow Classics professor, slid, strutted, pivoted on his toes, shook his booty. He was loose-hipped liquid sex. Sam—mild-mannered Sam—drove them all wild.

Especially me, thought Tamara.

Especially when he pulled her into the center of the room and twirled her around, over and over until she was dizzy with movement and lust and energy.

The air in the board room crackled. The mirrored ball spun. Everyone flooded the dance floor. They jumped; they shouted; they danced in couples, in groups, in one big circle. Everyone sang and screamed: *"Life goin' nowhere, Somebody help me, Ha ha ha ha, stayin' alive . . ."* Energy. Sex. Life. *"Ha, ha, ha, ha, We're stayin' alive . . . ,"* they yelled. They meant every word. And Marjorie captured it all on video.

We're out of control. Every single person in this room, including me, Joey realized.

It was only 9:30, and it felt like 3:00 in the morning.

While the rest of the city is going trick-or-treating, Grief Group One is having a Bacchanalian orgy in the board room, thanks to me.

Even as her raised arms waved from side to side and her hips gyrated and her voice sang to the music, questions surfaced through Joey's stupor. *Are they ready for this craziness?*

Then everyone was moving across the floor to Alli's song, "Y.M.C.A." Sam had tossed his jacket off to the side, and Del's shirt was open to the waist. Tamara's waitress cap sat cockeyed on her head, Joey's mini had lost half of its tassels. Rick's fluid moves defied description, and even Maggie, huge with child, danced up a storm. Only Dave was missing.

Why is he staying away? Joey wondered.

Maggie brought them all outside into the chilly Halloween night, where a fire blazed in the fire pit. She swayed to a Karen Carpenter song, which she dedicated to Jeff.

Then the slow dance morphed into the rhythmic chords of *Hair*, and that turned into Tamara appearing with a pair of scissors, cutting off a lock of her hair and tossing it into the fire. Soon everyone else was cutting a lock of their hair and throwing it in, dancing in a mad ceremonial romp around the blaze. Marjorie kept on shooting video. They were too nuts to stop, too wired to wind down. When the Jackson 5 came on, they streamed back into the board room and danced, wilder than ever.

I've got to slow this down, Joey thought. *But how?*

Alli skated by. "Come," she slurred, grabbing Joey's hand and dragging her to a dark corner of the room. "Did you know about Del?" She peered into Joey's face, then looked back at the dance floor and moaned softly.

"Did I know *what* about Del?"

"That he was a sex god?"

Joey shook her head. "No." *There are some other things I know about Del,* she dimly remembered with alarm. *What, exactly?*

"Look."

Alli took Joey's face in her hands and turned her head so she was looking squarely at him dancing. Del was mouthing the words as he pounded his feet, swiveled his hips, and shook his ass. Every inch of his body was one with the music. He was in ecstasy.

"I had no idea," Joey said.

"Me neither," Alli sighed. "And to think—he turned me down."

"When?"

"When I showed up at his house and told him I've always wanted to do it with a gay guy."

"With a come-on like that I can't imagine why he said no."

"I know—right?" Alli shrugged, missing the sarcasm.

"Maybe you'll get lucky tonight."

"I already am," Alli replied, sitting down so fast she almost fell off the beanbag chair. "Just seeing him dance makes me the luckiest girl in L.A."

Joey watched Alli watch the liquid motion of the man they'd known for nine months and never imagined had this side to him. Alli was rapt, her face keen with longing. Joey wondered if she was hungry for a time when tragedy was a word to describe a play, not something that Alli woke up with every morning.

They sat together, glued to the sight of Del coming alive. Until he grimaced, grabbed his chest, and collapsed.

Chapter Thirty-five

Tamara screamed. Joey ran over and crouched beside Del. He was deathly still.

"Somebody call a doctor," Alli yelled, terrified.

Joey felt time stop. The music continued to play. She smelled the vodka on Del's breath, the sandalwood incense she'd burned with Marjorie, and something she would later realize was the smell of fear. Her own fear.

"Do we call 911?" Maggie asked in a high-pitched voice. She grabbed Tamara's hand.

Marjorie was already punching in the number.

"Let's see if he comes to," Tamara said as Sam bent to help Del.

Joey shook off her terror and checked Del's pulse.

"He's breathing," Sam announced.

"C'mon, people," Joey ordered. "Let's give him some air."

Everyone moved back as Del opened his eyes. They were glassy and unfocused. "What's going on?"

Joey, instantly sober, stared at him with alarm. "You were dancing and you passed out. How do you feel?"

"Fine," Del slurred.

Del took in Joey and Sam hovering and the rest of them just staring. He drew a breath and color flooded back into his face.

"I'm fine. Just give me a minute."

"Would someone get him a glass of water?" Joey asked.

Marjorie called 911 back. "Cancel the earlier call."

Sam got the water, and Del slowly rose to his feet. "Are you sure you're all right?" Sam asked.

"We can take you to the hospital, man," Rick suggested.

"I told you, I'm fine," Del insisted curtly.

"But you were grabbing your chest. Like you had a heart problem." Joey put a hand on his arm.

Del pushed her hand away. "Nothing happened to my heart. It's hot in here. I must have gotten dehydrated, that's all. Would everyone calm down? Sheesh!" He shook his head in disbelief at the fuss they were making, with no trace of the wild animal he'd been moments before.

"Let me get you some more water," Sam suggested.

"I can get it myself," Del said. He walked unsteadily to the refreshments table as the rest of them looked at each other and looked away, instantly solemn.

To Joey, the colored glints of mirrored light now seemed to reveal them for what they were: widows and widowers decked out in foolish costumes. It was Halloween, and the specter of death, their old best friend, had just returned. *The party's over,* she realized.

"Okay," she announced in a deliberately light tone. "Let's break this disco down. We need to put the room back together, starting with that disco ball. Who's good on a ladder?"

Joey felt a flash of alarm when Sam climbed the ladder and Tamara helped him take down the mirrored ball. *What if he falls?* she worried. After Del, she felt acutely aware of the possible peril she'd put all of them in.

Marjorie began to collect the disco props. Del insisted on breaking down the fire pit despite Joey's protests. Alli bent to pick up the glitter from the floor. Her black lace thong revealed itself under her mini. They all looked. They all looked away. They were used to Alli by now.

Thirty minutes later the board room was back to normal, and everyone was gathered on the darkened parking lot.

"Anyone want to go trick-or-treating?" Alli called out.

"How about nightcaps at the Waverly Tavern?"

A round of yeses rang out, except for Sam. He had to get back to Andrew's babysitter. Tamara, who was driving Maggie home, exchanged a look with Sam that told Joey they'd see each other later at the duplex.

"I'm calling it a night, guys," Joey said. "And maybe you should too." She looked at Del.

"I've got rounds," he said, getting into his Porsche. He drove away before she could say a word.

Joey walked Maggie and Tamara to her car.

"God, I'm beat," Maggie said.

"Time to get you home. Put those little swollen ankles up." Tamara opened her car door.

"Oh, shit," Maggie yelped.

"What?" Tamara looked down at a trickle of water running down Maggie's legs. Joey looked, too. Around them, headlights were turning on. Cars were starting. Joey ran towards Sam's car as he headed to the exit, waving her hands in the beam of his headlights. Sam came to a stop. His car door opened. Rick came running to Joey. Alli skated over.

"Maggie's water just broke."

They ran back to Tamara's car, where Maggie was sitting calmly in the front seat.

"I'm thinking Elvira if it's a girl, Dracula for a boy. Anyone got a better name for a Halloween baby?"

In his living room Dave's head moved in time to the song from the

TV. His arms swung, his feet tried to boogie, even if they weren't sure they could.

It was Saturday night, and he was dancing without his sticks. Not exactly dancing, more like shuffling. He was throwing his own personal "Dirty Death Dance Disco Ball."

"Sun's coming out
Behind a cloud
Nothing to do
Nowhere to be
Da da da da . . . "

It was past 10:00, and the pretty blonde singer sang, shimmied, and shook on *Saturday Night Live.* He had the volume turned up loud so he wouldn't hear the phone.

"Please come," Alli had pleaded on his voicemail. "Just show up at Oasis on Saturday night. Please, Dave? The party won't be the same without you."

"Are you okay?" Joey had said.

"Where are you?" Sam asked.

"Pick up," Tamara said. "Pick up, Dave."

"Dammit."

"When the hell are you coming back?"

"You promised not to do this, Dave. You *need* to call me back." That was from Joey.

The toughest messages were from Maggie. "I thought we were friends," she said, "but friends don't scare each other like this. I don't understand what's going on. *Please* call me."

He hadn't called anyone back. What would he say?

Del had shown his hand on the night of the last Group Dave attended. After everyone else had driven away, Del had confronted Dave.

"You're a fucking liar," Del said. Then he told Dave what he'd found out about the night Caro died.

"And you're a fucking faggot," Dave had snarled back, feeling trapped and furious. He'd gotten into his car and peeled out.

Going to the "Dirty Death Dance Disco Ball" would've meant walking into a trap. There he'd be, surrounded by the Group. And there would be Del, probably wearing a devil costume and waiting for the perfect moment to expose Dave.

Dave didn't want to picture Maggie's face when she learned the truth. He'd lose her friendship, of course, and the thought of more loss made him want to puke.

The snap-happy lyrics pulled him back. Dave shuffled in time to the beat. He tried to convince himself that he was happy to be alone tonight, even if he knew better, until the beat changed, adding new percussion, except it wasn't in time to the tune. Somebody was banging, hard, on his door. He heard a woman's voice shouting. "Goddammit, Dave, open this door. Maggie's in labor, and she ordered me to come and get you."

Dave opened the door to find Tamara dressed in a tiny waitress outfit and black fishnets.

"Nice getup."

"I'll yell at you later," she promised as she marched in, strode to the hall closet, yanked it open, pulled out a jacket and tossed it his way. "But first I'm taking you to the hospital. Now."

Alli and Joey helped Maggie out of the car and into the Emergency entrance of the hospital. Sam and Rick drove off on a Chinese food run; Tamara was out on the Dave roundup.

"She's in labor," Joey told the security guard. "Where do we go?"

The guard pointed down the hall. "Admissions."

They walked Maggie over, stopping when her contractions hit. Alli timed them while Joey went ahead to get the process started. Soon Maggie was sitting in a chair at the window of a hostile intake clerk.

"But I have a birth plan," Maggie insisted. "I'm delivering in the Birthing Suite, not the Maternity Ward."

"I heard you the first time, Miss. You can sort all that out on the ninth floor."

"But the Birthing Suite isn't on the ninth floor!"

"And like I said, you can't enter this hospital until you've filled out these forms. So you'd better get started."

"What's the matter with you people? All you ever talk about is forms." Maggie's loud voice caused others to look their way. "I'm so sick of filling out fucking forms I could vomit."

The clerk shrugged. "You want to have your baby here, fill out those forms. Or have your husband fill them out for you." She closed the window firmly.

Maggie swept the stack of forms off the counter, and they scattered all over the floor. "My husband is *dead*, God damn you. I'm having his baby, and he'll never see it." She started sobbing through a contraction.

"Maggie," Joey soothed. "We'll help you."

"Of course we will," Alli said as she bent to pick up the forms.

They moved Maggie away from the clerk. Alli continued to time her contractions. For the next 15 minutes Joey wrote down Maggie's name, address, Social Security number, insurance carrier, policy number, etc., etc. It was only when she got to "Spouse's Information" that she understood the problem.

"Deceased," Joey wrote over and over again. That's when she realized the heartache an ordinary form could pose.

After all the forms were filled out and Maggie signed them, Joey brought them back to the window. The clerk slid it open, checked the forms, ripped off hospital copies, and handed them back to Joey along with a white plastic bracelet printed with Maggie's name and patient number.

"Tsk," the woman said with a shake of her head. "I wouldn't want to be *her* labor nurse. That's one angry woman."

"And you're one stupid cow," Joey snapped. She grabbed the forms and slammed the window closed for emphasis.

An hour later, Joey was sitting on a chair across from the Group in the waiting room of the Birthing Suite. Half-empty Chinese food cartons were spread all around them.

"Listen to this one, guys," Alli said, reading from a fortune cookie. "*Dreams are sweet but life is sweeter.*"

Joey wished this *was* a dream. At least then she could wake up and it would all be over. Instead, there they were, Maggie's team, in wilted disco costumes, feeding each other with chopsticks, downing black coffee by the gallon in hopes of getting sober, playing Words with Friends on their iPhones.

Joey shook her head at an evening that had gone off the rails and wouldn't end. She looked at Sam with regret. He had wanted to be anywhere but here. Alli was still wearing her orange skates, and Rick was in his skintight disco outfit. *We're hardly the poster children for a Grief Group,* Joey thought with a sinking heart. *Especially me.*

For the past hour they'd taken turns hanging out with Maggie. They all knew she'd been crying on and off and asking when Dave was coming. None of them knew if or when Dave would show.

Joey's head was pounding as she got up and walked to the women's room.

"What's wrong?" Rick asked from behind her.

"Where do I start?"

"How about at the beginning?"

If Joey had been thinking she would have realized she shouldn't be unloading to a member of Grief Group. But she was too upset to think. "I threw a party in the board room, where the Grief Group got drunk and disorderly, and I drank when I was supposed to be in charge, only I bailed. And if that wasn't enough, we could have lost Del." Her voice was shaking. "Everything I did tonight was reckless. I'm not a responsible leader, I'm an idiot. And now here's poor Sam, where he never wanted to be again. I shouldn't be in charge of a colony of ants, let alone all of you." Joey was close to tears by the time Rick put a kind hand on her shoulder.

"I think you're missing the point of the evening," he said.

"Did you not hear any of that?"

"Did you take a look at the Group?"

"Seriously?"

"Look again." He turned her around to face them.

The Group was sitting on couches, resting their feet in each other's laps, dueling with chopsticks, tossing fried noodles at each other.

"Yes?"

"Look at them," Rick insisted. "How old do they look?" Joey looked at Alli's wide smile and Sam's easy shoulders. She looked at Rick and she saw it. No worry lines, no creased foreheads. "We actually look our age," Rick confirmed, "for the first time since Group began, thanks to you."

Sam plucked dried noodles from his hair and wore them as earrings. Alli couldn't stop giggling.

"Still," Joey said. "I broke every rule in the book."

"Why did you throw that party?"

Joey thought for a moment. "I wanted you guys to have fun. To do what you might have done if you hadn't lost your spouse. I wanted you to have a good memory to look back on in a year of hell. I knew you were ready for it."

"You did that. It was a gift, Joey. Now will you relax?"

He reached over and began to rub her shoulders. For one moment she closed her eyes and stopped worrying about the fallout from this evening, about Rick's hands on her shoulders, about Del's problem and whether Dave would ever show up. She leaned against the corridor wall as Rick's fingers soothed away the tension in her neck and shoulders for a few delicious moments. Then she opened her eyes and remembered whose hands were on her shoulders.

"You're in Group. I'm your leader. Thank you, but this is another thing I shouldn't be doing." She moved away.

"No worries," Rick said, going back to the others.

Daniel. The full weight of how much she missed him came over Joey. His voice in her ear. His hands on her body. She shook her head to clear the memories as she spied Del striding by.

She followed him into a tiny break room lined with soda and coffee machines. He was putting coins into a machine as she entered.

"That dress looks a little worse for the wear," he said without turning.

"I have to talk to you."

"I'm on duty." He stabbed a button. Black coffee poured into a cup.

"I know this is not the time or the place, but you haven't returned any of my calls."

"Joey. I work in the ER. I don't even have time to return my mother's calls." Del reached for the full cup. "Right now I have a patient going up to Neurosurgery, so whatever this is, it will have to wait till the next Group." He crossed to the door.

Joey moved to block his exit. "You could have died tonight, Del."

"Spare me."

"I know you're on painkillers," she said. "Percodan or Oxy or . . . "

"I don't have time for this shit. I've got patients. . . . "

"And you've got a drug problem."

"Stop judging me," Del said.

"I'm not judging you. I'm concerned about you. I saw you popping pills at the swim party. You're restless and irritable. Tonight you almost went into cardiac arrest. You have all the symptoms of addiction."

"I've got work to do."

"I know how much pain you're in over losing Shawn. You couldn't save him, you can't save yourself, so you're self-medicating. But what if you make a mistake on a patient when you're high and the hospital finds out why?"

"Are you threatening to tell them your suspicions?" Del regarded her with hostility.

"Maybe it would be best if the hospital knew. Then you'd have to face this."

Del took a step towards her. She could smell his sweat and his fear. "You've got bigger problems than me," he said. "Someone in Group has been lying since day one, and you don't have a frigging clue."

Dave, Joey thought.

Del looked past her at the sound of the heavy double doors opening into the Birthing Suite. "Speak of the devil," he said, pointing behind her. Joey turned to see Dave slowly making his way down the hall.

"What has he been lying about?" she asked.

"Everything. His wife wasn't hit by a drunk driver."

"How do you know?"

"Because I can read people and he read phony as a three-dollar bill. So I did a little looking around and a little asking and found out what really happened."

"But . . . why would you do that?"

"Because you weren't on his case, so somebody had to do it." Out in the corridor, she heard the Group noisily greeting Dave. "Focus on a real problem, Joey, not one you've invented. Ask Dave to tell you what happened that night."

Del pushed past her and headed down the corridor towards Dave. As Joey watched they exchanged a tense look before Del passed him, shoving the double doors open so hard they smashed against the walls.

Joey was left in the doorway to catch her breath before heading out to greet her next "problem child."

Chapter Thirty-six

Seven hours later, when Dave walked into Maggie's birthing room again, a dozen pink and blue balloons scuttled across the ceiling. They'd been doing that all night, every time someone walked in or out, which had happened often. Because Maggie's labor was stalled.

Dave walked to her bed and watched her doze. She was exhausted from contractions and hooked to a fetal monitor. He looked down at the app he'd installed on his phone. It told him how long since the last contraction. As her closed eyelids blinked rapidly, Dave wondered, *Is she dreaming about her baby? Or about Jeff, the man who should be here instead of me?*

Alli dozed on one side of Maggie. Tamara rubbed her feet.

"Robin, the midwife, was just in here," Tamara whispered to Dave. She and Alli were still in their disco costumes.

"And . . . ?"

"I don't know."

"I'll go talk to her," Dave whispered.

Tamara went back to rubbing Maggie's feet. Dave headed out to find her midwife.

He thought about how Maggie had put together the perfect birth plan, everything from the choice of this cheerful room with a window in the Birthing Suite to the ideal midwife to the photos of Jeff on the bedside table to the teddy bears, one pink, one blue, waiting to greet her little one. Maggie had elected not to know the gender.

"This birth is going off without a hitch," she'd insisted in Group. "Not like the last nine damn months."

But the hitch is turning out to be her own body, Dave thought, *which is not cooperating to let her baby into the world.*

Throughout the night he'd seen Robin, a middle-aged woman with black braids and an air of supreme calm, check on Maggie every couple of hours. She'd gotten her up to walk the corridors and told her to rest when she could.

"I'm only here in case of emergency," Dave overheard her say to Joey at 3:00 AM.

"You're very calm," Joey observed.

"I've been at hundreds of births, and each one is different. Babies come when they're ready. I stay out of the way until I'm needed."

Dave walked down the corridor to stand in front of Robin, who was dozing, wrapped in a blue shawl. She woke up. "What's happening?"

"Nothing," Dave said. "She's taking her time and that's okay—right? I mean, for the baby."

"Let's see what the fetal monitor looks like," Robin said.

Dave followed behind her, past the waiting room where the Group snoozed on couches, sleeping close. They'd taken turns all night helping Maggie into and out of bed, walking her down the hall, rubbing her feet and her back, holding her hands, feeding her ice chips, reassuring her she could do this.

In Maggie's room Robin studied the fetal monitor. "The baby's heartbeat's depressed and Maggie's still stuck at nine centimeters."

"What does that mean?" Maggie asked, suddenly awake.

"If labor goes on much longer your baby could go into fetal distress." Her hands moved over Maggie's abdomen.

288 · LINDA SCHREYER AND JO-ANN LAUTMAN

"Then what happens?" Dave reached for Maggie's hand as another contraction caused her to moan in pain. She talked through gritted teeth. "What if that happens?" she repeated.

"They'll have to do a Caesarian."

"No. That's not in my birth plan." Maggie looked at Dave. "Tell Robin. No fucking Caesarian. I'm having my baby naturally."

Her voice was raw. Dave was determined to help her if he could. "Is there anything she can do to help her dilate all the way?"

Robin took Maggie's hands. "You're doing everything right, sweetie. You've got your team here. They're doing everything they can to help. You've been a trouper all night long but you're exhausted."

"Tell me what to do. I need to have this baby naturally." Maggie spoke with urgency.

"Okay," Robin agreed. "Let's get you up and walking again."

Tamara and Alli fetched Maggie's big pink robe and fuzzy slippers. Robin and Dave helped her get out of bed and onto her feet. When she doubled over in pain, Dave hesitated.

"Get her out there," Robin insisted. "She's got to be on her feet."

The women walked out of the room while Dave hung back. Joey joined the others in the labor walk as Maggie traveled down the hall, doubled over.

Robin watched. "She's tough, that one," she said to Dave.

"Anything else you can suggest?" Dave asked.

She hesitated. "Sometimes when this happens it's because some sadness hasn't been dealt with, something that blocks a joyous birth from taking place. Does that sound right?"

"She lost her husband nine months ago."

"Maggie told me. I've seen this happen before."

"And?"

Robin didn't answer for a moment. "Are you her boyfriend?"

"More like a friend who's a guy."

"Obviously you care about her. Maybe you can do something to help this along."

"Anything."

"She needs to get past where she's stuck because that's keeping this baby stuck, too. Perhaps there's something she's told you, something you know that can help her get past that?"

Robin's question rattled around in his head for a silent moment. As she moved away, a long-ago memory grabbed hold of Dave, something that might help Maggie.

He went to look for Tamara. Alli said she'd gone downstairs with Sam to make a call on her cell phone outside the hospital. Dave found her sitting in her parked car with Sam.

"Hey, pal," Dave said as he approached the car. "Can I hitch another ride?"

Thirty minutes later Tamara was waiting for Dave outside Maggie's apartment while she thought about her earlier call to Rosalba.

It was 6:00 in the morning when Rosalba answered on the first ring.

"It's Tamara. I'm still at the hospital. Is everything okay?"

"Ai, Meesy . . . " Rosalba started to cry.

"What is it?" Tamara's voice rose. "Did something happen to Maya?"

"She's been out all night. I tried calling you, but no reception."

"I'm coming home. I'll be there in half an hour." She ran to Sam. "Maya's missing. I've got to go home."

"I'll go with you."

As she raced out to the car Sam pulled out his cell. "Pick me up at the entrance," he yelled.

When she pulled up, Sam was standing outside looking calm. He opened the car door and poked his head in.

"Maya's fine."

"What?"

He got into the passenger seat. "I called the babysitter who was watching Andrew. Maya came down around midnight. She's been there ever since." Sam's babysitter said Maya was concerned about Andrew being without Sam for the whole night, a first. "She's sound asleep on the floor next to his crib right now."

"Oh, God," Tamara slumped. Terror oozed out of her pores, quickly replaced by anger. "What do I do with her? She scared Rosalba to death. And me, too."

"How about we sort this out when we get home later?"

"Hey pal," said a voice nearby. It was Dave.

Now, parked in front of Maggie's apartment, Tamara's tired brain was working overtime. *What is it about kids?* she thought. *Do they live just to torture us?*

The front door opened as she pondered questions with no answers. Dave walked towards her with something bulky under his arm. "Home, James," he said, sliding into the passenger seat.

She rolled down the window, and they drove to the hospital in tired silence. When they parked Dave reached for his poles.

"Give me that bundle," Tamara suggested.

"No. I can carry it *and* use the sticks."

They made slow progress to the Birthing Suite where they saw a knot of people huddled outside Maggie's room. Alli skated over.

"What's happening?" Dave asked.

"It's not going well." Her eyes were red. "The baby's in distress. The docs kicked us out. They're prepping her to go to the OR for a Caesarian."

Dave took his hands out of his metal poles. They clattered to the floor noisily as he shoved the bundle into Alli's arms. "Get that to Joey. Wait

for me to open it. Go!" Alli took off, skating down the hall like a roller
derby champ. Dave hooked his arm in Tamara's. "Help me get there. Fast."

As she struggled to steady him Rick jogged over. "Need a hand?"

"Please," Tamara begged.

"I've got to get to Maggie. Now."

Tamara let go of Dave as Rick lifted Dave's left arm, draped it over
his shoulder and half-lifted, half-dragged him down the hall and into
Maggie's room. Tamara ran after them, arriving as Dave pushed past the
knot of people to Maggie's side.

The small room was filled with an ob-gyn, a labor nurse, and an
anesthesiologist. They conferred hurriedly while Robin talked to Maggie.
Joey held the bundle Dave had just sent.

"No!" Maggie cried out.

"They have to do this, or you could lose the baby."

Maggie's loud wail filled the room as Dave got to her side. "Maybe
this will help," he said.

Tamara arrived as Dave reached for the bundle in Joey's hands, telling
her to hold onto one end. Dave started to unwrap it, backing up across
the room as the folded cloth unfurled into something so large it forced
the medical team to step into the doorway.

"What are you doing . . . ?" the ob-gyn asked angrily.

Dave ignored them, asking the rest of the Group to hold onto the
cloth until it was completely unfurled. Every Group member held up
Maggie's American flag, the one she'd brought to Group so long ago

Tears of joy and sorrow streamed down Maggie's cheeks. Dave handed
his end to Rick and came to her bedside. He leaned close, brushing the
hair off her forehead. "Jeff's here," he said softly, his voice breaking. "He's
right here with you." Maggie's tears turned to sobs. Dave stroked her
forehead. "You're not alone . . . "

As Maggie looked from Dave to the flag, something heavy lifted from inside her. A deep well of sorrow left her all at once. Tamara slipped her hand into Sam's. He held onto it tightly as the color rushed back into Maggie's face, and the medical team flooded back into the room, pushing past them.

"You people need to wait outside," ordered the ob-gyn.

"The baby's heartbeat is normal," Robin announced, watching the fetal monitor. Undeterred, the medical team moved forward, ready to spring into action while Robin felt Maggie's abdomen. "Are you ready to push?"

"Yes!" Maggie yelled.

"Go!" Robin ordered the medical team, except for the labor nurses. When the doctors protested, Robin protested louder. "I'm following my patient's directive," she repeated until they were gone. "You guys can stay," she told the surprised Group. They moved to the window to give her space. Dave joined them as Robin and the nurse helped Maggie sit up.

"Let's have a baby," Robin said.

A few pushes later, Grief Group One welcomed Maggie's tiny daughter as she slid into the world.

The Group peered with wonder and joy at the new life before them. They were honored to have been witness to a miracle.

Robin scooped up the baby and placed her on Maggie's belly. She laughed and cried as she held her daughter in her arms. Love didn't even begin to describe the look in her eyes.

While Robin cleaned up mother and baby, she and Maggie talked softly. "Dave?" Robin called out.

"Yes?"

"Can you come over?"

Dave moved to Maggie's side.

"Do you want to cut the cord?"

Dave looked at Maggie.

"Please," she said, the infant cradled in her arms.

A sob came from deep within Dave. Through his tears he managed to take the surgical scissors from Robin and cut the baby's cord before Robin swaddled the baby.

Alli's hand held Tamara's, who was holding onto Sam's; Rick and Joey leaned close. They were all barely breathing.

Dave reached for the American flag, folded it and wrapped the newborn in it over the swaddling blanket. He stood over mother and baby, tears rolling down his cheeks.

"Her name's Sophie," Maggie said softly, looking up at Dave. "Jeff wanted to name our first baby after his mother."

"Sophie . . . "

Maggie beckoned to the others. They gathered around the new life wrapped in the flag that had covered her father's coffin. Together they watched over Maggie and Jeff's daughter, the child he would never know. They marveled at the love between mother and baby. It was palpable. A solid, unbroken line of hope.

"We did it backwards," Joey murmured. "Backwards. We went from death to life."

Chapter Thirty-seven

Click.

Two weeks after the birth of Maggie's baby, on a brilliant blue-skied, unusually warm Veterans Day morning, Dave stood in the sand on Zuma Beach in Malibu, his back to the ocean, shooting the ancient sand city he'd stumbled upon.

Click.

He depressed the metal button on his Leica.

"Hey, Mister, did you build that thing?"

Dave looked over his camera. A skinny kid in faded board shorts looked down at the sand with amazement.

"Nope."

Dave shot again. The tide was coming in. No time to lose.

"Cool." The boy crouched down to get a better look. "It's, like, a whole city. And . . . whoa . . . are those, like, pyramids or something?"

"Uh-huh. And temples and cave dwellings and hieroglyphics . . . "

"Neato. Look at those walls that go all around it. How'd they make 'em look like bricks? And did you see those stairs that go from one house to the other?"

"Yup."

Click. Dave crouched, lost his balance and almost fell over.

TEARS AND TEQUILA · 295

"Whoa!" The kid reached over to steady him. "Are you okay, Mister?"

"Yeah. Thanks." The roar of the surf was growing louder. Dave walked to the opposite side of the city to take his last shots before it was too late. The boy jumped back as water surged over his feet and began to flood the city.

"Aaaggghhh!!!!!" he yelled.

Click.

"Whoever built this was nuts," the boy scoffed.

Dave took a shot. "Why?"

"'Cause it must've taken them, like, hours or all day or something, and it's gonna get wrecked in a second. Bye!" The boy kicked a little sand at the edifice, joining in its destruction before he ran off to dive into the ocean.

Dave faced the rising ocean. All this would be gone in moments. For one second he lowered the camera and looked down on the exquisite creation.

"Goodbye," he said.

He shot his last shots. Click. Of an ancient sand city of lost time. Click. And the hungry blue wave poised above it, hovering like a king cobra for one long instant as it swelled above the city. Click. Before the wave flooded the city, ravaged the walls, destroyed the temples, took down the winding staircases, and gobbled the pyramids. Click. Click. Click. Dave shot until he was standing a foot deep in the blue Pacific Ocean, looking down at a hundred tiny holes in the wet sand where an ancient city once stood.

He lowered his camera as the wave receded, put on the lens cover, and walked away, fighting tears. *Why does this hurt so much?*

As he walked to his car Dave watched wave after wave crash on the shore. Seagulls hung suspended in mid-air, their wings outstretched to catch the wind. Pelicans swooped, caught fish, swooped back up. A flock of Canada Geese flew across the cloudless sky. Watching their wings flap, he thought how easy it must be to fly straight to your destination instead of taking a treacherous, winding road like the one he'd traveled for the past nine months.

It's time to tell the truth.

The next Group was in two days. Dave planned to tell everyone then. But first he needed to tell Maggie.

"How do you want to spend Veterans Day?" he'd asked her on the phone. "I mean, there are parades and someone from the military is scheduled to speak at the Los Angeles National Cemetery in Westwood."

Maggie snorted. "I wouldn't be caught dead there. No pun intended."

"Okay." This was her first Veterans Day since Jeff died. Her call.

"Want to know why?"

"Sure."

"Because of the fucking flyover."

"The what?"

"You never heard of Air Combat USA? Neither did I, until I got a call from Jeff's major. They're going to fly over the National Cemetery in vintage fighter planes simulating aerial combat." She breathed out angrily. "Aerial combat? Wouldn't that be lovely? So I can picture Jeff's plane going down in flames."

"I understand," Dave said. "Where would you like to go?"

"I choose waffles," she said in a muffled voice that told Dave she was crying.

"Waffles, great. I know just the place."

"I choose waffles and life," she said in a broken voice.

They'd decided to have brunch before meeting the Group for a Veterans Day picnic in Griffith Park. They were relieved to have a plan for another endless holiday weekend.

As Dave walked to his car the kid boogie-boarded to shore.

"Hey!" he yelled. The kid ran up beside Dave, shaking off water like a mutt. "Is that thing all gone?"

"Yup."

"Bummer." The boy ran backwards alongside Dave. "I don't get it."

"What?"

"Why didn't the guy build it up there?" He pointed to the stretch of sand above the high water mark. "That way it could've stayed for maybe a month or a year."

Dave looked at the boy for the first time. He looked about 11 with a deep tan and slightly crossed blue eyes. "You've got a point," Dave agreed. *What does that remind me of, dammit?*

"Bye!" The kid was off again, running towards the waves, throwing himself back into the water.

Dave was exhausted by the time he made it to the parking lot. As he cleaned sand off his feet he was surrounded by cars disgorging kids with Frisbees who ran to the beach ahead of parents who trudged along with umbrellas and beach chairs.

We would have been a family, Dave thought before he could censor it.

Kevin and Melissa. He and Caro had picked out their names. First would come Kevin, who Dave hoped would be long and lean like Caro. She'd hoped he'd have Dave's sense of humor. They'd talked about the moment when Kevin would ask why his dad took so many pictures. "I'll tell him I'm obsessed with capturing moments in time that I never want to forget," Dan told Caro. "With preserving things I can't keep."

Like Caro, he realized, whom he'd frozen in amber, caught in a lie that had kept him company for the past nine months.

In his car, Dave stepped on the gas. *It's time to tell the truth,* his mind insisted, even as his stomach somersaulted at the thought. *But where will I be without that story?* he wondered as he pulled out onto Pacific Coast Highway.

He was relieved when gridlock proved to be the perfect distraction.

Chapter Thirty-eight

It was still there. On Veterans Day, the one-year anniversary of Bruce's suicide, his green windbreaker still hung in Maya's closet. How did Tamara know? She saw it when she checked to see if her daughter had stolen any clothes since the last time she'd looked.

"Find what you're looking for?" Maya stood in the doorway.

Caught, Tamara lied. "I wasn't sure if your blue sweater came back from the cleaners."

"Don't worry," Maya answered, walking in to get her sunglasses from the dresser. "I'm not a klepto anymore. Ready?"

Tamara waited for the fight to break out but Maya headed out again. So Tamara took one last glance around the room.

Posters of *The Runaways,* a recent movie about Joan Jett and the Blackhearts, were plastered on the hot pink walls alongside blowup photos of the real Joan Jett. Maya's 14th birthday present from Tamara, a polished pale wood and black Melody Maker Gibson guitar, the kind Jett played, was the most carefully tended item in the room.

The clothes rack listed beneath colored sweatshirts and ripped jeans; a long, light blue sock peeked like a tongue over the top of a half-open drawer. It was neat, for Maya.

Muchas cosas, muchas desordenar, Rosalba had insisted when they'd moved out of the old house. "The more things, the more mess," she'd translated, tossing dozens of garbage-bagfuls of Maya's junk.

Now, Tamara followed Maya to the front door, past a lit candle on a table next to Bruce's framed photo. Tamara saw her daughter's hand brush across her father's face as she passed by.

"Bye, Rosalba," Maya called out, walking out the door.

Rosalba came into the hallway, dishtowel in hand. "Bye, honey," she said. She exchanged looks with Tamara. "*Buena suerte* (Good luck)," Rosalba said, with an encouraging pat on Tamara's arm.

Maya walked down the steps of the duplex ahead of Tamara. A red and white-striped T-shirt and white jeans covered her slender body; Tamara smelled wildflower shampoo in her shiny blonde hair instead of stale Kools; Maya's eyelashes were no longer thick with globs of black mascara that made them look like hairy spiders; her only adornment was the hand-written note on the inside of her arm—"I LOVE U, DANA"—penned by her new best friend.

Tamara didn't know how it had happened, but Maya was coming back to her on a long, slow curve. Therapy had helped. Bruce's note had helped. Group had helped. Time had helped, most of all.

Even more surprising, love was back in Tamara's life. Not the love she and Bruce once had, a fire that flamed hot before it died. The love of a good friend and companion. Sam, kind father figure to Maya, father of the little boy she adored. Tamara's new significant other.

A thread of love ran between them, as plain as the square yellow vase on the dining room table. It was as unassuming as Tamara's fuzzy green robe. Somehow, love, which used to make a rare cameo appearance in her life, had taken on a starring role in all of their lives.

When Maya got to the bottom of the steps she collided with Andrew, who was scooting around the small tiled courtyard in his Batman walker.

"Ma!" Andrew yelled, his version of "Maya."

"Look at you. How fast can you go in that thing?"

Andrew shrieked with excitement when Maya vroomed him across the courtyard. Tamara saw the joy in Maya's eyes when she ran to Sam and put Andrew in his arms. She saw the warmth in Sam's face when he wished her happy shopping.

As Tamara unlocked the car she thought about Sam. They still hadn't slept together. They'd kissed. They had chemistry. They weren't seeing other people, and Tamara was ready for more. When Sam said he wasn't, she'd said fine, extra time was good. *Extra time to lose my muffintop,* she'd thought.

Two hours later, Tamara was collapsed in a chair at Macy's Teens, surrounded by bags of clothes. They'd been to Forever 21, Justice, Abercrombie's, and Wet Seal for tees and jeans and shorts and skirts. Now they were shopping for dresses.

"For the Father-Daughter Dinner Dance. Please?" Maya pleaded, coming out of the dressing room. She twirled in a lacy white mini-dress with a gold bolero jacket.

"You look amazing," Tamara said. *That damn dance,* she thought.

"Can I get it?" Maya asked in a high voice.

Tamara looked again. "Yes."

"OMG," Maya yelled. She held her phone at arm's length and sent a "selfie" to Dana.

As they waited on line to pay, Maya said, "It wasn't the clothes, Mom."

"What?"

"I didn't shoplift for the clothes."

Maya had never brought that troubling subject up before. Not in any session with the therapist that her grandparents had paid for, not in any of the dozens of fights she and Tamara had had around the dining room table with Rosalba playing referee, not in any of the screaming battles that ended with Maya or Tamara slamming off to their rooms.

The woman on line ahead of them looked to the side, like Tamara did when she didn't want to reveal she was eavesdropping. She didn't love talking about this in the line at Macy's, but she was not about to shush Maya now.

"So why did you do it?" Tamara asked.

"You used to promise to take me shopping on Saturdays. Then a client would call and you'd cancel on me. I got tired of waiting. I decided to get what I wanted."

"I'm sorry, honey. We needed the money. Your dad's business was . . . "

"I knew you didn't see those clients for the money. You preferred being with them. Like I preferred being with Daddy."

It was the truth. Maya had been a "Daddy's girl" from her first breath.

"Maybe shoplifting was my way of getting back at you."

As they inched along in the line, the woman turned around to look at them. Tamara stared her down. She didn't care who was listening. She'd waited for months to talk with Maya about this. So what if they were doing it in Macy's?

"That's very mature of you, honey."

"Dana and I talked about it the other day. We're in the *Reformed Klepto Club,* y'know? I'm sorry, Mom. I know I never said that before, but I didn't really understand. That must have been hard for you when you found out."

How did a 14-year-old get to be so wise?

"I'm sorry, too, Maya," Tamara said. "I've been a pretty lousy mom since your dad died."

"Bygones," Maya concluded. "Our turn," she said, dumping her load of clothes on the cashier's counter.

The moment was over.

Maya watched the cashier with an eagle eye as she figured out the sale price for each item. Tamara remembered shopping with Maya as a boisterous three-year-old. Tamara thought about the way Maya would run around the store, hiding under clothes-racks and scaring the daylights out of Tamara. She thought about the sullen teenager Maya had been until recently. Tamara glanced at the vibrant young woman by her side.

Maya wanted to be included in Tamara's life. Tamara wanted to be included in hers. *Are you watching, Bruce?* she thought, as her daughter reached for her hand and they walked out of the store.

Chapter Thirty-nine

Across town, Dave and Maggie were having brunch. "A super-stack of pancakes with hot apple pie topping and extra whipped cream," Maggie ordered. "And a side order of hash browns, crisp bacon, and hot maple scones with butter. Please."

The waiter scribbled on his pad.

"Two eggs, over easy, sausage," Dave said. "Hot coffee right away, please."

"Is that all?" the waiter asked.

"And a pineapple mango smoothie," Maggie added.

The waiter left. Dave began to tear his napkin into little pieces.

"What's up with you?" Maggie asked.

Dave opened his mouth to speak. Sophie, asleep in Maggie's arms, began to cry.

"Sssh," Maggie soothed, rocking her. "Be good for Uncle Davie, will you?"

Fourteen-day-old Sophie, who had straight black hair that made her look like a little Chinese baby, was dressed up for her first excursion to a café on Sunset. Wrapped in a blanket with tiny butterflies (from Alli), she wore a hand-knit pink and purple hat and vest (Tamara) over a pink onesie (Rick and the twins) and the tiniest fringed pink moccasins (Joey.)

Dave took out his camera and shot mama and baby. Picture perfect as they looked, he recalled how many times in the past two weeks he'd seen Maggie standing over the changing table with tears rolling down her cheeks. Hits of grief kept on coming.

"Asleep before the food comes," Maggie said to the baby in her arms. "You are one smart little girl." She kissed the top of the slumbering infant's head. The waiter set down Maggie's smoothie and handed Dave his coffee.

Dave took a long sip. As the warm brew slid down his throat, he remembered the perilous waters he was swimming in: he was on a first outing with the new family, getting ready to drop a nuclear bomb. *Mr. Sensitive*, he thought.

"I like this place," Maggie pronounced, slurping the last of her smoothie. "The corduroy upholstery's cool."

Dave didn't need to look around to check out the corduroy upholstery or the orange geraniums or the blue-and-white checked tablecloths. He knew it all by heart. "It's a great breakfast spot," he said.

They sat in silence. Dave drummed his fingers on the table.

"You and Caro used to come here, didn't you?"

Dave was surprised. "How did you know?"

"Because you're a mess. Are you okay being here?"

"I'm the one who suggested it—remember?" Maggie studied him quietly. He took a breath. "I need to, uh, talk about something. About the accident Caro was in that night . . . "

"Oh, wow. What about it?" Maggie was suddenly serious. But, as Dave opened his mouth before he lost his nerve, a wail came from Sophie. "Hang on," Maggie said. Sophie cried louder. "Are you hungry, sweetie?" Maggie pulled up her shirt to nurse her, but Sophie screamed even louder.

"Whoa," Dave said. "I've never heard her cry that loud. Have you?"

"I don't know," Maggie said in a tight voice.

Dave walked over to Maggie and helped her unwrap the baby, who was now screaming.

"Shit." Maggie regarded the brown stain in the baby's adorable outfit with dismay.

"You said it."

Sophie screamed in agreement.

"I have to change her." Maggie looked around, uncertain. "But where?"

"I'll take you to the bathroom. We can do this together." Dave tried to sound calm and in control. Maggie stood, holding Sophie. Dave, his nerves frayed, dropped the diaper bag when he slid it off the chair. Before he could pick it up he heard a cackle from behind him.

"What a little darling," cooed a stocky middle-aged waitress with long false eyelashes, blue eye shadow and a name tag: 'Stardust.' She picked up the diaper bag and smiled at Sophie, who was now red-faced, wailing, and looking nothing like a little darling. "How old is she?"

Maggie, sweating, shouted over the screaming. "Two weeks."

"Pee-yew," Stardust said, spying the spreading stain. "Come with me, honey. I raised five of these and cleaned up more shit than I could shovel." She turned to Dave. "Stay here, Dad, and drink your coffee. This is women's work." Stardust wrapped an arm around Maggie's waist and led her and Sophie to the restroom.

At the table Dave tried to calm down. But all he heard was the pounding of his pulse in his temples. And all he saw was the hungry blue wave hovering above the sand city of lost time. What did it remind him of?

Dave pushed his chair back and fled past the kitchen out to the back patio, where he stared over the city, unseeing.

What?

He remembered.

He and Caro lay side by side in bed in the hours before dawn, talking about death. He was flying to Sri Lanka the next day to meet a photography buddy from college. They were heading to shoot the aftermath of the tsunami.

"I just want you to know how much I love you before you go," Caro said softly, her brown hair spread over the pillow. "Because bad things can happen anytime, to anyone."

"Not to me. Superman!" He flexed his biceps.

She wasn't buying it. "Like that photographer who was just killed. One minute he was taking pictures. The next he was dead."

"Sweetheart, that was right after the tsunami. It's been over for weeks now. Nothing like that will happen to me."

"It could happen to any of us, Deek," Caro insisted. "You never know."

Dave knew he wasn't going to win this argument. He never did.

"I don't like thinking I could lose you at any moment," he said. "It's a scary thought." He pulled her close. Caro's dancer-slender body melded into his. Through her thin nightgown, her heart thrummed against his chest.

"That's why I do Buddhist meditation," she whispered. "To train myself not to dwell on fear. Or anger."

"But how can you tell if it's working? Is there some test you can take?"

"Silly. You can't know it here." Caro put her hand on his forehead. "It's not head business. You know it here." She put her hand on his chest. "It's heart business, Deek."

"I'm more interested in body business." He pushed back her hair and started to nuzzle her neck.

"Non-attachment," Caro whispered. "That's the goal."

"Non-attachment? What's that?" God, her skin felt soft.

"You live your life in every moment. You build, you love, knowing it can all go away like that." She snapped her fingers close to his ear. "Like a beautiful sand castle that's washed away by the next wave."

"Pretty poetic," Dave said as he pulled her nightgown over her head and they began to make love.

On the patio of the restaurant, Caro's vitality came roaring back to Dave on a tide of memory. The way she'd leaped across a stage, fearlessly. The way she'd loved him, fiercely. The way they'd fought, just as fiercely.

He remembered Caro, seven years after that conversation. After her mother and younger sister had died of breast cancer and Caro began to drink. Heavily. After she became someone Dave didn't know and often couldn't stand. And he became the enemy when he insisted she needed help.

It was a Saturday night 11 months earlier when Dave let himself into their house in Mar Vista. He plunked his suitcase down in the hall. He'd been out of town for two nights on VA business.

"Caro?" Dave called out.

Dirty dishes towered in the sink. Heat came off the TV. It felt like it had been on for days.

"Caro?" he yelled, heading up the stairs to their bedroom. The bed hadn't been slept in. He called Caro's best friend, who had no idea where she was. He called her older sister.

"Not again," she said.

It wasn't the first time Caro had stayed out all night. She'd come back swearing she'd been out with girlfriends, had "a bit much," and crashed on her girlfriend's couch. After the third time Dave wasn't sure he wanted to hear the truth.

This time was different. Dresser drawers were half open. Clothes were strewn all over the floor. The TV blared. She seemed to have left suddenly. Dave started calling hospitals, his hands shaking. None of them had Caro.

He rummaged through the pockets of her clothes until he found copies of bar bills. Then he set out to find her.

He drove from a bar in Silverlake to one in Hollywood to a club in Reseda to a bar in Calabasas that he recalled Caro talking about on the phone.

Loud music blasted when he opened the door into a dark and windowless room. Drinks were flowing, a live band played, the tiny dance floor was mobbed. Dave made his way to the bar, intending to show the bartender a photo of Caro on his iPhone. Then he saw her. Over in the black-and-white photo booth. Sitting on the lap of a guy from her work, someone Dave had met once or twice at a party.

"Phillip, Dave. Dave, Phillip," she giggled, unabashed as he looked down on them. "My husband, my lover," she giggled.

Dave wanted to wring her neck.

"Come," he demanded.

"Go away," she said, reaching for her drink.

"Come," Dave repeated. When he tried to pull her off the guy's lap Caro resisted. Phillip tried to come to Caro's aid, but he was wasted. Caro was tiny, and Dave's fury gave him strength. Adrenaline kicked in, and he managed to muscle her outside and across the parking lot. He was determined to get her into his car, get her home, load her up with black coffee, and get her to promise to get help. Again.

When they got to the car he opened the door and threw the keys on the seat. Caro pulled away from his grasp.

"You're hurting me," she said.

He grabbed her arm, harder. "Get in," he said.

Again, she pulled away. "Don't touch me," Caro said. "Don't you dare touch me. I'm six weeks pregnant."

Dave's mind spun back to the last time they'd made love. Months ago. Maybe four or five.

"That's right," Caro repeated, leaning so close he had to pull back from her booze-breath. "I'm having a baby, and it's Phillip's. So fuck you."

Dave slapped her across the face. Caro put her hand up to the palm print on her cheek.

"Fuck you!" she shouted.

"Let's go home," Dave shouted back. Maybe she was lying. She did that when she drank. He'd find out more in the morning.

One of his poles clattered to the ground as he tried to wrestle her into the car, but in an instant Caro slithered out of his grasp, slammed into the driver's seat, locked the door, started the car, and zigzagged out of the parking lot.

Dave started screaming her name when he saw her pull onto the wrong side of the dark stretch of road without stopping. He was still screaming it when he saw the lights of the oncoming semi truck.

When the semi slammed into his car Dave's screams were drowned out by the slam of metal on metal and the sight of the car flipping over and over with Caro at the wheel.

On the patio of the restaurant, the guilt that haunted Dave hovered like a jealous raven guarding its prey. The patio door opened. Maggie came toward him with a smile.

"Wow. Stardust changed Sophie and cleaned her up 1-2-3. Now she's sleeping, and the food's at the table, and you're not." She looked at Dave closely. "Are you okay?"

"I will be . . . I just . . . " He was having trouble breathing. Sweat dripped slowly down his face.

"Hey, it's me. Whatever it is, you can tell me." Maggie put a gentle hand on his arm.

Dave couldn't speak.

Maggie's hand remained on his arm. "You're a good person, Davie. I knew that the day I met you. Of course, back then, you were kind of a jerk, but you know what I mean." He tried for a smile that died on his lips. "I just hope you'll trust me enough to say what's got you so twisted up inside."

"It's not you, Maggie. It's me," Dave said finally, in a strangled voice. "I need a shot of courage to do this. I promise I'll tell you soon. Meanwhile, let's go eat, okay?"

They went back inside where Maggie demolished the rest of her breakfast, while Dave pushed his food around on his plate and Stardust showed Sophie off to every table until it was time to go to the picnic.

And Dave still hadn't found the right moment to tell Maggie the truth.

Chapter Forty

The brightly colored shiny, tiny train in Griffith Park's Travel Town pulled up with a loud toot-toot. Waiting in line in Maya's arms, baby Andrew screamed in delight. Tamara saw Rick's daughter, Moira, dance a little jig. Trevor tried to look bored.

"Any of you know where Joey is?" Rick asked Sam and Tamara.

"I think she went away for the weekend with Berta," Tamara said. "That's what Marjorie said when I picked Maya up from guitar."

"All aboard!" the conductor called. Sam and Tamara climbed into the sun-warmed seats of the small green train. Maya got on behind them; Alli boarded with her current date; Dave, looking pale, reached to steady Maggie and Sophie.

When the train started, Sam reached for Tamara's hand. She looked out the window as they bounced along the tracks. It had been an emotional afternoon.

An hour earlier the Group had finished picnicking on the lawn and were lying around in food comas.

"Stuffed," Alli declared.

Tamara would have nodded if she could have lifted her head off the grass. Next to her, Sam was sleeping on his back, snoring gently. Next to him, Andrew napped on the blanket.

Tamara heard loud laughter explode from a family picnicking nearby; folk songs drifted over from a guitar-playing group. A gentle breeze brought the happy screams of kids playing on the grass and the pungent scent of manure from the nearby pony rides.

She willed herself not to think about the ants nibbling Alli's take-out KFC or the deviled eggs hardening around the edges. She tuned out the crumbs attracting yellow-jackets and the last of the sushi sitting in the heat.

Tamara sat up. Someone *had* to clean the sushi before anyone ate it. Then she realized everyone was crashed out. Everyone but her and Dave, who was leaning against a tree across the lawn, next to where Maya played guitar and Moira and Trevor were reading. Tamara watched him light up yet again.

What's with him today? And Maggie. How is she doing?

Tamara spotted Maggie sitting on a bench, gazing at the baby in her arms. She looked like the picture of maternal bliss. Tamara knew better. *None of us is what we seem. Not anymore.*

She watched Maya talking with Moira and wondered what they were saying.

Dave's throat was sore from smoking, but he lit up again: anything to delay the truth he'd promised himself he would tell.

"Do you think my mommy can see us?" he heard Moira ask Maya. "Do you?"

"Yes. I think she's glad," said the little girl.

"Is she happy you're having fun?" Maya asked, strumming a chord.

"She's glad you're with us today," Moira said with a shy smile.

"Dessert," Alli yelled from across the lawn.

Moira and Trevor ran over to the group on the blankets. Maya stayed behind, strumming the guitar. She glanced over at Dave.

"What?" he asked. "Are you trying to bum a cigarette?"

Maya shook her head. "Even I know you're not going to make it if you keep that up." Dave ignored her. She indicated Moira. "Did you hear what she said?"

Dave nodded.

"If her mom can see us she probably wonders who's the nasty teenager corrupting her kids," Maya said.

"Don't say that. You're not so bad."

"Yes, I am. How am I supposed to be normal after what my dad did?"

Dave exhaled a smoke ring. "Normal is overrated. Joan Jett didn't have it so easy. It made her write some damn good songs." He stubbed out his cigarette.

Maya thought that over. "I wrote a song about my dad the other day," she said. "Want to hear it?"

Tamara was pulling Rosalba's red velvet cake out of the carrier when she heard Maya's voice echoing across the grass. She stopped to listen:

Angels of Mercy
Come to me
Angels of Mercy
Please come to me
Help me through the lonely nights
Tell me there's a morning light
Angels of Mercy
Please come to me . . .

Cold snaked up her spine as Maya's lyrics floated through the air. *My daughter will never be the same,* Tamara realized.

"Dessert," Alli yelled again. She rummaged through her bag and pulled out a slightly dented candle as Maya, Dave, and Maggie arrived at the blanket. "I wasn't sure you wanted to do this today," Alli said to Maggie. "I brought it just in case."

Everyone stopped talking.

"What's that for?" Maya asked over the silence.

Tamara's shoulders tightened.

"It's a memorial candle for Jeff, Maggie's husband. He was in the Marines," Sam explained.

Maya looked puzzled.

"Veterans Day is when we remember our soldiers," Rick said.

Tamara saw Maya's face color. "What about my dad? He died a year ago today."

"Our mom died a little more than two years ago," Moira said quietly.

"Two years and three months," Trevor corrected.

"How about lighting it for all of them?" Sam suggested.

Alli handed the candle to Maggie, who passed it to Dave to light. He passed it to Maya, who passed it to Trevor, then Moira, then Rick, Sam, Tamara, Dave, Alli, back to Maggie.

Sitting shoulder to shoulder they watched the flame flicker and burn. Andrew crawled over to Maya and climbed into her lap. "This guy got it the worst," she said, smoothing his hair. "He never even knew his mom."

"And Sophie," Moira said, looking at Maggie's sleeping daughter. "She'll never know her dad."

Tamara looked at her daughter and the twins. This was the first time they'd ever spoken in front of the Group. Everyone looked at the babies in silence.

"Losing a dad is bad enough," Moira said finally. "Losing a mom is the worst thing that can happen to you."

The miniature train hooted. The kids ran off. Everyone else quietly began to clean up.

"A kid's Group," Rick said. "That's what they need."

Sam and Tamara sat side by side on the train as Maya leaned forward from her seat behind them. "Why are we here?" she asked.

"What do you mean?" Tamara said.

Maya jerked her head at Maggie. "Isn't she supposed to be at a cemetery? I mean, that's where Abbie and her family are today."

"Who's Abbie?" Sam asked.

"My friend whose brother died in Afghanistan. Abbie and her family are at this soldier thing. Like a memorial. Maggie should be at that."

"She wanted to be any place but there. She wanted to be surrounded by life," Sam explained. "Everybody's different."

The train slowed as they passed the pony rides. Tamara looked out at mothers walking beside their kids, holding onto their little legs for dear life as they sat astride the slow-moving steeds. Fathers proudly recorded the event for posterity.

Bruce, Tamara thought. *Us,* she thought.

"I think it's wrong," Maya said.

"Why?" Sam asked.

"I think," Maya said, "people should go to cemeteries and visit people who died. And put flowers on their graves. I think that's the least you can do."

The train started up. Andrew screamed with delight. Sam looked out at the passing scenery. When Tamara looked out the window, all she saw was her shame looking back at her.

Later, when Tamara drove home on the freeway, long lines of red brake lights illuminated the dark road ahead.

"I talked about it with Dad," Maya said.

Tamara looked over at her. "About what?"

"Sam taking me to the Father–Daughter Dinner Dance. I didn't want to hurt his feelings, so I went to the cemetery."

Tamara tried to cover her shock. "When?"

"Two weeks ago. And I talked to his thingamajig."

"His what?"

"His gravestone. Is that what you call it?"

"But—how did you get there?"

"I took the bus."

Another secret. *How many more are there?* Tamara wondered.

"Dad understood about Sam taking me."

"I see."

Tamara looked at the road, unsure what to say next.

"But—how come it doesn't say, like, *Beloved Father and Husband* and stuff?"

"Doesn't it?" Tamara asked, trying to hide the fact that she'd never been to see it. "It should. I'll have to call them."

They drove in silence while Maya texted and Tamara imagined her 14-year-old daughter taking buses to Forest Lawn, finding out where Bruce was buried, walking through a graveyard alone. *I should have been with her.*

"You can go, you know." Maya put her hand on Tamara's arm. "I thought it would be hard . . . but it was good. It won't kill you, Mom."

Maya's tone was soft, her words simple. Tamara looked over to see if her daughter's face was filled with recrimination but Maya was leaning back against the headrest, eyes closed. No anger. No blame.

Above them, the night sky was filled with a galaxy of stars. When gridlock brought them to a stop Tamara saw pinpoints of light and realized she was looking at the cluster of bright stars in the constellation known as the Pleiades.

She remembered.

"Listen to this one," Bruce had said with excitement, the dog-eared book of baby names in his hand. It was a cool night in June, and an ocean breeze blew through their Westwood apartment. Their baby was due in three weeks, and they still had no girl's name. "Maya," he read.

"That's pretty. What does it mean?"

"That depends on the culture."

"Hang on," Tamara said, struggling to find a comfortable position. "Okay, go," she told Bruce irritably.

For the past couple of weeks they'd read girl's names out loud and rejected every one.

"Maya," Bruce repeated. "In Hebrew it means water; in Sanskrit she's the mother goddess; in Ancient Greece Maya was Aphrodite's daughter, and she's one of the stars in the Pleiades. . . . "

Maya.

The name reverberated through Tamara's body.

Maya.

She put her hand on her belly. Bruce stopped reading. His large hand joined hers.

"Do you think it might be too much for a little girl?" Tamara asked.

"Some say a person grows into their name." Bruce addressed her belly. "Hey. Are you our Maya? Kick if you want to *inspiya* us!"

Driving on the freeway Tamara looked up at the Pleiades twinkling above the city of angels. *A miracle.* She looked over at her sleeping daughter. *Another miracle.* Suddenly she saw the bond of love between them. Not the way they'd fought over the past year, not the tearing Tamara used to feel in her heart. As she looked over at Maya, all she saw was the love.

It rushed into her. It poured over her. It swelled into the car and out of the car and flew into the night. Their love shone clear up to the heavens, where the stars that bore her daughter's name winked down at them, millions of years old and new again every night.

"Shine, Maya, shine," Tamara prayed silently to the heavens.

"Shine, Maya, shine," Tamara prayed silently to her sleeping daughter.

"Shine," Tamara prayed silently to no one in particular as tears rolled down her cheeks and a fireball crossed the sky.

Chapter Forty-one

Joey and Kat were driving home from Santa Barbara when they saw the fireball cross the sky. They'd spent the hot Veterans Day weekend at Besa Del Mar after Berta cancelled on Joey at the last minute.

"My daughter and granddaughters are landing in about an hour," Berta told Joey when she came by to pick her up on Saturday morning. "Typical of them not to tell me until now."

Joey was crushed. "You're not going? Then neither am I."

"Nonsense," Berta said. "Go. Pick up a cute guy and teach him to waltz on the beach." They hugged and Joey started her car. "Wait," Berta said, walking towards her with something in her hands. "I spoke to him this morning."

"Who?"

"Daniel."

Panic rose in Joey's throat. "Why?"

"He called. He said you blocked his emails and deleted him, whatever that means. He asked me to show you this." Berta handed a cell phone to Joey. "I haven't seen it. I don't even know how to use the silly thing. I think you're supposed to press PLAY. Apparently, Daniel recorded this for you a while ago." She held out the cell phone. Joey hesitated. "Go ahead," Berta said. "It won't bite you."

Berta walked away. Joey sat in her car and looked at Daniel's face on the screen, frozen in time. He looked older. Her heart pounded as she pressed PLAY.

A video clip of Daniel in a hospital room began. "Hey, Joey. Someone wants to say hello." He focused the camera on a person in a full body cast with a halo around her head.

"Hey there, Joey. It's Lara." She tried to wave a hand. "My brother says you're awesome. Can't wait to meet you."

"That's my sister," Daniel said. The camera focused on a man sitting beside her. "And that's her fiancé, Bill. Say hi, Bill."

"Oy, Joey. How ya goin'?" Bill said.

Joey felt her pulse race. Daniel. His face. His body. His voice. His sister. Her fiancé. "Hang on," Daniel said as he moved into an empty room where he spoke in a quiet voice. "Berta told me Heidi fed you a whopper. Well, she left out some pieces of our story. Like her sleeping with my best friend. In our bed. Which broke up our marriage. Like I said, the woman's big trouble."

Daniel looked into the camera intensely. "Joey—listen to me. It's familial love I have for Lara. Not romantic love. God, not that. Never. That's what I have for *you*, Joey." Joey stared at Daniel's face. "As soon as I can get out of the mess Heidi made for me here I'll come back and clean up the mess she made for me there. I love you, Joey," he said. "I've loved you since the day I met you. We're in this. Together. Remember that."

Joey fought tears as Daniel's face froze. She watched the video two more times. Her hands shook as she got out of the car and gave the phone to Berta. She wanted to talk with her about what she'd seen, but Berta was on the landline with her daughter, giving her directions. They hugged goodbye, and Joey drove to Ferndale, her mind reeling.

When she walked past the manager's office she saw Kat at the desk, her head in her hands.

"What's the matter?" Joey asked.

"They fired my ass," Kat said.

"Ferndale?"

"Ferndale. Someone snitched about my spending Saturday nights at Neil's. And about letting you stay in the Baby Shit Suite. The bastards."

"Oh, God. I'm sorry, sweetie. I never should've taken the Baby Shit Suite."

"It's okay. I hate this job."

"What are you going to do now?" Joey asked.

"I don't know. To top it off, Neil asked me to move in."

"That's great."

Kat shook her head. "No it's not. He wants me to move to New Hampshire with him. He just got a job with the *New Hampshire Free Press*. It's a great newspaper. I don't know what to do."

Joey's heart beat faster. Kat moving to New Hampshire was terrible news but Joey was too distracted by Daniel's video to react. She sat next to Kat. "I don't know what to do either." She told Kat about Daniel.

"Oh, my God," Kat said. "So you were wrong the whole time. I knew it." They sat in silence, each absorbed in her own thoughts. "Wait," Kat said suddenly. "Why are you here? I thought you were going to Santa Barbara with Berta."

"She canceled. I didn't want to go alone."

"You don't have to," Kat said. "I'll go with you. Let's run away, get drunk, and get laid. Two commitment-phobes on vacation. We'll have a blast."

Joey and Kat spent Veterans Day weekend in an oceanfront room at Besa Del Mar and waltzed on the beach and talked until three in the morning. Kat ignored Neil's calls, and Joey swam laps in the pool and lay on a lounge chair, loving the kiss of the sun on her body, which was as good as it was going to get. Despite Daniel's video her bruised heart was still not ready to rekindle the romance.

"What's wrong with us?" Kat asked as they drank gin and tonics on the balcony at sunset. "Is it because our families were broken? Why can't we commit to these guys who want to commit to us?"

"I don't know," Joey said.

"We should wear signs that read 'Caution: Damaged Goods.'"

"I know," Joey said. "Why am I still asking the same questions I asked in ninth grade?"

"What questions?"

"Who am I and what do I want?"

"Don't ask me," Kat said. "I don't have a goddamn clue."

Kat went for a walk. Joey listened to the sounds from the beach. Sea gulls cried out. The gentle waves sounded like the ocean was breathing. She closed her eyes. Her mind quieted until a single sentence formed in her brain. She took a sheet of hotel stationery out of the desk and sat on the balcony, writing the words over and over again: "I am a grief counselor. I am a grief counselor." Joey's breathing quieted with the next wave.

"Maybe it's that simple," she said to Kat when she returned. "Maybe that's what I'm meant to be doing. Not getting my heart broken."

"Or fixed," Kat said, her cheeks flushed. She was buzzing with excitement. "Neil just called. He said if I hated it we can come back. So I'm going to give it a try. We're moving to New Hampshire in a week!" She reached for Joey. As they hugged, Joey realized she was about to lose another person she loved: Kat—the reason she'd moved to Los Angeles.

They left Santa Barbara on Monday afternoon, the sun on their skin, the sea in their eyes. On the drive back, Joey pictured life in her lonely apartment at Ferndale, the temporary village where she'd lived for the past nine months. Without Kat, without Daniel, it wouldn't be enough.

"Do you mind if we drive around?" she asked Kat.

"Do it," Kat said.

Joey got off the freeway in the West Valley, miles short of the Ferndale exit. For the next couple of hours, as darkness fell, they drove up and down small tree-lined streets that wove into each other. Joey headed up canyons, surprised to discover how much fun she had driving the curves.

They were happily lost when Joey pulled over on a small street that overlooked the lights of the Valley below.

"Look at that view," Kat said.

Joey saw the beauty of the limitless view, even as she remembered looking down on it with Daniel. She heard the quiet of the deep forest. Then she saw a sign in front of a grassy driveway—*For Lease*—that went back so far she could hardly see a house.

What she *could* see looked like a small stone cottage in the woods with steps up to a latticed porch and a yellow light burning inside. For no particular reason, her heart pounded. For no particular reason, her mind formed a word she hardly knew: *Home.*

"Let's drive down there," Kat said.

Joey took a chance, drove down the driveway, and lucked out. The owner, a heavy-set woman with messy auburn hair half-in, half-out of a bun, was just closing the front door.

"Hi. Can I take a look?" Joey asked.

The two-bedroom cottage had a clay-tiled roof and green shutters. There was a small grove of fruit trees in front and a vegetable garden in back that overflowed with ripe raspberry bushes. Inside, the owner led Joey through wainscoted rooms with wooden floors of tiger oak.

A fireplace in the dining room was made of the same gray stone as the exterior walls. The room had vaulted ceilings and a high shelf snaking around three of the four walls that would be perfect for her father's books.

"It's fabulous," Kat said.

"It reminds me of the house in Maine where I lived with my dad.

And my mom."

"If you can afford it, take it," Kat said.

"I can afford it," Joey said. "Thanks to you, I've been saving for months."

Joey took it on the spot, signing a two-year lease even as her heart pounded.

"Is it possible to start over?" she asked Kat as they drove to Ferndale.

"I hope so," Kat said. "That's what I'm banking on."

To rewind and start again, as if my mother's hair weren't brushing across my face as she left? Joey wondered as she drove.

They were almost at Ferndale when they saw the fireball streak across the sky.

Kat said it was a sign.

Joey decided Kat was right.

Chapter Forty-two

The next morning Joey's alarm never rang. When she woke up late, she realized her phone battery was dead. She left the phone behind as she raced to Oasis, put her things in the Quonset hut, and soaked Lexus and Armani in a tub of shallow water to hydrate them. She gave them some lettuce and apples and ran to tell Berta the news about her new place.

Berta's Bungalow was packed: art students, Tai Chi students, pottery students, fencing students. Everyone was there. And they were all crying. Grief like Joey had never seen was all around her. Before she could react Marjorie came to Joey's side and took her hands.

"It's Berta. She died in her sleep last night. I called and called you. . . . "

Joey's eyes opened wide. Tears gathered in the corners and spilled down her face. She looked at Marjorie as if she didn't know who she was and she didn't know what to do. Then Joey did what she always did at times like this.

She ran.

She drove all day and into the evening, paying no attention to where she was going. Her eyes were wild. Her grief felt too big for her body. Finally, as the moon rose, she found herself pulling into a familiar darkened parking lot.

Joey was crying in the orchid greenhouse at Miss Piggy's, crouched on the ground beneath the potting bench, surrounded by bags of pine bark and orchids that looked like bumblebees, down to the pollen baskets on their furry legs. She was crying amidst life, crying where she hoped not to be found.

That was where Demetrios found her.

A light turned on. "Who is there?"

"It's me. Josefina."

Demetrios walked towards her quickly. "Security called, said someone was in here. What is it?"

Joey struggled to speak. "Berta. My Yia-Yia. She died. In her sleep." Sobs escaped from her, unbidden. Demetrios' hands went to his chest. His deep brown eyes held Joey's in a well of compassion.

"Ohh . . . *Kalinihta* (good night), Sophia," he breathed, bowing his head.

Great heaves of sobs racked Joey's body. Demetrios stood beside her, steady and solid. Minutes passed. Her sobs began to subside. He reached his hand to her. "Stand."

"I can't."

"You must," Demetrios said.

She wanted to tell him she couldn't.

She wanted to be alone.

She wanted to see Berta painting at her easel.

She wanted to say goodbye.

She stood.

Demetrios took her hand in his. "We go outside, where God can hear us better." He walked her to the garden. "Just a minute."

Through the blur of her tears she saw Demetrios disappear into his office. She heard music come over the speakers. It was loud, rhythmic, and Greek. Demetrios came outside and threw off his jacket, rolled up his shirtsleeves, and began to snap his fingers. Beneath the starlit sky

Demetrios spread his arms wide. He put his left hand on her right shoulder and began to dance.

Joey didn't budge.

"Dance," he said. "Let yourself dance, Oh! Josefina."

"I can't," she cried.

"You can."

She shook her head. "Follow me," Demetrios insisted as the music wove through the night. He pulled her along as he moved to the left. To the right. Forward. Back. Her tears cascaded as he stood on one foot, hopped onto the other, moved to the right, to the left. He began again. Three steps forward. Three steps back. Joey sobbed as he raised his foot and bent at the knee. Three steps forward. Three steps back.

"Opa!"

His foot went to the opposite knee. His face was flushed. His breath was ragged. He dragged Joey along with him until she, too, began to be swept into the dance.

When they were done, Joey was winded. "What is it with you Greeks?" she asked, panting. "This is straight out of that movie *Zorba*."

"Written by Kazantzakis," he agreed. "He wrote, 'When Zorba's little boy died and everyone crying he danced. Everyone say he's mad. But it was the dancing, only the dancing, that stopped the pain.'" There was a sorrow in Demetrios' voice she'd never heard before. When Joey looked closer she saw the anguish in his eyes. "I dance," he said, "when I'm broken open."

"Are you talking about your son?" she asked softly. "The one who died?"

Demetrios bowed his head. "His name Yiannis."

They looked at each other across the chasm of their losses. Then Demetrios began to dance again. One foot up. One foot down. The delicate fronds of maidenhair ferns quivered as he passed. Lobelias fluttered and lady slippers trembled as Demetrios offered his grief to the night sky.

Later, as Joey drove away, the sight of him growing smaller and smaller as he danced alone, it came to her: Demetrios Pygmalion Phillippousis had just shared his personal tragedy to help her move beyond her pain.

For the rest of the long night Joey sat out on her balcony staring at the sky. She wanted Berta to be alive so badly it was all she could do to keep from howling at the full yellow moon.

Joey hoped the wide California sky could contain her pain. But as the hours passed she felt herself coming unspooled. After so many years, every tightly stitched seam she'd sewn over her grief burst open and the pain spilled out.

The most important people in her life had been scattered to the winds. Over and over again. Yet she'd hidden her grief like an old sock at the bottom of her gym drawer, to move aside when she was looking for something else. Now, losing Berta tipped her over the edge, and Joey found herself sinking to the bottom of a black hole.

For once, she stayed there, at the bottom of the hole. She went as low as she could go. And by the time the sun rose she felt she finally understood.

She would never forget Berta. She would never stop loving her. She would never stop loving her father, her grandfather, Nonna. She'd never stop loving any of them, even her mom, with the love of a five-year old.

But they would always be dead. Or gone. All of them. Always. And she couldn't push the grief down deep inside her any more. She would have to feel it. Carry in her heart and yet stay open-hearted and alive.

As she looked at the pink and orange streaks across the sky, suddenly, Joey knew what she needed to do.

Her eyes were so tired she could barely see the number she was dialing. She listened to the ringing. And just like that, as if no time had passed, Daniel's voice was in her ear.

"Hello?" he said.

"Come back," she said. "Please come back."

"Joey?" he asked, his voice rough with emotion.

"Berta died," she said, her voice trembling.

"Oh, God," he said.

"Will you come back?"

"I'm on a plane," Daniel said. "Ready for takeoff. See you tomorrow."

His phone clicked off. Joey pictured his face as the FASTEN SEAT BELTS sign lit up. She pictured his dark eyes and strong mouth, his large hands. Then she hung up, crawled into bed and fell into a dreamless sleep.

Twelve hours later it was dark when Joey woke. Dazed, she looked at her phone: 5:30 PM. "What day is it?" she wondered aloud.

It was Wednesday. *Grief Group.*

She showered, dressed, and drove to Oasis, arriving at 7:00. She had just enough time to go into *Berta's Bungalow* and sit by her easel, alone.

A black cloth covered the door. As soon as Joey walked through it she smelled sandalwood incense and heard the sound of chanting. The room was packed with students and teachers. All of Oasis had gathered to remember Berta.

Joey recognized Berta's daughters and granddaughters from their photos. She sat on a chair in the back and chanted with everyone until all she heard was the sound of *om*. She closed her eyes and inhaled Berta's essence. It was in the walls and the floor and the ceiling, in every painting and every square inch of *Berta's Bungalow*.

As Berta had taught her, she was everywhere.

Joey was walking to *Hummingbird* when she saw a fire in the fire pit. Her Grief Group was waiting for her.

"What are you doing here?" she asked.

"We came for someone who lost a friend," Sam said.

"A family member," Dave said.

"We came for you," Rick said to Joey.

"Please tell us," Alli said.

"Tell us about Berta," Maggie said.

"Sit down and tell us," Rick said.

Joey sat on a log by the fire and talked for a long time. She told them about Berta's laughter and her wisdom. Her St. Francis, Buddha, and menorahs. Her red bag with the green appliquéd parrot, her twig tea, and her paintings of the woman with the panther. She told them about the labyrinth and the cake that turned into a pickle.

As she talked Joey forgot she was their leader and they were her Group. And she learned what she should always have known: having Grief Group look deep into her eyes and say they knew what she meant was everything she needed.

"If there's a Labyrinth in heaven she's walking it," Tamara said.

Joey was chilled to the bone when she stumbled off the elevator and walked to her apartment. Someone was leaning against her front door, sound asleep.

"Daniel," she said in a strangled voice.

Daniel opened his eyes and Joey saw it. The light Berta talked about. She ran to him. "Thank God," she said as his arms closed around her. The familiar warmth of his body comforted her as nothing had since the day he'd left. The feel of his heart against hers. The scent of his skin. Days and nights of fear fell away. Months of believing something that was never true left her all at once.

She'd been wrong. She'd been terribly wrong. And she'd hurt them both.

"I'm so sorry," she said, over and over.

Finally, Daniel let her go. He lifted a hand and ran his fingers through her hair. "It grew," he said.

New lines were etched into his brow. Joey reached up to touch his streak of gray. "So did your streak." Words hung in the air between them. "Are you angry with me?" she asked.

Daniel looked deep into her eyes as he'd always done. His voice was quiet, thoughtful. "You did what you needed to do," he said. "And so did I."

She had many questions but the light in his eyes was the answer she needed. He took her hand in his. "Are we still in this? Together?" he asked.

Joey's heart hurt. "Together," she replied. Then she led him inside.

Much later, as she lay beside him, she said, "You came because of Berta?"

"No," Daniel said gently. "I didn't know about Berta. I'm so sorry." He stroked Joey's face. "I came to sign the papers. Oasis is sold."

Chapter Forty-three

Daniel and Joey sat in silence for a long time before he began to walk around her small living room. He told her about all the steps he'd taken to save Oasis. How many investors he'd met with in Australia.

"I tried to get them to put money into it. They told me I was nuts. 'A losing proposition,' some said. 'A money pit,' others called it. Nobody would help turn around a near-bankrupt business."

Between the expenses from Lara's accident and Heidi's fraudulent settlement claim, he'd had his hands full. Meanwhile, the balloon payment on the mortgage had come due. "And no bank would lend to me. I couldn't put my hands on that kind of money."

Joey had so many questions. She wanted to ask how it felt to lose Oasis. She wanted to ask how it felt to be away from her for months. And how it felt to see her again. She wanted to ask, but instead she listened to Daniel's familiar voice. And she watched him walk around the apartment in frustration until he came to a stop in front of her.

"I failed," he said, running a hand through his hair. She reached out and wrapped her arms around him.

"There was nothing more you could have done." She had deserted him when he needed her support. She had listened to her fears instead of believing in him. "I'm sorry I wasn't there for you."

Again, she searched his face for anger at her. It wasn't there. But she could see he was angry at himself. His body was stiff under her hands. Nothing she said would make him feel better.

"How much time do we have left at Oasis?" she asked.

"I sign the contract in a week. Then it goes into escrow."

Joey felt as if she'd been socked in the stomach.

The next morning the sky was a heartbreaking blue as Joey rode to Oasis on the back of Daniel's motorcycle. The familiar feel of his body under her hands comforted her. When they pulled into the parking lot the tie-dyed flags flew at half-mast for Berta. Joey felt the weight of the sorrow and joy of the last 24 hours.

"I wish I had time to mourn her," Daniel said as they got off the bike.

"You have Oasis to mourn," Joey replied.

Marjorie strode towards them with open arms. When Daniel told her the news of the sale her face crumpled. She and Daniel walked to the office, and Joey went straight to the Quonset hut. She carried the tortoise house out to the lawn to let Lexus and Armani bask in the sun.

"These are our last days here," she told them, "so at least you guys can enjoy yourselves."

She ignored the gnawing in her stomach as she mounted smoke detectors in every bungalow, a project she'd committed to a month ago. Now, it was a ridiculous task, but working with tools comforted her as it always had. She hammered and sawed and plastered and painted. She didn't want to think. She didn't want to feel.

Meanwhile, the news rocketed through Oasis.

"A buyer made an offer we couldn't refuse," Daniel said over and over again as he met with teachers. "We don't have a choice. Oasis is just not making enough money."

Joey was carrying a screen door across the parking lot when she saw

Heidi drive in. Daniel saw her, too. Joey put down the door and walked to him as Heidi got out of her car, yoga mat in hand.

"Get off the premises," Daniel said.

"Welcome back," Heidi said. "How was your trip?"

Joey stood shoulder to shoulder with Daniel.

"You know how it was. You made it a living hell," he snarled. His jaw was clenched. "Now get out of here."

"But yoga starts in10 minutes," Heidi said.

"Screw yoga," Daniel said. He was angrier than Joey had ever seen him. When he took a step towards Heidi, Joey thought he might hit her. "I knew you were sick," he said. "But I underestimated just how toxic you are. You went to such great lengths to screw me over—you must be nuts."

Heidi began to argue. Daniel took her by the arm and muscled her into her car. "Piss off!" he yelled and slammed the car door.

Joey moved to his side. He was shaking with anger. She put her hand on his arm as Heidi drove away slowly.

"Thank God," he said to Joey, his breathing fast. "Thank God for you."

Heidi drove straight to Gus Green's small, messy office.

"Hook, line, and sinker," she said, plopping into the visitor's chair by his desk. "The owner has no idea what we're doing."

"That makes two of us," Gus Green said. "Spell out this half-baked plan for me again, would you?"

Heidi could see Gus was nervous. The last thing she needed was a nervous partner. So she patiently repeated the plan. Next week Daniel would sign the offer from the Foundation, the straw buyers for Regency Properties.

"Then, after escrow closes, the Foundation transfers ownership to Regency. And poof! Up goes the Tower," Heidi said.

"Nothing fraudulent about that?" Gus Green said for the hundredth time.

"Of course not. Buyers buy places all the time and make promises they don't keep."

"So," Gus said. "Every *i* dotted? Every *t* crossed?"

"Of course," Heidi said in a soothing voice.

"And you remember the deal with the Foundation."

"They get 1 percent of the sale price. You told me. And speaking of percentages . . . ," Heidi said with her most beguiling smile.

After she drove home she took Scout for a walk. She began to laugh out loud at the rest of her conversation with Gus. She'd managed to convince the nitwit that she deserved a little more than he did in their split percentage from the seller.

"But I'm the licensed broker," Gus protested.

"And I'm the agent who brought in Oasis. And Regency. You never would have been in on this if it weren't for me."

In the end she'd promised him, "Next time you get the bigger cut." Gus Green didn't look at all happy, but Heidi had what she came for.

She saw no reason to add that her percentage from the seller, Daniel, was exactly the amount Daniel's father had stolen from hers.

"Soon we'll be even-Steven, Daniel," Heidi said, stopping for takeout.

Later, as she speared a piece of Kung Pao chicken with a chopstick, she checked out the Oasis website. Photos of the raucous Grief Group dancing around the fire at the Dirty Death Dance Disco Ball were everywhere. Marjorie's video on YouTube was the last nail in the coffin.

The zoning board would be no problem.

"Thank you, Ms. Unlicensed Everything," Heidi said to a photo of Joey in her costume. "I couldn't have done it without you."

Marjorie was going out to dinner with Daniel. Pleading exhaustion, Joey drove to Ferndale. She walked into Kat's place to find her surrounded by boxes.

"How the hell did I get six plaid shirts?" Kat asked. Then she looked up and saw the expression on Joey's face. "What happened?"

"Daniel came back."

"Oh my God," Kat said, scrambling to her feet. "First, Berta. Now Daniel's here. So why do you look like you were run over by a tank?"

"Because he has to sell Oasis. Right away."

"Oh, no."

"Oh, yes."

When Kat put her arms around Joey she allowed herself to feel the misery she'd been swallowing all day. "What can I do, sweetie?" Kat asked.

"Don't move to New Hampshire?" Joey smiled through her tears.

"Uhhh . . . ," Kat said.

"Okay, let's split a bottle and talk about anything but Oasis."

"Let's talk about your new place," Kat agreed, as she broke out an Amarone red wine she'd saved for special occasions.

"Jesus," Joey said. "I forgot all about that."

The week flew by. Joey was so busy she barely had time to attend Berta's funeral or time to think about losing Berta. Or Oasis. Or Kat, to New Hampshire.

Joey spent long days packing up tools in the Quonset hut; Daniel had decided anything that might be useful would go into storage.

Then it was 7:30, Wednesday evening. Grief Group.

Joey lit a candle on the scarred wooden coffee table in *Hummingbird*. She filled the handmade blue pottery bowl with chocolate-covered almonds. Her hands shook as they had nine months ago at the first Grief Group.

The last Grief Group.

They filed in slowly. They sat in their usual seats. A thick silence hung over the den.

"As you know, this is our last Grief Group at Oasis. But not our last Grief Group," Joey said. "We can keep meeting at each other's houses."

"My place first?" Tamara said.

"Then mine," Alli said.

"We'll take turns," Rick said.

"Is there anything you want to say while we're still here?"

Nobody said anything. Finally, Rick spoke. "If there was a word for the opposite of grief, that's what I felt in this room."

"Alive," Maggie said.

"Seen," Alli said. "Seen and heard."

"Having people look me in the eye and say, 'You're not alone,' meant everything," Sam said.

"Thank you for bearing with me at the worst time in my life," Alli said to Joey.

"You're one of those people," Sam said to Joey. "Who ran towards the tragedy. 9/11. The firemen running up the stairs when everyone else was running down."

"No," Joey said. "I'm not."

"Yes," Tamara said. "You ran towards us."

"Your courage, your bravery, were unbelievable," Dave said.

"No," Joey said again. "You're wrong."

"I'm the one who was wrong," Tamara said. "I was wrong when I said you couldn't help us. I've never been more wrong in my life."

"You were my direction home," Alli said simply.

Everyone nodded in agreement.

The pain in Joey's chest spread. It made her feel her heart might explode.

"I failed Del," she said.

"Del failed Del," Rick said. And Joey knew it was the truth. "You brought us back to life."

How could she have brought them back to life when she hadn't mourned her own losses? But as she looked around she realized they meant what they said. She took a deep breath to take in the wonder of it. And the love from all of them. Then she noticed Dave was standing near the doorway, half-in, half-out. He cleared his throat.

"There's something I need to say in this room." He paused. "I killed Caro," he said in the quietest of voices. "She never would have driven out of that parking lot or gotten into the accident if I hadn't slapped her."

Dave spoke for a long time about what happened that night and about his guilt. He spoke for a short, pained time about the feeling that shook him to his core: "How relieved I felt that she was dead." He looked down, deeply ashamed.

"We understand," Maggie said, moving to his side.

"It was an accident," Tamara said, moving to his other side.

Dave hung in the doorway.

"Please come in," Joey said.

When Dave hesitated the Group closed ranks around him and pulled him into the circle.

At the last meeting in Oasis, it was the first time he was ever fully there.

Chapter Forty-four

The next morning Tamara walked through Forest Lawn Cemetery, past the sign for Row C. Today was the day, she'd decided when she'd woken up. She owed it to Maya to visit Bruce's grave.

Suddenly, she found herself standing on the plain gray gravestone:

BRUCE SALVO
1976–2011

She wobbled off the stone and stared at the letters of his name. *So this is where he lives now. Nice digs,* she thought, smiling at her ability to make a pun at a time like this. *See? I'm okay. This wasn't so bad.*

A giggle started to rumble up from the burning she felt in the pit of her belly, and somehow, by the time it flamed up to her mouth, it turned into a sob, which morphed into a storm of sobs so fierce they took her by surprise.

She thought about the last time she'd seen Bruce, which made her sit down, hard, on the grass beside the grave. Her lipstick fell out of her purse and rolled away. She began to weep. She'd gone from zero to 120 in 10 seconds and had become the madwoman she was never going to be.

"How could you let me find you like that?" she said aloud, pounding

Bruce's gravestone with her fist. "God damn you. Damn you, Bruce. Daaaamn *you*!!"

She saw nearby mourners glancing at her with concern. Tamara didn't care. After one year of dry-eyed, angry grieving, she was finally coming undone.

When the waves of grief subsided Tamara could almost breathe again. But her mind was blank. Totally blank. She looked over at Bruce's tombstone and had no memories of him, not a single picture in her mind.

I must be done. I survived, she decided.

She stood and looked down at his gravestone one last time before she left.

BRUCE SALVO

1976–2011

Memories returned.

Snap. The soft air on the beach in Hawaii. Bruce's off-key tenor voice singing "Happy Birthday." The feel of the rough conch shell he'd put into her hand. The grin on his face. The iridescence of the string of pearls that spilled from it.

Snap. His voice called to her in a stage whisper from the top of the stairs: "We're up here." She looked up to see him holding six-month-old Maya, her head nestled into his shoulder. "She fell asleep, and I didn't want to put her down."

Snap. Her cold hand reached for his warm one in the movies.

Snap. She felt the irritation when she scanned the piles of paper, unopened mail, and unfinished projects that lined every surface of his home office. Bruce was hunched over his desk, his back to her, his head buried in a crossword. She closed the door, hard.

Snap. Veterans Day a year ago. The doorbell rang. The police. Snap.

The dingy room in the motel on Lincoln Boulevard where they'd found him. Snap. The floor covered with blood. Snap. A gun. Snap. Bruce on the floor with his face half-off. Snap. Snap. Snap.

Unwanted, violent images of her last sight of him filled Tamara's senses. For the first time she recalled it all. Yet even as her mental movie sent her reeling, she remembered.

The way Bruce cleared his throat before he spoke.

The warmth of his body lying next to hers in bed. A year ago. A lifetime ago.

Tamara sat beside his grave and felt the shock and sadness. She felt the pain she'd never wanted to feel. It sped through her bloodstream so fast she was amazed it didn't stop her heart. She'd been so sure that having these feelings would kill her.

She took a shaky breath and looked around. For the first time she saw that the grass looked like a velvet carpet studded with gray stone pillows. The sky was dotted with white clouds edged in charcoal. She smelled cinnamon from the scarlet carnations on the grave next to Bruce. She saw the purple sweater on the woman kneeling beside a grave a few rows away.

She retrieved her lipstick and her purse, slipped on her shoes, checked for grass stains on her skirt, and put her sunglasses back on.

I'm going now, Bruce.

She looked down at his grave again, and this time she didn't feel the rage or the sadness. She felt something tentative and new, a feeling she couldn't even name.

Then she knew what it was.

"I forgive you," she said.

She took off her sunglasses and put them on his gravestone. Then she walked away.

On the drive home Tamara called Sam from her car.

"Hi, it's me."

"Hi, you."

Tamara kept her eyes on the freeway. She needed to ask something of Sam and it scared her. *Do I know what we are to each other? Does it matter?*

"Sam?" she said, keeping her voice as casual as she could. "Would you take Maya to the Father-Daughter Dinner Dance at her school?"

There was a pause on the other end of the phone. Tamara's hands tightened on the steering wheel.

"It would be an honor," Sam said.

Tamara's eyes welled up. "Thank you," she said.

At the next red light she discovered a black billboard with white letters:

Well, you did ask for a sign.

—GOD

What is the sound that's trickling out of me like running water? Tamara wondered. Laughter, light as quicksilver poured through her, out of her, over her, flooding her body. She was alone in her car at a stoplight, laughing like a loon, something she had thought she'd never do again.

It felt wrong. "And God, it feels good," Tamara said as she drove onto the freeway and headed home.

Chapter Forty-five

Joey felt as if she were treading water before being swept away in a riptide. During the day she helped clean out the bungalows at Oasis; at night she packed up her things at Ferndale. She brought Lexus and Armani home to her tiny apartment and set them up on the balcony. "Soon, guys," she said. "Soon we're moving to a bigger, better place."

The day before the signing Joey was helping Marjorie clean out the last of the bungalows—*Rising Lotus*—when Marjorie suddenly said, "That's odd."

She showed Joey what she'd just found behind the shoe rack: an envelope addressed to Heidi Berne. The return address was Regency Properties with an embossed gold crown. "Where have I seen that gold crown before?" Marjorie asked.

"I don't know, but I've seen it, too," Joey said.

They opened the envelope. Inside was a color Xerox of yellow lined pages written in Heidi's signature red ink: *Ethics violations at Oasis: Requesting sexual favors from the director; hosting a party at leader's residence where alcohol was served to members of a Grief Group; trespassing on Oasis; hosting costume party in Oasis board room; serving alcohol; lighting fire . . .* The list went on. At the bottom of the page a note was written in Heidi's tiny handwriting: *This is the perfect way to show the zoning board what's going on there. Clearing the way for a sale to Regency. —H. Berne*

The words began to swim before Joey's eyes. She read a buck slip from Jonathan Caroon, Executive Vice President, Regency Properties that was paper-clipped to the paper: *"Good work, Heidi."*

"What the hell is all this?" Marjorie asked. Joey didn't know, but she couldn't stop her heart from racing. "What does Heidi have to do with Regency Properties?" Marjorie asked.

The image of the gold crown swam through Joey's mind. Suddenly she knew where she'd seen it before. Heidi's white canvas bag. The one she'd clutched in the office when they were locked in.

"Oh, my God." Joey grabbed the notes and ran to Daniel's office. Marjorie followed. He was packing papers into boxes. "Heidi's working with Regency Properties," Joey said. "Do you know who they are?"

Daniel frowned. "The company that builds shopping malls and office buildings?" She handed him the paper she'd found. "Shit," Daniel said. His face looked desperate.

"I don't understand," Marjorie said. "What's Heidi doing with Regency?"

"I'm not sure. But it sounds like they're the real buyers of Oasis."

"Then what's the Foundation?" Joey asked.

"God only knows," Daniel said bitterly. "Some shell company, probably. A nonprofit that satisfies the codicil in my grandmother's will."

Joey struggled to understand. Marjorie cursed under her breath.

"If Regency's the real buyer, they'll tear down this place and put up an office building," Daniel said in a hollow voice.

"Dammit. She sold it out from under you," Joey blazed. "She used things I did to mollify the zoning board."

"It's always Heidi," Daniel said between clenched teeth. "That woman can make more trouble in a day than most people do in a lifetime." He looked over at the portrait of his grandmother. "She couldn't stand Heidi from the moment they met."

"Ditto," Marjorie said.

"We've got to put a stop to this," Joey said.

Daniel's eyes looked black with despair. "I can't," he said. "In the end it's the same. Whatever the plan is, whether it's the Foundation or Regency that's buying us, I'm tapped out. The FMs are tapped out. No bank will lend to us. No investor will pony up the money. We owe too much to too many. Nobody can save Oasis." He walked to his grandmother's portrait. Joey came up alongside him. "You see that giant tree? It's a banyan in Queensland," Daniel said. "One of the oldest. My grandmother bought this property because of the giant pines. She always said she would tie her great-grandchildren to those trees if bulldozers ever came to tear down a single one." He looked at Joey with empty eyes. "Now they'll all be gone."

She put her hand on his arm. "Isn't there anything we can do?"

Marjorie stood beside them in silent support.

"Yes," Daniel said to Joey. "We can go home."

The next morning, the day of the signing, when Joey awakened, Daniel was looking out at the downpour. "Are you coming?" he asked.

"I can't," she said.

Daniel understood. But after an hour Joey drove there too. She couldn't stay away.

Wind shivered the needles of the giant pines as she drove into Oasis. A curtain of water sheeted off the sagging roofs of the bungalows. As she ran across the parking lot, umbrella high, Joey noticed it was filled with expensive cars.

It must be the Foundation. And lawyers. And realtors. And Regency. And God knows who else, she thought as she took the path to *Hummingbird.* The front door was open, and in she went. Straight through the waiting room and into the den.

When she looked around she saw them at the first meeting:

shell-shocked Sam; Tamara in sunglasses; Dave, deeply hidden and heart-broken; Daisy, covering her pain; Maggie and her flag, angry and lost; Alli, in fearful denial; Del, whom she'd helped as much as he'd allowed. She saw herself careening from her old life, struggling to carve out a new one.

She thanked the room for holding their pain and witnessing their transformations. She sent out a call for Del to get the support he needed. Then she saw the room as it was: a faded relic.

She turned to go, remembering the gift Berta talked about, the one nobody wanted, the gift that came from loss. She wondered if she would ever get it.

"There's someone here to see you," Marjorie said, poking her head in. "Gotta run."

A man with a long ponytail, a hand-painted tie, and bellbottom jeans came in. "Josephine Lerner?"

"Yes," Joey said.

"Steven Steiner. I'm a lawyer for—"

"You must be looking for the board room," Joey said.

"I'm here to see you, Ms. Lerner," he said. "I'm Berta Lobell's attorney. Can we sit?"

Mystified, Joey took a seat on one of the red plaid couches. Steven Steiner sat opposite her. He told her he'd been Berta's lawyer since he was 25. "Fresh out of Loyola. She was my first client. A one-of-a-kind," he said. "Berta knew her heart was giving out," he continued, opening his briefcase and handing Joey an unopened envelope. "She left this for you."

Josephine Lerner was hand-lettered in Berta's elegant cursive. With trembling hands Joey opened the envelope.

Dearest Joey,

I can't predict exactly when you will receive this, but I believe it will be soon. I hope by now the storm has passed. Knowing you, I'm sure you sailed right through it.

If my death made you feel you are more alone than ever, just go outside on a dark night and look up.

Don't you see me? You wrote my name in stars across the sky. You wrote all of ours. We will always be there. Just look up, dear one.

Love always, Berta

Tears choked Joey's throat as she folded the letter carefully.

Steven Steiner waited a few moments before speaking. "I'm also here to inform you that Berta stipulated a large bequest to you."

"What?"

"And she told me to tell you this: 'The way out is the way in.' Whatever that means," Steven Steiner said. He handed Joey another envelope. When she opened it something fluttered to the floor. She picked it up. It was a check. Made out to her. For an astronomical sum. Joey's eyes widened in disbelief. "Berta told you her last husband was Greek," Steven explained. "She didn't tell you what Giorgio did for a living. Did she?"

Joey couldn't speak. She shook her head.

"Giorgio started in tobacco and went into the shipping business. Cargo shipping. Like Onassis. But not exactly."

"Oh," Joey said, completely bewildered.

"Berta told me her husband used to call Onassis 'the little minnow.' Giorgio was known as 'ketos.' That's Greek for 'the big fish.'"

What was Berta's lawyer saying? Was it possible that Berta's first husband was bigger than Onassis? Was it possible that Berta, folksy, eccentric Berta, was a multi-millionaire?

"That's right," Steven Steiner said, seeing the wheels turning. "What you're thinking is right as rain." He closed his briefcase and stood. "Berta told me you should use this to make sure that 'everything and everyone you love is safe and sound.' Good bye and good luck, Ms. Lerner," he said, and walked out.

Joey sat for a moment in disbelief. Then she sprinted across the parking lot to the board room. She raced up the steps and threw open the door.

"Daniel! Stop," she yelled. "Don't sign the offer! We've got the money!"

Daniel was inexplicably alone. He gestured to a glossy brochure on the floor, where he'd tossed it. "One of the lawyers had this with him." It was a black brochure with a photograph of a 30-story office building, the Tower, to be built on the site of Oasis.

"I couldn't sign the offer," Daniel said. "Not when I saw that. I don't know how I'm going to find the money but I can't let them do this."

"This might help," Joey said. She handed him Berta's check.

Around the corner, Heidi was on her third cup of coffee at The Counter. She stared at her iPhone. Gus Green would be texting as soon as Daniel signed the binding offer. There'd be no way for him to get out of it. Not even when he found out her plan. Suddenly a message from Gus appeared: "Come now."

Heidi plunked down a couple of dollars and ran. She had no umbrella so she got soaked as she strode through the downpour. She didn't care.

When she walked into the parking lot she saw that a Mercedes and a Bentley were idling. She recognized Gloria Morgan from the Foundation behind the wheel of the Mercedes, Jonathan Caroon from Regency behind the wheel of the Bentley.

She gave them both a thumbs-up as she ran through the rain to Gus

Green's Ford Escort. They would all be going out to celebrate. She decided she'd go home and change into her hot pink Fendi suit. She was drenched by the time she tried the passenger door. Strangely, it was locked.

"Let me in," she demanded. Gus rolled down his window, leaving her in the downpour.

"Your ex didn't sign," he said.

"What?" Heidi said, reeling.

"He found out what you were up to. The Foundation and Regency have two words for you. The same two I have." He beckoned to Heidi. She leaned down. He whispered them in her ear.

Heidi pulled away, stung.

Gus Green drove out the driveway. The Mercedes and the Bentley followed. None of the drivers gave Heidi a backwards glance.

Joey and Daniel walked hand in hand to the parking lot.

"Now, what do I do?" they heard Heidi call out. She was soaked to the skin, yelling into the rain. "What do I do? Where do I go?"

"Go to hell," Daniel said. He opened the door of Joey's car, helped her close the umbrella, leaned down and kissed her. As Heidi ran into the office, Daniel got on his bike and drove out of the parking lot.

Joey followed him, looking in her rear view mirror at Oasis. Someone was standing near *Berta's Bungalow*. At first Joey thought it was Heidi. Then she saw it was Berta. She was waving jauntily with her paintbrush.

When Joey looked again Berta was gone.

Joey drove until the rundown bungalows of Oasis were so small they disappeared from view.

Epilogue

TEN MONTHS LATER

All she could see was the love.

In the dining room of Joey's wainscoted cottage, where the walls were painted a pale yellow and the rooms furnished with Nonna's antiques, Joey's father's books looked down on the gathering from the high bookshelves.

It was a Saturday night in mid-September, and Grief Group was sitting around the pine table with Joey and Daniel. They raised their glasses to the stars above and the lights of the city below. They were celebrating the imminent opening of the new venture.

Rick and his kids toasted with sparkling apple juice; Tamara and Sam clinked glasses of champagne; so did Dave and Maggie. Alli, pregnant by her new husband, Rod's college roommate, toasted with sparkling water. Baby Andrew walked around the living room under Maya's watchful eye. Maggie's daughter, Sophie, was crawling. Daniel and Joey raised their Foster's beers high.

They'd moved into the cottage 10 months earlier. In their spare time, in the evenings and on weekends, Joey had built bookshelves and cabinets, restored the moldings, and sanded the floors. At work they'd pored over the architect's plans and worked alongside contractors and carpenters, carefully preserving the giant trees while gutting bungalows and rebuilding.

When the long days were done Joey would hang up her tool belt in the gleaming new workshop and hop on the bike behind Daniel. Her hands, with a matching ring designed by his sister, would clasp Daniel's as they wound their way back to their cottage.

Some days they'd quit early, and Daniel would take her to Mount Sinai, where Joey sat on the grass beside a gravestone:

BERTA LOBELL

1925–2012

Joey would talk to Berta, her fingers tracing and retracing the letters of her name. Joey would tell her about her feelings, her days, about the new Oasis, her new home, and about her love for Daniel. She would breathe deeply, silently name all the colors she could see, place a stone on Berta's grave and walk back down the hill.

One day, Joey woke to find her pain was beginning to ease and her breath was evening out. When she walked barefoot in her back yard she realized she hadn't known what she was looking for when she'd gone west. Somehow, digging in the rubble of her life she'd struck gold.

For the first time she was growing roots. California roots.

Tonight, she looked at the faces of the widows and widowers and their children. Although they were moving on, there would be rough times ahead, Joey knew. Life was not a fairy tale.

So what is the legacy of death? Joey wondered.

The legacy is life. She heard the words as clearly as if Berta were whispering them in her ear.

Joey looked around the table again. She looked out the window at the stars in the night sky.

All she could see was the love.

THE SAN FERNANDO VALLEY COURIER
Bereavement Center to Open

The doors to Berta's Bungalow will open at THE NEW OASIS on September 20, 2013. Josephine Lerner will initiate the new center.

Maya and the Angels of Mercy will perform at the opening ceremonies.

Berta's Bungalow will be a freestanding safe haven in Los Angeles where people of all ages can go to rebuild their lives after the death of a loved one. The first Children's Group will be led by trained volunteer Group leaders Tamara Salvo and Dave Kline. Maya Salvo will be a co-leader.

END

Linda's Acknowledgments

After five years of terrific collaboration, I thank gutsy, spirited Jo-Ann Lautman, the grief maven without whom this book would never have been written. I thank my husband, Terry Crowe, who read and reread and advised on everything from the psychology of the characters to intricate plot developments. Thank you to Marion Rosenberg for her steadfast enthusiasm, superb copy-editing and expert guidance. Without you this book would still be in a drawer.

To Susan Ramer, whose first-look notes gave us confidence; Regina Ryan and Terry Gilman for their help with early drafts; the mental health professionals who reassured that Joey was leading the group appropriately.

To those who offered insightful comments, including Rhoda Pregerson and Riley K. Smith, Darlene Basch, Judy Bravard, Maggie Damon, Erica Di Bona, Jim Evers, Winifred Neisser, Nancy Ney, Linda Novack; members of the Second Generation Group and Sisters of the Pool. Thank you to Mimi Starrett who vetted Heidi's real estate shenanigans; Betsy Lautman and Lauren Schneider for the lively brainstorming session that birthed our title; Dan Lautman for all the proofreading and the inspiration for Joey's grandfather's Estwing hammer.

Thank you to Bethany Rooney, who inspired us to dig deeper with our characters; John Levey took time to read and advise; Karen Cease wowed us with her business savvy. To Leah Hager Cohen, Hope Edelman and Leora Galperin Krygier for their exquisite words; David Wilk at Prospecta Press for publishing; Tracy McGonigle for her imaginative cover design.

Gratitude to Syd Field, who taught me to write a story in three acts; Gloria Monty, Ann Howard Bailey, Bradley Bell, Lynn Marie Latham and Robert Guza, Jr., who trained me to write for 42 characters a week.

Thank you to the inspiration for Maggie's midwife—Ibu Robin Lim, 2011 CNN Hero of the Year; to Dr. Paula Bernstein, who corrected my mistakes about Maggie's labor and Rhoda Holabird, who walked the labyrinth with me; to Komala Frame's Australian grandmother, the inspiration for Zora. In memory of *Everywoman's Village,* the long-gone funky community center that inspired Oasis.

I'm grateful to Miss Baylinson, my red-haired fourth-grade teacher at PS 87, who told my mother I was a writer; to my father, Oscar Schreyer, a fine wordsmith, and my brother, Leslie, his wife Judy and daughter Gabri for the love and support. To my writing students—I learn from you every day.

To our talented and lively children—Evan and Jenna Sugerman, Jennifer Crowe, Marcelle Seelig, Gustavo Biermann, Fred Maher and adored grandchildren, Jazz, Micah and Ruby. You never complained, no matter how often I disappeared to write. Thank you for waiting for me to come back to your lives. To Swami Muktananda—who bestowed the name *Pravina* ("skillful" in Sanskrit) upon me when I was 28—thank you for saying that "one grows into one's name."

Finally, I thank the indelible legacy of my mother, artist Greta Schreyer and her father, Viennese master goldsmith Sigmund Loebl. Your DNA runs deep.

As a child of Holocaust survivors I grew up in a house of silent mourning. Nobody talked about what had happened to my grandparents. In writing this book I discovered that unspoken grief can find a voice and the healing of these characters led to my own healing.

For that, and more, I will always be grateful for what I've learned, from Jo-Ann Lautman, and on these pages.

Jo-Ann's Acknowledgments

With my love and appreciation to Linda, who was able to hear my voice and feel my feelings, and to Terry Crowe, our Friday actor and reader. To Susan Ramer, who believed in us, to Jessica and Jane Krell, who opened the door to Marion Rosenberg, our ultimate manager.

Everlasting thanks to my family and patient friends, to Rina Freedman, who always felt I could do it, whatever it was, to Terry Gilman, who cheered us on from the very first draft, and to Edie Lutnick, Hope Edelman, Lauren Schneider, and Melissa Rivers, for writing your praises of *Tears and Tequila*.

My thanks to Sarah Galvin, who kept the computer working through many titles, and then some . . . to Dr. Rick Shuman and Laurie, whose home was where I met Linda, and lastly to Carlo for giving me my angel.

About the Authors

Linda Schreyer is an award-winning television/screen-writer. She held staff writing positions on *General Hospital, Port Charles, Sunset Beach* (winning a Writers Guild Award nomination), and *The Bold and the Beautiful*; co-wrote the television movies *A Place at the Table* (receiving The Christopher Award and an Ollie Award) and *A House of Secrets and Lies*; wrote the screenplay, *Ohmigod!* for Touchstone Productions; and was sent to Moscow by Sony Pictures Television International to teach Russian writers to write for serial television. You can find her at http://imdb.com/name/nm0775365/.

Jo-Ann Lautman's name is synonymous with bereavement in Los Angeles. Former director of the bereavement program at Stephen S. Wise Temple, she was a member of the Cedars Sinai Medical Center Hospice team for eight years before she founded OUR HOUSE, a renowned grief support center based on the premise that grievers need understanding, support, and connection. Jo-Ann and her award-winning work have been featured in, among other publications, *People, Time Magazine*, the *Los Angeles Times*, the *Daily News*, and more. You can find her at www.ourhouse-grief.org.